VIKRAMADITYA VEERGATHA
BOOK I

THE
GUARDIANS
OF THE
HALAHALA

VIKRAMADITYA VEERGATHA
BOOK I

THE
GUARDIANS
OF THE
HALAHALA

SHATRUJEET NATH

JAICO PUBLISHING HOUSE

Ahmedabad Bangalore Bhopal Bhubaneswar Chennai
Delhi Hyderabad Kolkata Lucknow Mumbai

Published by Jaico Publishing House
A-2 Jash Chambers, 7-A Sir Phirozshah Mehta Road
Fort, Mumbai - 400 001
jaicopub@jaicobooks.com
www.jaicobooks.com

VIKRAMADITYA VEERGATHA: BOOK 1
THE GUARDIANS OF THE HALAHALA
ISBN 978-81-8495-638-2

First Jaico Impression: 2015
Second Jaico Impression: 2016

Page design and layout: Jojy Philip, Delhi

Printed by
Nutech Print Services-India
B-25/3, Okhla Industrial Area, Phase-II
New Delhi - 110 020

To
Sudha Anna, who never fails to entertain.
And Ritz, who never ceases to surprise.

Contents

Author's Note   ix
Index of Major Characters   xiii

Prologue   1
Hriiz   9
Giant   17
Arrivals   28
Council   47
Dagger   65
Veeshada   76
Nephew   88
Envoy   113
Andhaka   128
Dark   147
Fall   167
Brotherhood   190
Siege   212
Hellfires   232

Vishakha	244
Scouts	265
Oracle	288
Healer	306
Warnings	330
Borderworld	348
Maruts	370
Ghoulmaster	384
Rage	399

Author's Note

Readers familiar with Hindu mythology will be quick to realize that I have taken many liberties in the telling of this tale; that so many things in this book – and the others to come in this series – are departures from established myth and legend. But the very notion of 'established myth and legend' is flawed, for mythology is a wellspring of possibilities, where many versions of the same myth can coexist in harmony. This is the way mythology always has been, told and retold by bards and balladeers, each teller giving the story a new spin. It is my firm belief that this is what keeps myths alive. This ever changing, ever evolving narrative is the beauty of myths.

Myths being complex in nature, what I have also attempted here is simplifying them where possible, so that even readers with limited grasp of Hindu mythology can follow the thread of this story without being overwhelmed by an excess of detail and information. Whether I have succeeded or failed in this can only be determined by the reader.

As always, I owe my gratitude to a lot of people who have assisted and supported me in different ways to make this book a reality. My thanks to my sister-in-law Ritu Madan, and my friends Ravi Balakrishnan, Prasanna Singh, Shankar Ayyappan Kutty, Gaurrav Dhar and Saurabh Garg for their constructive feedback. Thanks also to Paul Thomas, Shekhar Shimpi, Vikram Gaikwad, Payal Juthani, Sandeep Kamal and his team at inCandlelight, and Sarang Kulkarni and Noopur Datye at WhiteCrow Designs for their help with various aspects of design.

This book wouldn't have been possible without my agent Kanishka Gupta and my publisher Akash Shah. My thanks to both, as well as to the team at Jaico: Sandhya Iyer, Srija Basu and Meera Menon. Also Savita Rao, Vijayakumar Arumugam, Nita Satikuwar and Vijay Thakur – thanks!

My parents Jyoti Prasad Nath and Shama Nath, my lovely wife Pragya, and my dear daughter Kaavya: I can't thank the four of you enough for your faith in me.

And a special note of appreciation for R Balki, Nandini Raghavendra, Sagarika Shah and Rensil D'Silva as well.

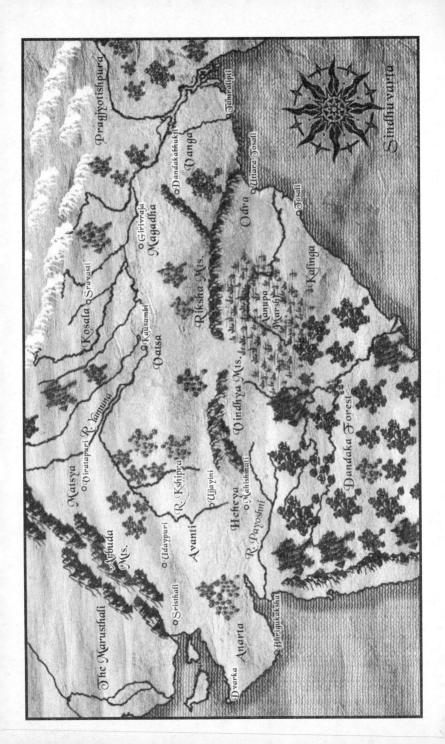

Index of Major Characters
(In alphabetical order)

Humans

THE KINGDOM OF AVANTI

Amara Simha	Councilor of Avanti
Angamitra	Captain of the samsaptakas
Atulyateja	Garrison commander of Udaypuri
Brichcha	Father of Shanku
Dattaka	Commander of the Sristhali command center
Dhanavantri	Councilor of Avanti & royal physician
Ghatakarpara	Councilor of Avanti; nephew of Vikramaditya & Vararuchi
Kalidasa	Councilor of Avanti
Kshapanaka	Councilor of Avanti & sister of queen Vishakha
Mahendraditya	Late king of Avanti; father of Vikramaditya, Vararuchi & Pralupi
Mother Oracle	Shanku's grandmother; head of the Wandering Tribe

Pralupi	Sister of Vikramaditya & Ghatakarpara's mother
Satyaveda	Governor of Malawa province
Shanku	Councilor of Avanti; granddaughter of the Mother Oracle
Upashruti	Mother of Vikramaditya & Pralupi; second wife of Mahendraditya
Ushantha	Mother of Vararuchi; first wife of Mahendraditya
Varahamihira	Councilor of Avanti
Vararuchi	Councilor of Avanti; half-brother of Vikramaditya
Vetala Bhatta	Chief councilor of Avanti; royal tutor
Vikramaditya	King of Avanti
Vishakha	Wife of Vikramaditya; Kshapanaka's sister

THE KINGDOM OF MAGADHA

Daipayana	General of the Magadhan army
Kapila	Second son of Siddhasena of Magadha
Shoorasena	Elder son of Siddhasena of Magadha
Siddhasena	King of Magadha; ally of Avanti

THE KINGDOM OF VATSA

Chandravardhan	King of Vatsa; ally of Avanti
Himavardhan	Brother of Chandravardhan; father of Ghatakarpara
Shashivardhan	Son of Chandravardhan of Vatsa
Yashobhavi	Councilor of Vatsa

THE KINGDOM OF KOSALA

| Bhoomipala | King of Kosala; ally of Avanti |
| Pallavan | Envoy & councilor of Kosala |

The Kingdom of Heheya

Harihara   King of Heheya; ally of Avanti
Rukma   Daughter of Harihara of Heheya

The Kingdom of Matsya

Baanahasta   King of Matsya; ally of Avanti

The Anarta Federation

Yugandhara   Chief of the Anarta Federation; ally of Avanti

The Republic of Vanga

Sudasan   Chancellor of the Republic of Vanga

Devas

Brihaspati   Royal chaplain of the devas
Dasra   Captain of the Ashvins & twin brother of Nasatya
Indra   Lord of the devas; king of Devaloka
Jayanta   Son of Indra
Narada   Envoy of Devaloka & advisor to Indra
Nasatya   Captain of the Ashvins & twin brother of Dasra
The Ashvins   Elite cavalry of Devaloka, led by Nasatya & Dasra
The Maruts   The seven sons of Diti
Urvashi   Apsara of Devaloka & mistress of Indra

Asuras

Andhaka   The blind rakshasa
Diti   Sorceress & matriarch of the asuras
Hiranyaksha   Lord of the asuras; king of Patala
Holika   Sister-consort of Hiranyaksha & witch

                        queen of Patala
Shukracharya   High priest of the asuras
Veeshada   The thief of the Halahala

Others

Betaal   The Ghoulmaster; lord of the
                        Borderworld
Shiva   The Omniscient One

Prologue

*T*he flame appeared in the sky sometime during the fifth night of the Churning, while the devas and the asuras slumbered heavily on opposite shores of the White Lake.

It wasn't discovered until daybreak though, when a couple of devas emerged from their grand pavilion to view the bewildering sight in the western sky. Soon, the lake's northern shore was thronging with devas, their din rousing the asuras on the southern shore. The asuras, too, came out of their tents, shaking their heads, perplexed by the jagged, teardrop-shaped flame hanging overhead.

Wonder slowly changed to unease on both sides of the large lake, as the rising sun crested the young peaks of the Himalayas. For instead of being diminished by the sun, the brightness of the flame increased in ferocity; a glare in the sky like a sultry, malevolent eye.

Recognizing it for an omen, the asuras and devas exchanged emissaries, each side trying to gauge what the other made of the phenomenon. Being the more timid of the two, the devas proposed calling a halt to the Churning, and waiting for the omen to wear itself out. But the asuras, spurred by their greed to find the magical Elixir hidden in the depths of the White Lake, goaded the devas to abandon caution and return to the task of churning the lake.

The devas, who were greatly outnumbered by the asuras, saw that the latter were fully prepared to take on the Churning all by themselves. They also realized that should this happen, the asuras would stake full claim to the Elixir, with its promise of eternal youth. Unwilling to forgo their share of the Elixir, the devas were left with no choice but to accept the asuras' proposal.

Thus, the two rival clans of demigods, born of a common father but torn apart by the lust for power, set about the chore of churning the White Lake for the sixth consecutive day.

All day they toiled, as the flame glowered over their heads. They heaved and pulled, but the water yielded nothing. Fatigue grew on them, dull and cankerous – still they persevered, hauling on hope with bruised and blistered hands.

Then, a little before sundown, a black boulder emerged from the bottom of the muddy, turbulent lake. It bobbed in the water, heavy yet light, the eddying currents splashing against it, washing it slowly toward the far shore.

The Churning was brought to a halt. The asuras and devas hastened to take a closer look at the rock. It was large and made of obsidian, and required half a dozen devas and asuras to drag it ashore. Once the stone was a safe distance from the water's edge, the rival kinsmen crowded around, gaping at it in gluttonous fascination.

They knew their quest for the Elixir was finally over!

What they saw, deep in the core of the volcanic glass, was an iridescent blue light, emanating from a softly swirling mass buried inside the stone. The swirl was flecked with a thousand gold and silver particles that burned like scintillas upon catching the rays of the setting sun. The blue light radiated at regular intervals, flashing seductively through the rock's polished black surface like a beacon in the night.

The fat flame above burned blood red and spread across the sky like an impure stain, but the devas and asuras were too entranced to notice the change. They summoned a council, and after some deliberation, determined that the rock should be cracked open and the Elixir be distributed among them right away. As the impatient devas and asuras jostled one another to line up, one of the devas struck the rock with his heavy mace. On the third blow, a slender crack appeared on the stone's surface, and at once, a faint tendril of iridescent blue vapor escaped into the open. The gathered demigods raised shouts of exultation...

But almost immediately, cheer turned to dismay, and dismay to horror.

Gripped by morbid waves of fear, they watched the unfortunate deva drop his mace and claw at his throat. His face started to convulse violently, a half-scream gurgling in the folds of his larynx. His eyes began bulging out of the sockets, the skin peeling off his contorted face. He slumped to the ground in agony as his steaming flesh melted off his bones, his entrails spilt out of his stomach and his body dissolved into a bloodied, messy pulp that settled into the sandy soil with a rasping, dying moan.

As more blue mist emerged from the boulder, a sulfuric stench filled the air, overpowering the smoldering reek of the deva's corpse. Within moments, the devas and asuras closest to the boulder started to choke and fall.

The toxic fumes enveloped the trees nearby, making birds tumble off their perches, their feathers catching fire before they hit the ground. Plants and shrubs shriveled to a burned crisp and the White Lake's surface boiled and frothed eerily at the shores. Tremors rose from deep underground, and sizzling fissures appeared on the earth's surface.

Up in the sky, the red, oppressive flame engulfed the sun, changing color to a vile, iridescent blue.

Panic-stricken, the devas and asuras took flight, seeking refuge in the forests by the lake. But borne by the breeze, the noxious vapor followed them, claiming asura and deva without discrimination and wreaking havoc on nature.

Sage Brihaspati, the chaplain of the devas, held a hurried consultation with Sage Shukracharya, the high priest of the asuras. The bitter adversaries for once agreed that the devas and asuras had erred in judging the rock's contents. This was no life-prolonging Elixir. On the contrary, it was the accursed Halahala – the primordial poison, which, if not trapped in a vacuum, could destroy all Creation.

The Churning had dislodged the boulder from the abyss of the White Lake, and by breaking it in their eagerness to imbibe the Elixir, the devas and asuras had unwittingly breached the Halahala's protective vacuum, unleashing the scourge upon themselves.

Brihaspati and Shukracharya went to work, intoning the most arcane of mantras, conjuring up spell after spell to contain the Halahala. But the fracture was too deep and wide, and the toxin too potent, for any of it to have an effect. Devas and asuras continued to succumb as steam from the White Lake rose to fuse with the Halahala and form a dense, miasmic cloud that rained scalding, acidic pellets over the mountains.

Frantic in the face of the growing terror, the two sages sought out the ancient gods Brahma and Vishnu for assistance. The gods, however, confessed to their helplessness and instructed the devas and asuras to take the boulder to Shiva the Omniscient, for Shiva was the only force in the three worlds capable of destroying the Halahala.

Two dozen of the hardiest devas and asuras were marshaled to escort the poison-spewing boulder to Shiva's abode on Mount Kailasa. Brihaspati and Shukracharya cast powerful spells on each of them to temporarily ward off the effects of the Halahala, and the procession set forth. For three days, the group travelled through the windblown mountains, braving blinding blizzards and freezing temperatures. And all through their journey, they had the company of the angry blue flame in the sky.

Finally, on the third night, when the effects of Brihaspati and Shukracharya's spells had begun wearing off, the group staggered up to the mouth of the Eternal Cave, Shiva's dwelling.

Without waiting to hear the terrifying account, Shiva the Omniscient demanded the toxic boulder from the devas and asuras. Taking the rock in one hand, the most ancient of gods cracked it open on the floor of the cave. Raising the split stone to his lips, he swiftly poured the blue, viscous Halahala down his throat.

The poison singed and seared Shiva's mouth and gullet, and he broke out into a feverish sweat. His dark skin turned ashen and blistered, and his muscular neck turned iridescent blue as the acidic fluid caught in his throat and crackled into flames. The god's bearded face bloated to bursting, and his eyes rolled back till the whites as he let out a fearsome bellow that crashed over the mountains, triggering mighty avalanches.

The devas and asuras huddled in fright as Shiva smote the ground with his gigantic trident, splitting the stony floor into two. Where the trident struck, water gushed forth from a subterranean river, and the god drank from the fountain long and deep, quenching the Halahala's fire. He then slumped to the ground to lay still, his body racked by spasms.

At long last, the mighty god raised his head and looked at the devas and asuras, his eyes tired but placid – and they understood the poison had been vanquished.

Overhead, the night sky was empty, rid of the flaming omen.

The asuras and devas rejoiced, embracing each other in relief, their enmity briefly forgotten. But as Shiva sat nursing his tender throat, his face was grave. He knew something the joyous devas and asuras didn't.

The Halahala hadn't been entirely destroyed.

The curse of the Halahala had just begun. Now nothing could prevent the three worlds from plunging into the darkness of greed.

And the darkness of war.

Many Thousand Years Later...

Hriiz

The four horsemen of the Frontier Guard stood at the top of a high ridge, watching the dull orange sun edge into the purple haze that obscured the far horizon. Down below them was the Marusthali, flat and parched, a spidery network of cracks on its surface running infinitely westward. Behind them rose the rocky folds of the Arbuda Range, dividing the wasted desert from the fertile vastness of Sindhuvarta, which lay to the east.

And all around was the bleak stillness of the mountains.

The murky haze had smothered nearly half the sun when a bearded vulture swept lazily into the horsemen's field of vision. The large bird circled a couple of times, before angling away sharply toward a far outcrop. As it disappeared behind the rocks, a chill wind suddenly sprang up from the Marusthali, plucking at the men's clothes and ruffling their hair, which was dry and matted with dust.

One of them, a grizzled veteran, wearing a bronze medallion fashioned in the form of a sun-crest, pulled his cloak tighter around himself and cursed under his breath. The other horsemen exchanged sly smiles.

"Cold's already getting to you, captain?" the biggest man in the group derided, his handsome young face twisting in a mocking grin.

"Humph!" the older man grunted, continuing to gaze over the darkening desert.

"Why don't you retire and give the sun of Avanti a chance to warm your old bones, captain?" the handsome lieutenant persisted with his needling. "Leave this business of hunting the Hunas and Sakas to younger blood."

The captain turned a cold eye on the cocky youngster. When he spoke, his voice was harsh and caustic.

"Count yourself lucky to have the luxury of hunting the Hunas and the Sakas, lieutenant. Because when I was your age, *they* were the hunters – and *we* the hunted. And these bones that you make fun of..." He paused and raised his chin toward the western horizon. "They have grown old pushing the Huna and Saka hordes back into the Great Desert. Don't you forget that!"

A stiff silence followed, broken by the youngest in the group – a reedy lad not a day older than twenty.

"It must have been something... driving the invaders out of Sindhuvarta." He looked wistfully at the last sliver of the dying sun. "I sometimes wish I was born a decade earlier. Then, perhaps..."

As the boy's voice trailed off, the captain sized him up, shaking his head. "You kids can't cease talking about fighting the Hunas and Sakas, can you? Your heads are just full of stories you heard as little brats. But you have no idea what it was really like." His uneasy eyes returned to scan the empty desert. "I fear that you might wish them upon yourselves with your eagerness for combat."

"You speak as if the Hunas and Sakas are more demon than human," the young lieutenant butted in, still smirking. "Perhaps the fear comes with age."

"And with ignorance comes bravado," the captain snorted in reply. "None of you fellows have ever met a Huna or Saka in battle, so what would you know."

"Let me assure you that the three of us are perfectly capable of dealing with any Hunas or Sakas we find in these hills, captain." The young lieutenant's voice turned combative as he squared his shoulders and gripped the pommel of his sword purposefully. With a slight jeer, he added, "That should give you all the freedom to deal with the cold."

"Oh, I'm sure you must be awesome with that sword," the captain retorted, his voice rising as he picked up the challenge. "After all, you have mastered your craft by hacking at those practice dummies in training school for years."

The mounting tension hung around them like a sullen mist. But before things could spiral out of control, the fourth horseman, a young man with calm eyes, quickly moved in to defuse the situation.

"It's not like we had a choice, captain," he chuckled disarmingly. "You old men put the fear of Avanti into the invaders, and brought peace to Sindhuvarta. So now we have to be content with plunging our swords into practice dummies, patrolling these dead mountains and sparring with one another verbally. Yet, we mustn't be judged without being given a fair chance to prove our worth, should we?"

The veteran considered the point before inclining his head. "I guess you're right," he sighed deeply. "It is in the nature of the bloodied sword to doubt the strength of untested metal."

"As it is in the nature of the new blade to discount the sharpness of old iron," the younger man smiled, tactfully acknowledging the captain's climbdown. After the briefest of pauses, he added, "All the same, I'm glad the glory of Avanti has prevailed."

"The glory of Avanti shall always prevail," the lieutenant returned to the conversation, but now his tone was sober and placatory, too. "May our kingdom prosper under King Vikramaditya!"

The other horsemen nodded and turned to the desert. Now that peace was brokered, they sat in the dwindling light for a while. The captain spoke again to break the hush.

"Our watch is over. It's time to return to the outpost."

Turning his horse around, he made his way back toward a jagged cleft in the mountains. The others filed after him quietly.

Fifteen minutes later, the patrol rode into a small basin surrounded by cliffs. Night had fallen, but the horsemen picked their way with practiced ease, the noses of their horses pointed toward three flickering points of light that gradually grew to reveal small torches.

The torchlight also threw the contours of three small wooden buildings into focus.

As the quartet approached the buildings, the captain, who was leading the way, observed the outpost's cook and an off-duty guard seated at a verandah, hunched over a *chaturanga* board spread out between them. Both men sat still, immersed in thought as they devised their game strategies.

The captain swore silently at the cook. Silly oaf, still at his bloody game when he should be in the kitchen getting dinner ready!

Deciding that the cook needed a ticking off, the captain dismounted, tethered his horse to a nearby rail and marched briskly toward the verandah. He was still ten meters from the house, when he sensed something was wrong.

The two men had not moved a muscle since he'd spotted them – surely they must have heard the horses trotting in. And even if they had missed that, the noise of his leather sandals crunching on gravel was loud enough to wake the dead. One of them ought to have noticed *that*. But both men just sat staring at the *chaturanga* board as the torch threw shadows around them.

It suddenly dawned upon the captain that the outpost was strangely silent. Yes, the stationed unit was small, and some soldiers were probably still out on patrol... Yet, there ought to have been *some* degree of activity, but there wasn't any.

Something else was odd, too. No smell of burning firewood anywhere. Not from the kitchen, not from the fires that should have been lit to fight the chill.

Working on instinct, the captain drew his sword, dropped to a crouch and pussyfooted forward, his eyes darting from the verandah to the shadows lurking behind the building. Somewhere behind him, the lieutenant and the boy were laughing at some joke, but the captain's mind barely registered this. He was preoccupied with the two men on the verandah.

As he drew closer, the captain's eyes grew wide in horror as he noticed the hilt of a large knife protruding from the cook's back, plumb in between the shoulder blades. Circling cautiously, the captain came in full view of the guard seated opposite the cook – and the first thing he saw was the guard's tunic, soaked in blood from a neat slash that had opened the guard's throat. The two men were propped up by spears that dug into their sides, preventing the bodies from keeling over under their weight.

In a flash the captain knew that the whole thing was a trap.

"Everything okay, captain?" hollered the horseman who had prevented a flare-up on the ridge.

Choking back waves of nausea and panic, the captain turned and stumbled away from the building, flailing frantically at his men, who were now approaching him tentatively.

"No..." he croaked. "No... we're trapped. They are back."

The three soldiers stared at the captain. "Who are back?" the lieutenant asked sharply, drawing his sword. The other two did likewise, peering at the verandah in confusion.

"*They*... the Hunas and the Sakas," the captain's voice rose a pitch and quavered.

"What?"

The captain turned, raised his sword with both hands and scanned the darkness. Instantly, the three others, too, turned to face the dark, their swords on the ready. Slowly, facing outward, they stepped back toward one another to form a tight protective circle, their eyes peeled for danger.

Suddenly, a thin whistling noise filled the air. Before the soldiers could even make sense of it, a heavy arrow smacked into the thin boy's head, cracking his skull and burying itself an inch above his left temple. The boy was dead before he slumped to the ground.

The other three had just about realized what had

happened when a second arrow skewered into the lieutenant's neck, ripping through muscle and tissue, its head emerging from the other side. The lieutenant coughed in surprise and blood gurgled from his lips as he fell on his face with a heavy thud.

The fourth horseman, the peacemaker, wasn't so lucky. The arrow that was shot at him was aimed at his neck, but owing to sudden movement on his part, it smashed into his left jaw, splitting open his cheek and breaking his jawbone. The young man howled in agony and dropped to his knees, before toppling sideways and convulsing in the mud.

The captain whirled around a couple of times, sword waving drunkenly as he waited for the inevitable fourth arrow to claim him. However, nothing came out of the dark. The seconds went by, and the captain felt the alarm rising inside him as the pounding of his blood filled his ears.

Then he heard another sound – the gentle clip-clop of hooves.

Slowly, from the far reaches of the shadows, a ring of horsemen emerged. As they drew near the torchlights, the captain noticed the shamanic *hriiz* branded on the horsemen's foreheads. He hadn't seen the *hriiz* in nearly ten years. The captain raised his sword, blinking rapidly to clear the cold sweat and fear from his eyes.

"Drop your sword, old man. Don't make us kill you."

The horseman had spoken in fluent Avanti, but there was no mistaking the coarse desert tongue of the Hunas – or the intent behind the words. The captain lowered his arms, his sword dropping with a clatter. At his feet, the young guardsman began moaning again, clutching his face tenderly.

"You are wise, so you will live," the Huna chieftain spoke again. "You will live so that you can let your king know that we are coming back. And tell him, this time we intend to take Sindhuvarta. *All of it*."

Three Huna horsemen dismounted. As they approached him, the captain began backing away hurriedly. But two of them grabbed him by his arms, pinning him between them.

"You... you said you shall let me g-go," the veteran bleated, wriggling in fear.

"I did, and you shall. But we can't let you come back to fight us again, can we?" The Huna chief's eyes gleamed wickedly. Turning to one of the captain's captors, he issued an order. "*Ah'khat waa*."

Right away, two Hunas began dragging the captain toward the verandah, while the third followed, pulling a machete out of his belt. The captain could instantly see the horror in store for him unfolding before his eyes – the Hunas chopping all his fingers off, and him never being able to wield a weapon ever again.

"No, please... no, no. I beg you, please... have mercy... No..."

The Huna chieftain watched the squirming and blathering captain being led away. He then hoisted a spear out of his saddle, dismounted, and walked up to the young soldier still writhing in the dirt. As the captain's screams began shredding the night, the chieftain plunged his spear expertly between the young man's ribs.

The soldier's body heaved once and went still.

Giant

The bullock cart trundled through the heavy drizzle, its big wooden wheels squeaking and grinding arduously on the paved limestone road that led up to the darkened palace.

It was the sound of the wheels that first alerted the two guards at the palace gates. They emerged from a makeshift shelter and peered into the rain, their eyes seeking to validate what their ears had already told them. Their vigil was rewarded when the cart slowly materialized out of the darkness and lumbered to a halt in front of them.

"Who's there?" one of the guards demanded, raising a burning torch. His long spear pointed at the figure of a man seated to the front of the cart, huddling from the rain under a thick shawl.

The figure shrugged the shawl off his head to reveal a round, chubby face that cascaded onto his chest in a series of double chins. The man had thick, rubbery lips that easily broke into a smile, and even in the dim torchlight, his big black eyes twinkled with mirth.

"Just a humble cartman making deliveries, sir... though if you ask these two oxen, they'll swear there are seven men on this cart." The cartman grinned and threw the shawl off to show his broad girth – and a tremendous paunch that defined it. "See?"

"Very funny," the guard snapped, though not without humor. Pointing to the back of the cart, he asked, "What have you there?"

"*Soma*, sir."

"*Soma*?" The second guard raised his eyebrows suspiciously. "For whom?"

"For King Kulabheda, the new king of Heheya. A tribute from the *soma* traders from the north, along with their salutations." With a wink, the cartman added in a sly undertone, "Not that the two of you can't have a little. It's really good stuff, I assure you. Nicely distilled. Your king would be none the wiser should two small flagons of it disappear."

While one of the guard's eyes lit up at the suggestion, the other walked around the cart imperviously, studying the six large urns loaded on to its back. Made of earthenware, the urns were each five feet high, their wide mouths covered by lids.

"Why are you making the delivery so late at night?" the guard asked.

"The rains have left the road from the north in bad shape, sir," the cartman explained. "I had to drive carefully so the *soma* didn't spill over, and that slowed me down. I also lost my way a bit in the dark outside Mahishmati. And, as I said, these blasted oxen... they really move as if they bear the burden of not one but *seven* men."

"Hmmm... I need to check the urns before I let you through."

"Go ahead, sir. Satisfy yourself." With a merry chuckle, the cartman added, "Though I still recommend your flagon as the best way to satisfy yourself."

The guard hoisted himself onto the cart. Raising his torch, he opened the lid of the first urn and peered in. The rich, fragrant, cardinal red wine, filled almost to the brim, glimmered in the torchlight.

"Don't let too much of the rain get into the urns, sir," the cartman grinned cheekily. "I'm sure your king won't fancy his *soma* diluted."

The guard hurriedly closed the lid, before conducting a perfunctory scrutiny of the other urns. Each was full of wine. Satisfied, he jumped off the cart. What he had failed to notice in the dark, however, were the thin, hollow, reeds that had been sticking an inch out of the surface of the wine – one reed in each urn.

He signalled the other guard to open the palace gates. "Go on," he shooed the cartman. "The granaries and storehouses are to the left. The guards inside will guide you."

Once the cart was inside the palace compound and the gates shut, the guard turned to his mate. "That was really good *soma*." Then, as the drizzle intensified, he added a tad regretfully, "Perhaps we should have filled our flagons after all."

Five minutes later, two porters were carefully unloading the heavy urns from the cart and lugging them into a storehouse to the rear of the compound. The cartman stood beside a soldier, watching the porters.

"You can go," the soldier growled insolently at the cartman once the last urn had been unloaded.

"If you don't mind, I'd like to see that last urn stored away safely, sir," the cartman spoke in an ingratiating manner. "My payment depends on it."

The soldier grunted in mild annoyance, but waited until the porters emerged from the storehouse. The soldier dismissed them, turned to the cartman and jerked his head.

"Leave."

"Er… shouldn't you lead me to your king so that I may offer my respects and inform him of this delivery?" the cartman hesitated, his eyes observing the porters as they disappeared from sight.

For a second, the soldier glowered at the fat little man in disbelief. "I'll have your tongue for your impudence, you dog," he exploded at last, making a threatening gesture with his spear. "Get lost."

"Yes sir."

Chastised, the cartman quickly waddled to the front of the cart and began preparing to leave. However, he watched the soldier out of the corner of his eye, and the moment the soldier dropped guard and relaxed, he pulled out an ironwood quarterstaff from under the cart. With confounding dexterity and speed, he then smacked the soldier expertly on the left temple. The soldier sank to the ground, knocked cold.

Stepping over the prone soldier, the cartman entered the storehouse that was packed to the rafters with provisions in sacks and chests. The six urns stood lined up against a wall. Walking up to the urns, the cartman rapped his staff against each, three times in quick succession.

Off came the urns' lids, and from each emerged a man, *soma* dripping off his body. The men leaped out of the urns nimbly, freeing their swords from their scabbards before their feet touched the ground.

"Pthoo!" One of the men spat out a reed. "It felt like we would be spending the rest of the night inside those urns, breathing out of those reeds."

The man's voice rang with authority. Clearly the leader of the group, he was around thirty, extremely large, broad-chested and powerfully built, with heavy muscular arms and shoulders. His swarthy, clean-shaven face was handsome in a brutal sort of way, and he seemed like someone accustomed to using his fists and sword to drive a point.

"Well, you had enough *soma* to keep you company till daybreak," the cartman grinned. "So what are you complaining about?"

"My friend Dhanavantri, I'm complaining about how you kept telling those guards that the cart has seven men on it," the big man wrung some wine out of his shoulder-length hair before tying it into a high, crude ponytail. "What if they had become suspicious?"

"The killing would have started at the palace gates then, what else? And don't tell me that would have been a problem for any of us."

As the men smiled wolfishly at one another, Dhanavantri continued, "Anyway, what I told the guards was the truth. My experience tells me that the more truthful you are, the less people are inclined to believe you."

The leader shook his head in mock horror. "And my experience tells me that you have to leave. If you and the cart are not back at the palace gates quickly, the guards could get suspicious and raise an alarm."

Dhanavantri nodded. "I shall be waiting with the horses outside the city. I'll see you tomorrow morning."

Once their fat friend had departed, the leader raised his heavy scimitar. Running a thumb on its keen edge, he looked at the men around him. "I repeat one last time... Avoid all unnecessary violence. Most of the guards, soldiers and palace staff are still loyal to King Harihara – they're just afraid of

Kulabheda and his elite Royal Guards. You will kill only the Royal Guards. Take down as many of them as possible." Seeing the men nod, he added, "Okay, let's go."

The men slipped out of the storeroom, silent as shadows, and fanned out across the palace compound.

* * *

In one of the palace bedrooms, a strong, well-built man lurched drunkenly over a bed, looking down at a young woman who lay trembling on plush velvet cushions. The woman was in her early twenties, her lustrous eyes large with fear in her pallid face.

"You…" the man pointed accusingly at the woman, holding on to the bedpost with his other hand. "You… I could have forced myself on you. I can marry you by force, you know that. But instead, I am asking… I, Kulabheda, am *asking* you to marry me."

The woman quailed as Kulabheda slurred and ranted on top of her. At last, mustering courage, she pleaded. "Please… please don't do this. My father will reward you handsomely if you will let…"

"Your father will… *reward* me?" Kulabheda interrupted, throwing his head back in uproarious laughter. "No, no… Princess Rukma, I'm afraid Harihara is in no position to reward *anyone*. For he is below us in the dungeons, with nothing left to give. I have taken everything he had. His kingdom, his treasury… *everything*. If anything, *I* am in a position to reward your father – with his and your own mother's life."

"Please have mercy on them," the princess whimpered.

"I will, I promise you." Kulabheda sobered down just enough to quaff a goblet of *soma* that he held in his hand.

"All I want is your assent in marriage," he continued, wiping his lips crudely with the back of his hand. "Agree, and your parents will come to no harm. You have my word. And imagine – by marrying me you can be queen of Heheya! Queen of the very kingdom you grew up in. How many princesses are blessed with such luck?"

"Why are you doing this to us?"

"Why? You ask *why*?" Kulabheda's face darkened and he flung aside the empty goblet in rage. "You spoke of your father rewarding me... I was your father's most loyal general; I served him and Heheya faithfully for years. But when the time comes for him to give you away in marriage, he chooses to favor some silly prince or the other over me! That's the reward I get for my loyalty." Kulabheda paused to catch his breath and grunted. "Perhaps he thinks a soldier isn't worthy of a royal princess. So I've decided to seek your hand as king of Heheya."

"I'm... I'm sure my father didn't mean ill," Rukma tried to reason. "He would have given you anything else had you asked for it."

"I wanted *you*, but he ignored me," Kulabheda leaned over the princess, his bloodshot eyes drunk with lust. He licked his lips lasciviously, his face inches from the princess's. "So now I am left with no choice but to take what is mine."

Suddenly, Kulabheda threw himself on the princess, pinning her down with his weight. As he plunged his head into the soft curve of her neck in crazed passion, Rukma wriggled in desperation and let out a shriek.

A moment later, the bedroom door was kicked open with a loud bang.

As the door swung clumsily on a broken hinge, a giant

of a man wearing a high ponytail barged in, brandishing a heavy scimitar. His face, however, was hidden in shadow.

"Who are you?" Kulabheda demanded, swiveling around.

"Your nemesis," the intruder answered. With a smirk in his voice, he added, "How interesting to know that the new king of Heheya cultivates an interest in wrestling with women."

Kulabheda pushed himself off the bed, his eyes flashing with anger. "The new king of Heheya also feasts on the corpse of the person he has killed," he said, reaching for his sword on the side table.

As he straightened, the giant stepped into the light. Fear swelled in Kulabheda's eyes on recognizing the man. "Oh, it's you!"

Just then, alerted by the crashing in of the door, three Royal Guards came rushing to the bedroom. Swords raised, they launched themselves at the intruder. But in a series of fluid, lightning-fast moves, the man parried the attack, severing a guard's arm and carving open the stomachs of the other two.

Seeing that the intruder was busy fighting the guards, Kulabheda raised his sword and lunged at the man's broad back, which was turned to him. But at the last moment, the giant spun around and wove out of the way of Kulabheda's sword. Thrown off balance, Kulabheda stumbled forward – straight into the tip of the other's scimitar aimed directly at his chest. The heavy sword pierced the flesh and buried itself firmly in Kulabheda's heart.

As the giant pulled his scimitar free, blood welled out of the wound and Kulabheda fell on the carpeted floor, lifeless.

The intruder straightened and looked at the cowering princess, her face white with shock and fear.

"Fear not, Princess Rukma. You are safe," he reassured.

"I come from the court of King Vikramaditya of Avanti. I am here under orders from King Vikramaditya to free King Harihara."

The man bent to grab Kulabheda's head by the hair and lifted it off the floor. He raised his scimitar, and then looked at the princess, who was staring at him in wide-eyed horror.

"Please close your eyes," he said.

Rukma nodded and screwed her eyes shut, shielding her face with a forearm for added precaution. The scimitar descended, hacking Kulabheda's head clean off his body.

With the head in one hand, the giant strode up to an indoor balcony that overlooked a large, enclosed atrium. The hall below was teeming with confused soldiers, many of them already scrambling up the curved staircase that led to the bedchambers and boudoirs.

"Stop and listen to me," the man commanded, his voice echoing through the courtyard. As the soldiers stared up at him in awe, he raised the severed head high. "Kulabheda is dead."

A collective gasp arose from the soldiers while the man continued addressing them. "Harihara is once again your king, and you will obey him. King Harihara's orders are to arrest every one of Kulabheda's Royal Guards. If any of them resist – you are free to kill them."

An enthusiastic murmur spread through the hall; some soldiers began hailing King Harihara. In the din, one of the men who had arrived in the urns came up to the giant and whispered into his ear. The leader nodded, tossed Kulabheda's head down into the atrium and marched off.

A little later, the giant and two of his men, accompanied by some of King Harihara's loyalist guards, descended a narrow winding staircase that led to the dungeons beneath the palace. As they approached a cell set to the back, the guards began shouting.

"Hail King Harihara! Glory to Heheya!"

One of the guards unlocked the cell and entered it. In a moment, an elderly couple and three bookish ministers shuffled into the torchlight, their eyes blinking in a mixture of surprise, exultation and relief.

"King Harihara, do accept my salutations on King Vikramaditya's behalf," said the giant, bowing with his hands folded.

The old man smiled and looked at the queen and his ministers. "I knew Vikramaditya would do everything in his capacity to assist an old ally in trouble. What I didn't expect was that he would send one of his best warriors to do the job." Turning back to the large man, he said, "It feels really good to see you, Kalidasa."

"You, too, your honor," Kalidasa bowed again.

Harihara looked quizzically at the scimitar in Kalidasa's hand. "I take it that Kulabheda is no more?"

"He isn't, your honor," the giant shook his head as he sheathed the bloodstained blade.

"And our daughter?" the queen spoke with a quaver.

"Princess Rukma is safe, Queen Mother," Kalidasa assured her.

"Thank God for that." King Harihara began leading the way out of the dungeon. As he mounted the stairs, he spoke to Kalidasa over his shoulder. "I presume you are here to escort me to Ujjayini as well?"

"Yes, your honor. We need to leave at the earliest, so that we are well in time for King Vikramaditya's *rajasuya yajna* the day after. Heheya being one of Avanti's oldest allies, my king insists on your presence at the *yajna*."

"The honor is mine," Harihara smiled with pride. "But do we have time for a bath and a decent dinner at least? That bastard Kulabheda fed us nothing but gruel the past week."

"Certainly, your honor," Kalidasa nodded. "With your permission, we shall leave Mahishmati at sunrise tomorrow, so that we can be in Ujjayini by nightfall."

Arrivals

The sun had yet to shake off its slumber when the small boat slipped through the dark water, its prow pointing toward a row of bathing *ghat*s that lined the eastern bank of the river Kshipra. There was sufficient daylight, though – enough to make out the *ghat*'s steps, which were dotted with early bathers, leading up steeply from the waterline. At the top of the steps were numerous large peepal trees, all still in shadow, from which flocks of birds periodically burst forth into the early morning sky. Behind the trees rose the ancient, white marble ramparts of Ujjayini, capital of Avanti.

The sadhu sat to the front of the boat, taking in the scene with his deep, wide-set eyes, his fingers playing absentmindedly with a prayer bead made of *rudraksh* seeds. He was of medium height, muscular, his dark skin covered by a thin layer of ash. He wore a black dhoti and turban, and his broad and handsome face was covered by a rich black beard that reached down to his chest.

"Are you going for the feast as well, gurudev?"

The sadhu turned around to look at the wizened boatman, who had put forth the question. He stared at the boatman for a moment, as if in incomprehension.

"The feast..." boatman repeated, pointing toward Ujjayini. His tone seemed to imply that what he was alluding to should have been glaringly obvious. "The feast in celebration of King Vikramaditya's *rajasuya yajna*."

The sadhu looked at the city's ramparts and nodded distractedly. He neither spoke nor turned to look at the boatman; clearly, the sadhu didn't fancy a chat.

"People from all over the kingdom are coming for the feast." The boatman either didn't get the hint – or chose to ignore it. "I myself have ferried nearly a thousand people to the city over the last two days. You are the first today, gurudev, but I am sure more will follow as the sun gains height."

The sadhu continued staring at the ramparts.

"I will be going as well," the boatman appeared happy to carry on a one-sided conversation. "And why not, I ask you? After all, the feast is in honor of our king – if we citizens of Avanti don't celebrate it, who will? Don't you agree?"

The sadhu condescended with a small nod, in the hope that the matter would end there. He immediately paid the price for his mistake.

"Actually, gurudev, it's not only Avanti that is celebrating," the boatman launched into another vigorous explanation. "The royal courts of Matya, Vatsa, Kosala, Magadha and Heheya are also attending the *yajna*, and I hear even some subjects of these kingdoms have journeyed to Ujjayini for the occasion." He paused for a fraction of a second as a new thought occurred to him. "Is your holiness also from one of these kingdoms?"

The sadhu turned and considered the boatman. There was something unsettling in his gaze that made the boatman look away nervously. At last, the sadhu shook his head and returned his attention to the walls of Ujjayini, which were now framed by the golden glow of the newborn sun. The boatman, for his part, didn't hazard any more words.

A few minutes later, the boat nudged the bathing *ghat*. Picking up a staff and a cloth bundle that lay beside him, the sadhu disembarked.

"What do I owe you?" he asked, fumbling at the folds of his dhoti.

"Gurudev, you are a holy man… I can't accept money from you…" the boatman began obsequiously, but his manner suggested tokenism. And when the sadhu proffered a coin, he reached for it without the slightest demur, eyes gleaming in joy. "Thank you, gurudev. The palace grounds are easy to find. You just have to walk through the gate at that corner…"

The sadhu raised a hand to hush the boatman. "I have come from very far and I have travelled long. I know how to find my way."

Ascending the ghat's steps, the sadhu ran a quick hand around the cloth bundle, patting it gently, as if feeling for something. For a moment, he couldn't seem to find what he was looking for, and his features turned anxious. But when his palm brushed against a hard, pointed object at the bottom of the bundle, he exhaled in relief.

The dagger was safe. All that remained was to seek out the man it was meant for; the man who was somewhere inside Ujjayini's walls… somewhere inside the royal palace.

***

Queen Mother Upashruti leaned out of the ornate, canopied balcony adjoining her bedroom, breathed in the scented morning air and smiled contentedly to herself.

Life was finally being kind to her.

From where she stood, she could see the broad sweep of the expansive lake that surrounded the royal palace of Avanti on all four sides. The lake was full of pink lotuses in various stages of bloom, and stately swans glided here and there on its surface. The far edges of the lake were lined with jacaranda and gulmohar trees, on which kingfishers sat making a meal of the day's first catch. The palace causeway spanning the lake was to the queen's left, although she couldn't see it now because of the bedazzling sunlight reflecting off the water.

Turning to her right, Queen Upashruti looked across the lake toward the palace grounds, on the other side of a wide thicket of deciduous trees and shrubs. Her ears caught the faint bustle of human activity coming from that direction, and she again smiled softly. The queen knew the grounds were full of people preparing for the *rajasuya yajna*.

Once the priests invoked the blessings of ancient gods and performed the sacrificial rites, the son born from her womb would assume the title of samrat – overlord of Sindhuvarta. And the kings of all the neighboring kingdoms – many already reduced to vassal states, still others only nominally independent – would swear allegiance to her son and the throne of Avanti. Life was indeed becoming kind to her.

The *rajasuya yajna*, the pure honey-gold sunlight splashed over Ujjayini, the tranquility and contentment borne by the morning breeze… None of these was imaginable even ten years ago, when not a day passed without news of a costly victory or a demoralizing upset in battle, coming from one quarter of

Sindhuvarta or the other. The uncertainty had started much earlier, of course, not long after Upashruti first entered the palace of Ujjayini as King Mahendraditya's bride. The barbaric hordes from the Marusthali had already swamped the faraway principalities of Salwa and Gosringa, but the threat turned real with the Hunas and Sakas making steady progress eastward, swallowing the kingdoms of Nishada, Malawa and Kunti before laying siege to Avanti and Matsya.

It had taken all of Mahendraditya's acumen and courage to stitch an alliance against the invaders, but the Hunas and Sakas had proved intractable. The queen still remembered the night when, hiding in the Labyrinth with the rest of the royal household, cradling the young Vikramaditya to her chest, she had learned that Mahendraditya had been mortally wounded by the sword of an unknown Saka warrior. She remembered the king lying on his bed, his life ebbing away from him as he held her hand and entreated her not to lose hope, even as the barbarians swarmed barely a few miles outside Ujjayini. She remembered the despair come crashing down on her as the king's hand went limp in hers.

With the passing of her husband, Queen Upashruti had felt that it was all over – that Avanti would inevitably fall. Yet, remarkably enough, Mahendraditya's death served as a rallying point for the allied forces of Sindhuvarta's kingdoms, and first under the command of Acharya Vetala Bhatta, and later under Vikramaditya himself, the invaders' resilience was broken. Not only were the Hunas and Sakas dislodged from Avanti and Matsya, every tract of Sindhuvarta claimed by the barbarians was systematically prised back. So, in the Queen Mother's mind, the *rajasuya yajna* was an opportunity for all the kingdoms of Sindhuvarta to formally offer their gratitude to her son.

The queen's thoughts were interrupted by the creaking of a door. Turning around, she saw one of her handmaidens standing a little inside her bedroom.

"Your highness, Princess Pralupi and Prince Himavardhan are here to see you," she announced. Seeing her queen incline her head, the handmaiden pulled the door open wide to admit a woman and a man.

It was obvious that the woman who led the way into the darkened bedroom was Queen Upashruti's daughter. Age – and the softness of their faces – was where mother and daughter differed. The queen habitually wore a benign expression, but Princess Pralupi's face had a rough angularity, accentuated by a sour turn of the mouth, almost as if she was carrying life's bitterness with her.

"How are you, my angel? I'm so glad to see you…" Queen Upashruti's eyes shone as she embraced her daughter. "They told me you came last night."

"Yes mother," Pralupi replied vaguely as she disengaged herself from the queen's clasp.

The Queen Mother searched her daughter's face for a moment, then, remembering her manners, turned to Prince Himavardhan. "How are you, prince? I trust you had a good journey from Vatsa and are rested?"

The man, who was cradling a white rabbit in his arms, smiled shyly at the queen before dropping his gaze, but he didn't respond to her questions. Although in his mid-forties, the prince had the demeanor of a child, and his eyes rarely made contact with others. He merely stood staring at the marble floor, gently stroking the rabbit.

The queen didn't seem particularly bothered by this, and returned her attention to Pralupi. "Good, good. I hope the two of you are going to stay in Ujjayini for some time. I would love both of you to do that – and so would your brother."

Princess Pralupi nodded noncommittally. But before any more words could be exchanged, the prince suddenly shuffled up to the queen's bed, his eyes shining eagerly. Reaching the bed, he began running his hand over the cobalt blue velvet bedcover. He then turned to Pralupi.

"Sso ssoft," he lisped, his voice was full of awe.

The queen smiled indulgently and turned back to her daughter. "How is King Chandravardhan?"

"He's here," Pralupi answered flatly. "You'll see him at the *yajna*, I suppose."

The queen nodded, and then tried another track. "Did you meet Ghatakarpara?"

"Not yet. We arrived late last night."

"Oh, he's grown into a nice strong lad." Queen Upashruti's voice brimmed with the doting pride that is unique to grandparents when talking about their grandchildren. "The Acharya has been training him well. One day, your son will make this family proud."

"But he'll never become a king, will he?" Pralupi pouted petulantly.

"Why do you say that?" the queen's voice was sharp.

"Mother, everyone knows Ghatakarpara is the ideal candidate for ruling Vatsa. But he won't – because he's not the son of King Chandravardhan. He's the offspring of the king's imbecile brother. So instead of my son, Chandravardhan's incompetent drunkard of a son Shashivardhan will ascend Vatsa's throne…"

"Hush dear," the queen waved her hands urgently to silence Pralupi. Casting a glance at Himavardhan, who was sulking at his wife, the queen added, "Keep a hold on your tongue and your emotions."

Pralupi turned to her husband. "Why don't you go and look at the swans on the lake?" she pointed toward the balcony.

The prince's face lit up and he trotted off. Pralupi took her mother's elbow and propelled her out of Himavardhan's earshot.

"Why don't you speak to Vikramaditya?" she whispered. "He loves you and will listen to you."

"Speak to him about what?" Queen Upashruti looked puzzled.

"Making Ghatakarpara the next king of Vatsa."

The queen took a step back in surprise. "But dear, Shashivardhan is the rightful heir to Vatsa's…"

"Rightful?" The princess's eyes flashed with jealousy and hatred. "If Shashivardhan were the rightful heir to Chandravardhan, he should have been here for today's *yajna*. Isn't that what's expected of a crown prince? But no, while the rest of the royal household is here, Shashivardhan is in Kausambi, probably drowning himself in *soma* and squandering the treasury's riches in some gambling house. Rightful, humph!"

Queen Upashruti cast her eyes around helplessly, as if seeking a satisfactory answer in the dark recesses of the room. "But why would Chandravardhan even listen to your brother?"

"Why *wouldn't* he?" Pralupi pursued the matter. "Vikramaditya is about to become samrat, the most powerful man in Sindhuvarta. Chandravardhan is already a vassal of Avanti. Avanti's army is infinitely superior to Vatsa's – and the kingdom relies on our trade routes for its economy. Chandravardhan's survival depends on us; he can't refuse if

Vikramaditya asks that Ghatakarpara be made his successor. Chandravardhan is smart enough to know that if he refuses, Avanti can crush him."

"Your brother will never agree to this," the queen's eyes were round with distress.

"I don't see why," the princess's voice was tinged with outrage at the possibility. "Doesn't he love his nephew? Wouldn't he want his nephew to rule a kingdom of his own?"

"Of course Vikrama loves Ghatakarpara, dear... " the queen fumbled, "But I don't think he will listen..."

At that moment, Himavardhan returned from the balcony. He held the rabbit up with both hands. "He wantss food."

"I'm talking to mother," said Pralupi wearily, forcing some gentleness into her voice. "We'll feed him in a little while. Please go and watch the swans."

"No," Himavardhan stamped his foot adamantly, his mouth sagging. "Now, now... He wantss food."

Pralupi looked at her husband in exasperation, before giving in with a nod. As the prince walked toward the bedroom door, she turned back to the queen. "Talk to Vikramaditya, mother," she hissed. "If not for me, at least do it for your grandson."

Queen Upashruti watched the door close behind her daughter and son-in-law and sighed. Perhaps she would broach the subject with Vikramaditya after the *rajasuya yajna*, she thought without relish.

* * *

Two pairs of eyes followed Princess Pralupi and her husband as they walked out of the queen's boudoir, descended a flight of stairs, crossed an open courtyard and disappeared down a corridor.

The eyes belonged to two men who sat on an ironwork bench, just inside an arched arbor laced with sweet-smelling jasmine. One of them was in his late fifties, lean and tall, his austere face highlighted by a pair of shrewd black eyes under bushy gray eyebrows that complemented a thick crop of gray beard. The few wisps of hair that had escaped from under his deep purple turban were of the same gray hue. Acharya Vetala Bhatta, royal tutor and chief advisor to the king of Avanti, wore his age with pride and dignity.

"Did she come to meet you?" Vetala Bhatta finally broke the silence, gesturing toward the retreating form of Princess Pralupi.

The man seated beside the Acharya shook his head. He was much younger, a shade over forty, short and lean in build. His body was sinewy, the muscles constantly rippling under his skin like trapped energy looking for an outlet. Locks of jet-black hair fell down to his shoulders, and he sported a heavy black moustache on his lip and a bright red *tilaka* on his forehead.

"No. Why would she? She doesn't care much for me... never did. I'm only her half-brother, born to her father of another woman."

Vetala Bhatta glanced sharply at his companion. "I don't think that's true – she *does* care for you. She just doesn't show it easily."

The younger man turned and smiled at the Acharya sadly. "You know that's a lie, raj-guru."

Vetala Bhatta gave this some thought before inclining his head. It was a lie and Vararuchi, half-brother to Princess Pralupi and King Vikramaditya, had seen through it.

"The truth is that Pralupi probably doesn't care much for anyone other than herself," the Acharya said, choosing honesty this time, and speaking from his experience of having tutored the children for years and seen them grow up. "So, don't judge her too harshly."

"I don't," replied Vararuchi. "Actually, I feel a strange sympathy for her. She is the princess of Avanti, the most powerful kingdom in Sindhuvarta, but she has to live with a man who can barely take care of himself. I don't think father acted wisely when he decided to marry her off to Himavardhan. She deserved better. I'll never understand why he did it."

"Those were hard times, Vararuchi... you were old enough, so you should know that," Vetala Bhatta reminded patiently. "The Hunas and Sakas had to be repelled, and Avanti needed to form strong alliances to fight the invaders. Chandravardhan of Vatsa was an obvious choice, but he declined to accept Pralupi's hand in marriage. Instead, Chandravardhan proposed her marriage to his brother and... Well, King Mahendraditya made that choice for Avanti."

The two men sat quietly for a while. It was obvious that despite the difference in age – and their relationship as mentor and pupil – the two shared a close bond. At last, Vararuchi raised his face to the clear blue sky.

"Father would be a very proud man today. He always believed that Vikramaditya was destined to achieve great things... he would often tell me so when we went hunting," the sadness lifted from Vararuchi's eyes as he spoke. "Today his son, the king of Avanti, will become samrat of Sindhuvarta."

Vetala Bhatta studied Vararuchi briefly before nodding. "Yes, he would be proud – of *both* his sons. Of his younger son, who will soon be Samrat Vikramaditya... and of you, for having ruled Avanti wisely till Vikramaditya was old enough to become king." The Acharya clapped Vararuchi warmly on the shoulder and smiled. "Vikramaditya and the court of Avanti owe you a great deal."

The younger man returned the smile. "Thank you for your kindness, raj-guru. But everything I did was out of love for my little brother. And because of the promise I made to father on his deathbed. I gave him my word that as his elder son, I would always stand by my brother and ensure that Avanti's glory remains untarnished."

The Acharya squinted up at the sun and quickly began rising to his feet. "In that case, you had better hurry up and get ready. The auspicious hour for your brother's *yajna* is nearly upon us."

***

A metronomic clanging of temple bells and gongs rent the morning calm, sending droves of frightened pigeons into flight. Below, under an ancient banyan tree, stood the royal temple, white smoke wafting out of its doors and windows. The atmosphere was redolent with the scent of *sambrani* and camphor, while somber incantations pervaded the space between each toll of the bells. Outside the temple, junior priests clad in white stood in two rows, their lips moving silently as they repeated the mantras and hymns being recited inside.

Behind the priests and slightly to the left, a group of four men were standing, conversing in low voices. They were Acharya Vetala Bhatta, Vararuchi, Dhanavantri and Amara Simha, the last a short, brawny man with a barrel-like chest and heavily muscled arms. His head was a shock of reddish-brown hair, and his large beard and big curling moustache were the same color. He had fierce black eyes that tended to stare combatively at everything.

The pealing of the bells and the incantations ceased, signaling the end of a sacred rite. As the priests outside began raising salutations to the gods, three figures emerged from the temple's smoky sanctum. While the first was a Brahman priest, senior in age and bearing, the second was Queen Upashruti.

The third was a tall and stately man of about thirty-five. He had a calm and assured gait, and it was plain that authority rested easily on his broad shoulders. Glossy, black hair reached down to his shoulders, while perceptive black eyes gazed out from under finely arched eyebrows. A rich moustache complemented the strong, chiselled chin. The man possessed a unique kinetic magnetism, and all eyes were drawn to him the moment he emerged into the open.

Glancing in the direction of Vetala Bhatta, the man spoke briefly to the head priest. He then approached the Acharya, folded his hands and bowed deeply.

"Bless me, raj-guru," he said.

"You have my blessings, my king," the royal councilor replied.

"I seek your blessings not as your king, but as your pupil," the man insisted. "Guide me with your wisdom as you have in the past, and help me lead Avanti to even greater glory."

Vetala Bhatta's face softened and he smiled. "You have my blessings, Vikramaditya. As samrat of Sindhuvarta, may you rule wisely and justly, and be known as the greatest of kings."

Vikramaditya turned to Vararuchi and bowed. "I seek your blessings too, brother."

"You already have more than that," Vararuchi smiled at the king. "My life is at your service, brother. Lead Avanti well, Samrat Vikramaditya."

The king looked down at Vararuchi affectionately. "I am not samrat yet, brother. Not till the *yajna* is over."

"To father and me, you always were samrat."

At a loss for words, Vikramaditya stared at Vararuchi for a moment. Then, in a rush of emotion, he embraced his brother. As they disengaged, Vararuchi spoke again.

"Mother sends you her blessings."

The king looked at his brother in surprise. "Oh, but isn't she coming for the *yajna*?"

"A palanquin was sent to fetch her, but she couldn't come. It's the arthritis."

"Is it getting worse?" Vikramaditya searched Vararuchi's face in concern.

"She's in great pain," the elder brother shrugged, his eyes clouding with worry.

"Why doesn't she..." The king interrupted his train of thought and addressed Dhanavantri. "Isn't there something you can do for *badi-maa*?"

"Why wasn't I informed about this earlier?" The fat councilor regarded Vararuchi with the peculiar reproach that practitioners of medicine reserve, when confronted with ailments that have aggravated owing to lack of care or indifference. Turning back to Vikramaditya, he said, "I had prescribed her some medications a while back, and I believed she had got better. Nobody told me that she's... Anyway, I will pay her a visit as soon as we're done with the *yajna*."

Reassured, the king turned his attention to the Acharya.

"Has everyone else arrived?"

"Chandravardhan and his court are here. As are King Baanahasta, King Bhoomipala, and the five chiefs of the Anarta Federation. And I've just been told that King

Siddhasena and his sons from Magadha arrived at the palace a little while ago."

"And King Harihara?" Vikramaditya glanced back at Dhanavantri.

"We escorted him safely to Ujjayini last night."

"He was a friend of father's, and is one of our oldest allies," the king nodded in satisfaction. He began walking toward the palace grounds, where the sacrificial fire was lit, and palace staff and priests were busy preparing for the *yajna*. As the others fell in step, Vikramaditya turned to Dhanavantri.

"So Kulabheda didn't really present any problems, did he?"

"Hardly," Dhanavantri shrugged his fat shoulders. "From what Kalidasa tells me, the rogue was too busy getting drunk on *soma* and courting Princess Rukma to offer much resistance."

"Well, at least he gave Kalidasa and you a break from the monotony of peace," the king smiled. "Kalidasa keeps insisting that this peace is getting too tedious."

"And so he gets rewarded with a battle, while my axe accumulates rust from lack of use," Amara Simha grumbled good-naturedly. "Some people have all the luck."

"I admit it was unfair to have denied you a battle, Amara Simha," the Acharya permitted himself a grin. "Unpardonable."

"Yes, but sending both Kalidasa and Amara Simha to remove Kulabheda would have been like using a hammer to crush an ant," Vararuchi remarked, putting a friendly arm around Amara Simha's hefty shoulders.

"Then I should have been sent to Heheya instead of Kalidasa," Amara Simha insisted stubbornly.

"If you had gone there, King Harihara's palace would have needed a lot of rebuilding before it became habitable again," Dhanavantri chuckled and poked Amara Simha in the ribs. "And that would have been the end of the Avanti-Heheya alliance."

The men laughed heartily as the concourse slowly threaded its way toward the palace grounds. Not far away, seated under a neem tree, a sadhu watched the group closely, his keen eyes observing Vikramaditya, the same sadhu the boatman had ferried to Ujjayini earlier that morning.

The sadhu had found the man he had come for.

***

In a large room in the royal palace, a young man of around twenty stood before a full-length mirror made of bronze and tin alloy. Though not very tall, he was well-proportioned, possessing the natural agility of youth toned by hours spent in martial training. His fair, clean-shaven face was rakishly handsome, his large, black eyes full of vitality – and a touch of haughtiness that comes naturally to the high-born.

Using an ivory comb, the young man carefully brushed the thick mop of hair away from his forehead, before applying kohl to his eyes. When he was done, he pulled on a cloak and pinned a gold ceremonial medallion of Avanti to it. Finally, he picked up a short sword from a side table and thrust it into a scabbard slung at his waist.

He was admiring his reflection in the polished metal one last time when someone knocked at his door.

"Come in," he called, his eyes still on the mirror.

The door opened to admit a sentry. "A rider from the garrison of Udaypuri seeks an audience, your honor," he announced.

"The rider wants to see *me*?" The young man turned, his eyebrows rising fractionally. He then shook his head in confusion, a few locks of hair slipping out of place and falling partially over his eyes. "What for? He should report to the command center here. That's the protocol."

"He insists on delivering his message in person, your honor."

"Then tell him he will have to wait. It's almost time for the *yajna* and I have to be with the king."

"I told the rider as much, but he says it's urgent, your honor," the sentry shifted his weight from one leg to the other. "He says he has something very important to share."

The young man frowned, but nodded as intrigue got the better of him. The sentry went out, and moments later, the rider stood at the door, covered in dust from head to toe. His eyes were red from lack of sleep, and from the way he swayed, it appeared he was on the brink of exhaustion.

"Salutations to Prince Ghatakarpara... Glory to Avanti and..."

Prince Ghatakarpara raised an impatient hand to stay the rider, then beckoned him in. "You say this is urgent, so get on with it."

The rider shut the door behind him and moved forward. "I bring a personal message from Atulyateja, garrison commander of Udaypuri," he rasped hoarsely. "Three days ago..."

"Atulyateja has sent you?" Ghatakarpara's face cleared and he smiled. "How is my old friend? I've seen so little of him since he left Ujjayini to take command of his own garrison."

The rider was silent, unsure about how to respond to this. The prince sensed the rider's uncertainty and snapped out of his reverie.

"What's the message that Atulyateja has for me?" he demanded, leaning theatrically against an ornamental colonnade.

"Your honor, three days ago, a captain of the Frontier Guard was found unconscious in the hills close to Udaypuri. All the fingers on the captain's hands were missing, and he had lost a lot of blood. The physicians and nurses at the garrison tended to him, and yesterday afternoon he finally regained consciousness."

"Continue." The young prince injected lazy authority into his voice.

"The captain says that he was part of a patrol stationed at the edge of the Arbuda Mountains – the western edge, close to the Great Desert."

Ghatakarpara dropped the studied poise and went rigid. He sensed what was coming.

"It seems his outpost was destroyed and all his men were massacred." The rider paused to swallow hard. "The captain says the attackers were the band of Hunas."

"How can he be sure?" Ghatakarpara narrowed his eyes.

"He says they all had the *hriiz* on their foreheads."

"How did the captain survive the attack?"

"They chopped off his fingers and let him go – with a message for our king. They told him they are coming back to conquer Sindhuvarta."

The rider's words and their horrific implications sent a chill through the prince.

"Commander Atulyateja instructed me to deliver this to you in confidence, as he didn't want to cause unnecessary panic, your honor."

Ghatakarpara responded with a grim nod. He saw why Atulyateja had dispatched a rider instead of using the *suryayantras* to communicate the news to Ujjayini. The *suryayantra* system would have been faster, but far less discreet. Too many people would have learned of the attack, and once tongues started wagging, nothing could prevent distress and fear from spreading among the populace.

"I shall have a message for the commander this afternoon," he muttered, jaw clenched tight. "Meanwhile, get some rest – and don't breathe a word about any of this to anyone."

As the rider's footsteps faded down the corridor, Ghatakarpara rubbed his chin and stared down at the floor. *They had the* hriiz *on their foreheads*. He had seen the distinctive sigil of the scorpion on a few toothless old slaves in the market... and he had heard many gruesome tales about the cruel men who wore it.

They are coming back to conquer Sindhuvarta.

The king needed to be told about this immediately.

The prince took three big strides and threw open the door to the gallery. But at that precise moment, the roll of drums and the shrill call of trumpets from the palace grounds echoed in his ears, heralding the start of the *rajasuya yajna*.

Ghatakarpara cursed. He would now have to wait till the *yajna* was over to share the ominous news with the king and the rest of the council.

Council

With every passing moment, the sulk on Ghatakarpara's face grew longer, as he slouched against a marbled parapet and stared into the brooding green waters of the lake lapping against the palace walls. He was at the bottom of a wide landscaped terrace abutting the banquet hall, a canopy of blazing red gulmohars sheltering him from the bright afternoon sun. Behind him, a little to the left, an elaborate fountain of cavorting water sprites and mermaids made a loud splash, muting the chorus of revelry coming from the banquet hall and drowning out the hum that issued from the direction of the palace grounds, where the feast for the subjects of Avanti was underway.

"What are you doing here all by yourself?"

The young prince started at the sound of the voice, even though it had a soft, soothing cadence that served up the image of rich, golden honey. He turned to see a tall, sensuous woman, half-hidden by the fronds of an exotic

shrub, looking at him from the top of the winding pathway
that led down to the fountain.

"Is everything all right?" the woman asked, a shadow of
concern falling across her face.

Ghatakarpara nodded, his breath catching in his throat,
rendering him incapable of speech. Kshapanaka invariably
had that effect on him. In fact, he was certain she had that
effect on most men.

The prince watched with adoring eyes as Kshapanaka
stepped past the shrub and descended a low flight of steps
to join him. In her mid-twenties, Kshapanaka was tall and
graceful, yet she possessed an athletic build that spoke of
formal military training. Her eyes were large and languid
in her dusky, chiselled face, but the prince could see an
impetuous spark dancing in their depths. Her hair hung
around her shoulders in alluring curls, highlighting the arch
of her slender neck.

"So, what's the matter?" Kshapanaka leaned on the
parapet and studied Ghatakarpara's face earnestly, before
transferring her gaze to the far shores of the lake. "I can see
something's troubling you."

"No, not really," the prince shook his head, subconscious-
ly marveling at the woman's perceptiveness.

"Then why are you here when everyone else is inside?"
Kshapanaka inclined her head toward the banquet hall.

"Oh, that. I was just getting bored."

"Are you sure there's nothing else?"

There was something about the way Kshapanaka looked
at Ghatakarpara as she posed the question that breached
the boy's defenses.

"Well... I mean all of them are so stuffy and full of
themselves, bragging about the battles they've fought or how

cleverly they rule their kingdoms," the words came out in a rush as the resistance melted away and the prince bared his heart to the beautiful woman standing by his side. "Just because someone has fought a few battles doesn't mean those who haven't are fools and shouldn't be taken seriously."

Kshapanaka looked at Ghatakarpara in silence for a moment. "And who isn't taking you seriously?"

"Uncle Vararuchi," the prince muttered in a voice pebbled with resentment.

"What makes you think he doesn't take you seriously?" Kshapanaka arched her eyebrows.

"I needed to tell the king something, but when I approached him, uncle Vararuchi stopped me. He said the king was busy attending to the guests and that I was not to disturb him. I told uncle Vararuchi that it was important, but he just shooed me away." After a moment's pause, the prince shook his head vehemently. "Everyone around treats me as if I'm still a kid."

"That's because you *behave* like one."

Aghast, Ghatakarpara turned sharply toward Kshapanaka. He had confided in her expecting her to be supportive, but instead, she had stung him with that remark. He opened his mouth in protest, but changed his mind and turned away, seeking refuge in injured silence.

"Only a kid would think of bothering the king on a day when he's playing host to so many kings of Sindhuvarta," Kshapanaka said matter-of-factly.

"I had... I have some very important news for the king," Ghatakarpara spoke hotly. "*Very*, *very* important news..."

"Did you tell Vararuchi what this news was?"

"No," the prince mumbled.

"Maybe you should have, and then allowed *him* to decide

if it was something worth troubling the king with. But no, you wanted to impress the king by delivering the big news to him yourself." Shaking her head, Kshapanaka pushed herself off the parapet and turned to depart. "Craving attention is a childish instinct, and not a sign of maturity."

Watching Kshapanaka leave his side, a sudden sense of shame and loss overcame the prince, and his face crumbled. Swallowing hard, he addressed her entreatingly, urgently. "Don't you want to know the news that I am in possession of?"

The woman broke her stride, turned, and considered Ghatakarpara evenly. "It's for you to decide whom you want to share it with."

"A rider came to me this morning from the garrison of Udaypuri." The prince took a couple of steps toward Kshapanaka. "The garrison commander has sent a report of one of our border outposts being attacked by a band of Hunas."

Kshapanaka stood rooted to the spot, staring hard at Ghatakarpara with narrowed eyes.

"It seems all the Frontier Guards at the outpost were killed, but a captain was allowed to go…"

Kshapanaka raised a hand to stop the prince, and then beckoned him quickly. "We mustn't lose any time in delivering this news to Vararuchi or the raj-guru. Come…"

* * *

Acharya Vetala Bhatta and Kshapanaka huddled in a remote corner of the terrace, listening intently to Ghatakarpara's account without interruption. When the prince had finished, the royal advisor, before speaking, once again cast his eyes around to make sure they couldn't be overheard.

"This rider who brought the news... where is he?"

"I've asked him to wait to hear from me... and speak nothing of this to anyone," answered Ghatakarpara.

"Yes, we might need him to take a message back to Udaypuri," the Acharya nodded. "But first, we must consult with the king."

"How do we do that now?" asked Kshapanaka, glancing toward the banquet hall, which was echoing with talk and laughter.

"Not now. We can't," the raj-guru frowned. "It'll have to be later tonight – or maybe tomorrow. Until then we keep this to ourselves, though I will share this with Vararuchi. There's no point in..."

Before Vetala Bhatta could complete articulating his thoughts, he was interrupted by a loud voice that came from the direction of the banquet hall.

"Acharya, my friend... how are you!"

Startled, the raj-guru turned around to see who had hailed him. He was relieved to find two elderly men, well out of earshot, walking toward them, smiling broadly.

"Come, King Chandravardhan, King Harihara... come, come," the Acharya's face lit up with familiarity and he took a few steps toward the approaching men; however, he looked briefly back at Kshapanaka and Ghatakarpara once. "Remember, not a mention of anything to anyone," he warned under his breath.

Kshapanaka and Ghatakarpara watched respectfully as the raj-guru exchanged greetings with Harihara and Chandravardhan. A bulky man of medium height, decidedly much the worse for wear, Chandravardhan had a flabby, mustachioed face that had the flush of a habitual drinker. There was also evidence of this in the pronounced slur in his speech, yet his voice was strong and authoritative, a vestige of the power he had commanded in his distant youth.

"What are you people conspiring about here?" he demanded of the Acharya in jest.

"Mundane matters of the palace, your honor," the raj-guru smiled amiably.

"Bah, today you must let all that be and celebrate." Chandravardhan drank deeply from the huge goblet of *soma* that he held in his right hand. "Today you must celebrate my friend and brother Vikramaditya!"

"Assuredly," the Acharya humored Chandravardhan as he escorted the two guests into the shade. "I'm sure you have met Kshapanaka and the king's nephew, Ghatakarpara."

At the sight of Kshapanaka, Chandravardhan stopped and placed a hand over his heart theatrically. "Oh, if this isn't our answer to the heavenly apsaras! Had I been but twenty years younger, I would be on my knees right now, begging for your hand in marriage."

The king of Vatsa threw his head back and laughed uproariously to blunt his slight indiscretion, and the others joined him in good humor. Sobering down, Chandravardhan next turned his attention to Ghatakarpara and nodded with satisfaction.

"It's nice to see my young nephew growing into a strong man," he said, grabbing the prince by the shoulder and feeling the hardness of his muscles. "Train well under the Acharya," he added, pointing to the raj-guru. "If you master half of what he teaches you, I promise no man will best you in battle."

"I will, sir," the prince said respectfully.

Harihara, who had been smiling benignly all this while, turned to Kshapanaka. "How is the firstborn Princess of the Nishada? Is she... better now?"

For a matter of a second, an unsettling silence fell over the group. Vetala Bhatta coughed softly into his hand as he gave Kshapanaka a quick, sidelong glance. Ghatakarpara folded his hands and studied the floor, while Chandravardhan sought refuge in the goblet of wine. Kshapanaka, however, only smiled politely before replying.

"I'm afraid the kingdom of Nishada exists only in memory, your honor," she said cryptically. "We are now the daughters of Avanti." After the slightest of pauses, she added, "No, my sister isn't any better, but neither has her condition worsened."

The king of Heheya nodded abashedly, his eyes betraying that he knew he had broached a sensitive topic. Luckily, the situation was rescued by the appearance of a minor palace official.

"Raj-guru, the samrat wishes all of you to join him inside the council chamber to discuss a matter of utmost urgency," the minion bowed low and withdrew respectfully.

As the Acharya exchanged mystified glances with Kshapanaka and Ghatakarpara, Harihara looked around in surprise. "What does Vikramaditya want with us now?" He appeared relieved that something had come up to break the awkwardness of the moment.

"I'm not sure, your honor," Vetala Bhatta shrugged.

"There's only one way of finding out," snorted Chandravardhan, leading the way back inside.

***

The council chamber was large and lofty, ventilated by a long row of windows that ran along one side of the room, overlooking the lake. A northerly breeze ruffled the gossamer curtains on the windows, but failed to stir the brocade tapestries hung on the inside walls, framing battle weapons and other heirlooms of the Aditya dynasty.

The chamber was dominated by an enormous bronze council table, its surface emblazoned with the heraldic sun-crest of Avanti. Crafted in gold and inlaid with coral and lapis lazuli, the crest represented a complex, eight-pointed solar motif that spanned the breadth of the broad table, around which were arranged a number of high chairs. Some two dozen of these were presently occupied, with Samrat Vikramaditya seated at the head of the table.

The king looked around at the assembly, taking in the air of mystery that hung over the table as he ascertained that everyone who mattered was in the room.

"I know this is most unexpected, and I hate to tear you away from the lovely banquet spread downstairs," he spoke at last in measured tones, taking care to engage each and every pair of eyes that regarded him with curiosity. "But a matter of some concern has come up, and considering we are all here under one roof, I think it is best we discuss it forthwith. It's something that the good king of Matsya has brought to my notice..."

Vikramaditya paused and gestured to the man seated to his immediate right. "Would you be so kind as to share what you've told me with everyone, King Baanahasta?"

Baanahasta bowed and stood up. He was lean and tall, with a dark angular face that was covered with a sharp, pointed beard, which he was prone to stroke during conversation.

"Pardon me for breaking up the celebrations, for what I'm about to say might amount to nothing," he said, clearing his throat. "But the samrat believes there might be something in it."

"You have our full attention," Chandravardhan spoke with the clear intention of cutting to the chase, even though his words didn't seem to imply this.

"Yes," said Baanahasta. "The point is that we have been receiving some disturbing reports in Matsya. I admit the reports aren't official; they come from opium farmers living in the hills, from goatherds... even mountain bandits captured by my soldiers. But there's a pattern in what they say."

He paused and drew a deep breath. "They all claim to have seen Saka horsemen roaming the hills that border my kingdom."

Baanahasta's words were greeted with a shocked silence that seemed to last forever. It was finally broken by a short, stocky man with a thick salt-and-pepper beard. This was Bhoomipala, the king of Kosala.

"Have your border patrols reported any of these sightings?" Bhoomipala asked in his high, nasal voice.

"I'm afraid not," Baanahasta coughed apologetically. "Like I said, these reports aren't official. It appears the Saka horsemen aren't present in large numbers. That's probably why my patrols haven't seen them."

"Since when have the Saka horsemen been observed in your territory, your honor?" the Acharya butted in, fixing a piercing gaze on Matsya's ruler.

"The reports started coming in about two weeks ago. So the sightings could have happened... who knows... a month ago, maybe more," Baanahasta shrugged.

"Do we know if the horsemen have ever attacked or even threatened any of your subjects?" It was Vikramaditya's turn to put a question.

"Some reports say they ransacked a farm or two, but it appears to have been solely for the purpose of obtaining food," replied Baanahasta. "Provisions and livestock were stolen, but no one was threatened or came to any bodily harm."

"Then perhaps they're there only to reconnoitre the locality," Chandravardhan grunted. "Or they could be a small group that has broken away from the larger Saka tribe… Outcasts, if you know what I mean. Now they don't know where to go, so they've been reduced to scavenging the hills… It's possible."

The council chamber acquired a meditative quality as everyone tried to grapple with the import of the revelation. It was cut short, however, when a husky voice drawled insolently from lower down the table.

"Is the samrat of Sindhuvarta going to take the reports of Matsya's lowly shepherds, farmers and brigands seriously?"

All heads turned to survey the man who had just spoken. In his early thirties, he was tall and broad-shouldered, his handsome face wearing a stylish beard and moustache that fenced his thin lips, which had a perpetual smirk at one corner. He had light green eyes, which were regarding Vikramaditya with poorly concealed arrogance.

The samrat stared levelly back at the man, taking his time to reply. When he did, his voice was firm. "Yes. Because dismissing such reports, however unreliable they may seem, would be immensely stupid. We all know that the Hunas and Sakas are cunning and fearsome adversaries, and we can't have them gaining a foothold in Sindhuvarta again."

Shrugging his shoulders, the other man lolled back in his chair and looked lazily up at the ceiling. "I think we're all making too much of this."

"You may be right, Shoorasena," Vikramaditya's tone had undergone a subtle change as he met the challenge to his authority head-on. "But Sindhuvarta has suffered far too much under the occupation of the Hunas and Sakas. It took great sacrifices from all our kingdoms to rid our lands of the invaders. Your own father…"

The samrat paused to point to the frail, white-haired man sitting beside Shoorasena, his shoulders stooped with age. "…the respected King Siddhasena, lost two of his brothers in battle. King Bhoomipala lost a son, Vararuchi and I lost our father… We've all lost a lot to win that war. By taking this lightly, we will be insulting the memory of the martyrs who fought for Sindhuvarta. That is not acceptable to me."

Shoorasena looked at Vikramaditya for a moment, then glanced quickly around the table, assessing the mood. On receiving hard, disapproving glares from virtually everyone, he dropped his eyes, nodded and retreated into a surly silence.

Vetala Bhatta took the opportunity to rise from his seat. "There is another good reason to believe that the reports in Matsya are correct," his tone was grave. "A piece of news came in from our garrison at Udaypuri just this morning. I intended giving it to the samrat later in the evening, but now I might as well share it with everyone here."

Quickly and without preamble, the raj-guru told the gathering about the Huna attack on the Frontier Guard outpost. As he spoke, the sense of disquiet heightened in the room, and worried looks crisscrossed in every direction.

"It's plain that the Huna-Saka Confederacy has renewed its interest in Sindhuvarta," the Acharya concluded. "The Sakas are scouting Matsya, whereas the Hunas are eyeing Avanti's borders."

"This is very distressing," said Baanahasta, rubbing his chin through his beard anxiously, suddenly awake to the prospect of a genuine threat to his kingdom.

"How many men did we lose in the attack?" Amara Simha asked, his voice bristling.

The raj-guru looked inquiringly at Ghatakarpara, who shrugged to indicate that the rider hadn't made any mention of this.

"Those border outposts are small, so maybe a dozen men," the Acharya hazarded a guess.

"We need to start moving troops to the border immediately," Vikramaditya spoke decisively. "Brother Vararuchi, please ensure that ten thousand infantry units, three thousand archers and three thousand cavalrymen of the Imperial Army are dispatched by tomorrow morning, with instructions to set up camps to the north and south of Udaypuri. And notify the commander of the Royal Engineers to start reinforcing all border defenses and secure them against attack."

"Would you want me to travel to Udaypuri as well to oversee the troop movements, samrat?"

"Someone from the palace would have to go," Vikramaditya conceded. "Let's consult and decide on that shortly. For now, let the troops leave immediately."

Vararuchi acknowledged the command, and the king turned to Kalidasa, who had been standing impassively to one side all the while, his massive arms folded across his chest. "I would like you to start preparing your *samsaptakas* for deployment at short notice."

"All two thousand of them are fully ready for battle, samrat," said the big man. "They only await an order from you."

"Good," Vikramaditya nodded in satisfaction.

King Harihara stood up. "I shall have three thousand of Heheya's best soldiers and a thousand horsemen at your disposal in two days, Samrat Vikramaditya," he volunteered.

"Thank you," the samrat bowed.

"I shall send you five thousand soldiers as well," pledged Chandravardhan, before looking across to Baanahasta. "And to help guard Matsya's border, you will have another five thousand of Vatsa's best, along with my elite heavy cavalry brigade."

A turbaned young man seated lower down the table got to his feet. Well over six feet tall, he was lean and handsome, with soulful brown eyes and a small, clipped moustache. "I speak on behalf of all the five chiefs of the Anarta Federation, samrat," he announced. "Each of us shall send three thousand troops to be shared between Avanti and Matsya."

"The kingdoms of Sindhuvarta are much obliged to all of you, Chief Yugandhara," replied Vikramaditya, making it a point to acknowledge all five Anarta chieftains with a bow.

It was King Bhoomipala's turn to rise. "I commit to send eight thousand troops and two thousand archers to Matsya," he said. "King Baanahasta will have them under his command in a week."

Once the king of Kosala had resumed his seat, all eyes were directed toward Siddhasena, who sat hunched in his chair, staring weakly at the table with watery eyes. When no sound came from the old king for a while, Vikramaditya addressed him gently.

"Your honor, can we expect some support from the kingdom of Magadha in the event of an attack from the Hunas and Sakas?"

Siddhasena raised his head to the samrat and opened

his mouth reluctantly. But before he could frame his reply, Shoorasena interrupted his father.

"The army of Magadha is preparing for a big campaign against the republic of Vanga. We're afraid we won't have enough troops to spare you."

As eyebrows rose in surprise around the table, Vikrama-ditya scrutinized Siddhasena closely. "But why are you going to war against Vanga, King Siddhasena? They are a peace-loving people."

"They are challenging the sovereignty of Magadha," Shoorasena again answered for his father. "Vanga is encouraging the sedition of the Kikata tribe from Magadha by supporting the Kikata rebels."

Before anyone else could utter a word, Vararuchi leaned forward and addressed Shoorasena. "The samrat's questions are directed at the king of Magadha, not you," he said, his tone simmering with hostility. "Allow the king to answer them."

"Our king is not answerable to others on affairs that pertain to the integrity of the state of Magadha."

This time, the speaker was a dark man seated to Siddhasena's left. He was in his late twenties, and had truculent, beady eyes and a thick black moustache. This was Shoorasena's younger brother Kapila, although they bore no physical resemblance to one another.

"Enough!" Chandravardhan thundered, rising from his seat. Leaning his hands on the table, he stared at the brothers. "We are not here to listen to you boys talk. Vararuchi is right. Let your father speak for himself."

The atmosphere in the council chamber was charged as fierce stares were exchanged, but King Siddhasena raised a placatory hand before more damage could be done.

"Calm down, please. Calm down," he entreated in a quavering voice. "Pardon Shoorasena and Kapila, King Chandravardhan, for they are young."

The king of Vatsa snorted in disgust, but sat down out of respect for the older king. Siddhasena meanwhile glanced at his sons flanking him.

"Let me speak," he said, before turning to Vikramaditya. "Samrat, I request you to pardon my sons for their indiscretion as well. But they bear you no ill will. As proof of that, the kingdom of Magadha promises to allocate troops for the defense of Sindhuvarta."

As Shoorasena and Kapila stared stonily at the table, Vikramaditya inclined his head. "We are grateful for that, good king," he said, deciding against pressing the matter. "We would never doubt your word." Looking up at the gathering, he added, "Well, that takes care of things for the time being. Let us return to the banquet."

"About time," Chandravardhan grumbled to Harihara, as everyone began filing out of the chamber. "But I dare say, the last half hour has wholly ruined my appetite," he added without cheer.

* * *

Night had fallen over Ujjayini, and the palace was quiet after the day's hustle-bustle. The royal guests had retired to their rooms after a light dinner, though no one partook in much food or conversation – the combined effect of the afternoon's rich banquet and the sobering meeting in the council chamber.

In the eastern wing of the palace, two figures walked down a wide passageway, conversing in undertones. The taller of the two was Vikramaditya, while the other was

Dhanavantri, his bloated shadow bobbing behind him in the light of the flickering lamps.

On reaching a carved wooden door at the end of the passage, the king raised his hand and knocked lightly on the wood. A moment later, a young girl opened the door, bowed reverentially, and made room for Vikramaditya to pass. Dhanavantri followed, struggling a bit to squeeze his expansive middle through the gap.

The room was a bedchamber, in the center of which stood a large, four-poster sandalwood bed. The lace curtains veiling the bed were drawn aside, and a woman lay propped up on the satin bedcovers. Two maids stood on either side of the bed wielding large fans, with which they stirred the still air over the woman's head. An elderly matron sat by the side of the bed, and as Vikramaditya and Dhanavantri approached, she stood up and moved respectfully some distance away.

Walking up to the bed, the king looked down at the woman. She was of about thirty, her face thin and pale white. The face had once been attractive, but now it wore signs of waste, with heavy dark circles under the eyes that stared ahead blankly, showing no acknowledgment of the activity around her.

Vikramaditya sat down beside the woman, gently picked up her frail hand and stroked it lovingly, but the woman remained unresponsive in her vegetative state. Turning to the matron, he asked, "Has she been fed?"

"Yes, your honor. Princess Kshapanaka personally came to feed her this evening."

"Did she eat well?"

The matron, who was clearly a nursemaid, hesitated. "Yes... a little, your honor. She... she eats less and less..."

Dhanavantri came around to the other side of the bed. "Is she being administered her medicines as I instructed?" he asked. There was none of the usual flippant joviality in his voice.

"Without fail, sir," replied the nurse.

The physician bent down and felt the woman's pulse. Next he checked her pupils, before drawing back to stand patiently, while the king sat looking at the wan, expressionless face.

At last, the samrat slowly placed the woman's hand back on her lap. He then caressed her forehead for a while, before sighing deeply and rising. He nodded to the matron who bowed in return, cast one more lingering glance at the woman on the bed, and walked out of the room.

The king and Dhanavantri retraced their steps down the passage in silence. On arriving at the end of the passage, where it forked, Vikramaditya stopped to consider his companion with sad eyes.

"Do you think her condition is worsening?" he asked.

"It's hard to say, samrat."

The king was quiet for a moment. "But we can be reasonably sure she isn't ever going to get better, right?"

Dhanavantri looked away, not having the heart to answer the question.

Interpreting Dhanavantri's silence correctly, Vikramaditya swallowed hard and stared vacantly at the opposite wall. "I wish I could reach out to her... somehow. Speak to her and tell her I love her and that I am waiting for her..." He turned to Dhanavantri once again, his eyes pleading. "She's been like this for two years. Isn't there some cure for this, somewhere?"

"You know that I've tried everything I can. Unfortunately, nothing has worked so far."

"Yes, you've tried your best, I know," the king hung his head in dejection. "If the affliction is beyond even the finest physician in Sindhuvarta, I have to accept it as my fate."

Dhanavantri reached up and placed a comforting hand on the samrat's shoulder. "Don't lose hope, friend. I promise you that I shall keep trying to bring her back. Now get some rest."

"You sleep well, too, my friend," replied the king.

The two men parted, the royal physician taking the flight of steps down to the level below, Vikramaditya turning into the passage that led to his bedchamber.

As the sound of the men's footsteps receded, a figure slowly detached itself from the shadow of a big pillar in the hallway downstairs. The light from a faraway lamp immediately fell on the figure, revealing a man's dark, bearded face under a black turban.

It was the sadhu from the boat.

The sadhu paused stealthily, looking right and left to ascertain no one was around. The coast was clear, so he began mounting the stairway leading toward the king's bedroom. As he crept his way up, he reached into the rough shawl he was wearing – and his fingers curled around the hilt of the long dagger that was carefully tucked away into the folds of his dhoti.

Dagger

The cloaked rider had been on the road for nearly two hours, and though the steed was a strong beast in the prime of health, it was beginning to show signs of fatigue, its mouth foaming from exertion. This wasn't surprising, considering the rider had ridden swiftly and without stop since leaving Ujjayini's gates, just after sundown and a little before dinner was served at the palace.

"Please talk to your grandmother and ask her to get us some news from the Great Desert," Vikramaditya had said, speaking to the rider in the privacy of his royal chamber. "The sooner we get some information, the better we can plan our defense against the Hunas."

The path that the rider had taken led westward from Ujjayini, and after an hour's ride, it had petered into rocky, scrub-laden hills. The rider had pressed on until, at the end of the second hour, the horse had drawn up to the rim of a flat, open plain. Two small fires burned in the middle of the plain, their diffused glow silhouetting a few crude tents pitched on the dusty ground.

As the rider dismounted and began stroking the neck of the tired horse, the high-pitched trill of a nocturnal bird split the stillness from the right. Almost immediately, another bird answered the first one's call from the darkness to the left. The rider paused for a moment, and then looking skyward, let out a warble that was a close imitation of the first two calls. Then, taking the horse by the bridle, the rider began walking toward the glow of the fires.

Halfway to the tents, three figures emerged from the darkness and stood in the rider's way.

"Greetings, sister," one of the figures spoke in a friendly voice. "What brings you in search of the Wandering Tribe at this hour?"

"I'm here to speak to the Mother Oracle."

"Ah!" The three figures fell in step with the rider. "But how did you know where to find us?"

"You forget that I too have the blood of the nomads in me. The snowflake that melts on a mountaintop intuitively knows the way back to the distant sea."

The rider and the three escorts reached the tents. Stepping into the ring of light cast by the fires, the rider shrugged off the cloak to reveal the face of a young girl, a little over twenty. Petite in build, she had sharp elfin features, with large black eyes that flashed in the firelight. Black hair curled profusely around her fair face, which, at the moment, was smiling impishly at the familiar faces seated around the fire.

"Shankubala, how are they treating you at the royal palace?" fussed a dark woman of around fifty, drawing the rider close to the fire and thrusting a wooden bowl of spicy broth into her hands. "Come, you must be hungry and tired. Drink that!"

"It's been a long time since you visited us, Shanku. Look how tall your nephew has grown," said a man, pointing to a boy of ten who smiled shyly and slipped into one of the tents.

It was a while before the niceties of familial reunion were complete and Shanku was allowed a private audience with her grandmother. Sitting opposite the old crone in a tiny tent lit by a small lamp, watching the wrinkled face and rheumy eyes, the girl wondered how to bring up the matter that had brought her to the tent. But she was spared from making the decision.

"My child, you are a pleasing sight," the old lady cawed through her toothless mouth. "You are blessed with your mother's beauty, but those big eyes are your father's... curse his deceitful heart! I'll never know what your mother fancied in him – he's brought nothing but disgrace to the Wandering Tribe. But you're not here to discuss the family, are you? Tell me what you want."

Shanku spoke for a few minutes, outlining what the king of Avanti wished from her grandmother. The old woman nodded quietly as she listened, and when the girl was done, she sat back and gazed at the tent's roof for a while.

"The winds from the west won't blow this way for at least a week, if not more," the hag said at last. "But let me listen to what the migratory birds have to say. They may have something that your king might find of value."

"What about the clouds?" Shanku inquired.

"Yes, I shall try to read the clouds as well, but it depends on whether they come from the direction of the Great Desert."

Shanku nodded. "I shall return tomorrow night, grandmother. I hope you would have learned something of use."

"And if I have not?" the old woman eyed the younger one closely.

"Then I shall return again on the day after."

Shanku took her leave and was about to exit the tent when her grandmother called to her.

"Do you see your father, child?"

Shanku turned around and considered her grandmother silently. "I haven't in a long time," she murmured at last.

"And are they kind to you at the palace of Ujjayini... even after what he did? Otherwise, you could always come back to us. You're always welcome here."

The girl nodded again. "I know that. But no, everyone there is very kind to me... especially the king."

"In that case, come back and sit down, child," the hag said solemnly, patting the ground by her side. "I have had a vision that your king should know about."

***

Vikramaditya sat at a low table made of teak and ivory, bending over a palm leaf manuscript, his back to the door of his bedchamber.

The light from two lamps placed on the table fell on the palm leaves, revealing lines of lyrical verse written in Sanskrit. The king read each line carefully, pausing now and then to smile in appreciation, or to make small annotations in the margin. The palace was still, and the only sounds were the rustling of the dry palm leaves and the occasional scratching of the king's quill. Outside the palace, somewhere on the gulmohars overhanging the lake, a jungle nightjar chuckled intermittently.

The samrat was so completely engrossed in the manuscript that he almost failed to notice the light draught that blew across the room as the door to his chamber opened and closed silently. However, at the last moment, he observed the sudden flicker of the lamps as they caught the breeze, and his face stiffened.

Without demonstrating the slightest hint of alertness, the king placed the quill back in the inkpot and returned his gaze to the manuscript. Yet, his right hand went under the table, searching for the short sword strapped underneath, hidden from view. Listening for footfalls, he quietly pulled the sword free. Taking a deep breath, he rose in an abrupt crouch and turned around, the sword extending straight out in front of him.

Three paces from the tip of the sword stood the sadhu, the sword pointing at his chest.

"Who are you?" Vikramaditya demanded gruffly, scanning the room for signs of more intruders. Satisfied that there was none, he fixed his eyes on the sadhu. "What do you want? How did you get in here?"

"It doesn't matter how I got in here," the sadhu replied. "And as to who I am and what I want... it's a long story. Can we sit down and talk?"

Vikramaditya looked at the sadhu with narrowed eyes, his sword unwavering. "What do you have concealed in your hand under the shawl?" he demanded.

The sadhu smiled and drew his hand out of the shawl. As the light from the lamps glinted off the blade of the dagger that the intruder held, the samrat levelled his sword menacingly. The sadhu promptly raised his left hand to stay the king.

"I come in peace and I mean you no harm, Samrat Vikramaditya," he said. The sadhu then switched his grip on the hilt, so that the dagger lay, inoffensive, on his upturned palm. "I have come to give you this dagger and leave it in your safekeeping."

"Why? What's so special about this dagger?" The king still didn't lower his guard.

The sadhu paused a moment before answering. "It is the most powerful weapon in the three worlds, samrat."

Vikramaditya stared from the sadhu to the dagger, and then back at the sadhu, his eyes clouded with skepticism.

"It is something that both the gods of Devaloka and the demons of Patala covet," the sadhu continued in a somber voice. "Both devas and asuras will do anything to get their hands on this dagger... *anything*."

The samrat held the sadhu's gaze, his mouth turning downward at the corners in a disbelieving smirk.

"Is that so? Then why have you brought it to me?"

"I want you to protect it and keep it from falling into their possession."

* * *

At the other end of the palace, in a corner bedroom, Kapila squatted on a divan, staring into the depths of the flagon of *soma* in his hand. He watched the rich liquid swirling inside the flagon for a while, then raised anxious eyes to Shoorasena, who stood by a window with his hands clutched behind him, looking out into the night.

"What do we do now?" Kapila addressed his brother's broad back.

Shoorasena turned his face inward fractionally, as if meaning to reply, but then changed his mind and went back to staring outside.

"Father has committed himself to sending Magadha's troops to shore up Matsya and Avanti's defenses," Kapila pressed on, his voice low but marked with urgency. "Now how are we to move against Vanga?"

Shoorasena continued gazing into the dark in silence.

"We are left with no choice but to put the campaign against Vanga on hold," Kapila sighed, his face drooping with regret.

"There will be *no* change in our plans," Shoorasena spun around and snarled at his younger brother. "We have to attack Vanga and gain control of its iron mines. We need cheap iron ore to begin the rapid militarization of Magadha. Without that iron, expanding our army will be next to impossible. And let's not forget Tamralipti – we capture the port, we control the sea trade between Sindhuvarta and the eastern kingdoms of Sribhoja and Srivijaya."

"I know, brother. But if some of our troops are to be diverted for the protection of Sindhuvarta, our push into Vanga might fail."

"Yes, we need each and every soldier of Magadha on that front." Shoorasena went and sat down beside Kapila. "Confound it, we should never have let father come here! He's never been capable of standing up for Magadha. Always bowing to the wishes of Avanti... First to King Mahendraditya, then to that bully Vararuchi, and now to Vikramaditya... *Samrat Vikramaditya*," he scoffed, his voice choking with envy.

"And let's not forget Vikramaditya's glorified flunkey, Chandravardhan," Kapila gritted his teeth in anger. "It disgusted me to see father apologise to that fat pig."

"Chandravardhan, Baanahasta, Bhoomipala... they're all stooges of Avanti," Shoorasena spat out in disdain. "They hail Avanti as the protector of Sindhuvarta, but the fools are completely blind to the fact that Avanti is using *their* armies to defend Sindhuvarta. Then, once Avanti has cleverly cornered all the glory of victory, all the other kingdoms fall over one another in gratitude and applaud when the king of Avanti crowns himself as the samrat of Sindhuvarta!"

"It isn't just glory that Avanti has claimed for itself, brother," Kapila interjected. "Look at how it has taken possession of the erstwhile kingdoms of Gosringa, Nishada, Malawa and Kunti in the name of liberating them from the Hunas and Sakas. Gosringa, Nishada and Malawa are now provinces of Avanti, while Kunti is little more than a protectorate. Avanti has expanded on the blood and bones of its neighbors, yet Chandravardhan and the other blinkered idiots can't stop singing its praise." Kapila paused and his shoulders slumped in dejection. "But why blame only them? Even Magadha has always conducted itself in this servile fashion."

"Not anymore," Shoorasena growled darkly, rising from the divan. Looking up at the ornate ceiling of the room, he shook his head. "Once we have conquered Vanga and the other eastern kingdoms of Odra, Kalinga and Pragjyotishpura, our power will rival that of Avanti. Then Avanti and its puppet kingdoms won't dare talk down to us, I promise."

"Indeed. But right now we must address the issue of the promise that father has made to Vikramaditya." Kapila rose from his seat as well. "We have to figure out a way of ensuring that the whole of Magadha's army stays at our disposal."

"Don't worry," Shoorasena placed a reassuring hand on his brother's shoulder. "I will find a way."

***

Vikramaditya frowned as he examined the dagger closely, turning it this way and that in the light of the lamps. Occasionally, he cast a mistrustful eye on the sadhu, who stood to one side, unperturbed.

As far as the king could make out, the weapon was rather primitive, comprising a hilt made of polished obsidian, to which was attached a thin, long blade. The dagger's edge was sharp, but by no means the keenest that he had come across.

There was absolutely nothing in the knife to substantiate the sadhu's claim.

"*This...* is the most powerful weapon in the three worlds?" the samrat appraised the intruder, his tone sarcastic.

The sadhu nodded. "Its power rests not in its blade, but in its hilt."

The king once again cast his eye over the obsidian hilt, then looked at the sadhu and gave an impatient shake of his head. "Your story is all nonsense," he said. "Tell me what you really want, or I shall..."

"Hold the dagger against the light and look through the hilt," the sadhu spoke imperiously.

Vikramaditya narrowed his eyes at the sadhu's irreverent tone.

"Go on," the trespasser urged, lowering himself into a cushioned chair without invitation.

The king glared at the sadhu for a moment. Then he slowly raised the dagger to the light, his expression still thoroughly unconvinced. Yet, a moment later, his face underwent a dramatic transformation as he stared, mesmerized, at the dagger.

For in the opaque blackness of the hilt, he saw a strange light.

It wasn't the dull, yellowish light of the lamps refracting

through the glassy stone. It wasn't even a light coming *through* the stone. It was a light coming from *within* the inky blackness of the hilt, iridescent blue, speckled with gold and silver motes, pulsating with life.

After what seemed to him like eons, Vikramaditya lowered the dagger and turned to the sadhu.

"What is inside this hilt?" he asked in a hushed awe.

"What do you know about the Halahala?" Instead of answering, the sadhu posed a question of his own.

"The Halahala...?" The king paused in surprise. "It was that all-destroying poison that the devas and asuras accidentally churned out of the White Lake while looking for the Elixir."

"Yes, the scourge from the White Lake," the sadhu nodded, pointing to the dagger's hilt.

Vikramaditya stared at the dagger in his hand, then looked back to the sadhu in confusion. "You're saying that what I saw in this hilt is that Halahala?"

"A very, very small portion of it, yes. Yet, infinitely potent and capable of doing immense harm..."

"But... but that can't be," the samrat argued. "The Halahala was destroyed by the mighty Shiva before it could annihilate the three worlds."

"No, not all of it," the sadhu shook his head in regret. "One little portion of the toxin escaped destruction due to great greed and cunning – the portion now in your hands. And unfortunately, knowledge of the poison's existence has spawned even greater greed and cunning – the greed and cunning to possess the Halahala at any cost."

"How do you know this?" the king's voice was filled with wonder.

"Like I said, it's a long story, so pull yourself a chair. I shall tell you the untold story of the Halahala – which began with a little-known but sly asura by the name of Veeshada."

Veeshada

Veeshada was one of the asuras the sages Brihaspati and Shukracharya picked to transport the Halahala from the shores of the White Lake to Mount Kailasa," the sadhu commenced his narrative. "Much as all the other devas and asuras who were assigned the task, he was of formidable character, with mastery over the dark arts."

"Now, even by asura standards, Veeshada was blessed with an extremely crafty and calculative mind, and as the band of devas and asuras made their way over the Himalayas with the deadly Halahala, a devious plan hatched in Veeshada's head."

"The asura had witnessed the havoc that the Halahala had caused, and it dawned on him that a poison with such devastating effects would be of great value to the asuras in their struggle for supremacy against the devas. He understood that a small quantity of the Halahala was all that was needed to shift the balance of power in favor of the asuras – they could perpetually hold Devaloka to ransom under its threat."

As the sadhu paused to collect his thoughts, Vikramaditya listened in rapt attention. "From Brihaspati and Shukracharya's conversations, Veeshada had also gathered that before the rock had been broken, the Halahala was contained in a vacuum inside the boulder," the sadhu continued. "So, as the group journeyed to Mount Kailasa, Veeshada secretly fashioned a dagger with an obsidian hilt, and created a small chamber within the hilt."

The samrat's eyes widened, and he once again raised the dagger and held it delicately to the lamps, marveling at the blue light beating inside the hilt.

"On the second night of the journey, as a furious blizzard swept through the mountains and the devas and asuras huddled from the cold and slept, Veeshada sneaked a few ounces of the Halahala into the chamber concealed in his dagger's hilt. Using his magical powers, he then sealed the stolen poison into a vacuum before fleeing into the night, making for the asura dominions."

"Didn't the rest of the devas and asuras notice Veeshada's absence the next morning?" Vikramaditya interjected.

"They did, but they assumed that he had blundered in the dark and was claimed by the blizzard," the sadhu answered. "And anyway, their main concern was bringing the stone to the Eternal Cave. So they suspected nothing of Veeshada's treachery – until I told them about it."

"*You* told them?" The king's eyebrows rose sharply. Pausing to place the dagger back on the table, he asked, "Who are you? You still haven't told me how you know all this."

The sadhu smiled... and for a brief moment, he seemed to fade a little in the light of the guttering lamps. Then, as the king blinked rapidly, certain that his eyes were playing tricks on him, the sadhu appeared to grow in form. At the same time, a mellow phosphorescence enveloped the figure for a fleeting moment.

And in that moment, as the cosmic beat of the *damaru* roared in his ears, Vikramaditya saw the white, crescent moon adorning the sadhu's matted locks, and noticed the tinge of blue iridescence around his throat.

The vision was gone in a flash, and when the king looked again, all he saw was the sadhu seated before him, quietly stroking his beard. But Vikramaditya knew what he had seen was no illusion. Without taking his eyes off his visitor, he rose from his seat and dropped to his knees with folded his hands.

"Pardon my insolence, Mahadeva, but I did not recognize you because of your disguise," he whispered.

"It is just as well," Shiva smiled benignly. "Had people been able to see through it, the whole purpose of a disguise would have been defeated."

"I am blessed, gurudev," the king remained on his knees, his head bowed.

"Rise, samrat, and take your seat," Shiva commanded. "Time is short and I have much to tell you about the Halahala."

The king returned to his chair and Shiva took up the thread of his narrative.

"Once I had consumed the Halahala, the devas and the asuras were overjoyed. But I put a stop to their rejoicing by informing them of Veeshada's flight. I told them where to find the asura, and commanded them to retrieve the dagger and bring it to me."

"But gurudev, you are the Omniscient One, the mightiest of the ancient gods," Vikramaditya interrupted. "Why did you have to send the devas and asuras after Veeshada when you knew where he was and could have stopped him yourself?"

"Indeed I am omniscient, but it was not in my destiny to stop Veeshada," answered Shiva. "It was in the destiny of the devas and asuras to prevent him from doing his mischief – just as it is now in your destiny to prevent them from doing theirs. Now let me get on with my story."

The king bowed in acknowledgment, and Shiva continued. "The devas and asuras did as I bid them, and for two days they pursued Veeshada. They finally cornered him in an underground cavern and ordered him to yield the dagger. The wily asura, however, tried to incite his brethren against the devas, telling them how they could rule over the devas with the help of the Halahala. The uneasy standoff ended when a deva finally slew Veeshada and took control of the dagger. But the damage was done."

Shiva paused and looked at the dagger with sad eyes. "Veeshada had succeeded in opening the devas' and asuras' eyes to the true power of the Halahala. He had kindled in their hearts the greed to possess the dagger. Even when they returned to Kailasa, their reluctance to part with the dagger was plain on their faces. What I had feared had come to pass. I saw the Halahala would never again be safe from the devas and the asuras."

"But couldn't you have put an end to the matter by consuming the remaining Halahala as well, Mahadeva?"

"The Halahala is the most hazardous of substances in all three worlds," Shiva spoke with patience. "Even the ancient gods dread it, which was why it was cast into the depths of the White Lake in the hope that it would never be found. It nearly destroyed me when I swallowed it the first time. There is no way I could survive a second exposure to the poison."

Rising from his seat, Shiva strolled over to the window. He stood for a while in silence, before turning back to Vikramaditya. "You see my predicament, samrat?" he asked. "Here I am in possession of a poison that cannot be destroyed, one that both asuras and devas desperately crave after. But I cannot allow either to get hold of the Halahala – for if one or the other succeeds, the fragile equilibrium of the cosmos will be broken and the three worlds will topple into chaos. So, ever since that fateful day so many thousand years ago, I have been forced to protect this dagger from the evenly matched rivals."

"Forgive my ignorance, gurudev, but the Halahala would give the celestial devas a great advantage over the demonic asuras of Patala," the king pointed out. "Isn't this desirable for the triumph of good over evil?"

"The universe is all about balance, samrat," Shiva shook his head. "The forces of light and darkness are meant to keep a check on one another. If one becomes too powerful and starts overrunning the other, that balance will be upset. For the tyranny of virtue is as unbearable as the stranglehold of vice."

Shiva paused and gave a dry chuckle. "And as you will discover for yourself, the devas are not above deceit and viciousness when it comes to getting what they want. So, the question of good triumphing evil doesn't arise."

The room was silent for a while as Vikramaditya pondered over Shiva's words. At last, raising his head, he asked, "Why have you brought the Halahala to my safekeeping, Mahadeva?"

"What choice do I have? I can trust neither deva nor

asura with it. The only option left is to entrust the dagger in the care of mankind, the neutral force between Devaloka and Patala. And there's no better man than you for this task, samrat."

"But can't you continue protecting the dagger, gurudev?" the king protested. "No deva or asura would dare take the Halahala from *you*. It is safest in your hands."

"You are right," Shiva conceded. "But I am a *yogi* in pursuit of transcendence through meditation. The Halahala is a constant distraction, tying me down to the material world. It prevents me from fulfilling my dharma and achieving enlightenment. For thousands of years I have been bound by the responsibility of protecting the dagger – to have done otherwise would be putting the universe at risk. But I cannot be untrue to myself and my dharma any longer. It is time to bequeath the Halahala to its rightful custodian and set myself free."

Vikramaditya once again lapsed into brooding silence. When he finally addressed Shiva, his voice was troubled.

"It is a privilege that you have chosen me to guard this dagger, gurudev. But I fear that I will fail in honoring your trust. The responsibility of protecting the Halahala from the gods of Devaloka and the demons of Patala is too heavy a burden for one man to bear."

"Yet I don't doubt your capabilities for a moment, Samrat Vikramaditya," Shiva responded levelly. "Else, I wouldn't have made a journey this far. And who says you are alone? You have nine of the best warriors on earth by your side. And if I must add, you and your Council of Nine don't have a choice in this matter – all your destinies are already interlinked with that of the Halahala."

Following a silence that seemed to last forever, the king

heaved a huge sigh and looked into Shiva's face. "As you wish, Mahadeva," he said, his voice ringing with resolve. "My Council of Nine and I swear to protect this dagger till our last breath."

"I am grateful to hear that." Shiva seemed reassured by Vikramaditya's words. "I can now return to the Eternal Cave in the knowledge that the dagger is safe with the Guardians of the Halahala."

***

The ambience within the council chamber was sepulchral, the air perfectly still, as though eavesdropping on every word being uttered in the room. Even the thin lace curtains on the windows hung straight down, heavy like hessian, as if mindful of the seriousness of the occasion.

"Did Mahadeva give any indication of what the devas and the asuras would do next?"

The question came from Acharya Vetala Bhatta, who was sitting at the council table, next to Vikramaditya.

"No, he didn't," the king answered, looking around the table.

To his left were the raj-guru, Kalidasa, Kshapanaka, Shanku and Dhanavantri. To the right of the table were seated Vararuchi, Ghatakarpara, Amara Simha and another man in his early fifties. He was of medium build, with a brown, clean-shaven face scarred with pockmarks. A long mane of white hair swept back from his broad forehead, and his eyes were deep and pensive under thick white eyebrows. A black, wooden crutch rested against the arm of his chair.

"All he said was that it wouldn't be long before they come to know that the dagger is in Avanti," Vikramaditya continued. "And that it is inevitable that both sides would make efforts to claim it."

"And these efforts would include the use of force," Amara Simha leaned his brawny forearms on the table, his ferocious eyes following the pattern of the sun-crest ensign on its surface.

"In all probability, yes," the samrat responded, although Amara Simha hadn't exactly posed a question. "But the Omniscient One did say that the devas and asuras will probably try other means first."

"Yes… Appeals to our conscience, bribery, subtle threats, dire warnings…" the Acharya nodded. "Force will probably be the last resort – when everything else fails."

"Not to forget, there might be outright attempts to steal the dagger through trickery as well," cautioned Vararuchi. "Both devas and asuras are masters of the dark arts."

As heads nodded around the table in agreement, the king addressed Vetala Bhatta. "We have to assume that the devas and asuras will take recourse to magic, raj-guru. We will need some potent spells to protect the dagger."

"I will do what I can," the Acharya heaved a sigh, mild worry lines creasing his brow. "But we must realize that the devas and asuras possess knowledge of sorcery that far exceeds what is known to man."

"We will have to do the best we can," said Vikramaditya.

There was a moment's pause in the conversation. It was broken by Kshapanaka.

"What should we expect once the devas or the asuras decide to use force against us?"

"I don't know – but the Omniscient One did say that we have to be prepared for the worst things imaginable in the three worlds."

Anxious glances were exchanged as everyone shifted uncomfortably in their chairs. The king turned to the pockmarked man seated beside Amara Simha. "A lot would probably depend on your inventions, Varahamihira."

The elderly man nodded once, but offered no verbal response.

Vararuchi leaned forward and craned his neck to look at Varahamihira. "Do you have any suggestions?" he prodded.

Varahamihira shrugged and spread his hands. "What can I say? I wouldn't know what to do until I have an idea of what we are dealing with."

As the councilors nodded in acknowledgment, Ghatakar-para spoke forcefully. "We should start by strengthening Ujjayini's fortifications. We should rebuild the moats, and have more guards manning the city walls and gates. We should deploy more forces..."

"And *where* exactly should we deploy these forces, young man?" asked Vetala Bhatta, eyeing the prince with severity. "We are talking about the possibility of being attacked by demons and demigods, not some kingdom from across the border. The attacks, when they do come, could come from anywhere – over land, by air, through water. They could materialize in any shape, size or form. Varahamihira is right... we have no idea what we will be up against."

"Then how are we to prepare ourselves for what is to come?" asked Kshapanaka, even though she knew that the question had no satisfactory answer.

Another ripple of nervousness ran through the chamber. As if to allay it, Varahamihira said, "I shall begin some experiments, anyway. There are a couple of ideas that I had conceived some time ago that I have neglected... Let me get back to them and see what I can develop. If not against the devas and asuras, they might come in handy against the Hunas and Sakas."

"Yes, with the Hunas and Sakas we at least know what to expect," Kalidasa muttered with a mild shrug and a wry smile.

"Let's hope so," Vararuchi added quickly.

"That's right," said Vikramaditya, addressing the council in a tone intended to dispel the air of uncertainty and rally confidence. "Let us focus our energy on dealing with a real and immediate threat. We can figure out a way of tackling the devas and asuras later." Turning to Vararuchi, he asked, "What progress have we made on the troop deployments?"

"The three thousand cavalrymen you had asked to be sent to Udaypuri left last night, samrat. The infantry units and archers will be on their way in the next hour. I have also sent a message to Atulyateja, the garrison commander of Udaypuri, informing him of the troop movements, and instructing him to begin establishing camps and command centers along the border. He has also been told to strengthen the Frontier Guard patrols and increase the number of scouts all along the Arbuda Range."

"We should inform the provincial governors of Malawa and Gosringa about the troop movements as well," reminded Kalidasa. "The local militia can then be brought in to aid the Imperial Army and the Frontier Guard."

"I have already dispatched a message to Governor Satyaveda, as the garrison of Udaypuri falls under the jurisdiction of Malawa province," said Vararuchi. "But I shall make sure the governor of Gosringa is also informed immediately."

"Have the Royal Engineers been pressed into action?" asked the Acharya.

"They have, raj-guru. All the forts and outposts along the border are being fortified."

"Good," Vikramaditya nodded in approval. "Now let's decide who should go to Udaypuri to coordinate things."

"I can go," Kshapanaka and Kalidasa volunteered in unison, without a moment's pause.

"I'm ready too," Vararuchi offered a moment later.

Ghatakarpara raised his hand and leaned forward, meaning to speak, but he was interrupted by Dhanavantri.

"I recommend we send our friend Amara Simha," said the physician, pointing across the table and grinning. "He's just been sitting around here, complaining of boredom, and putting on weight. The exercise will do him good. And to be honest, I'm tired of seeing his sulking face around the palace. Sending him away would be a pleasant change of scenery – for him, *and* for the rest of us."

Smiles broke out around the table and the mood lightened almost immediately. Amara Simha glared at Dhanavantri for a moment, then grinning self-consciously, he stood up.

"As long as there is a promise of a good fight ahead, I would be more than pleased to go, samrat," he said, rubbing his hands and cracking his knuckles in anticipation of action.

"Well then, that's settled. You can leave tomorrow morning," said the king. "One last thing..."

Vikramaditya's eyes sought Shanku out, who, as usual, had remained quiet and unobtrusive throughout the lengthy discussion.

"Did you meet the Mother Oracle last night?" the samrat asked.

"I did. She told me that she will try and read the elements for news from the west. I am to return to her tonight."

"When you meet her, thank her and the Wandering Tribe on my behalf," the king inclined his head in a gracious gesture.

Vikramaditya was settling back in his chair as Shanku spoke.

"There is something else that she *did* tell me though, samrat…" Aware that all eyes were on her, the girl hesitated.

"Yes?" the king looked at her encouragingly.

"She told me that she had a vision. She didn't say what it was, but she asked me to warn you that the sun is on the wane, and that a great eclipse is coming to devour the sun."

As silence descended on the room, Varahamihira shook his head. "That's not possible, girl," he was emphatic. "My calculations show that the next solar eclipse isn't due in two hundred years."

Shanku paused before answering, her words taking on a prophetic ring. "The sun my grandmother was referring to is the royal emblem of the Aditya dynasty, noble councilors. The sun-crest of Avanti…"

Nephew

The sky was a striking blue, stretched and washed clean, with not a speck of cloud from horizon to horizon. Nothing moved in the azure emptiness save for a solitary Brahminy kite, soaring high above the snow-capped mountain range, the cold air currents lifting its light body further and further up into the still, early morning sky. Down below lay miles and miles of glaciers, reflecting the harsh glare of the sun so that the ridged landscape was lit up in a bright, yellow-white glow.

The kite sailed in a northeasterly direction, heading toward the majestic bulk of Mount Meru, towering over its sister peaks like a giant among dwarfs. Nearing the large mountain barring its path, the bird gained altitude yet again, till it finally crested the summit and crossed over into Devaloka.

Almost immediately, the mountain of Meru fell away to reveal the breathtaking city of Amaravati, nestling amid the mist-laden hill slopes and valleys beneath, its spires and turrets shimmering in the sunlight like morning dew.

Descending sharply, the kite skimmed over the sprawling capital of Devaloka, making straight for a splendid, multitiered palace located at the heart of the city. Surrounded on all sides by a ring of rocky cliffs, the palace was built on an enormous rock of gray basalt that thrust upward from the center of a wide, bottomless abyss. The palace's colorful domes and turrets, fluttering with pennants, caught the bright sunlight, throwing the shadows of the yawning trench into stark contrast. To the north and south, two broad wooden drawbridges were thrown over the moat-like abyss, linking the palace to the surrounding hills and the rest of Amaravati.

As it drew near the palace, the kite began undergoing a remarkable metamorphosis. Its body enlarged in size and muscularity, the reddish brown plumage giving way to tawny fur-covered skin. The bird's legs simultaneously transformed into those of a lion, and a long tail sprouted from its rump. Only its head and wings retained their original form, though gaining proportionately in size to balance the rest of the body.

The beast alighted on one of the palace's many balconies, landing with a crouch, its wings beating heavily against the stone parapet. As it straightened, its face assumed manlike features – completing its transformation from kite to garuda, a member of the immortal scouts of Devaloka.

On entering the palace, the garuda strode through the halls and winding passageways with familiarity, none of the minor devas on guard duty challenging its progress. The beast made its way deep into the belly of the palace, till it came to a huge door made of sturdy wood, from behind which came muffled sounds of metal clanging against metal. Pushing the door open, the garuda entered a semicircular balcony that looked down on a spacious mud pit, where an intense fight was underway.

A dozen devas bearing swords and spears were circling a colossal figure standing in the center of the mud pit. The figure was incredibly muscular, his burly torso and powerful arms glistening with sweat as he crouched and watched the ring around him. His bearing was regal, his broad face haughty under a thick golden beard that almost reached down to his chest. His unprotected head was covered with long blonde hair that matched his beard.

As the garuda watched, four devas leaped unexpectedly at the giant, who fended off their blows with a bulky shield made of bronze. The giant then fought back, hacking at his attackers with a heavy sword, forcing them to fall back in haste. As the devas resumed circling him, the figure sneered at them.

"Is that the best you've got?" he mocked. "A dainty apsara can inflict more damage than all of you put together. Come on…"

Goaded by the challenge, the devas collectively hurled themselves at the giant, but he stood his ground, deftly parrying their assault. And when he counterattacked, some of the devas lost their swords, while a few more were knocked flat on their backs. The devas retreated yet again, leaving the giant standing in the middle.

"That's better," he said, catching his breath. Throwing down his sword and shield, he added, "Tomorrow, I will practice barehanded combat. You may go."

Once the devas had withdrawn and the giant began toweling himself, a palace official approached him and whispered softly in his ear. The giant turned and looked up at the garuda, his blue eyes sharp and calculative. He nodded, indicating that the garuda had permission to join him.

The garuda walked into the mud pit, its wings folded respectfully. "My salutations to Indra, mighty king of the devas," it said, bowing deeply to the towering figure.

Indra acknowledged the beast with another nod. "What news do you bring?"

As the garuda began speaking, Indra listened with growing interest, his eyes shining with excitement.

"Are you absolutely certain about this?" he asked, once the garuda had fallen silent.

"Yes, master of Devaloka. I saw the Omniscient One give Veeshada's dagger to the king."

"Samrat Vikramaditya, king of Avanti," Indra wondered aloud. "A human being in possession of the Halahala... a *puny* human being..."

Forcing himself back to the present with a shake of his head, the king of the devas looked down at the garuda. "You may leave," he said, before turning brusquely to the palace official who stood a little distance away.

"Request Guru Brihaspati and Narada to meet me in my chamber," he ordered.

* * *

"I didn't make a mistake by agreeing to protect the Halahala, did I raj-guru?"

"No you didn't, Vikrama. It is man's dharma to accept his destiny with grace and courage."

The samrat and the Acharya were alone, standing by a detached dovecote located on a wooded hillock on the southern shore of the palace lake. The privacy that the place afforded gave Vetala Bhatta the freedom to address the king intimately – just as he always had before Vikramaditya ascended the throne of Avanti on the day he turned eighteen.

"Besides, you have already given your word to the Omniscient One," the raj-guru smiled gently, to take the sting out of a mild rebuke. "So, now is not the time to ask such questions."

The king nodded quietly, chewing his lip as he scattered handfuls of grain on the ground, which was teeming with cooing and fluttering pigeons.

"I just wonder if I should have taken you and Vararuchi and the rest of the council into confidence first," he said at last. "I feel that by accepting responsibility of the dagger, I have forced a decision on the council."

The Acharya appraised the samrat for a moment before answering. "You do yourself and the Council of Nine great injustice by believing so, Vikrama. The council swears its unquestioning allegiance to you, not because you are the king of Avanti, but because you are a man of integrity and honor. The council trusts you to do what is *right* – not what is *convenient*. We respect that in you, Vikrama, and are proud to be your councilors. You and the council are one, and your decision is the council's decision. Always remember that."

"I will, Acharya," promised Vikramaditya, his voice flooding with relief and gratitude.

"And I can assure you that had the responsibility of guarding the Halahala been placed before them, the council's decision wouldn't have been different from yours. The honor that comes from fulfilling a duty imposed by the mighty Shiva outweighs every threat under the sun."

The two men turned away from the feeding pigeons and began retracing their steps. Their conversation drifted to the threat from the Hunas and the preparations underway to secure the frontier from attack. But on reaching the top of the hill, the samrat spied a caravan of chariots and horses wending its way in the distance, heading northward beyond Ujjayini's gates. He stopped to watch the procession through the trees.

"King Siddhasena," said the raj-guru, as he joined the king. "The last of our royal guests returning home."

Vikramaditya was silent for a while. When he finally spoke, his voice was dry and hard.

"Did you manage speaking to the old king about Magadha's campaign against Vanga?"

"I spoke to him briefly about it over dinner last night," the Acharya replied. "He was very vague in his answers – I almost got the impression he didn't want to talk about it."

"What did he say?"

"He just said that the decision to wage war against Vanga was made in consultation with Magadha's royal council."

"Did he say *he* made the decision?"

"No," Vetala Bhatta shrugged. "As I said, he was very evasive."

"I don't think King Siddhasena is in control of Magadha any longer," said Vikramaditya. After a short pause, he asked, "Is there a serious threat of a Kikata uprising against Magadha?"

"Not that I know of," the raj-guru shook his head doubtfully. "The Kikata tribe is too small and insignificant to revolt against the might of Magadha. I shall ask for reports from our spies anyway."

The king nodded in agreement. "Even assuming the Kikatas are restive, would the republic of Vanga lend them support against Magadha?"

"The idea seems farfetched. Vanga has always maintained neutrality in such matters. The republic is known for its noninterference in the territorial disputes of other kingdoms."

"Precisely. So the question we need answered is this." Vikramaditya narrowed his eyes shrewdly at Vetala Bhatta. "What is Prince Shoorasena's real motive behind engaging Vanga in a conflict?"

The king and his chief advisor stood watching the procession slowly disappear over a far hill, when they heard footsteps scrambling up the path. Turning around, Vikramaditya's eyebrows rose in surprise on seeing Ghatakarpara appear over a rise. At the same instant, the young man saw the king.

"Uncle, I was told I might find you here," panted Ghatakarpara. "Please, can I have a word with you?"

The king nodded as his nephew drew close. But at that moment, Vetala Bhatta, who was hidden from sight behind a tree, stepped into Ghatakarpara's line of vision. On seeing the Acharya, the prince stopped short and looked around waveringly.

"Yes?" said the samrat.

"It's not... nothing urgent," Ghatakarpara fumbled awkwardly. "I... we can talk later."

Sensing the reason behind the boy's hesitation, Vikramaditya said, "There's no better time to talk than now." Inclining his head toward the raj-guru, he added, "You are among friends, and among friends there are no secrets. Speak boldly, young man."

The prince fidgeted for a moment, stealing glances at the Acharya. Then, summoning up his courage, he said, "I mean to... I mean, I *want* to go to Udaypuri."

The king and the raj-guru stared at one another in surprise. "What for?" asked Vikramaditya.

"To fight the Hunas," Ghatakarpara blurted out. "I want

an opportunity to go to the frontlines. I want to volunteer to oversee the war preparations. I want..."

"Hold on, hold on," the samrat quelled the outburst with raised hands. "There is no battle happening anywhere with the Hunas – at least not right now. And Amara Simha has already volunteered to go to Udaypuri."

"Then please let me go with him, uncle... please," the prince pleaded.

The king once again exchanged a glance with Vetala Bhatta. "But you still need to complete your training here."

"Uncle, *please*," Ghatakarpara was now virtually on his knees, begging. "My best friend is already a garrison commander. If Atulyateja is fit enough for battle, why not me? The Acharya knows that I've trained well..." He petitioned the raj-guru with beseeching eyes. "Please tell the samrat what you told me the other day."

Vikramaditya looked at the Acharya, who merely nodded once. But the king also noticed the faint, indulgent smile on Vetala Bhatta's face. Turning back, the samrat considered the prince for a moment.

"Fine, you can go."

"Yes!" Ghatakarpara almost leaped in elation, his eyes alight with joy. Immediately, the king raised a cautionary finger.

"But... but... you have to promise me that you will stay close to Amara Simha and follow his orders. If I hear you have been doing otherwise, I will come and yank you back here by the ear." Vikramaditya smiled to take the edge off his words.

"I promise, uncle. I promise. Thank you."

"Good. Prepare to leave with Amara Simha. I shall send word that you will be joining him."

The prince bounded down the hill, unable to restrain his excitement. As the king watched him fondly, he sighed and addressed the raj-guru. "Another of your wards is ready to leave the protection of his nest."

"Yes," the Acharya smiled with pride. "He is desperate to win your approval, which is natural at his age."

"Are you sure he is ready for whatever is to come?" Vikramaditya asked with sudden concern.

"Oh yes," the chief advisor's tone was confident. "He has a few soft spots and some rough edges – but nothing that life at the frontier can't remedy. Between Amara Simha and a couple of battles, Pralupi's son will discover the stuff he is made of."

***

The elderly woman sitting opposite Vararuchi and Dhanavantri had a kind, good-natured face. She was plump in a comforting, maternal sort of way, her chubby cheeks dimpling every time she smiled, which was often. Her eyes, almost reduced to slits on account of the fat that had accumulated around them, revealed a charitable disposition, and her overall appearance was one of self-contentment.

Vararuchi looked up from the plate set before him and caught the woman's eye. "The food is marvelous, mother," he said between mouthfuls.

"Ummph, just fantastic…" Dhanavantri agreed with the earnest appreciation of a gourmet.

"It's very simple fare," the woman waved a self-depreciating hand. "Had I known the two of you would drop in, I would have ensured a more sumptuous spread. Why didn't you send word?"

Vararuchi merely grunted and shook his head, too busy enjoying the food to respond.

"We decided to come so I could take a look at your leg, *badi-maa*. Lunch was never part of the plan," Dhanavantri paused and grinned cheekily. "Though in retrospect, we couldn't have timed the visit better."

The woman smile indulgently and ladled some more gravy onto the councilors' plates. "I'm so glad for my arthritis," she remarked. "Thanks to it, I at least got to see both of you. You people come by less and less these days."

Although there was a hint of disappointment in her voice, there was no rancour – because that was one emotion that Ushantha, first wife of King Mahendraditya, was quite incapable of summoning. In fact, it was this attribute of hers, above all others, that had appealed most to the late king of Avanti. For as long as the king had known her, Ushantha had never grumbled or nursed a grudge, choosing to smile her way through adversity instead.

Dhanavantri, who had cleverly interpreted Ushantha's words as being directed mainly at her son, remained silent. Vararuchi too, however, desisted from making any comments.

"Things are very busy at the palace these days?" Again Ushantha's question was matter-of-fact, meant neither to stoke nor play on Vararuchi's guilt.

The councilors eyed one another, their minds going to Veeshada's dagger at the same time. "Yes mother. And they'll probably become even busier now," said Vararuchi truthfully, but without elaboration.

Dhanavantri saw the woman's face fall. "That means I will see even lesser of you."

Then, as evidence of her inability to harbor sadness for

long, Ushantha brightened. "But of course, as councilors of Vikrama, you're bound to be busy – after all, he's now the samrat of Sindhuvarta." Her voice glowed with genuine happiness for her stepson. "Upashruti will be so proud of Vikrama."

Neither Ushantha nor Dhanavantri, who had his head buried in a bowl of sweet yogurt, noticed a shadow pass over Vararuchi's face at the mention of Queen Upashruti. In a flash it was gone, replaced with a smile.

"We are all proud of Vikrama," said Vararuchi, pushing his empty plate toward a servant who was waiting to clear the table.

With lunch coming to a close, Ushantha and the councilors adjourned to a big bedroom upstairs. The bedroom gave onto a large balcony that offered a panoramic view of the countryside, lush green with paddy fields segmented into little squares by narrow footpaths and canals, stretching all the way to the distant purple hills. Here and there, mango and *jamun* trees spread their shade for weary travelers and the farmhands taking their siesta. The air was still in the shimmering afternoon heat, with only the faraway metallic tunk-tunk-tunk of a coppersmith barbet disturbing the silence. The scent of frangipani floated in from the open windows.

"I've brought you a liniment of *guggul* and turmeric, *badi-maa*," said Dhanavantri, extracting two earthenware jars from a cloth bag slung over his shoulder. He handed the jars to an old maid for safekeeping. "These are to be applied on the joints every morning and night for the next one month. You can also use warm fomentation to ease the pain. And please, no more cold water baths."

Ushantha, who sat propped up on a bed, pulled a face,

but quickly offered a placatory smile on seeing the physician wag a fat finger at her in warning.

"This should give her relief," Dhanavantri assured Vararuchi as he rose from the bedside. However, turning back to Ushantha, he added, "I still think you should come and live in the palace, *badi-maa*. It has all the conveniences, and you will get to see all of us more often. And I will get a chance to tend to your leg more regularly."

"No, no..." Ushantha shook her head emphatically. "I'm far happier in the countryside, where I was born and raised. You will recall that I did stay in Ujjayini during the Huna occupation – but life in the city is too stressful for me. I shall move out of here the day you find me a place in Ujjayini that offers me this..." She waved her arm toward the wide balcony and the rustic tranquility that lay piled outside.

Following the sweep of the woman's hand, Dhanavantri was forced to admit that *badi-maa* had a cogent argument against shifting to Ujjayini. "No city can match the calm of the countryside," he nodded in understanding. "If this gives you peace and happiness, so be it."

Later, as Vararuchi and Dhanavantri rode back toward Ujjayini in silence, each lost in his private thoughts, Vararuchi pondered over the physician's invitation to his mother to come and live in the palace. The moment Dhanavantri had made the suggestion, Vararuchi had known what Ushantha's reaction would be. He also knew the real reason behind his mother's reluctance to come to the palace.

Brahman by birth, Ushantha had always known that her marriage to Mahendraditya was a contravention of tradition – Kshatriya kings were ordained to wed Kshatriya princesses, and only children begot by such alliances were legitimate heirs to the throne. Ushantha had also known that tradition would impose upon Mahendraditya to marry a Kshatriya, who would then bear him the rightful heir of Avanti. So, she had stubbornly resisted the idea of shifting to the palace, and when Queen Upashruti arrived as Mahendraditya's new bride, Ushantha had made it a point to keep as far away from Ujjayini as was possible. Vararuchi recalled how it had taken all of Mahendraditya and the Acharya's skills to persuade his mother to live in Ujjayini during the Huna invasion, and how she had left the city the moment Avanti was rid of the attackers.

"Your *chhoti-maa* is the queen of Avanti, but both she and I know that hers is a marriage of convenience," Ushantha had once explained to him. "I am the one true love of your father. And while there's a lot that a woman can bear, no woman can live with the knowledge that her husband loves another more dearly. Upashruti doesn't have a choice in the matter, but by residing in Ujjayini, I don't want to be a constant reminder of her lower status in the king's life."

Vararuchi turned to look back at the old mansion that he had explored endlessly as a child, before Mahendraditya had taken him to the palace to be placed under the Acharya's tutelage. It stood all by itself in the middle of the paddy fields, now half-concealed by a thick copse of trees, wrapped in moldering solitude. The sight depressed him, yet Vararuchi realized that his mother was right in picking it as her sanctuary. Despite everything he had done for Vikramaditya and the royal household, he knew Queen Upashruti disliked him intensely for who he was; the Queen Mother's jealousy would have known no bounds had Ushantha also been in the palace.

Heaving a sigh, Vararuchi faced east again. The two-hour ride back to Ujjayini, which lay across the Kshipra, would be full of bitter memories.

* * *

The tantric *mandala*, drawn with turmeric paste and vermilion, was crude in design but complex in character. Covering almost the entire surface of the rough-hewn granite table, it was made up of an elaborate grid of concentric circles and dissecting radials set inside a six-pointed star. The intervening chambers of the grid were patterned with obscure markings and hieroglyphics, and small mounds of white cowrie shells were placed on the six vertices of the star. At its vortex, where the radials came together, six pieces of human vertebrae lay in a random scatter.

It was these bones that consumed the interest of Sage Shukracharya. He leaned over the table, propping himself with spread fingers, and stared minutely at the vertebrae, assessing their relative distances to one another and the distances between them and the cowrie shells.

Although a deva by descent, the sage wasn't very tall, yet he was strongly built, with broad shoulders and a deep chest matted with graying hair. His face, lit by the glow of a smoky lamp, appeared fair, and was covered with a thick iron-gray beard and moustache under a curved, beak-like nose. The highlight of the face, though, was the black eye-patch that the sage wore over his left eye – which called attention to his good eye, burning with feverish intensity as it darted from one corner of the *mandala* to another.

After analyzing the bones for a while, the sage picked a pair up. Cupping them in his hands, he closed his eye and breathed an ancient mantra, before casting them back onto the *mandala*. Bending in eagerness, he once again peered at the bones. With rising excitement, he repeated the procedure a third and a fourth time, picking different sets of bones and invoking different mantras on each occasion. Every time he threw down the vertebrae, his breathing quickened, until sweat stood out on his brow.

Having collected and thrown all six bones down the fifth time, Shukracharya almost ceased breathing as he interpreted the mystic signs. Finally, he raised his head and fixed a glazed eye into space, his lips spreading in a slow smile of triumph. Snapping back into action, the sage swept the vertebrae into a leather pouch with a definite sense of purpose. He tucked the pouch into his waistband, snuffed out the lamp's flame between forefinger and thumb and marched out of the sparse room.

The sage traversed a series of labyrinthine passages lit by dim torches, each passage leading deeper into the bowels of Patala, till he came to a dead end, his path blocked by a solid wall of hard rock. Raising the index finger of his right hand, Shukracharya drew a large rectangle on the rock face, where a portal magically opened. Passing through this gap, the sage stepped onto a high ledge that was cut into the sheer rock cliff that rose steeply behind him. Below him, the crevice plunged to meet the raging currents of the Patala Ganga, the accursed river doomed to flow inside Patala for eternity.

Across the wide chasm, on the opposite bank of the Patala Ganga, stood a large edifice made of polished volcanic glass, black in color – the famed black crystal palace of Hiranyakashipu, Hiranyaksha and Holika, the sibling-consorts who ruled the asura dominions. The structure, a jagged ring of spiked towers – ten in number, and uneven in size and height – jutted out of the ground like a fossilized eruption, the tower in the center of the cluster rising high into the black sky littered with stars. Diffused starlight reflected off the towers' smooth, flat sides, while their edges and angularities gleamed white and sharp, like razorblades.

His eye fixed on the palace, Shukracharya stepped off the ledge, heedless of the perilous gorge that stretched in front of him. For a fraction of a second, his feet hovered over empty space, high above the churning rapids of the river. Then, out of nowhere, a Mind Bridge appeared underfoot, thin as gossamer and frail as the mist, to support the sage in his crossing of the chasm. Once the sage was back on firm ground on the opposite bank, the mysterious Mind Bridge unraveled and dissipated in the eddying wind.

Inside the palace, Shukracharya made his way through countless halls and antechambers guarded by vampire bhootas and pishachas, who paid deep obeisance to the sage as he passed by. At last, the sage arrived at the Court of the Golden Triad, where several high-ranking asuras were already gathered around the foot of a wide throne, also made of black crystal. Asura lord Hiranyaksha was presiding over the assembly, while his sister-consort, the Witch Queen Holika, sat to his right.

"No, this will not do," Hiranyaksha's voice rumbled in displeasure. "We shouldn't be happy with ourselves for harrying the outlying colonies of the devas. What are we? Scavenging crows, nibbling at bits and leftovers? No, we are the mighty asuras, descended from Diti. We must strike at the very heart of Devaloka. Our aim should be to take Amaravati."

"Amaravati is extremely well defended, my lord," cautioned one of the assembled asura generals. "We have tried to take it many times and failed."

"So are we to accept that the devas are unconquerable?" Holika's tone was icy as she considered the general with her cold blue eyes, set deep in a face that was both enticing and forbidding in its beauty. Her red lips were full and inviting, yet a subtle hint of menace lurked just under their surface. Her complexion, like the rest of her body, was lustrous gold, but there was a sinister aspect to the shadows that formed from her features.

The asura general wilted under the Witch Queen's gaze.

"The devas and unconquerable? Never!" Hiranyaksha smacked his thigh with his fist as he glared over the assembly. "We will take Amaravati apart brick by brick, even if it's the last thing we do. I want all of you to devise plans to invade Devaloka. When my dear brother returns from his penance to take his place by my and Holika's side, I want to gift him Amaravati. And its ruler in chains."

"Noble thoughts indeed," remarked Shukracharya, making his way into the court. "Hiranyakashipu would be very pleased to see Indra as a prisoner in Patala."

"Greetings, mahaguru," Hiranyaksha rose from his high crystal throne at the sight of the sage. The asura lord was an imposing figure, tall and heavy, a pair of thick ram horns on his forehead adding to his stature. His dark, hairless face was craggy but handsome, with deep lines running down his cheeks to a strong, stern jaw. His eyes were bright golden in color, the same shade as Holika's skin, but they retained a dark, brooding quality as they appraised Shukracharya.

"I'm glad you agree that it's time to take Devaloka," Hiranyaksha continued as he descended the steps from his throne to meet his high priest. Gesturing toward a vacant seat flanking the throne, he added, "Do join the discussion, mahaguru. Your wisdom and guidance would be invaluable, as always."

The sage made no move to accept the seat. "Much as I see the need to move against the devas, there are more important things to discuss right now," Shukracharya looked the asura king in the eye before glancing at Holika, who had climbed halfway down the steps. "The bones have spoken and revealed some very important tidings."

"Yes mahaguru?" Hiranyaksha's face was impassive as granite as he towered over the sage.

"The Halahala…" Shukracharya nodded and paused. The court fell silent as everyone present drew in their breaths. "It no longer enjoys the protection of the Omniscient One."

"Then where is it?" asked Hiranyaksha with anxiety. "Have the devas got…"

"No," the high priest shook his head. "Not yet. It is in the possession of a human king named Vikramaditya."

"A *human* king…?" Surprised murmurs spread through the court. "How did it come into this human being's possession?"

"The bones tell me that it was given to him by the Omniscient One himself," Shukracharya replied. As more wonder went around the court, the sage added, "According to the bones, this king is a formidable force. But, at the end of the day, he is only human. I fear that the devas will make a move to claim Veeshada's dagger from him without much delay."

"We mustn't allow that to happen," Hiranyaksha glowered.

"Do the devas know of this development, mahaguru?" the Witch Queen posed the question, blue eyes clouding with worry.

"They do," the high priest confirmed. "The news was delivered to Indra a little while ago."

"Then there's no time to lose, lord," Holika exchanged a grim look with her consort-brother. "We have to take the dagger from this human king before they can."

* * *

Dusk had fallen over Ujjayini and the first stars had made their appearance, growing in brightness as the day diminished in size and strength, the western sky fading from orange to ashen pink to purple. Lamplights came on all around the busy city, its thoroughfares swelling with shoppers, its markets and squares echoing with the hoarse cries of hawkers selling grain, fruit and sweetmeats. In street corners, magicians and jugglers strove to outdo one another in entertaining passersby, as small knots of young men and women loitered about, strutting and preening in age-old courtship rituals. Old men sat under awnings swapping stories, chewing *tambulam* and rolling dice, while elsewhere, the chime of temple bells drew the more devout out of their homes. Down by the riverside, where boats were being lashed to their moorings, the taverns were well on their way to achieving full capacity.

The royal palace was silent in contrast, with only the plaintive melody of an evening *raga* issuing from a chamber set to the back of the palace.

The music came from a pair of *rudra veena*s being played by Vikramaditya and Vararuchi, the strains perfectly synchronized as the brothers pitted their skills in a sporting effort to outdo one another. Over a series of elaborate *alankaras* the ensemble rose to a crescendo, building to a point where both men virtually abandoned themselves to the enchantment of harmony. When at last the strings of the two *veena*s fell silent, they raised their heads and looked at each other, smiling in delight and mutual admiration.

"That was a simply beautiful, Vikrama," said Queen Upashruti, who had entered the chamber while the brothers were playing. Her eyes shone as she gazed at Vikramaditya in appreciation.

"Thank you, mother," the king replied as he laid his *veena* down and stood up. "But I do think Vararuchi played better than I did. He always does." He turned to smile at his brother, who was standing respectfully to one side. "He's the one who taught me this wonderful *raga* that he learned during his travels through the Southern Kingdoms."

The queen gave Vararuchi a passing glance, struggling to bring on a token smile that barely turned the corners of her mouth. When she spoke, she reserved her praise for her own son. "Then you have mastered it well, Vikrama."

Vararuchi, on whose face the joy appeared to have died, offered a broken smile of his own before turning to Vikramaditya. Swallowing hard, he bowed. "Allow me to take my leave, samrat," his voice and manner were stiff and formal. "I shall see you tomorrow morning."

"Why are you going so soon?" the king protested, even as Queen Upashruti maintained a cold silence, refusing to make eye contact with Vararuchi or be drawn into the conversation. "I was hoping we could play one more *raga*."

"I have... some work," Vararuchi replied, groping for an excuse. "I need to talk to Amara Simha... about Ghatakarpara. Just making sure he takes care of the lad."

"Of course he will," Vikramaditya sounded perplexed, but seeing Vararuchi's resolve, he inclined his head. "But if you think it's important, I won't stop you. Sleep well, dear brother."

Vararuchi turned and bowed to Queen Upashruti. "Permit me to leave, queen mother," he said.

Keeping her face averted, the queen nodded, but made no further acknowledgment of Vararuchi. She waited for her stepson to leave the room before approaching Vikrama-ditya.

"Are you sure it's wise to send Ghatakarpara away?" she asked, her voice brimming with grandmotherly concern.

"Hmmm? Oh yes, mother," the king answered. His expression was suddenly distracted. "He's not a child any longer, and he's not alone. Amara Simha will be with him."

Queen Upashruti watched her son turn and go to a balcony, where he stood quietly, leaning against the rails. She followed him, and was surprised to see a pall of sadness clouding his face.

"What's the matter?" she asked in alarm.

Vikramaditya sighed and shook his head. "Nothing much, mother," he said in a melancholic voice. "It's just that the *raga* we were playing was... is... one of Vishakha's favorites."

The queen's face fell and she looked away. When she turned back to her son, her tone was gentle but insistent. "It's been nearly two years, Vikrama," she said, placing a hand on his forearm. "How much longer will you wait?"

The king continued staring into the night without reply.

"No one believes she is going to get better," Queen Upashruti pressed the matter. "Deep in your heart, even *you* know this. Why are you turning your face from the truth? There's a full life before you – you have to move on."

The king maintained a stubborn silence.

"King Harihara came to me yesterday," the queen spoke to fill the silence. "He asked me if you would accept Princess Rukma's hand in marriage. She is a nice girl and I..."

"Why is King Harihara doing this?" Vikramaditya brushed his mother's hand off with a mixture of anger and exasperation. "What's wrong with him? He knows about Vishakha, still he has the gall... I was under the impression he'd come to Ujjayini for the *yajna*."

"There's no harm in considering Harihara's proposal," the queen persevered. "After all, it's a tradition among Kshatriya kings to take more than one wife, so there's..."

"No mother, that won't happen," Vikramaditya spoke with vehemence. "How can you even think I would consider something like this when you know that Vishakha is in the palace – just *six* rooms away?"

Turning around, the king walked back into the room. Queen Upashruti tailed her son, meaning to say something conciliatory, but the king spoke first.

"Mother, I have loved Vishakha from as far back as I can remember. Probably from the day the late king Vallabha brought her and Kshapanaka to Avanti and left them in the safety of this palace. I cannot turn my back on the woman I have loved and married just because of... her condition. It doesn't matter if two years have passed or five. I will wait for her."

The queen again opened her mouth, but was once again interrupted by Vikramaditya. This time, however, his voice was gentler, more persuasive. "And how do we know she will not get better? Dhanavantri, Kshapanaka and the nurses are tending to her, and Dhanavantri has promised to do everything to find a cure." Coming close to the queen, he added, "Please mother, we need to believe that Vishakha will get better. She needs our faith."

Queen Upashruti looked up into her son's eyes and nodded, conscious that he was not amenable to reason.

"King Harihara will be disappointed," she sighed sadly.

"Mother, I'm certain he will find other suitable matches for the princess of Heheya."

At that moment, they were disturbed by the sound of the door opening. Looking around, they saw Princess Pralupi flounce into the room.

"Come, child," said Queen Upashruti, approaching her daughter, intending to welcome her, but the princess pushed past her mother and walked up to Vikramaditya, her eyes flashing in anger.

"I hear you have decided to send Ghatakarpara to the frontier?" she demanded. "Why?"

"Well, he is definitely going to Udaypuri," the king answered evenly. "But the point about my *sending* him there doesn't exactly count as *he* was the one who volunteered to go."

"Ghatakarpara is still a boy and doesn't know right from wrong," Pralupi snapped back. "As his uncle, you have to tell him what's good for him."

"On the contrary, your son is old enough to think for himself," answered Vikramaditya. "It's time we all stopped making decisions for him."

"Ghatakarpara's place is in the palace," the king's sister dug in adamantly.

"A young prince's place is where he is needed most and where he can learn the art of administering a kingdom. The frontier will teach him things he would otherwise never learn."

"What if something happens to him there?"

"In times like these, things could happen to people anywhere. But to answer your question, it's a risk everyone who bears a sword for Avanti has to live with."

Princess Pralupi stared at her brother defiantly. Then, after a moment's pause, she asked, "And what decision have you made about my son's future?"

"What do you mean?" the king looked flummoxed. "I just told you he has expressed a desire to go to the frontier and I have conceded to his wish."

The princess turned sharply to Queen Upashruti. "You haven't spoken about it yet, mother?" she asked accusingly. "You said you would."

The queen stepped forward, looking perturbed. "We will talk about this later, dear. Now is not the time…"

"What is all this, mother?" Vikramaditya interjected, narrowing his eyes in suspicion.

"Later… I will tell you everything…"

But before the queen could complete her sentence, Pralupi turned back to face her brother.

"I want Chandravardhan to make Ghatakarpara the next king of Vatsa."

"What?" Vikramaditya's face registered utter amazement.

"Yes, and you have to convince Chandravardhan to do this. He will listen to you. He *has* to listen to you."

"No," the king shook his head, frowning. "I won't do anything of the sort. Chandravardhan's son Shashivardhan is the legal heir…"

"Shashivardhan is a drunkard and a gambler," Pralupi hissed.

"That may or may not be true, but it doesn't give me the authority to tell Chandravardhan to make Ghatakarpara his successor. Chandravardhan has been a trusted friend and ally of Avanti, and has stood by me. I won't abuse that trust and friendship by doing what you ask."

"Even if it means Vatsa getting an incompetent king like Shashivardhan?"

"Vatsa is an independent kingdom, sister," Vikramaditya explained patiently. "It is *not* our vassal state, as some might like to believe. And Avanti does not interfere in how our allies run their kingdoms. That was one of the principles our father lived by. Let us not trouble the soul of King Mahendraditya by breaching that rule."

Pralupi stared at the floor in frustration, her fists clenched. When she looked up, her eyes were welling with tears.

"You don't love your nephew, and you don't want him to become a king," she said spitefully. "You just want him to remain in this palace as one of your faithful councilors, following you around and obeying orders like a dog."

She turned and stomped out of the chamber, tears streaming down her cheeks.

Envoy

Let me warn you that I intend reporting your behavior to the royal court of Ujjayini. I will not tolerate such outright disrespect to the office of the governor of Malawa."

The high-pitched, nasal voice belonged to one of the two men seated in a stately room inside the fort of Udaypuri. The speaker was thin and tall, and had a large head that tended to stoop and bob forward as he spoke, giving him a vulture-like appearance. His dark, clean-shaven face showed signs of aging, and his gray hair was thinning under his official turban.

In direct contrast, the man across the table was in his early twenties, with an open and earnest face, pink in complexion. He had square shoulders that hinted at a military background, and he wore his hair short, which complemented a clipped, black moustache.

"My intention was never to disrespect you or your office, sir…" the younger man began, but he was immediately interrupted by the other.

"Then how do you explain your decision to send a rider directly to the palace, commander?" the older man railed. "You are aware that protocol demands that all reports gathered in the province of Malawa should first be tabled before me. *I* am the governor of Malawa, and *I* should be the one informing the palace of what's happening in and around my province. But because of your impertinence, the *palace* sends me news that there's a perceived threat from the Hunas on our border. Do you know how silly you have made me look?"

"My apologies, Governor Satyaveda... I would most certainly have delivered the report to you had you been present in Udaypuri at the time. But unfortunately you were deep in the jungles on your hunting expedition..."

"Then you should have waited patiently for my return instead of bypassing me," the governor bristled with indignation.

"Sir, as you can see, the matter pertained to a Huna incursion on Avanti," the younger man insisted. "They had attacked one of our outposts, killed seventeen of my men and left a warning for our samrat. As in-charge of this garrison, I surmised that the news had to reach Ujjayini without delay."

"You are a garrison commander of the Frontier Guard, not of the Imperial Army," Satyaveda quibbled, his ego not permitting him to back down. "The Frontier Guard reports to the governor, and you stepped out of line by not reporting to me. Worse, when I sent word asking you to come and meet me, you didn't show up for two days."

"Sir, I have been at the border, seeing to the defenses. I just returned this morning and here I am."

"Well, your overall conduct has been less than satisfactory, commander," the governor grumbled. "You broke the rules by not following proper reporting procedures..."

"Had procedures been followed, in all probability, the palace would still be oblivious of the Huna attack on that outpost, Satyaveda," a voice boomed, silencing the governor.

Startled, the men at the table turned to see Amara Simha striding in, followed by Ghatakarpara. Satyaveda jumped to his feet, his chair scraping on the stony floor.

"What a pleasure, Councilor Amara Simha," he twittered obsequiously, hurrying forward to meet the bulky warrior. "Greetings to you too, prince. Pardon me, but I wasn't informed that the two of you were coming to Udaypuri. Otherwise, I would have come to receive you in person. Why didn't you send word, councilor?"

"Obviously, even we are lagging in the procedures and protocols department," snorted Amara Simha, eyeing the garrison commander, who fought to stifle a smile.

"Please don't say that," said Satyaveda, sounding flustered. "Come, please be seated…"

"Would you rather that every procedure be followed, even if that means leaving Avanti unprepared and vulnerable to a sudden Huna attack?" Amara Simha demanded, ignoring the governor's invitation and placing his large hands on his hips.

"No, no, not at all," stammered Satyaveda. "That's not what I meant, no."

"So you agree Commander Atulyateja here did the right thing by giving top priority to the security of Avanti?"

"Oh yes, absolutely. I mean…"

"Good. That shows we are all on the same side," Amara Simha spoke decisively. "So let's get down to business."

As Amara Simha lowered himself into a chair, the governor nervously watched Ghatakarpara approach Atul-yateja with a broad smile. His eyebrows shot up in anxiety when he saw the two young men embrace each other.

"How are you, my brother?" asked Ghatakarpara, slapping Atulyateja on the back.

"Faring well, prince," the commander answered with a smile as he disengaged himself.

"We miss you in Ujjayini, especially when we go swimming in the holy Kshipra," said Ghatakarpara, his eyes twinkling. "Just last week, Jayaati and I were talking about how old Mother Jaala tied the three of us up and took us to the City Watch tribunal when she caught us sneaking firewater out of her brewery. You had a soft spot for her second daughter, remember?"

Atulyateja smiled in embarrassment, conscious of the older men scrutinizing them. Realizing this, the prince also checked himself. As he approached the table to sit down, he added, "Thank you for sending the rider to me with the report on the Huna attack, brother."

Once everyone was seated, Amara Simha turned to the governor. "Let's take a look at the plans."

Satyaveda looked uncertainly from Amara Simha to Ghatakarpara. "Plans…?"

"Yes, the plans. The defenses that have been put in place, where troops have been deployed, where scouts have been positioned… maps, you know, maps."

"I… don't have those," Satyaveda glanced at the three men, clearly at a loss.

"Then what have you been doing here, governor?" Amara Simha was brusque. "Other than ranting about protocols not being observed, that is?"

"I have the maps and everything else in my room," the garrison commander interjected quietly.

"So why are we wasting our time here?" Amara Simha

got to his feet. Snapping his fingers, he added, "Come, let's go there."

As Amara Simha and Ghatakarpara headed for the door, the governor of Malawa rushed up to Atulyateja and caught him by the arm to slow him down.

"Why didn't you tell me that you had sent the rider to Prince Ghatakarpara?" he whispered. "And you never told me that the two of you were such close friends."

"You never asked, sir."

"I know, silly of me," Satyaveda fawned over the commander. "Anyway, let's forget about what I said earlier, okay? I was just stressed by this whole thing about the Hunas... I see you did the right thing by not waiting for me. Good, good... Now go with them, commander. And if you want any help with anything, just ask."

* * *

Vikramaditya and Kalidasa stood in front of a large red pavilion, which had been set up on a knoll overlooking a swathe of dry scrubland. Lower down and to the right of the pavilion were four tents pitched together, where a dozen *samsaptakas* – members of Avanti's elite Warriors of the Oath – were huddled in discussion.

Squinting in the glare of the midday sun, the king carefully inspected the sparse landscape, but all he could see was barren, undulating earth, scattered with clumps of stunted vegetation. Other than the vague shimmer of the horizon, nothing moved.

Yet, the king knew that somewhere out in the scrubland were five young soldiers of the Imperial Army – the last five remaining cadets of the original thirty-two who had volunteered to join the service of the *samsaptakas*.

"Can you see any of them?" Vikramaditya glanced at Kalidasa.

"No," the giant replied with a small smile of satisfaction. "These five are very good. All of them are worthy of enlisting with the Warriors of the Oath."

A few more minutes passed before Angamitra, a young captain of the *samsaptakas* and Kalidasa's trusted deputy, detached himself from the group near the tents and approached the foot of the knoll. Looking up at Kalidasa, he spoke.

"We think it's time, commander."

On seeing Kalidasa nod in assent, the captain marched back to the tents and issued a command. Five *samsaptakas* immediately sallied some distance into the scrubland, each bearing a shield in his arm. As the samrat and Kalidasa watched with interest, one of the *samsaptakas* suddenly barked an order.

"Charge!"

Instantly, five disheveled figures rose, ghost-like, from under the burning dust of the scrub, throwing off their camouflage of prickly bushes. They were armed with broad swords, which they brandished wildly as they ran, screaming, toward the row of waiting *samsaptakas*.

Four of the cadets reached the *samsaptakas* and began striking at them with great ferocity, but the *samsaptakas* used their shields with dexterity to fend off the deadly swords. The fifth cadet, however, stumbled and fell halfway to his target. Pushing himself upright, he swayed groggily for a moment before slumping to the ground with fatigue.

"Halt," commanded Angamitra, and the four cadets ceased their attack. Meanwhile, two *samsaptakas* from the tents ran to the fallen cadet. Lifting him gently, they proceeded to carry him back into the shade.

"It looks like only four cadets will be taking the Death Oath, not five," said the king, shaking his head. "I feel sorry for that boy. He almost made it."

"I should have expected this," Kalidasa grimaced. "A few always fall at the last hurdle."

"It's not surprising," Vikramaditya turned and entered the welcoming shade of the pavilion. "They hardly get any sleep, and they eat and drink practically nothing for weeks. And of course, the exercises are grueling. There's only so much punishment the body can take."

"The funny bit is that the real punishment starts only *after* cadets earn a place among the *samsaptakas*," remarked Kalidasa, following the king into the pavilion. "One year of the most hellish training... I sometimes feel the cadets who *don't* qualify are the lucky ones."

Vikramaditya smiled as he sat down at a table laden with food. "Yet, there isn't a soldier in Avanti who hasn't dreamt of becoming a *samsaptaka* and serving under the commander of the Warriors of the Oath."

"It is my honor to lead such fearless and capable men," Kalidasa replied graciously, joining the king at the table.

Silence prevailed as the two men chewed their food. At last, Kalidasa looked across at the samrat.

"You are yet to give me your opinion on something that I shared with you," he said.

Vikramaditya stared at Kalidasa with a blank face, trying hard to recall what the latter was alluding to. Then his eyes lit up and he smacked the table.

"Ah, the new poem you've written!"

"So you haven't entirely forgotten about it," Kalidasa gave a playful smile.

"Of course not... I was going through it the night the Omniscient One brought the dagger." The king paused and sighed. "So much has happened since then that it slipped my mind."

Kalidasa nodded. "So what do you think of it?"

"I confess I haven't finished it," Vikramaditya replied. "But from what I've read, it's rich and exquisitely beautiful, as usual. I'd even say possibly your best so far."

"Amara Simha thinks so too," Kalidasa smiled self-consciously at the praise.

"There you are – straight from the critic whose opinion really matters," the samrat spread his hands as if to rest his case. "Few men have studied Sanskrit grammar and verse as well as Amara Simha has. If he says you're the most talented poet and playwright in Sindhuvarta, the debate ends there."

"I have *you* to thank for that, Vikrama. I owe you everything I have today – including my name."

"You owe me nothing but brotherhood and friendship," the samrat smiled affectionately. "And I owe you the same. And as far as your writing is concerned, credit goes only to your passion, and the way you have applied yourself to the craft."

The men returned their attention to the food, but the king couldn't help but marvel at the giant sitting opposite him. He still recalled that blustery evening outside the town of Lava, the red flag fluttering atop the old Kali temple at the edge of the forest. The boy was around eight, and had been found cowering inside the temple, a haunted look in his eyes. He had barely spoken when the guards had brought him to Vikramaditya, and when he eventually did, it was plain that he had no memory of who he was and how he had got to the temple.

Taking pity on him, Vikramaditya – himself not a day older than fourteen – had brought the boy to Ujjayini. There the boy, whom Vikramaditya named Kalidasa after the goddess Kali, had grown as a member of the palace household, training under Vetala Bhatta and Amara Simha, mastering the art of war and verse with equal élan. And it was during those growing years that Kalidasa and Vikramaditya had forged a tight bond of friendship and loyalty.

The two men dined in silence for a while before Vikramaditya glanced at his friend. "I loved the way you have described the beauty of Ujjayini in your poem," he said.

"That wasn't very hard," Kalidasa brushed off the compliment with a shrug. "Ujjayini is the most beautiful city on earth, so it came naturally."

The king nodded. "You have also celebrated the beauty of Ujjayini's women in much detail." He paused to glance at Kalidasa, his eyes twinkling mischievously. "Did you mean its women in general or was there a specific woman in mind while you were writing?"

The giant looked up at the king, then dropped his gaze to his plate, a shy smile on his lips.

"Why don't the two of you marry?" Vikramaditya said abruptly. "You like Shanku a great deal, and even though she may be adept at hiding her feelings, I know she has immense admiration for you. You really should ask her…" He paused suddenly, his face growing serious. "Or, does the thought of her father's treachery bother you?"

"No, that has nothing to do with it," Kalidasa spoke sharply, betraying his feelings for the girl. "I see no reason why she should suffer because of what her father did."

"Then where's the problem?"

"I am a *samsaptaka*, Vikrama," Kalidasa sighed. "I have taken the Death Oath – the oath to return from battle either victorious or dead. I can't wed Shanku knowing that every time I ride into battle, death is my only companion."

The king was about to respond when the door flaps of the pavilion parted and a rider entered.

"Salutations to Samrat Vikramaditya," he said, bowing. "I bring a message from Acharya Vetala Bhatta."

"What is the message?" the samrat demanded.

In reply, the messenger proffered a rolled palm leaf scroll that he held in his hands. The king took the scroll, his eyebrows rising at the sight of the wax seal bearing the sun-crest of Avanti. The message from the raj-guru was important, urgent and confidential, he surmised.

Breaking open the seal, Vikramaditya read the short note inside. He then nodded to the rider and spoke briskly to Kalidasa. "We need to leave for Ujjayini straightaway."

In a matter of minutes, the king and Kalidasa were on horseback, making their way across the scrubland, an escort of eight horsemen trailing some distance behind them.

"What did the Acharya's message say?" Kalidasa's curiosity finally got the better of him.

"We have a visitor at the palace," Vikramaditya replied, urging his horse into a gallop. "A visitor from Devaloka, an envoy of the devas."

* * *

"You must pardon me for the delay, deva," said Vikrama-ditya, approaching the council table. "I was out of Ujjayini and it's an hour's ride back to the palace."

"No apology is needed, samrat," the deva answered with a

wave of his hand and a charming smile. "You have important matters to attend to, and I came unannounced. But I was very well looked after by the Acharya and the rest of your council – indeed, the hospitality of Avanti is without parallel."

"Thank you, good deva." The king's tone was guarded, conscious of the deva's attempt to flatter. He took in the visitor's stately robes and the elegant, handsome face with its sharp nose and broad forehead, which was crowned by a fine crop of silvery hair.

"Address me as Narada, please. There should be no formality between friends." Brown eyes twinkled amiably as the deva considered the faces around the table.

As his councilors exchanged glances, the king lowered himself into his seat at the head of the table and inclined his head. "Now if I may ask, what can we do for you?"

Narada's smile broadened as he drew himself closer to the table. "I have come to propose friendship on behalf of the devas – friendship that would be beneficial to both of us."

"We have never had a deva calling on us before and broaching the topic of friendship, so the timing of your visit is striking," Vikramaditya smiled thinly in response. "If I'm right, your proposal has to do with the dagger, doesn't it?"

For a moment, Narada was taken aback by the bluntness of the question. But he quickly regained his composure. "It's not just about the dagger, samrat. As I said, I'm here to offer a hand of friendship. We must both realize that we should work together to undo the evil designs of the asuras. If peace and prosperity have to prevail in Devaloka and on earth, our cooperation is critical."

Anticipating a response from Vikramaditya, the deva paused. But when he saw none coming, he resumed his well-rehearsed speech.

"I can promise that you will benefit greatly by befriending us," he said. "We are aware that you and your allies face a serious threat from the barbarian tribes to the west of Sindhuvarta. We can help you counter that. There's trouble brewing in the east – we can assist you with that as well. Accept our friendship and you won't regret it, samrat." As an afterthought, he added, "You must know that we devas seek your friendship because we see you as a worthy ally against the asuras."

"We are always happy to make new friends," Vikramaditya spoke after giving the emissary's words some thought.

"Excellent," Narada beamed at the council members. "Lord Indra would be pleased to hear this." He looked around the table expectantly, but the king and his councilors said nothing.

"I take it that you are willing to give us possession of the dagger?" the deva asked.

"So the devas *do* want the dagger in exchange for their friendship," the council chamber echoed with the sarcasm in Vikramaditya's voice. "That means your offer of friendship is conditional. How come you didn't mention this earlier?"

"It's... it's just a token... to seal our alliance." For the first time, Narada faltered, groping for words. "Don't look at it as a precondition."

"In that case, we could give you something else as a token of our friendship. That would work just as well as the dagger, wouldn't it?"

The visitor was quiet as he gauged the mood of the men around him. At last he shook his head. "I'm afraid it has to be the dagger, samrat."

"If we are going to be allies, how does it matter who has the dagger?" asked Vikramaditya.

"We devas can protect it better against the vicious asuras," said Narada. "We want to free you from the responsibility of having to guard it from them."

The king appraised the envoy for a while. At last, drawing himself erect, he said, "The only one who can free us from this responsibility is the one who placed the dagger in our hands, deva. We have given our word to the Omniscient One – and we intend keeping it."

"Don't make a hasty decision, samrat," Narada entreated, barely keeping the disappointment out of his voice. "I am more than willing to wait."

"Hasty or not, the decision has been made," Vikramaditya smiled. "I have nothing to add."

Narada rose from his seat. His face had lost all the earlier charm, and his poise was missing. "The storm of war is already building in and around Sindhuvarta," his voice had become gravelly, like a low snarl from a dark cave. "Soon, the asuras will also be at your doors. You shouldn't have squandered the opportunity of making friends with the devas, samrat."

"The way you put it, it seems we will now have to bear the consequences of denying Indra possession of the Halahala," replied Vikramaditya, rising from his chair. "But we are prepared for it. Let your king know that."

* * *

Hiranyaksha's face was etched with impatience as he gazed out of an arched, crenulated window overlooking the boiling torrents of the Patala Ganga. Every now and then, he cast his eyes over his shoulder, looking into the chamber in the direction of a large crystal table where Shukracharya stood bending over a *mandala*. Beyond the table, on a divan at the far end of the chamber, Holika sat nursing an infant, her keen eyes observing the high priest as he shuffled the six pieces of vertebrae around the *mandala*.

"Aha!" Shukracharya finally broke the silence, his voice bearing a ring of triumph.

"What is it, mahaguru?" Hiranyaksha took four long strides to the table.

The sage raised his head, his single eye burning with excitement. Seeing the asura lord's dark face staring down at him, eyebrows raised in inquiry, Shukracharya's lips peeled back in a wide grin.

"Brihaspati's mission has been a washout. Narada is returning to Devaloka empty-handed – just as I had expected," he gloated. "The fool employed the usual tricks to get Vikramaditya to part with the dagger, but he failed utterly in shaking the human king's resolve."

"And the dagger is still safe in Ujjayini?" the Witch Queen asked from the divan. Her eagerness lent her voice a shrill edge, upsetting the baby suckling at her breast. Puckering its mouth, it studied her face with its large golden eyes, which were facsimiles of Hiranyaksha's.

"Very much," the sage answered, consulting the six bone pieces just to be sure.

"With all due respect, I still think we took a big risk in letting the devas make the first move," Hiranyaksha grunted, stepping away from the table and walking back to the window.

"Not at all," Shukracharya insisted. "It was a calculated gamble. I was right in concluding that Vikramaditya couldn't be swayed into surrendering the Halahala through induce-ments and threats. But I knew Brihaspati would try that tack, so I let him be frustrated. Now the devas have wasted time and effort, and have nothing to show for it."

"But we have to act quickly now," the asura lord

growled, raising his voice to make himself heard over the noise of the doomed river. "Indra isn't going to take this rejection lightly."

"Indeed, mahaguru," Holika urged. Setting the gurgling infant down on the divan, she rose and approached the high priest. "The devas are bound to redouble their efforts, and the next time they will certainly use force. We must preempt them."

"Yes, the time to make our move has come," Shukracharya concurred, clearing the table. Looking at the asura lord, he added, "You may give the orders to prepare for battle."

"The preparations are already underway, mahaguru," Hiranyaksha's golden eyes gleamed in his granite-hard face. "A force of pishachas is being assembled, and I have summoned the dead-eyed rakshasa Andhaka to seek your blessings and lead an assault on Ujjayini."

Andhaka

King Siddhasena closed his eyes and inhaled deeply, filling his aged lungs with the cool, early-morning air infused with the sweet fragrance of jasmine and frangipani.

He was seated on a stone bench in the middle of a large, leafy garden, with none for company other than his loyal bodyguard Sajaya, who stood a few paces to his left. Further to the left, some way behind the guard, was an ornate gazebo with five iron swings arranged around a central fountain. The pathway at Siddhasena's feet led out from the gazebo and meandered across the garden toward the royal palace of Magadha, which was partially visible from between the flowering shrubs and trees.

For a while, the king sat quietly, soaking in the peace and silence. Then, opening his eyes, he reached for his wooden stick, while raising his left hand toward his bodyguard, signaling a desire to be helped to his feet.

The guard took a step forward, but was interrupted by an authoritative voice that cut through the morning calm.

"Let it be, soldier. I shall assist the king."

Even as Siddhasena raised his head to look down the path, his face clouded at the familiarity of the voice, his old eyes registering weariness. And on catching sight of Shoorasena's approach, the king's mouth turned down at the corners, as if full of some bitter aftertaste. Still, he looked back at his bodyguard and nodded.

"Come," said Shoorasena, offering his father a hand.

Once the king had gained his feet, Shoorasena took a firm grip of the old man's hand. Putting his other arm protectively around his father's shoulders, the prince began leading the way down the path, with the guard following them at a respectful distance.

Having walked some distance, Shoorasena looked down at the stooping figure by his side. "Father, I hear that last night you signed an order to dispatch three thousand Magadhan soldiers and three thousand of our archers to Matsya. Is that true?"

Siddhasena sighed inwardly. The question hadn't come as a surprise to him; he had foreseen its inevitability the instant he had issued the command to send the reinforcements to Matsya. But the speed with which the news had travelled to his son's ears was astonishing.

"Yes," he replied at last.

"Why?" the prince asked urgently, keeping his voice down. "We had discussed the matter, and I thought we had decided not to send any troops from Magadha."

"No son, you've got it wrong," Siddhasena corrected. "The fact is that we had only *discussed* the matter – we had not made *any* decision on whether to send our troops or not."

Shoorasena didn't respond immediately, but the old king could sense his son's jaw go rigid in anger.

"So now you've decided to issue the order without taking anyone in the royal council into confidence," the prince muttered.

The king knew exactly what his son meant by 'anyone in the royal council'. For Shoorasena, the only person who mattered in the royal council was himself.

"As king of Magadha, I had to do it," answered Siddhasena. "The Sakas are scouting Matsya and King Baanahasta is in trouble."

"Baanahasta has enough help coming his way from the kingdoms of Vatsa and Kosala," Shoorasena shot back.

"If the Hunas and Sakas begin attacking Sindhuvarta, no amount of help would be enough, son," the old king shook his head. "Besides, King Baanahasta has been an old ally, and Magadha cannot desert him in the time of need."

Shoorasena maintained a frosty silence as he helped his father up a path that gave onto a wide terrace at the northern extremity of the palace garden.

"And most importantly, I have given Samrat Vikramaditya my word that we would send troops to defend Sindhuvarta," the king added. "It is my duty to honor that promise."

Walking on to the terrace, the prince guided his father to its edge, which was protected by a high stone parapet. The land fell away from the terrace, rolling down small hills to meet the plain below, where lay Girivraja, the capital of Magadha. The two men gazed down at the panoramic view of the city for a while before Shoorasena broke the silence.

"Father, your latest decision is a setback to our campaign plans against Vanga. Even before we went to Ujjayini and heard of the threat from the Hunas and Sakas, you had assured the royal council of Magadha that you would support that campaign. It seems as if *that* promise means nothing to you any longer."

"I don't understand your obsession with waging war against Vanga," Siddhasena began shrilly, but he dropped his voice to a murmur when he felt his son's hand tighten on his shoulder. "The republic has never meant us any harm," the old king winced at the pressure being exerted on his feeble body.

"They are backing the Kikata rebellion, father. They need to be taught a lesson."

"Spare me that lie, please," Siddhasena shrugged and wriggled to ease himself out of his son's crushing grasp. "I know there isn't even a remote threat of an organized rebellion from the Kikatas. Yes, as among most tribes we have subjugated, a few Kikatas may bear a grudge against us. But the great majority is perfectly happy under Magadhan rule. They are also quite loyal to Magadha. Look at Sajaya..."

The king inclined his head toward the bodyguard, who now stood quietly at the far end of the terrace. "He has been with me for more than two decades. His conduct is above reproach, his loyalty to Magadha above question."

Shoorasena again lapsed into silence, observing Girivraja down below, which was beginning to come alive with activity, its thoroughfares filling with carts and caravans making for the bazaars. Glancing up at the sky, the prince then turned to casually survey the terrace and the gardens beyond.

"As you wish, father," he said at last with a shrug. "The sun is gaining in height as well as in heat. Let us return to the palace."

Taking his hand, the prince began escorting Siddhasena

toward a broad flight of stairs that led down from the terrace to the lower levels of the palace.

"When do the troops depart for Matsya?" Shoorasena asked as they reached the top of the high stairway.

"By nightfall," the king replied as he gripped the prince's hand and began a stiff, labored descent. "These steps are too steep. We should have taken the other route back."

"This one gets to the palace quicker," Shoorasena said blandly.

Siddhasena had negotiated the top five steps when the prince suddenly wrenched his hand free from the old man's grasp. As the king looked up at his son in surprise, Shoorasena gave him a violent shove.

The king rocked and swayed, his hands flailing as he fought to retrieve his balance. Then, just when it looked as if Siddhasena had regained control, Shoorasena pushed him again, this time with even greater force.

Siddhasena stared at his son in wide-eyed horror as the realization finally sank in, and he opened his mouth as if meaning to say something. But the words died somewhere in the king's old, sad heart, and all that emerged from his throat was a grieving, gasping moan – a last wail of defeat at having failed as a father.

Slowly, after teetering on the steps for what seemed like an eternity, Siddhasena toppled over and rolled down the stairs, his frail body flopping and bouncing, bones snapping and cracking each time his body made an impact on the stone steps. Reaching the bottom of the stairway, the old king's body came to a halt in a jumble of misshapen limbs, the scrawny neck twisted at an unnatural angle, blood pooling quickly under the head.

Shoorasena heard a rush of footsteps from behind.

Turning around, he saw the bodyguard Sajaya appear at the top of the stairs. Swallowing nervously, the prince pointed to the body lying far below them.

"Father..." he said, his voice shaking with emotion. "He slipped and fell."

Too shocked for words, the unsuspecting guard gaped at the king's crumpled body. Then, moving as if he was in a trance, he descended the steps to stand beside Shoorasena. "The good king is no more," the guard's lips moved in a whisper.

The sight of his dead master was so riveting that the guard failed to observe the prince draw a heavy sword from his scabbard. It was only moments before Shoorasena stabbed him in the abdomen that Sajaya realized he was being attacked – but it was too late for him to defend himself. As he clutched his stomach and doubled over, he stared up at Shoorasena in surprise.

"Why... my lord," he mumbled, his voice slurring, incoherent with pain.

In response, Shoorasena yanked the sword out of Sajaya's stomach, tearing more flesh and tissue in the process. The guard screamed in agony as blood began oozing freely from between his fingers. He took a step back and tried to straighten, and immediately Shoorasena swung the sword.

The murderous blade arced through the air before slicing through Sajaya's neck, severing his head. The guard's body collapsed on the stairs in a heavy sprawl, but his head rolled all the way down till it came to rest by Siddhasena's feet, the unseeing eyes looking up at the dead king in bewilderment.

Sajaya's scream had drawn attention, and within moments, guards and palace hands came rushing to the stairs. Those at the bottom flocked to the body of Siddhasena and the guard's head, while those who came from the direction of the garden formed a semicircle at the top of the stairs. A deathly hush fell over everyone as they stared from the dead king to Sajaya's headless body to Shoorasena standing on the steps, holding the bloodied sword.

"The Kikata bodyguard pushed my father down the stairs," the prince thundered, pointing to Sajaya's body. "I saw him do it and I killed him."

As a horrified murmur rose from all around the stairway, Shoorasena raised his sword heavenward. "The Kikatas have taken the kind and beloved king of Magadha from us," he screamed vengefully. "I swear I will make them and their allies pay with blood."

In a matter of seconds, a chant arose from the assembled guards and palace hands, a chant filled with rage and sorrow, growing rapidly in size and volume.

"Death to the Kikatas," they roared in a rising frenzy of bloodlust. "Death to Vanga."

* * *

The rain was coming down in sheets, pounding the earth as if venting an old pent-up rage. Yet Shanku pressed through the downpour, her horse's hooves squelching in the soggy mud as the beast struggled to keep a solid footing. The heavy droplets stung her repeatedly in the face, blinding her; still, the girl persevered, bending low over the neck of her mount and drawing the hood of her cloak over her head for meager protection.

Her grandmother had spoken, and from what she had heard, Shanku knew she had to convey the tidings to her king without delay.

The girl did not slow her pace even after entering Ujjayini, and the subjects of Avanti watched in wonder as the horse thundered through the drenched streets toward the palace, splashing through puddles and kicking up dirt in its wake. On reaching the palace, the horse charged across the palace causeway at full gallop, forcing the palace guards to draw the gates shut in alarm.

"It's me," Shanku said tersely as she reined in her horse and threw off her hood for identification. "Let me pass."

In a matter of a few minutes, she found herself in the council chamber, where Vikramaditya, Vararuchi, Vetala Bhatta and Dhanavantri were pouring over tax records. Shanku stood inside the door, diffident and unsure whether to intrude upon the councilors as they debated levying additional taxes to raise funds for the royal treasury.

"If we are looking at a long and protracted war against the Hunas and Sakas, we have no choice but to raise taxes," Vararuchi was saying. "Or we have to abolish some subsidies."

"Doing away with subsidies means the poor and less privileged will have to bear the brunt," the samrat shook his head in disagreement. "Better raise taxes from the rich, if we have to."

"We should definitely increase duties on iron, bronze and lumber," the Acharya pointed out. "If nothing else, that would result in a drop in demand, so our armories won't end up facing a shortage."

As the others nodded in agreement, Dhanavantri piped in. "We can also start raising the rates of fines and penalties. We did that during the last war. Someone is always breaking the law somewhere…"

The four men were so immersed in discussion that they wouldn't have noticed Shanku standing in the shadows, had it not been for a sudden fit of sneezing that overcame her.

"Child, what are you doing there?" the Acharya looked at her in surprise. "Why didn't you come inside?"

As Shanku approached the council table, the men saw that she was dripping wet.

"What happened to you?" the king inquired as he straightened.

"I was caught in the rain, samrat," Shanku replied.

"I can see that, but what were you doing outside in this weather?"

"I had gone to visit the Mother Oracle, samrat. She has some news for you."

"That's fine, but why didn't you go and dry yourself before coming here?" Vetala Bhatta spoke kindly. "You're completely soaked and you might catch a chill."

"I thought it was important to deliver the news first, raj-guru."

Vikramaditya inclined his head in acceptance "What does the Mother Oracle say?" he asked.

"She says that the birds speak of a great wall of dust rising far away in the west."

"A wall of dust..." Vararuchi looked from his brother to the Acharya. "The Mother Oracle must mean the dust that rises from the desert floor as a huge army rides eastward."

As all five councilors exchanged ominous glances, Vikram-aditya nodded to Shanku. "We owe your grandmother a debt of gratitude. Thank you."

The king was about to turn his attention back to the tax logs when the girl spoke again. "There is one more thing, samrat. The Mother Oracle spoke of a more immediate danger to Avanti."

"What's that?" All four heads turned sharply her way.

"She has warned of a sightless evil that is heading northward to bring terror upon Ujjayini."

As the men looked at one another in alarm, Dhanavantri spoke. "Northward from *where*?"

"The Mother Oracle didn't say," Shanku replied. "She only revealed that she read the signs in the rain clouds coming from the south."

"Did she tell you anything else about this... sightless evil?" asked Vikramaditya.

Seeing that she had the full attention of all four men, Shanku nodded. "She said that the sightless evil has been unleashed to recover something – something that was gifted to the king by an ancient god."

***

It was the most miserable day in the life of the miserable young soldier standing guard on the northern bank of the Payoshni. That, at least, was the soldier's own opinion, as he sheltered under the large banyan tree and cursed.

He cursed the rain hammering down from the gray sky overhead. He cursed the damp cold seeping into his stiff joints. He cursed the marauding mosquitoes hovering above his head and humming in his ears and ravaging his exposed arms, ankles, neck and face. And he cursed his decision to enlist with the army of Heheya.

But of all the things that the soldier cursed that morning, the one he cursed most was the ill-fated day he was ordered to report to the garrison of Payoshni for duty.

Slapping his right cheek in a vain attempt to kill a mosquito, the soldier peered southward through the curtain of rain. Not far ahead flowed the Payoshni, a lethargic swamp of a river, its surface green with water plants and slime – slime so thick that the heavy raindrops bounced off it, instead of penetrating it.

And across the broad river, on the other side of Heheya's border, arose a thick, dark wall of trees, stretching away to the south, all the way to the horizon and beyond.

Dandaka, the Forest of the Exiles.

A limitless expanse of dense, steaming jungle, Dandaka was the most inhospitable region in all of Sindhuvarta, home to the most ferocious of wild beasts, the vilest of pestilence... and the lost race of danavas, demonic forest spirits who, it was believed, ruled the jungle from the fabled fortress town of Janasthana.

Dandaka was also a penitentiary for the lowest scum of human society.

For it was to this forest that the kingdoms of Sindhuvarta invariably banished their worst criminal offenders – traitors, murders, rapists and pedophiles. Because it was said that while it was possible for convicts to cheat death at the gallows, there was no escaping the horrors of Dandaka. Or *the forest of no return*, as some called it.

In reality, this was an exaggeration. The past had seen two instances of exiled criminals fleeing Dandaka – by banding together in groups to increase their chances of getting out alive – and trying to sneak back into civilization. Some of these fugitives had been apprehended and sent back, while others had been killed for putting up resistance. Yet, the rumor ran that a small handful had successfully eluded capture and resettled across Sindhuvarta.

It was to prevent such escapes from becoming routine that the garrison of Payoshni was established at the head of the Payoshni Pass – the only point along the river's cliff-bound northern bank that offered a passage between the kingdom of Heheya and the Dandaka Forest. This had earned the garrison the nickname Gateway Garrison; though given the nature of the southbound traffic it encountered, it was also commonly referred to as the Arse of Sindhuvarta.

The soldier keeping watch under the banyan tree couldn't agree more with that description of the place. Swatting a fat mosquito that had alighted on the tender spot under his elbow, he cursed again and surveyed his surroundings.

Before him stretched the marshy riverbank, on which was drawn up an old boat that was used to ferry the exiles across the river. To his right and left, the land rose sharply to form the vertiginous, sheer-faced cliffs that ran along the northern bank for miles and miles – a formidable wall capable of deterring the stoutest of outcasts looking for a way out of Dandaka. Behind him was the narrow defile of the Payoshni Pass, a natural bottleneck.

On the other side of the pass the soldier could discern the buildings of the godforsaken garrison, hidden amid a forest which had once been a part of the Dandaka, ages before the Payoshni had carved the terrain, setting it free. It now extended north a couple of miles before yielding to the flat, arable lands of Heheya.

The guard returned his gaze to the river, lazily wondering when his replacement would arrive to relieve him. The thought of returning to the relative warmth and dryness of the garrison distracted the soldier to the extent that he missed observing the figures creeping along the edge of the forest, on the other side of the Payoshni. It was by sheer luck that at the last moment a movement caught his eye, as the last of the figures slipped into the river.

Suddenly on alert, the soldier watched the gray-green waters carefully.

While it was too far to be certain – and the rain was intense enough to impair visibility – he thought he saw what looked like a row of heads bobbing in the water amid the hyacinths. Knowing that the Payoshni was infested with crocodiles, he was on the verge of dismissing the whole thing when he noticed the line begin moving toward the northern bank.

A moment later, as the rain unexpectedly let up, he saw the unmistakable movement of arms splashing in the water, as the figures began swimming.

Slipping out from under the tree, the soldier ran headlong toward the garrison. A few soldiers were standing guard outside the buildings, and as soon as he was within calling distance, the soldier began hollering to get their attention.

"Sound the alarm, sound the alarm," he shouted frantically. "Some exiles are trying to escape from the forest."

Even though this wasn't a common occurrence at the garrison, within a couple of minutes, roughly fifty soldiers and a dozen cavalrymen had assembled and begun moving efficiently toward the river. As they crossed the Payoshni Pass and approached the river, the men drew their weapons and fanned out with drill-like precision.

On reaching the river crossing, however, the soldiers saw no sign of human activity – neither in the sluggish river, nor on either of its banks.

"Surrender immediately," ordered one of the horsemen, a young commander. Scouring the area around, he added, "Resistance is useless. You are surrounded by the army of Heheya – there is nowhere to run. Show yourselves."

Nothing happened.

The rain had now reduced to a steady drizzle. A few soldiers scouted the trees nearby, while some others, led by the commander, moved warily to the river's edge and inspected the water and the docked boat. The commander then studied the opposite bank for a while before shaking his head.

"There's nothing here. Where's the soldier who raised the alarm?"

The commander's horse suddenly whinnied and shifted skittishly, but no one paid it much attention. The sentry stepped forward.

"Are you sure you saw someone trying to cross the river?" asked the commander, twitching the reins to control his horse. "Or were you just hallucinating?"

"I saw some figures swimming in the river, sir. I'm quite certain."

"Well, there's no one here, soldier," the commander made a broad sweep with his arm. "The only way anyone could have got out of here is by heading toward the garrison. We know that didn't happen because we came that way."

"Maybe they retreated back into the forest," the soldier tried defending himself.

"Maybe…" chuckled another of the horsemen. "Or maybe you had too much firewater last night and the effects haven't fully worn off."

The soldiers had just begun sniggering at the remark and lowering their weapons when there was a loud, turbulent splash in the river, followed by a most hideous roar.

The next moment, a large, horned ogre rose out of the Payoshni, shaking the water plants off its black, hairy body. As the soldiers stood rooted to the ground in terror, the beast lunged at the commander and grabbed him by the shoulders, plucking him off his horse.

Then, in one single movement, it opened its large gaping mouth, bristling with sharp jagged teeth, and bit the commander's head clean off his torso.

At the same instant, around thirty reptilian forms with horns on their heads, smaller in size to the ogre but more agile, leaped out of the muddy water with savage shrieks. Running, leaping and scampering on all fours, the smaller beasts attacked the stunned soldiers, slashing at them with long retractable talons and biting into their necks and shoulders with their teeth.

As the sense of self-preservation finally kicked in, some of Heheya's soldiers took flight, while the braver ones drew their weapons to defend themselves. Those who stayed to put up a fight managed inflicting some injuries on the smaller beasts, but they quailed when the monster that had claimed their commander stepped ashore.

Over twelve feet in height, the ogre had the legs, body and head of a goat, the head crowned with a pair of large horns that arced backwards. But its big, muscular arms and face were humanoid – at least partially. The monster had an abominably large mouth, which opened wide by unhinging at the jaw and cheeks. A pair of small nostrils pointed to a nonexistent nose, above which were two dead eyes, devoid of irises. The two eyeballs, white and smooth as marble, stared unseeingly in front.

Yet, blindness seemed to pose no problems to the rampaging beast.

Because Andhaka, the rakshasa sent to Sindhuvarta by the asura lord Hiranyaksha, relied on a keen sense of smell, touch and hearing to inflict mayhem.

Spitting the crushed pulp of the commander's head out of his mouth, Andhaka flung the body over his shoulder into the

Payoshni. He then caught a couple of soldiers in his hands and squeezed hard, the soldiers' bones cracking and imploding under pressure. One of the cavalrymen immediately charged at the ogre, only to have his head twisted and ripped out of his shoulders. And an archer, who shot two futile arrows at the rakshasa, was punished by being hurled against the side of a cliff, his head splitting open on impact.

The more courageous soldiers of the garrison battled hard, but they quickly began wilting under the brutal assault led by Andhaka. And the last of the fight went out of them when they saw a fresh horde of beasts issue out of the Dandaka Forest and throw themselves eagerly into the river.

The surviving soldiers scattered, running toward the garrison's fortifications for cover, screaming at the top of their lungs for assistance. But Andhaka and his army of pishachas gave pursuit, leaving a trail of carnage that extended from the river crossing all the way inside the garrison of Payoshni.

* * *

The courtyard was filled with five hundred devas mounted on horseback, standing in five orderly columns. The afternoon sun glinted off their bronze armors and shields, while a light breeze ruffled the hackles on their helmets and flapped at the banner of Devaloka in the hands of one of them. The only sounds were the impatient clink of horse hooves on stone and an occasional murmur from the palace councilors who lined the galleries overlooking the courtyard.

At the head of the five columns were two devas astride their black mounts, both horses significantly larger in size than the beasts behind them. Unlike the rest of the devas in the courtyard, the two commanders were bareheaded –

and judging from their straight golden hair, sharp noses and droopy eyes, it was plain that the two were twins.

The somber silence was broken by the hollow sound of a gong struck somewhere inside the palace. As the heavy peal rolled and crashed against the cliffs surrounding the palace, an official appeared at an empty balcony high above the courtyard.

"Indra, king of Devaloka, is here to grant an audience to the Brotherhood of the Ashvins," he announced, before withdrawing.

A moment later, the towering figure of Indra stepped on to the balcony. He was followed by a lissome apsara of great beauty, tall and pleasantly endowed, her fair face in direct contrast to her vivacious black eyes and rich brown hair that fell seductively on her bare shoulders in great abundance.

As the apsara came and stood by his side, Indra leaned his huge hands on the stone parapet, and gazed down into the courtyard. Immediately, the two devas at the head of the cavalry columns dismounted and bowed their heads.

"The Brotherhood of the Ashvins awaits your permission to ride to Sindhuvarta, mighty king," said one of the twins, raising his head.

"You have my permission, commanders," Indra's voice boomed across the courtyard. "Ride to Ujjayini and bring me Veeshada's dagger." He paused, then added with a scowl, "And remember... if there is even a shred of opposition, show no mercy. The human king doesn't deserve any."

Bowing once again, the twins mounted their horses. Then, donning their helmets, they turned around and rode out of the large gate at the far end of the courtyard. The rest of the cavalry followed, gathering speed as they rode away from the palace.

Indra watched the riders depart, a smile spreading over his broad, bearded face. "Fetch me some *soma*, my dear," he said, addressing the apsara. "Let me drink to the success of the Brotherhood of the Ashvins."

"As you wish, lord," the apsara answered. She entered the room adjoining the balcony and returned shortly with a goblet brimming with the rich wine.

Indra gulped down half the contents of the goblet and let out a sigh of satisfaction. "Soon, the Halahala will be ours," he said, beaming to himself. "For millennia I have waited for this day, this moment."

"But lord, isn't it too early to assume the Ashvins will succeed?" the apsara tilted her head saucily, her enigmatic eyes on Indra. "What makes you think the human king will give up without a fight?"

"My dear Urvashi, for *his* sake and the sake of his precious little kingdom, I hope he isn't foolish enough to come in their way," Indra replied, his voice bubbling with scorn. He paused as the roar of hoof beats rushing across the southern drawbridge filled the air, echoing from the abyss surrounding the palace.

"Do you hear that?" Indra asked, taking the apsara by the shoulder and drawing her close. "The dreaded Ashvin cavalry of Devaloka, led by the able Nasatya and Dasra. Those horse hooves can pound the soil of Avanti into infertile dust, and those riders can reduce the city of Ujjayini to rubble."

"But it seems to me that the human king isn't easily intimidated," Urvashi fluttered her eyelids flirtatiously, her tone teasing. "Poor Narada literally had the palace door slammed on his face."

The king of the devas threw his head back and emptied

the goblet. Then, bringing his face close to Urvashi's, he whispered softly in her ear. "If the human king tries to thwart me again, I promise to strike unspeakable fear in his heart."

His hand dropped and went around the apsara's slender waist, groping and squeezing her bare midriff in arousal. "He had the audacity to rebuff my offer of friendship – I will now make him feel the crushing might and fury of Indra's enmity."

Dark

There was still an hour to sundown, but the heavy clouds hanging over Ujjayini had darkened the city, forcing its inhabitants to light the lamps early. Intermittent rain and squally winds continued to lash the capital, keeping most of the citizenry off the streets.

Within the council chamber, two palace attendants bearing small torches moved on silent feet, igniting lamps that stood in recesses in the walls. A third attendant went around the room, closing the windows to keep the draft from extinguishing the freshly-lit lamps.

Vikramaditya and his councilors sat around the table, waiting patiently for the attendants to finish their chore. The glow from the lamps gradually dispelled the gloom, and in their light, it was possible to see a large map of Sindhuvarta, woven in red satin and embroidered with gold threads, spread out on the council table.

At last, when all the lamps were lit and all the windows shuttered, the three attendants bowed deeply and backed out of the chamber. The king waited for the heavy door to shut before he looked at Vararuchi.

"Yes," he said, taking a deep breath. "You were saying something before we were interrupted…"

"I was saying that the four thousand soldiers and thousand horsemen that King Harihara had promised us are already in Avanti, on their way to Udaypuri," Vararuchi replied. "So we can now divert some of *our* soldiers to the south."

"It is something we could consider," the samrat nodded, though the idea appeared to trouble him.

"Yes, but the point is where do we station them?" Dhanavantri asked. Pointing to the map on the table, he added, "The Mother Oracle has only said that this… sightless evil, whatever it is, will come from the south. In geographical terms, the south is a very broad area – it could apply to *any* point south of Ujjayini. If we know nothing about where this thing will come from, where do we position our troops?"

"Not to mention that we know nothing about *when* it will come either," remarked Varahamihira, rubbing his pockmarked chin morosely.

"The troops should stay on standby in the garrison of Ujjayini," Vikramaditya spoke with firmness. "If they are here, they can be dispatched wherever necessary the moment we receive some concrete information about this… thing."

"That's being practical," agreed Vetala Bhatta, glancing around the table. "It's better than spreading ourselves thin trying to plug all possible entry points to the south."

As heads nodded in agreement, Kshapanaka spoke. "How many troops of the Imperial Army do we put on standby?"

The councilors looked at one another indecisively.

"As Vararuchi said, we have an additional four thousand soldiers and thousand horsemen from Heheya on the way to the border," Dhanavantri shrugged his fat shoulders. "Perhaps an equal number will suffice?"

"We also need to keep enough troops ready for quick deployment to the west," the Acharya pointed out. "Let's not forget what the Mother Oracle said about the wall of dust."

"Then perhaps half that number?" Vararuchi looked at his brother inquiringly. "With maybe five hundred archers to give them support?"

While Vikramaditya considered this, Kalidasa cleared his throat. "The Warriors of the Oath are also at our disposal, samrat," he reminded.

"Yes, but let's keep them in reserve," the king answered. "The *samsaptakas* should be the last line of defense – when everything else fails."

Turning to Vararuchi, he added, "How many troops we shall need to counter this sightless entity is anybody's guess. But for now, a thousand infantry units and five hundred of cavalry and archers each would be fine, I suppose. We can also rope in two or three contingents of the City Watch, if necessary. And anyway some of us – or maybe most of us – would have to lead the defense."

Seeing that the matter was settled, Vetala Bhatta addressed Vararuchi and Varahamihira. "If the soldiers are being stationed at Ujjayini, we will need a system in place to relay messages swiftly from the south."

"I have already deployed a network of riders to the south, raj-guru," said Vararuchi. "I realized that owing to the rainy conditions, we cannot bank on the *suryayantras* to transmit signals. And even flares aren't entirely dependable in this weather, given the damp and poor visibility."

"Riders make sense," the Acharya nodded in satisfaction.

At that moment, there was a light knock on the door of the council chamber. As the councilors turned, the door opened to admit a palace hand.

"Salutations to the samrat and the Council of Nine," said the attendant before addressing the Acharya. "Pardon the interruption, but a rider awaits you in your private chamber, raj-guru. He says he has an important message to deliver."

Vetala Bhatta exchanged a glance with Vikramaditya, who nodded. The chief councilor rose from the table and exited the room. Meanwhile, the samrat turned to Vararuchi.

"How are things at the border? King Chandravardhan had said he would send five thousand soldiers…"

"I have checked on that," Vararuchi reassured the king. "There's been a delay, but his troops are crossing over from Vatsa as we speak."

"What about the reinforcements from the Anarta Federation?"

"Of the fifteen thousand troops that Chief Yugandhara had promised, nine thousand have arrived. Unfortunately, I have already dispatched all nine thousand to King Baanahasta's court in Viratapuri – I thought it would be a good idea to strengthen Matsya's borders against an eventuality." Vararuchi ran his fingers through his hair ruefully. "Perhaps I should have retained half the number and sent them to Udaypuri instead. We could then have kept more of our soldiers here on standby to deal with…"

"No! Our soldiers need to be in the frontline," Vikram-aditya interrupted, getting the drift of his brother's thoughts. "Vatsa, Heheya and the Anartas have pledged their support in the understanding that the might of Avanti's Imperial Army will be at the frontier, standing shoulder to shoulder with their own troops in the defense of Sindhuvarta. The forces they've sent are reinforcements, not substitutes for our soldiers. Keeping the invaders out is a shared responsibility, so no matter what, we shouldn't hold more of our own troops back for Avanti's narrow gains. Whatever is coming from the south is a headache, but we'll have to make do with the two thousand units we've already decided on. Let's tackle this without breaching the trust of our allies."

Smarting and chastised by the king's words, no one spoke for a while. It was the royal physician who broke the pause by bringing a subtle change to the topic. "Any news from Amara Simha?"

"Nothing today, so I surmise everything is under control. But his message yesterday did say that he has begun overseeing troop deployments along the frontier." As an afterthought, Vararuchi added, "The message also made special mention of Satyaveda being a pompous, sniveling fool."

Knowing smiles cropped up around the table, the councilors' heads shaking in resignation. Even Shanku shed her habitual reserve, permitting herself a tinkle of laughter.

"The governor must have rubbed Amara Simha the wrong way and had his head chewed off," Dhanavantri chuckled.

"What else did Amara Simha expect from him!" exclaimed Varahamihira. "We very well know how unbear-able Satyaveda can be. I find it hard to believe that the governor comes from the same noble ancestry as Acharya Vedavidya and Councilor Sagopana – may their souls rest in peace." With an exaggerated shudder, he added, "Imagine our plight if we had to suffer Satyaveda at this table every day?"

"Seeing him being packed off to Malawa was such a relief," agreed Vararuchi. "We don't thank the Acharya enough for that."

"Let's not be too harsh on the man," Vikramaditya intervened with a smile. "I concede he is too full of himself and a tad incompetent, but he is otherwise quite harmless."

"Pride and incompetence – what more harm need anyone inflict on his fellow beings, my king?" Dhanavantri shot back with a grin.

Once the ripple of laughter subsided, the samrat addressed his brother again. "Did Amara Simha say anything about how Ghatakarpara is faring?" The king's voice had a faint trace of avuncular concern in it.

"No, he didn't," replied Vararuchi. "But he had a note of praise for Ghatakarpara's friend Atulyateja – the garrison commander at Udaypuri. He said the boy was resourceful and efficient, and was being a big help in coordinating troop movements."

"Then perhaps he should be rewarded with a transfer to the Imperial Army," suggested Varahamihira.

Seeing the heads around the table nod in agreement, Kshapanaka spoke up. "Your intentions are honorable, Varahamihira, but I disagree. If all the best soldiers are drafted into the Imperial Army, what happens to the Frontier Guard? To stand on its legs, the Frontier Guard also needs young men of talent and caliber."

Varahamihira gave this thoughtful consideration. "You're right," he said at last. "Stuffing the Imperial Army with the best brains defeats the purpose of creating a strong Frontier Guard. We must..." He paused as his glance went to the door, where Vetala Bhatta had just made a re-entry. "What happened, raj-guru? Is there a problem?"

The Acharya remained silent as he returned to the table, lowered himself into his chair and studied the faces looking at him. When he turned to the samrat, his tone was sober and measured. "The rider has brought news from our spies in the east. King Siddhasena is dead."

A hush fell over the chamber, which was broken by Dhanavantri. "Poor man, he didn't look too well to me when he was here for the *rajasuya yajna*. I intended prescribing him..."

"Siddhasena didn't die of illness or age," the raj-guru interrupted the royal physician. "He was apparently killed– pushed down a flight of steps in the palace of Girivraja."

The expressions on the councilors' faces turned to shock and revulsion.

"Who pushed him?" Vikramaditya demanded.

"It seems it was his bodyguard, Sajaya."

"That's impossible," cried Vararuchi. "I have seen Sajaya in battle by Siddhasena's side. He is the sort of soldier who is prepared to give his life for his king. He couldn't have been disloyal to Siddhasena."

"Yet, it is being made out as a Kikata conspiracy against Magadha," the Acharya shrugged. "Sajaya belonged to the Kikata tribe."

"Were there any witnesses to the guard's act?" the samrat leaned forward and scrutinized Vetala Bhatta's face closely.

"There was one – Shoorasena himself."

The king raised his eyebrows in surprise. "And the guard has admitted to killing the king?"

The raj-guru shook his head slowly. "It seems he was killed by Shoorasena in revenge."

As the councilors digested this news, the samrat leaned back in his chair. "Things are not going well in Magadha," he said, staring into the distance.

"Not well, meaning...?" Vararuchi asked cautiously.

"I mean what's happening in Magadha is bad news for the rest of us in Sindhuvarta." Vikramaditya looked at the puzzled faces staring at him. "I'll explain... When the deva Narada was here, trying to buy our friendship and negotiate an agreement for the dagger, there was something that he said which struck me."

The king paused for breath, and Kalidasa cut in. "I remember him saying that there is trouble brewing in the east."

"Precisely," said Vikramaditya, snapping his fingers. "Perhaps this was what Narada was referring to."

The councilors exchanged glances, their faces pensive. At last Varahamihira spoke.

"The Hunas and Sakas in the west, a sightless, nameless evil from the south, and now Magadha to the east... I wonder what nasty surprises the north has in store for us."

* * *

Muffled footsteps accompanied the hooded figure as it slipped through the darkened bylanes of Udaypuri, keeping to the shadows as far as possible. The figure was moving in a northerly direction, away from the fort and the town center, heading toward the seamier quarters of Udaypuri, where the houses got progressively smaller, and the streets became narrower and more squalid.

The only thing that appeared to increase in this congested

part of the garrison town was poverty. And organized crime.

Yet, the figure pressed forward without the slightest hint of trepidation, leaping over open, overflowing drains, and twisting in and out of the stench-filled maze with familiarity. Finally, having climbed up a small deserted alley, the figure came to a halt in front of an anonymous building with a rough, wooden door.

Making a quick check of the surroundings, the figure rapped on the door, four times in quick succession. Almost immediately, a latch rattled inside, and the door opened a few inches. Dim light squeezed out of the crack, as a rough voice spoke from behind the door.

"Who is it?"

"It's me," the figure mumbled, pushing the hood back to expose his head and face.

The man inside raised a lamp in inspection. The next moment, the door swung open to admit the visitor.

"Welcome, sir," said the man, ushering the guest into an anteroom before bolting the door behind him.

"It hasn't started, I hope?" the visitor inquired as he shrugged off his cloak.

"No sir. We have a little more time to go." After a pause, the usher added, "Your friend is awaiting you in the last room."

The visitor walked past the anteroom into a long passage with doors on both sides. Making his way to the far end of the passage, he pushed a door open without bothering to knock.

A fat, middle-aged man was inside the room, seated on a battered divan. This was Aatreya, one of the biggest merchants of millet and turmeric in the province of Malawa.

"Come, come," said Aatreya, looking up with a smile. Patting the vacant spot on the divan, he added, "Do be seated. For a moment I thought you wouldn't be coming today – I've been waiting for half an hour. What took you so long, governor?"

"There's no way I wouldn't have come," Satyaveda hummed in response, pressing a few rebellious strands of hair back on to his sparse scalp. "After all, tonight's fight is special. It's just that there are these guests from the royal palace whom I had to entertain – that's what delayed me."

Once the governor made himself comfortable, Aatreya leaned closer to him. "So, do you have anything useful for me?" he asked, dropping his voice.

Satyaveda searched the folds of his robe and extracted a crude palm leaf scroll. Handing it to the merchant, he said, "This has all the information on the troops that have been deployed along the frontier of Malawa. The strength of troops at key points, defense installations, signal systems that have been set up... everything."

"Excellent," Aatreya beamed. "I shall have this sent across tomorrow."

"Careful you don't lose it – I got my hands on it with a lot of difficulty. Also, let the courier know that the garrison is now under the command of Councilor Amara Simha, who is personally overseeing troop movements. I'm sure your friends from the desert would remember him."

"*Our* friends from the desert," Aatreya corrected. "I assume the councilor is one of the guests from Ujjayini whom you're busy entertaining?"

"Yes," replied Satyaveda. "The other is Ghatakarpara, the king's nephew."

"Nice, nice... This information should fetch us a bonus."

Aatreya reached into a bag he was carrying and pulled out a small pouch tied with a string. He shook the pouch and grinned at the heavy jingle of coins. "Here's your share for the previous bit of information."

The governor smiled as he accepted the pouch. "Come now, let's go. We shouldn't miss the fight," he said, rising.

The two men retraced their steps down the passage and turned left into a filthy storeroom, where the man who had ushered in Satyaveda sat on a stool. On seeing the guests, he rose and went to a large metal chest standing in one corner. Pushing the chest aside, he opened a trapdoor on the floor.

Satyaveda and Aatreya slid through the concealed trapdoor and climbed down a rough, wooden ladder. At the bottom of the ladder was a small room, with a window set in the far wall. The window was covered with a wire mesh, through which lamplight poured in. The murmur of conversation also wafted in from the direction of the window.

Satyaveda approached the window and looked out, his eyes shining in anticipation. The window overlooked a mud pit, with wooden seats arranged around it in rising tiers. The crude amphitheater was packed with men of the working class, talking and shouting jovially. On opposite sides of the mud pit sat two men, each holding a large gamecock. One bird was black and the other was reddish brown.

"Which one would it be, sirs?"

The governor turned to see the usher standing behind him and Aatreya. "I will go with the defender, of course," said Satyaveda, throwing the pouch that he had just received from the merchant to the usher.

"A costly mistake, my friend," smiled Aatreya, handing another pouch to the usher. "My money is on the black challenger tonight. I've heard he's quite a champion in the province of Gosringa."

"But there's only one champion in Malawa and that's my red king."

"Red king indeed... red with his own blood tonight, I say," chuckled Aatreya as he joined Satyaveda at the window.

"His blood or the challenger's... we'll see," the governor retorted.

The two men watched the mud pit from their private cubicle, one of three reserved for special guests of the house. Guests born into nobility or holding offices of rank and privilege; people who couldn't be seen mingling with the rabble of Udaypuri. Yet, people wealthy enough to wager huge sums of money on the illegal sport of cockfighting.

A referee stepped into the mud pit and started reading out the rules, but his voice was almost drowned by the cheering of the men around the arena. At last, the referee stepped back and gestured for the fight to commence. Instantly, the gamecocks flew from their owners' grasps and began circling one another, hackles raised.

As a roar went up around the mud pit, Satyaveda licked his lips and watched the birds, his eyes popping out of their sockets, perspiration beading his brow. And when the cocks lunged at one another, filled with murderous rage, the governor's eyes partially closed in ecstasy.

It wasn't the prospect of winning a wager that excited Satyaveda. At one level, he didn't particularly care if his favorite red king was slaughtered by the black challenger and he had to leave the clandestine arena empty-handed. What really set his pulse racing was the sight of the birds hacking and pecking at one another, feathers flying in all

directions as they clawed and gouged in a desperate struggle
to stay alive.

The thrill these bloody fights offered was the only thing
the governor lived for these days.

Besides the deep, bottomless yearning for revenge, that is.

*　*　*

Dhanavantri awoke with a start.

For a second or two, disoriented, he stared at the dimness
around him. Then his mind slowly registered the soft glow
of a low-lit lamp, the insistent pressure of a hand shaking
his leg, and a woman's voice coming from somewhere near
the foot of his bed.

"Get up…"

The physician struggled to push himself up on one
elbow. "What is it?" he mumbled, blinking his eyes at the
small, stout silhouette of his wife Madari standing by the
bedside.

"The samrat has sent for you," answered Madari.
"There's a chariot waiting outside to take you to the palace.
It seems you are needed at the queen's bedchamber."

"Why? What's happened?" The physician's voice rose
sharply in alarm as he slid off the bed. "Is the queen all
right?"

"The messenger with the chariot says Vishakha spoke…
and she moved her eyes."

"What!"

Dhanavantri stopped in his tracks and looked at his wife
in amazement.

"He doesn't appear to know anything more than that,"
Madari shrugged.

The physician gathered himself with an effort. "Let the

messenger know that I will be with him in a moment," he said.

When Dhanavantri hurried into Vishakha's chamber ten minutes later, he was greeted by the anxious yet hopeful faces of the palace household. Vikramaditya stood by one side of Vishakha's bed, while on the other, Kshapanaka sat stroking her sister's hand gently. Queen Mother Upashruti sat on a stool beside Kshapanaka, conversing with the nurse in low tones. The Acharya, Vararuchi and Kalidasa had arranged themselves a little behind the king.

Vishakha herself, however, lay inert on her bed, staring vacantly into space.

Approaching the bed, the physician looked around the room. "Who can tell me exactly what happened?" he asked softly.

"They said she spoke," said Kshapanaka looking up, her lips quivering, eyes moist with joy. "She's recovering."

Dhanavantri nodded, overcome by a sudden surge of compassion for Kshapanaka. As a junior physician, he had had occasion to treat King Vallabha for gout, and it was during those visits to the kingdom of Nishada that he had first seen the sisters as little girls. Even back then, Kshapanaka and Vishakha had shared a close bond, one that grew stronger after their father left them in the protection of Avanti, so he could fight the Hunas without fearing for their safety. It was the girls' attachment and interdependence that had helped them overcome the trauma of the massacre at Vallabha's court, the tragedy bringing the sisters even closer in the years that followed.

And then the horrible accident had occurred. Dhanavantri was aware that Vishakha's condition had not only deprived Kshapanaka of her closest companion, it had also orphaned her emotionally. Which was why, for two years, she had lavished Vishakha with all her care and attention, doing everything in her capacity to revive the queen's old self. So, it was only natural that a small spark of hope had now been kindled in the younger sister's heart.

"Who heard the queen speak?" he looked around the bedchamber, gulping at the small lump that had formed in his throat.

Two maids stepped forward in response to the question.

"What did she say?" asked Dhanavantri. "Tell me everything in detail."

"Your honor, as usual, I was seated by the queen when I noticed that a draft had begun blowing through the room," said one of the maids, speaking with remarkable coherence.

"When was this?" the physician interrupted.

"About fifteen minutes ago, sir. I realized the queen would feel cold, so I asked her to fetch a quilt." The maid pointed to the girl standing next to her. "It was while we were tucking the quilt around the queen that she spoke."

"Are you sure?"

"Yes, your honor. We both heard her."

The second girl looked at Dhanavantri with big, round eyes and nodded.

"What did the queen say?"

"We are not sure, your honor, because her words came out in a moan. But it sounded like 'rain water'."

Again, the second girl nodded in agreement.

The physician glanced quickly at the faces around. "Is that all? I was told she moved her eyes as well."

"Yes, your honor. We were startled, so we looked at the queen. And she seemed to look straight at us. I mean, not like... usual. Then her eyes moved. First a slight flicker to the left… then she looked that way." The maid pointed toward the window at the end of the room. "She stared into that side for a little while. Then she looked back at us and…"

The maid's face fell in disappointment. "…and she was back like this."

"Okay, I want…" Dhanavantri was about to issue a set of instructions when Vetala Bhatta took a step forward.

"I can try to read the queen's mind again," he offered. With a short pause, he added, "If I have the permission of everyone here, that is. Especially you." The raj-guru looked at Dhanavantri.

Before the physician had a chance to reply, Vikramaditya spun around to face the Acharya. "Would you do it for us?" he asked eagerly. "You will see what's in her mind?"

"I can try… if our physician permits."

"I see no harm in it, so why not?" Dhanavantri stepped back to make room for the chief advisor.

"Fetch me my spear," the Acharya commanded.

A couple of minutes later, Vetala Bhatta stood at the foot of the bed, eyes closed, one hand gripping the spear, which was adorned with two human skulls near its sharp, pointed tip. His other hand was rolled into a fist and was pressed against his chest. The raj-guru moved his lips in whispers, the incantations barely audible in the heavy, loaded silence. The skulls on the spear burned a dull red, light emerging from their cavities, as if lit from inside. The sight of the glowing skulls made the two maids shrink back in fear.

After a considerable passage of time – it could have been minutes but it seemed like hours to those in the bedchamber – the raj-guru opened his eyes and lowered his hand. He observed Vishakha's face for a moment, then looked up at the ring of expectant faces.

"I could see or read nothing," he announced with a solemn sigh. "All I was able to hear was the galloping of horse hooves, same as the last few times. Her mind is otherwise completely dark. Nothing's changed – I'm sorry for getting your hopes up."

As the Acharya moved away, Kshapanaka's eyes brimmed and a tear rolled down her cheek. Queen Upashruti immediately put a comforting arm around her. Dhanavantri stole a quick glance at the samrat, who looked away from the bed in disappointment.

"Okay… Here onwards, I want the queen to be under constant observation," the physician said, stepping forward to fill the vacuum with some hope. As he bent to examine Vishakha, he added, "If such an occurrence were to happen again, we shouldn't miss it. Now I suggest we leave the queen to rest."

As the room began clearing, Kshapanaka looked from Vikramaditya to Dhanavantri with pleading eyes. "I'd like to stay awhile," she said. "Can I?"

The king and the physician nodded before joining the others on the way out. Once they were out of the room, everyone huddled around Dhanavantri.

"What do you make of this?" inquired Queen Upashruti.

"It's hard to say, queen mother," the physician shrugged.

"This has never happened in the last two years," pointed out Vikramaditya. "It *has* to be a sign of recovery."

"Probably a partial return of consciousness," Dhanavantri agreed. "We will know for sure only if we observe it happening a few more times."

"Is there some new medicine that you recently administered her?" probed the raj-guru.

"Well, it's not really recent, but I have been prescribing

her dosages of *ashwagandha* for the last five months. I've only lately discovered that *ashwagandha* has some curative properties for memory disorders. Perhaps the medicine is slowly taking effect."

"Can't the process be speeded up then?" the king looked at Dhanavantri hopefully. "Maybe you could increase the potency or something…"

"Perhaps," the physician was noncommittal. "But first we have to see if there's a recurrence of what happened tonight. Till we know for sure, everything would be guesswork."

* * *

Vararuchi had barely stretched himself on his bed with the intention of retiring for the night when there was a knock on the door.

Heaving a weary sigh, he propped himself up. "Who is it?" he demanded.

The door to his bedroom opened to admit light from the passage outside. A palace attendant stood in the lit doorway.

"A rider insists on seeing you, your honor," the attendant said apologetically. "He says he brings an urgent message from the south."

Vararuchi was up like a bolt. "Allow him in," he commanded.

Swinging his feet off the bed, he went to a corner of the room, where a small lamp burned in a recess. Picking the lamp up, Vararuchi was in the process of lighting a larger one with five wicks when the rider presented himself. Vararuchi could see that the man had ridden hard in the rain, his clothes wet and streaked with mud.

"Salutations, your honor," he said.

"To you too, soldier. Now tell me…" Vararuchi paused impatiently.

"Your honor, some bizarre reports are emerging from the south, suggesting strange disturbances…"

"From *where* in the south?" Vararuchi interrupted sharply. "I mean in which parts of southern Avanti are the disturbances happening?"

The rider paused doubtfully for a moment. "Not in Avanti, your honor," he spoke at last. "The reports are coming from the kingdom of Heheya."

Vararuchi stared at the rider for a moment, nonplussed. "Heheya?"

"Yes, your honor. You had asked for all reports coming from the south, so my captain decided that even this should be brought to your notice. Because of its… *strangeness*."

Vararuchi nodded. "What do the reports from Heheya say?"

"It appears there have been a series of attacks in Heheya since morning, your honor. A couple of garrisons were ruthlessly stormed, and two or three villages have been entirely destroyed. The unconfirmed death toll is close to three hundred."

"Who are the people conducting these attacks?" Vararuchi stared at the rider in shock and incomprehension.

"That's the funny bit, your honor," the rider continued. "According to the reports, the attackers aren't men… but strange *beasts* that came out of the Dandaka Forest. One report even said that the attackers were an army of demonic pishachas."

"What?"

"Yes, your honor. The report says that some survivors also spoke of the pishachas being led by a giant, demon-like creature that was a cross between a goat and a man. It seems this creature is blind, but kills without mercy…"

"Wait, wait, wait…" Vararuchi's expression was suddenly tense. "This creature is supposed to be *blind*?"

"According to one report," the rider nodded in mystification.

A sightless evil that is heading northward…

Vararuchi strode over to a shelf above a large table. Reaching up, he took down a roll of blue silk, which he unfurled and spread over the table. He then beckoned the rider to his side.

"Do we have any idea where the attacks took place?"

The rider looked down at the map of Sindhuvarta and nodded. "The first attack was reported at the garrison of Payoshni, your honor," he said, pointing a finger at the Payoshni Pass. "The next attack was at this village here, then the one here. In the afternoon, a second garrison was attacked at this point…"

As the rider traced the route of the attacks in Heheya, Vararuchi virtually stopped breathing. The rider's finger was marking a straight path north across Heheya – and if the finger continued following the path further north into Avanti, it would inevitably reach Ujjayini.

…heading northward to bring terror upon Ujjayini…

Fall

The sky was still pitch dark over Mahishmati, the heavy clouds blotting out the faint light of predawn in the east. Strong gusts of wind whipped through the city, driving the rain hard, herding the soldiers patrolling the palace walls and the streets below deeper and deeper into doorways in search of dryness and warmth. Occasionally, one or two of them would thrust their heads out from under the eaves and scan the darkness before ducking back into shelter.

For all the rain and the dark, the unease in the soldiers' manner was palpable, the way they huddled suggesting that they sought protection from more than just the wind and rain. Where torchlight fell on their faces, fear and uncertainty crisscrossed their eyes.

"Don't we have any more news yet?" King Harihara demanded a trifle querulously. "I had asked for reports every quarter of an hour. It's nearly three-quarters of an hour since the last report – what's happening?"

The king was standing by a south-facing window high above ground level, looking out into the wet blackness that surrounded his palace. In his hands he held a map of Heheya, embroidered in purple silk, which he kept folding and wringing absentmindedly. His old face was pinched, dark circles forming under his tired, sleep-deprived eyes.

"The next report should be here any moment, your honor," a minister replied without conviction. The minister then turned to an attendant and spoke in an undertone, "Check if anything has come in. Quick."

Harihara turned away from the window and faced his council of ministers. "Are we certain that the southern and eastern walls of Mahishmati are fully fortified?"

"Yes, your honor." It was the turn of another of the ministers to answer. "We have placed many contingents of archers and swordsmen to the south and east, and have barricaded all four gates."

"So there's absolutely no way the… these pishachas can enter the city, right?"

There was a worrisome pause before the first minister spoke. "We have done what we can, your honor," he said nervously. "Anyway, we have also deployed more soldiers throughout the city… in case…"

As the minister's words tapered off ominously, Harihara sighed and turned back to the window, his fingers fidgeting with the map. While he would have liked his council to reassure him, the king was acutely aware that there was not a soul in Heheya who knew how to deal with the menace that was wreaking havoc across his kingdom. Two garrisons and four villages completely destroyed; the dead numbering close to five hundred.

A shudder ran through Harihara as he thought of

what might happen if the gates of Mahishmati were to be breached.

"What do these pishachas want?" he asked, although it was clear that the question wasn't addressed to anyone in particular. Turning back, he looked at his ministers, the strain showing in his face. "And why Heheya – what harm have *we* done them?"

The ministers looked at one another, clearly as much at a loss for answers. But before any of them could hazard a response, the door to the chamber opened to admit the attendant, followed by a rider. From their appearance, it was evident that they had brought some news of import.

"Your honor, a report has come…" the attendant began.

"What's the news?" Harihara asked, stepping toward the rider anxiously. "Do hurry up."

"Your honor, the threat has passed Mahishmati."

The stunned silence was so complete that for a short while, the chamber was filled with the eerie keening of the wind and the splattering of rain on the palace walls.

"What do you mean, soldier?" one of the ministers demanded, the relief plain in his voice despite the sharpness of the tone.

"Sir, the pishacha army crossed Mahishmati a few miles to the east, but instead of turning toward the city, it continued going northward."

"Northward?" The king unfurled the silken map on a table and pulled a lamp close as he summoned the rider. "Show me what you mean."

As the ministers gathered around, the rider pointed to the map. "The beasts passed Mahishmati at this point, but instead of changing course and making for the city, they continued in a straight line."

"Really?" asked Harihara in a quavering whisper, as if fearful of bursting the bubble of good fortune that seemed to have magically enveloped this capital.

"Yes, your honor. Your commanders had some men follow the pishachas, just to be sure. It's clear the beasts are not coming this way. They are heading straight for the hills that lie between us and the kingdom of Avanti."

Harihara looked around at his ministers in bewilderment. "But there's nothing in those barren hills... So, what do these beasts really want?"

* * *

Amara Simha bounded up the stairs leading to the roof of the fort, two steps at a time.

Although the stairway was steep and winding – and despite his heavy build – the councilor displayed no signs of breathlessness, and when he emerged on to the fort's wide, flat roof, the only evidence of the strenuous climb was a mild flush on his big, bearded face.

"Are there any new updates from Sristhali?" he demanded, striding toward a small group of soldiers gathered at one corner of the roof, which afforded an unobstructed view of Udaypuri on all four sides.

The soldiers stood around a *suryayantra*, a large contraption full of levers and cogwheels and mechanical arms, to which were fitted tin alloy mirrors of various sizes. In the group were Ghatakarpara and Atulyateja, while a little to the left of the soldiers two figures hovered uncertainly – Governor Satyaveda and his lackey Chirayu, both patently out of their depth with respect to what the military men were doing.

"None sir," answered Atulyateja, turning to the councilor.

"Hmmm…" Amara Simha grimaced as he joined the men around the *suryayantra*. Placing his hands on his hips, he squinted at a hill located to the west of the fort, at the edge of the bustling town. Next, he raised his eyes and studied the patchy clouds floating north across the early morning sky.

"What do we know for certain about this Huna scout?" he asked at length.

"We know that he was captured by our troops somewhere near the border town of Sristhali last night," said Atulyateja. "He has been confined to a cell and is being kept under guard at the command center at Sristhali. We also know that he has somehow broken his right leg, and that he appears to be delirious and in considerable pain."

"Not to forget, so far, he has resisted all efforts at interrogation," Ghatakarpara butted in. "Either due to the delirium, or because he doesn't understand us or is pretending not to."

"If he's a scout, it's unlikely that he *doesn't* understand what we're saying," muttered Amara Simha grimly. "Scouts everywhere undergo basic language training. And even the delirium could be just a sham."

"Absolutely correct," interjected Satyaveda, who had sidled up to Amara Simha. "I have always said that these Hunas are not to be trusted in the least bit."

Amara Simha stared blankly at the governor for a moment, debating whether the inane statement merited any response. Deciding against it, he turned back to Atulyateja with a shake of his head.

"Anyway… have they got a translator at the Sristhali command center?"

"We don't know, sir," the garrison commander shrugged.

At that moment, a series of dull flashes of light began emitting from the hill to the west. The men on the roof immediately focused their attention on the flashes. After a couple of minutes, the flashes ceased.

"What does the message say?" Amara Simha demanded impatiently of a soldier who was busy decoding the signals on a strip of palm leaf.

"Sir... it says... they can't escort the prisoner to Udaypuri... for some reason..." the soldier spoke haltingly as he made sense of what was on the palm leaf. "The message was not clear, because the sun probably went behind the clouds while they were transmitting."

"Brilliant invention by Varahamihira, but on days like this, it's completely unreliable," Amara Simha glared at the *suryayantra* on the roof in frustration.

"Ask them to resend the message," ordered Atulyateja.

A soldier began operating a lever on the heliotrope on the roof, but he was stopped by Amara Simha's voice.

"No, we'll only end up wasting more time before the sun gets fully blocked out." The councilor looked up at the sky once again, noting the steady buildup of clouds. "If they can't escort the Huna scout here, *we* shall go there."

Amara Simha addressed the soldier operating the *suryayantra*. "Let the Sristhali command center know that I am coming to interview the prisoner. Inform them to keep the scout under heavy protection – and keep him in a condition fit for interrogation." As the soldier began calibrating the levers to align the various mirrors to catch and reflect the rays of the sun, the councilor added, "Also tell them to have a good translator at hand. And make sure the message reaches Sristhali at any cost."

The machine began transmitting Amara Simha's message

to the hill, where another group of soldiers were operating another heliotrope on a mobile platform. The solar signals would then be relayed further and further south, till the message was finally delivered to its destination.

"I want you to take charge of things here till I'm back, commander," Amara Simha spoke to Atulyateja. "I expect to be back in two days."

"Very good, sir."

"And you…" Amara Simha addressed Ghatakarpara. "You will accompany me to Sristhali."

"I can?" The prince's face lit up at this unexpected offer.

"Yes, of course," the councilor replied as he began marching off the roof. "It's time you saw a little more of the frontier."

Amara Simha was halfway to the door when he heard the quick shuffle of feet behind him. Almost immediately, he was addressed by a wheedling voice.

"If you don't mind, can I have a quick word with you?"

The councilor stopped and turned to see Satyaveda trotting up to him. "Yes, governor?"

"I would very much like to accompany you and the prince to Sristhali…" said Satyaveda, hastily adding, "With your permission, of course."

Amara Simha's eyebrows rose in surprise. "What for? I mean… why would you want to go to Sristhali?"

"I am due to visit the town on routine inspection anyway," the governor wrung his hands together as if he were washing them. "Also, I would like to see this culprit we have apprehended. This Huna scout…"

The councilor looked around vaguely, unsure about what to say, wondering how he would deal with concentrated doses of Satyaveda's stupidity and cloying formality for two full days. At last, unable to find a good enough excuse to turn the governor down, he nodded.

"You may come if you wish to. But I'd appreciate it if you could hurry up a bit. I want to leave as soon as possible and be in Sristhali before sundown."

* * *

"Your honor, the stable master says he can't give us more than three hundred and thirty fresh horses."

"What does he mean he *can't* give us?" Vararuchi demanded, turning his horse around to glare at the young captain who had addressed him. "I didn't ask him for a favor. Tell him it's an order – we need at least one thousand fresh horses."

"I did tell him, your honor. But… he says it's not possible."

"Who is this fool?" Vararuchi snapped, his eyes flaming with indignation. "Ask him to present himself…"

However, before Vararuchi could finish, Kalidasa raised a restraining hand and spoke in a calm voice. "I shall talk to him and see what the problem is, brother." Getting off his horse, the giant addressed the captain. "Lead me to the stable master."

As Kalidasa and the captain walked away, Vararuchi shook his head irritably and turned back to survey the southern horizon. The rain had ceased three hours ago, but the sky was still overcast, though there was a promise of sunlight in the thinning of the clouds to the west.

Vararuchi, Kalidasa and Varahamihira had left Ujjayini just before daybreak, leading a force of fifteen hundred horsemen and ten chariots south toward the Avanti-Heheya border. On the basis of the reports that had come from

Heheya, everyone agreed that the demonic army heading north was likely to cross into Avanti near the village of Trehi sometime later that afternoon, and that it was best to confront it as close to the border – and as far away from human habitation – as possible.

The samrat and his councilors had also concluded that in the interest of speed, the force should consist solely of cavalrymen – so the infantry and archer units had been jettisoned in favor of a larger contingent of horsemen. However, at the insistence of Varahamihira, the ten chariots that he had engineered for the Imperial Army not long ago were also included into the division. In hindsight, though, that looked like a bad idea – the heavy chariots were proving to be unwieldy and cumbersome in the wet, mud-soaked terrain.

The division was now at a horse station roughly halfway to the border. The soldiers had broken for a quick breakfast, as fresh horses were being harnessed for the remainder of the ride – and the battle to come. Wisps of gray smoke from the cooking fires lingered in the still, damp air above the station, and from where he sat on a wooded knoll, Vararuchi could hear the clanging of plates and pans over the nickering of horses. The smell of horse manure lay thick and heavy, like an invisible blanket, over the station.

"We must try and get past the village of Trehi before noon," a voice spoke at Vararuchi's elbow. "Otherwise, this demon army will reach there first and Trehi will most certainly be destroyed."

"I'm hoping we can," Vararuchi looked down at Varahamihira, who had climbed up the knoll with surprising quietness. The engineer stood by Vararuchi's horse, leaning on his wooden crutch. A stump that ended above the ankle dangled from under the hem of his dhoti – all that remained of Varahamihira's right leg after meeting a Huna axe in battle years ago.

"I'm really hoping we can," Vararuchi repeated with feeling, returning his gaze to the horizon. "But we're already running behind time. We're too slow. We need to move faster."

Varahamihira noticed the emphasis in Vararuchi's words. "Once we have fresh horses, we can pick up speed," he said.

"Right," Vararuchi replied tightly, keeping his gaze averted.

"You don't like the idea of having the chariots," the engineer's eyes twinkled as he smiled.

"Well, they *are* slowing us down," Vararuchi admitted with a shrug.

"Agreed, but we need them. We don't have any archers, so we must have some sort of range weapons."

Vararuchi looked back to Varahamihira. "The chariots have hardly been through any trials. Are you certain they will work?"

"We shall find out today."

Vararuchi turned away with a dissatisfied frown to see Kalidasa come up the knoll. He raised his eyebrows in inquiry, but was disappointed when he saw the giant's somber face.

"The stable master doesn't have a thousand fresh horses to spare," said Kalidasa. "At the most he can give us three hundred and fifty, maybe sixty. But honestly, even that looks difficult, as some horses are still recovering from illness."

"But how's that possible?" asked Vararuchi in consternation. "This is a large station."

"Apparently, most of the horses that were here have been relocated to the west to service troop movements along the frontier. The stable master says that if he had been given a day's notice, he could have made arrangements."

"Had we had a day's notice, we wouldn't have needed fresh horses," Vararuchi said glumly. "If only all troubles gave a day's notice before coming."

"I have anyway asked the stable master to replace as many horses as possible," said Kalidasa. "And feed and water the rest. His men have started their work. We should be able to leave shortly."

Vararuchi nodded before returning to scan the southern horizon. With more than three hours of journey to go and less than a quarter of his cavalry replenished, the mounts would be on the threshold of exhaustion when his men met the pishachas crossing over from Heheya.

The prospect of the battle suddenly appeared even bleaker to Vararuchi.

* * *

The distant rumbling of thunder permeated Kshapanaka's sleep, making her stir and open her eyes. She looked around vaguely for a moment, before turning to Vishakha, propped up in bed. Studying her sister's blank face, Kshapanaka addressed one of the maids in the room.

"The queen didn't speak or move, did she?"

"No, your honor."

"Are you certain?" The anxiety on Kshapanaka's face was mirrored in her voice.

"Yes, princess," the elderly nurse replied in place of the maid. "I was watching over the queen while you had dozed off." Approaching Kshapanaka, the nurse added kindly, "You must go and get some sleep. You haven't slept all night."

Kshapanaka sighed and looked down at her lap, where a half-embroidered silk scarf lay along with a needle and a ball of fine yarn. She had been working on the scarf all morning, yet very little progress had been made, as her mind kept drifting to the events of the night before. Every minute or so, she had gazed at her sister, hoping that Vishakha would move or utter something – she had even tried speaking to the queen, repeating the words 'rain water' a few times, in a desperate bid to draw a response.

But Vishakha had remained stubbornly indifferent, lost in a private world that no one had been able to fathom or breach for two years... ever since the day of that near-fatal accident. The day when joy had been so cruelly torn out of Kshapanaka and Vikramaditya's lives, to be replaced with a shroud of irreparable sadness.

"I'll go in a little while," Kshapanaka answered the nurse, picking up the embroidery. Even though she could feel the tiredness grating under her eyelids, she added, "I'm not so sleepy right now."

The needle went in and out of the silken scarf for a while, but as the memories came flooding back, Kshapanaka's eyes prickled with tears and her hands dropped to her lap, limp and tired.

Nishada was for the large part a hazy blot, though she did have faint recollections of Itti *tai* narrating stories to her and Vishakha by the palace pond, and of her father lifting her onto his shoulders, so she could pluck the ripe *ber* fruits growing in the royal orchards. Their arrival in Ujjayini was vivid, though, the size of the palace and its surrounding lake stirring awe in her. The initial years in

Avanti had been carefree, the palace ringing with the shouts and laughter of children oblivious of the uncertainties and dangers lurking beyond the palace walls. But Kshapanaka's first painful memory was the news of the Hunas sacking the kingdom of Nishada, and executing King Vallabha and the entire palace household in cold blood. She would never forget the helplessness she had felt watching Vishakha lie sobbing on Queen Upashruti's lap that night...

With nowhere to go, the orphaned sisters continued to reside in Ujjayini, where the harsh realities of the times slowly became more and more obvious. Not a day went by without bad news, as one by one, the raiding Hunas and Sakas conquered smaller kingdoms like Nishada. And even when the larger kingdoms of Sindhuvarta rallied together, tidings of defeat and death were commonplace.

Kshapanaka remembered the day King Mahendraditya was brought back from the battlefront, grievously injured from a stab wound in his abdomen. She remembered watching his funeral procession leave the palace a few days later, and Vararuchi take an oath to rule Avanti till Vikramaditya was old enough to be king.

With time, under the watchful tutelage of Acharya Vetala Bhatta, the children of the palace grew into skilled warriors – all except Vishakha, who abhorred violence in any form. Meanwhile, first under Vararuchi's fierce leadership, and then – following his coronation – under Vikramaditya's command, the kingdoms of Sindhuvarta regrouped, and inch by inch began forcing the invaders back till the last of the barbarian horsemen fled into the haze of the Great Desert.

In the years of peace that followed, Vikramaditya wed Vishakha – a foregone conclusion, considering the couple had set their hearts on one another very early. The palace of Ujjayini quickly became a bower of great happiness and tranquility, but all that changed one sunny winter morning when calamity returned with a vengeance.

That morning was indelibly branded in Kshapanaka's mind, the glorious sunlight even now searing her soul, her heart pounding to the beat of horse hooves as Vishakha's laughter, sparkling like freshly melted snow, filled her ears...

The sisters had been riding in a meadow outside Ujjayini, ribbing each other playfully, when Kshapanaka had dared Vishakha to try and ride her horse. Although Vishakha was the more proficient rider, Kshapanaka's mount was a notorious temperamental beast that few could master. Vishakha, however, accepted the challenge. A few gentle rounds around the meadow seemed to indicate that Vishakha had got the better of the horse, so she upped the pace to a full gallop, laughing gaily all the while at Kshapanaka's astonishment.

Then suddenly, without warning, the horse had reared, bucked and kicked wildly. Before either sister could react, Vishakha was thrown off the saddle, her head striking a rock protruding from the grass. Dhanavantri had later diagnosed that the fall had probably caused Vishakha a severe brain injury.

All Kshapanaka knew was that it was the moment when her sister had gone away...

"Princess, the queen mother is here," the nurse whispered gently in her ear.

Kshapanaka snapped out of her thoughts, deftly wiping her wet eyes before turning to the foot of the bed, where Queen Upashruti stood flanked by Princess Pralupi and Dhanavantri. Prince Himavardhan stood behind his wife, his mouth hanging open as he stared at Vishakha's inert form.

"Child, you look dreadful," the Queen Mother exclaimed, observing Kshapanaka's drawn face with concern.

"It's nothing, mother," Kshapanaka struggled to summon a smile as she stood up. "I just haven't slept much."

"You haven't been up all night, have you?" Queen Upashruti paused before surveying the nurse and the maids with a critical shake of her head. "Why didn't you make sure the princess caught some sleep?" she demanded sharply.

Before the nurse and maids could say anything in their defense, the queen came around the bed and took Kshapanaka tenderly by the shoulders.

"Go and get some rest, child," she said in a gentle, maternal fashion, almost bringing Kshapanaka to tears again. "We are all here to look after Vishakha. I promise that you will be informed if your sister shows even the slightest sign of revival."

Kshapanaka smiled gratefully at Queen Upashruti. At that moment, however, Himavardhan slipped from Pralupi's shadow and approached Kshapanaka, his eyes on the embroidered scarf in her hands. He stared at the piece of cloth for a moment before sticking a hand out for it.

"I want," he said, looking at Kshapanaka awkwardly, his voice adamant. "I want."

Kshapanaka smiled wanly and unfurled the scarf, but didn't hand it over to the prince. "Do you like it?" she asked.

The man nodded, his eyes shining with eagerness.

"It is not fully done, see?" Kshapanaka explained kindly, turning the scarf around to display the work. "Let me finish it. Then I promise to give this to you. Is that alright?"

Himavardhan smiled and nodded his agreement before retreating to Pralupi, who exchanged a small smile of appreciation with Kshapanaka. A small crisis had been averted.

Once Kshapanaka took her leave, everyone turned their attention to Vishakha. Dhanavantri once again checked her pulse and pupils, and gave the nurse a set of instructions.

For a while, the Queen Mother stood watching Vishakha. When she saw that Dhanavantri was done, she nodded to Pralupi to signal that it was time to depart. "I shall be with the child for a while. You may leave."

As Pralupi exited the bedroom with Himavardhan trailing her, there was another roll of thunder, this time closer, coming from the north.

"The thunder is almost constant. More rain in the offing, I suppose," remarked Queen Upashruti to no one in particular.

Dhanavantri nodded, but when he looked toward the open window, his eyes were uneasy. Something gave the physician the impression that it was not thunder, but the distant beat of horse hooves being carried their way by the wind.

* * *

The state room at the palace of Girivraja was crammed with councilors, courtiers and palace attendants, pressed shoulder to shoulder in three tight concentric rings that went all the way back to the walls in descending order of rank and nobility. This formation left an open space in the center of the room, where Shoorasena and Kapila sat on their high chairs. Facing them was an elderly man with a gentle, soft-spoken disposition – Pallavan, a special envoy from the court of Kosala.

"Do accept my heartfelt condolences on behalf of King Bhoomipala and the entire kingdom of Kosala," the envoy addressed the brothers. "King Siddhasena was a dear friend of Kosala, one of the most honorable of men. His passing is not just a loss to Magadha, but the whole of Sindhuvarta."

The brothers exchanged fleeting glances before Shoorasena spoke. "Thank you for your kindness, noble sir. The commiserations of King Bhoomipala and his subjects are well appreciated by Magadha's royal council – and its grieving citizenry."

Pallavan paused to reflect briefly on the prince's choice of words. Earlier that morning, his cavalcade had passed through the streets of Girivraja en route to the palace, and from what he could tell, more than grief, Magadha's citizens were displaying signs of murder and pillage. He had witnessed armed mobs roaming the capital, looting and burning houses and establishments belonging to Kikatas with impunity, and his cavalcade had heard of fleeing Kikatas being hunted down and killed in the countryside.

It was plain that the rioting mobs had the sympathy, if not the active support, of Magadha's law enforcement machinery – and by extension, that of the state.

"Indeed a sad moment," the envoy shook his head mournfully. "A moment of blind insanity that took the good king away. But we should show good judgment and restraint in these trying times."

"It was not blind insanity that cost the king his life," Shoorasena corrected Pallavan tartly. The prince was smart enough to see where the envoy was trying to lead the conversation. "On the contrary, it was an act of calculated wickedness on the part of the Kikatas, backed by the republic of Vanga. An act aimed to strike at the very heart of Magadha's sovereignty, an act that has rendered the people of Magadha fatherless. So, they are understandably angry."

"Yet their rage could end up claiming innocents lives," Pallavan tried to reason through the rhetoric. "After all, the Kikatas are Magadha's subjects as well."

"They plot against us and we are expected to protect them?" Shoorasena scoffed as he looked around the room with a cold smile that was meant to rally support. "I wonder if the good diplomat would advise *his* royal court to show as much magnanimity toward Kosala's own enemies."

Pallavan noticed heads nod and a sneer spread around the room. Gauging the belligerent mood, he concluded that this wasn't a track worth pursuing. Anyway, the fate of the Kikatas wasn't his problem – he was in Girivraja with a very clear mandate, the first of which had been to pay Kosala's condolences to Magadha.

That he had done. Now it was time to broach the second topic on his agenda.

"As you see fit... lord," he said, struggling to find the right form of address for Shoorasena. With King Siddhasena dead, it was logical to assume that Shoorasena, the crown prince, was successor. Yet, there had been no formal coronation or announcement to that effect; neither did Shoorasena show any indication of being the new king. Even this meeting was taking place in the state room, and not in the royal court that housed the throne of Magadha. A meeting there would have helped decode the new power structure at Magadha.

"Before I take the royal council's leave, there is one more matter that I would like to discuss," the envoy chose his words carefully. "With your permission...?"

Shoorasena waved a hand in weary condescension.

"The late king had promised to Matsya three thousand soldiers and three thousand archers as reinforcement against a possible Saka threat."

Pallavan could sense Shoorasena stiffen and pass a sidelong glance at Kapila.

"I'm afraid you have your facts wrong," the prince shook his head. "Father never made any specific commitments about sending Magadhan troops to Matsya."

"But he did... prince," Pallavan hesitated, casting a quick eye around the room. "Last week, your father sent written messages to King Baanahasta, King Chandravardhan, King Bhoomipala and Samrat Vikramaditya, confirming that the three thousand soldiers and three thousand archers would leave Magadha for Matsya's borders."

Shoorasena sat still in his chair, his brow furrowing over eyes that looked stunned at what had just been revealed. At last, he shook his head softly, "It... it's not possible."

"It is true," insisted Pallavan, beginning to enjoy the prince's discomfiture in a twisted sort of way. "My king received the message in Kosala five days ago – that's how I know. And the message was from King Siddhasena, for it bore his royal seal."

Shoorasena chewed on his upper lip and looked around at the circle of councilors and courtiers, who, in turn, shuffled their feet and exchanged furtive glances. The envoy's shrewd mind understood that the news of Siddhasena's messages to the other kings had unsettled the whole bunch.

"Okay, perhaps father did send those messages," Shoorasena broke the silence. "What of it?"

"The kings of Sindhuvarta sincerely hope that the late king's promise to Matsya will be honored, lord."

"Must you be in so much of a hurry... like... like vultures?" Shoorasena demanded hotly, taking recourse to indignation. "The ashes of my father's pyre are still warm."

"Do pardon us, but war may soon be upon Sindhuvarta,"

Pallavan spoke gently. "The old king would have understood the urgency. Besides, like his ashes, his promise is also warm."

"If the promise was his, he should be the one to fulfill it."

Pallavan appraised the tall prince carefully. He seemed to have regained his composure, and from the manner in which he sat in his chair – back upright, chest thrown out and the chin thrust combatively in front – it was clear that he had had enough with fudging around the matter.

"Are you saying..."

"I am saying we are not bound to fulfill that promise," Shoorasena's voice had acquired a decisive ring, and the envoy immediately sensed the mood perking up in the room. "If the king made that promise, he did so without consulting the royal council of Magadha. So the council cannot be held accountable for that. So, unfortunately, his promise dies with him."

"Wouldn't you reconsider this in the name of your father?" the diplomat pressed. "The kingdoms of Sindhuvarta face a threat..."

"The kingdoms of Sindhuvarta should learn to deal with their own problems," Shoorasena snorted. "Magadha is faced with a serious challenge from the Kikatas and Vanga, but do you see me running from one kingdom to another for help? We make do with what we have – my suggestion to all your kings is to learn to do the same."

The prince rose from his seat, his manner implying that the interview was over. "Do stay for lunch, noble sir," he added. "I'm told the royal kitchen has prepared a sumptuous spread of the choicest culinary treats of Magadha especially for you."

As Pallavan left the state room, Shoorasena's voice echoing in his ears, he realized that it didn't need a formal coronation or a throne – or a royal council, for that matter – to see where authority and power was vested in Girivraja.

* * *

A dour drizzle beat down upon the plain, mingling with the mist rolling in from the nearby mountain passes, reducing visibility even further.

The fifteen hundred horsemen stood in three rows, facing south, those in the foremost row bearing long lances to skewer the vanguard of an attack. The horsemen in the rows behind, armed with swords and shields, were to engage in melee combat once the lancers blunted the opening assault.

Sitting astride his horse, Kalidasa moved back and forth in front of the cavalry, inspecting the troops closely, on the lookout for any telltale signs of fear or lethargy. They could afford neither if the reports from Heheya were anything to go by.

Vararuchi, for his part, sat still on his horse, his eyes narrowed on the misty slopes of the mountain range that formed a natural border between Avanti and Heheya. He didn't like the rain and the mist, nor did the sight of the heavy clouds covering the hilltops strike his fancy. All three obstructed vision – always a handicap in battle – which was why he had sent four scouts into the hills, to try and get an estimate of what his division was up against.

None of the scouts had returned with reports.

The plain where Ujjayini's troops were positioned was actually a flat-bottomed valley south of the village of Trehi. The division had crossed Trehi a little after noon, but had immediately encountered a minor stream that had broken its banks on account of the torrential rain. The cavalry was able to ford the bloated river, but Varahamihira's chariots struggled in the slushy mud. On seeing that they were losing time, the three councilors thought it best to proceed minus the ten chariots.

The rain increased in density, forcing Vararuchi to repeatedly wipe the water from his eyes as he stared at the mountains. The only sound was the omnipresent, hollow splash of water striking the wet earth.

Then, as Vararuchi watched, a dark shape materialized from the edge of the hills, charging toward the troops through the mist and the rain.

"Attention, men!" Vararuchi shouted as he uncoiled a thin, flexible sword measuring just over six feet in length. The weapon was an *urumi*, a sword favored by the warriors of the Southern Kingdoms.

Immediately, the lancers brought down their spears, the tips pointing straight ahead, aligned with the heads of their horses. Kalidasa simultaneously drew his broad scimitar as he rode up to Vararuchi.

The shape drew nearer and Vararuchi saw that it was one of his scouts. "Hold position," he ordered the cavalry.

As the scout rode up to Vararuchi and Kalidasa, they noticed his face, mauled with terror. Before either councilor could say anything, the scout spoke, the words tumbling out in a rush.

"They are in the hills... I saw them eat them... Behind me..." he babbled hysterically.

"Who are in the hills?" Kalidasa demanded with firmness.

"They... the pishachas... They were eating two of our scouts."

"What?"

"Yes." The scout turned and pointed to the hills with a quaking finger. "They saw me too and now they're coming after me. There!"

Kalidasa and Vararuchi craned their necks and peered into the swirling mist, but they could discern nothing out of the ordinary.

Vararuchi shrugged and was about to address the scout when the air above the plain was lacerated by a series of shrill cries that drowned out the noise of the rain. A moment later, dozens of misshapen figures emerged from the mist, leaping and scrambling at great speed toward the rows of waiting horsemen.

Brotherhood

The old potter was at the bottom of the clay pit, standing ankle-deep in the chalky alkaline mud oozing and bubbling with rain water. The potter was raking the clay into large tin bins, which he then passed on to his apprentice, a young boy of about twelve who stood at the lip of the pit. The boy, in turn, loaded the heavy bins on to the back of a mournful mule that transported the clay to the pottery located some distance from the pit.

The rain was little more than a drizzle now, but the rumbling in the sky had become incessant, increasing in volume with every passing moment. The potter paused now and then to look up at the clouds, his ear cocked as he tried to make sense of the unusual noise filling the air.

It was after the apprentice had made his fifth trip to the pottery that the source of the sound was revealed. The potter was busy filling the bins for the next round when he heard the boy's high-pitched shout above the rumbling.

"Aapa, aapa… look!"

"What is it?" the potter demanded, raising his head. But from where he stood, he could see neither the boy nor the object that the boy was drawing his attention to.

"Aapa... come up and see this." The apprentice appeared at the top of the pit, his young face flushed with excitement and fear as he beckoned his master, pointing vigorously at something beyond the potter's line of vision.

His curiosity piqued, the potter crawled up the pit, cursing profusely as his feet kept sliding and getting sucked into the viscous mud. But the moment he hoisted himself on to firm ground and looked up, his expression changed to openmouthed wonder. Still on all fours, he stared at the spectacle unfolding before his eyes.

The clay pit and the pottery were in the middle of a desolate plain, scantly covered with vegetation. Far to the south and the west were paddy fields, beyond which lay a scattering of farmers' huts. Further to the west on the horizon was Ujjayini, its ramparts more imagined than visible in the grayness of the atmosphere.

What caught the potter and his apprentice's attention, though, lay much closer at hand.

A huge rainbow had broken through the gray-black clouds overhead, its tip arcing to earth roughly half a mile from the clay pit. At the point where the rainbow touched the ground, a vaporous portal shimmered – and through it emerged a horde of helmeted horsemen bearing bronze shields and longbows. The steeds were large, black beasts snorting powerfully and stamping the ground in impatience, and there was something menacing about the riders as they spurred their horses forward.

As the figures by the clay pit instinctively sank to the ground to escape detection, the horsemen milled around, waiting for the last of them to descend from the rainbow pathway. Once the entire cavalry was firmly on Avanti's soil, the portal vaporized, and the rainbow gradually diffused and disappeared. Meanwhile, the horsemen regrouped into disciplined columns, and at some sort of a command from their leader, they began riding away from the clay pit.

The potter and his apprentice slowly pushed themselves upright, their eyes fixed on the retreating horsemen.

"Who are they, aapa?" the boy finally asked in a dazed voice.

Watching the horsemen pick up pace and gallop away in the direction of Ujjayini, the potter shook his head. "I don't know. But they're definitely not human. And something tells me they are here to cause trouble."

* * *

The flesh-eating pishachas hurtled through the mist and the rain, fangs bared, screeching and whooping their lungs out in an insane display of intimidation.

Vararuchi wrapped his fingers tightly around the hilt of the *urumi* and waited, bracing himself for the moment the beasts would collide against the wall of Avanti's horsemen. His eyes flitted right and left as he took in the scale of the attack, and then he focused all his attention on the three pishachas that were heading straight his way. Drawing his breath, he raised his shield and outstretched his sinewy right hand, the *urumi* dangling free of any encumbrance.

"Hold position," he shouted, his eyes locking with those of a pishacha in the forefront, one that had picked him as its target.

The beast rapidly narrowed the gap, and Vararuchi was able to make out its gray scaly skin, the membranous webbings

that covered large parts of its body, and the bulging head
with its slanted reptilian eyes and sharp, pointed horns. He
also noticed the creature's snarling mouth, lined with razor-
sharp teeth, and the retractable claws on all four limbs.

When the three pishachas coming at him were less than
ten yards away, Vararuchi raised his hand fractionally. At
the same time, he dug his heels into the flanks of his horse
and shouted out his order.

"Attack!"

As the cavalry lunged forward, lances aimed squarely
at the oncoming beasts, the pishacha in front of Vararuchi
leaped high in the air, flinging itself at the general with feral
rage. The same instant, Vararuchi launched his horse, the
urumi swirling over his head. Wielding the supple blade
expertly, he caught the pishacha in mid-leap – the *urumi*
slashing at the beast's face, opening it into two from the
mouth. As the creature screamed in agony, Vararuchi used
his shield to toss its falling body to one side. Even before it
hit the ground, Vararuchi moved in on the next pishacha,
the *urumi* flailing viciously in the air.

To Vararuchi's right, Kalidasa was also in the thick of
battle, keeping the murderous attack at bay by hacking at
the beasts with his scimitar.

The lancers, though, were struggling to fend off the
pishachas.

Owing to the speed and nimbleness of the beasts, the
lancers were finding it hard to aim their heavy spears. Quite
a few lancers had failed to pin the attackers back, and they
were now paying a hefty price by having their faces and
limbs mutilated by the beasts' talons and teeth.

"Drop your spears... drop your spears," Kalidasa
roared as he dug his scimitar between the ribs of a pishacha

that was gnawing at a lancer's exposed neck. "Use your swords instead," he added, cleaving the head of another beast into two.

The cavalry responded to Kalidasa's command swiftly, and almost immediately Avanti's troops began beating back the pishacha offensive. The battle raged with intensity, but with Kalidasa and Vararuchi leading by example, the horsemen gradually began gaining an upper hand.

Then, as the rain thinned and the clouds above the plain lightened, a bestial howl echoed from the direction of the hills. Shivering involuntarily at the sound, Avanti's soldiers turned to see Andhaka lumber into view from one of the passes, his foul face contorted with rage and bloodlust. And in his wake, more pishachas came scampering and shrieking.

The moment he caught sight of Andhaka, Vararuchi concluded this had to be the demon leading the pishachas, as mentioned in the reports from Heheya. And observing the rakshasa's white eyes, he realized this was the sightless evil from the Mother Oracle's prophesy. Vararuchi instantly turned his horse and rode up to Kalidasa.

"We have to bring that thing down, brother," he shouted, pointing to Andhaka.

With a nod Kalidasa turned around and called to the cavalry. "We need some lancers."

Half a dozen horsemen with lances volunteered right away. The two councilors spurred their horses forward, hewing a crude and bloody path through the writhing mass of pishachas, making straight for the rakshasa. The lancers followed their commanders in, while the rest of the cavalry focused on the fresh onslaught from the hills.

Kalidasa, Vararuchi and the lancers spread themselves around Andhaka, circling him warily. Two of the lancers attacked suddenly, thrusting their spears at him. The rakshasa, however, sensed the horsemen's moves – while he deftly parried one thrust, he caught the second spear and yanked hard, unseating the lancer from his horse. As the soldier fell to the ground, Andhaka raised one foot and smashed it down hard on the lancer's head. The crunching and popping of the soldier's skull was audible above the rumble of battle.

In a sudden rush of fury, Vararuchi charged at the rakshasa, the *urumi* scything through the air. The blade glanced off Andhaka's shoulder, barely cutting through the ogre's thick matted hide. Yet, the attack irked the rakshasa enough to draw forth an angry bellow. Immediately, the horses reared up in alarm.

As the men fought to regain control of their mounts, Andhaka swung his arms at the circle around him, smiting two lancers and one of the horses hard. The rakshasa also smelled the horses' fear, and he began roaring repeatedly to unsettle the animals even more. The move paid off – the horses bucked and reared in fright, a few even turning around and bolting.

Realizing the futility of staying on horseback, Kalidasa and Vararuchi leaped to the ground and began attacking Andhaka. The ogre, however, was impervious to their weapons and fought back with ferocity – Kalidasa was knocked to the ground twice, both times narrowly escaping the rakshasa's trampling foot.

Elsewhere on the battlefield, the pishachas were running amok, overwhelming the cavalry.

Seeing that Avanti's horses were tiring and that the tide was gradually turning against them, Vararuchi cast aside his *urumi*, grabbed a fallen spear and closed in on Andhaka.

Finding Vararuchi within his grasp, the rakshasa grabbed him and raised him up in the air. Vararuchi, who had been expecting this, immediately tried to spear Andhaka in the head, but the ogre intercepted the descending lance and snapped it in two.

Then, even as Kalidasa slashed wildly at him and Vararuchi struggled in his grip, the rakshasa opened his mouth wide with the intention of biting off his captive's head.

Andhaka's gaping mouth was barely two feet from his face, the ogre's nauseous breath washing over him, when Vararuchi felt something whoosh past him. The next instant, he heard a fleshy thwack somewhere close by, and sensed the rakshasa's grip loosening. A moment later, he slipped from Andhaka's grasp and dropped to the ground.

Regaining his feet, Vararuchi looked up in surprise to see a five-foot-long shaft protruding from the left side of the ogre's head. As he watched, another heavy arrow smashed into the base of Andhaka's thick neck, the arrowhead embedding itself deep as the distinct sound of vertebrae snapping came to Vararuchi's ears. Andhaka's head jerked back violently, dislocating from his heavy shoulders.

The rakshasa uttered a deep guttural moan and staggered back, black bilious blood drenching his left arm and upper body. He rocked uncertainly for a while, clawing feebly at the thick shafts sticking out from his neck and head, when a third arrow hammered into his chest, breaking the ribcage on impact. Andhaka crashed to the ground, his body twitching a couple of times before going into a lifeless slump.

An agonized wail arose from the pishachas, a wail that went back and forth across the plain as the fall of Andhaka was relayed. Almost immediately the beasts seemed to lose the will to fight, turning tail and fleeing back toward the hills. Avanti's cavalry attempted to give chase, but the fatigued horses clearly weren't up to the task and the endeavor was soon abandoned.

Walking over to the dead rakshasa, Vararuchi knelt down to inspect the inert form closely. As Kalidasa came over and stood by his side, Vararuchi reached out and tried to yank the bulky arrow out of Andhaka's chest. The shaft was buried deep and didn't budge an inch.

"The thing works," he said looking up at Kalidasa, eyes wide with relief and wonder. "Just as Varahamihira had said it would."

Kalidasa nodded and turned his gaze to the north of the plain, where a row of chariots were heading in the direction of the battlefield. He could make out Varahamihira seated in the foremost of the chariots.

"I'm glad he figured out a way of crossing that river and getting here in time," said Kalidasa, waving an arm at the approaching chariots. "Otherwise you and I would most probably have ended up as feasts for the vultures."

"You, probably…" Vararuchi agreed, rising to his feet. "Me, most definitely."

* * *

"You are here because you… want a dagger from the samrat, right?"

The captain of the City Watch studied the two horsemen with uncertainty, his fingers picking nervously on the bronze medallion that he wore on his chest. From his expression, it was clear that the captain hadn't the faintest notion of what the horsemen were alluding to.

"Yes," Nasatya nodded, looking thoroughly bored at having to deal with the captain's inferior intellect. "That's exactly what I told you."

"So you... the two of you are seeking an appointment with the samrat... for the dagger. Is that right?"

As the captain spoke, he kept shifting his gaze around. There was something unnerving about the two horsemen's thin long faces, their lank golden hair, and the way they looked at everything with cold, hooded eyes. He wondered who these horsemen were – and how they had come so close to Ujjayini without being intercepted by any of the other units of Avanti's army.

"No, we are *not* seeking any appointment, because we don't particularly care about meeting your king," the second horseman, Dasra, said curtly. "We would be happy to wait right here, as long as your king just hands over the dagger to us."

Although taken aback by this brazen display of disrespect, the captain merely cleared his throat. "So, you would like the palace to be informed that you are here for this dagger."

"Yes," Nasatya spoke again. "And while you're at it, my advice would be to hurry things up a bit. We are not used to being kept waiting."

"Indeed," Dasra snorted, exchanging a caustic smile with his brother. "Else, we might be tempted to dispense with courtesy and ride into your pretty little city without invitation."

The undercurrent of hostility wasn't lost on the captain, who stole a glance beyond the shoulders of the two horsemen. A little distance away stood a phalanx of cavalrymen, helmeted and armed to the teeth with bows, swords and shields. In the captain's opinion, they numbered roughly five hundred, and he was painfully aware that his own platoon of the City Watch, with less than twenty men, was hopelessly outnumbered. Worse, they were quite some distance outside Ujjayini's walls, in a plain to the east of the city.

In case of an eventuality, there was no question of expecting speedy reinforcements.

"And who shall I say wants the dagger?" he asked, mustering some confidence.

"The Brotherhood of the Ashvins from the court of Indra, king of the devas," replied Nasatya.

***

"Aren't you glad that we brought these chariots along, after all?"

Varahamihira cocked an eyebrow and smiled at Vararuchi, who was leaning against one of the chariots and running an appreciative hand along the stock of a heavy, wooden ballista that was mounted on the back of the chariot. An arrow measuring a little over five feet was already wedged in the ballista's sliding trough, ready to be fired at short notice.

"They slowed us down quite a bit, but yes, in the end they also proved to be life savers," agreed Vararuchi, his gaze lingering on the contraption. "Without this thing, we would never have managed to kill that monster." Heaving a huge sigh, he looked at Varahamihira. "Remarkable thing you've designed. We must induct more of these into the Imperial Army."

The troops were resting in the shoulder of the hills bordering the village of Trehi. A few fires had been lit, and soldiers dispatched to Trehi to fetch provisions for a late lunch. The wounded were being tended to, while the dead were still being counted and laid out by the edge of the plain. As the horses grazed fitfully in the hills, the men sat around in small clumps talking in subdued tones, their expressions ranging from fatigue to relief to triumph.

"But how did you manage crossing the river?" asked Kalidasa, tying a crude bandage around his badly scraped knee. "The chariots just kept sinking in the mud when we crossed it."

"We moved a little to the east and found a point where the ground was harder and the currents less strong," Varahamihira explained, as he hobbled on his crutch and sat down beside Kalidasa. "Still, we had to abandon two of the chariots. That's what delayed us."

"I think you made it against the odds, and you made it in the nick of time."

"Yes, though you almost got me killed with that first arrow. The slightest error in your aim and I would be lying there." Vararuchi pointed to the row of bodies being laid out.

"The way I saw it, with your head almost inside the monster's mouth, you were as good as dead," Varahamihira said with an offhand shrug. "I figured being struck by Avanti's arrows was a more dignified way of dying."

As Kalidasa and Varahamihira exchanged cheeky grins, Vararuchi pressed a palm to his forehead in mock exasperation. Just then, a captain approached the councilors. "Your honor," he addressed Vararuchi. "We have taken the final count."

"So what are the damages like?"

"Two hundred and forty two men dead, and over three hundred and fifty injured, some fifty of them very grievously, your honor. A few of them won't pull through, I'm afraid. We've also lost about seventy horses."

Vararuchi stared at the row of dead soldiers somberly for a moment. "What about the attackers?"

"We have counted some four hundred and thirty pishacha bodies. Apart from that big one."

Varahamihira opened his mouth to say something, but he was cut short by an agonized scream from one of the soldiers being lifted onto a makeshift stretcher. The soldier's upper arm and shoulder was a mass of bloodied, mangled tissue, the white of the bone showing where a pishacha's teeth had torn off a sizeable chunk of flesh.

Varahamihira winced, waiting for the scream to die down. Once silence was restored, he asked, "Have we captured any of the attackers alive?"

"None, your honor. They all managed to flee."

"I want all the pishachas and that monster to be dumped into a pit and burned to ash," instructed Vararuchi, his face clouding with rage.

"Yes, your honor. And... what about our dead?" the captain gestured to the line behind him. "Are we taking them back with us?"

"Ujjayini is just half a day's journey," said Vararuchi with a brusque nod. "Avanti's fallen deserve to have their last rites performed on the banks of the sacred Kshipra."

***

"From their manner, it is plain that they want to intimidate us into giving up the Halahala, or provoke us into a confrontation," said Vetala Bhatta, glancing from the samrat to Kshapanaka. Dhanavantri was standing by the Acharya's side, while Shanku, as always, hung back deferentially. "No kind words or sweet enticements of the kind Narada dished out the other day."

The king and the four councilors were in a private chamber annexed to the royal court, holding a hurried consultation over the demand placed by the horsemen from Devaloka.

"With a force that's just five hundred strong, I don't think intimidation is a particularly good strategy to adopt," Dhanavantri shrugged his fat shoulders.

"Well, if the idea is to intimidate, it's not going to work, no matter what their numerical strength is," said Vikramaditya hotly. "And if they are spoiling for a fight, they shall not return disappointed. Acharya, please inform the City Watch to barricade the gates and set up archers along the walls. And let the Imperial garrison know that I want a thousand cavalrymen and infantrymen each to ride with me into battle."

"Surely you're not planning to go out there yourself, samrat?" The raj-guru assessed the king with his shrewd eyes.

"Of course I am." Vikramaditya looked at Vetala Bhatta in surprise. "By refusing to come to the court of Ujjayini and insisting that *we* go to them with the dagger, the Ashvins have issued a direct challenge to Avanti. I have decided to accept it – though I will give them one opportunity to change their minds and return in peace."

"But if you ride into battle, you'd be playing straight into their hands, Vikrama."

The samrat considered the Acharya narrowly, even as the other three councilors exchanged puzzled glances.

"Those horsemen aren't fools – they probably know we won't surrender the dagger without a fight. What they expect, however, is that you will be provoked by their insolence and will ride out to meet them. If you do that, they would have succeeded in dictating the terms of the engagement. Without raising a finger, they would have got the king of Avanti to leave his palace and come to them, instead of the other way round."

"Mind games..." the king nodded ponderingly. "I see what you mean, Acharya."

"Yes. Your going there would mean that you concede that the Ashvins are important enough to merit your attention – we mustn't give the Ashvin commanders that satisfaction. The message from the court of Ujjayini should convey that the king of Avanti cannot be bothered by a band of horsemen and their petty threats."

"But the Ashvins have made the first move by ordering us to yield the dagger," Vikramaditya contested. "It's an open challenge, and not responding to it would be cowardice. We can't just ignore the challenge by hiding inside the palace gates; we have to counter it."

"I said nothing about ignoring the challenge," the raj-guru pointed out. "I only said *you* shouldn't be the one seen to be affected by it."

A pregnant pause ensued, the stillness so intense that the hushed murmurs in the adjoining court magnified into a steady, monotonous drone. Vetala Bhatta looked at the four faces around him, his gaze finally settling on the samrat.

"With your permission, let the four of us deal with the Brotherhood of the Ashvins."

* * *

The cavalcade from Kosala wound its way down the wooded hill, the gates to the palace of Magadha slowly receding from view.

Pallavan, who was seated inside a shuttered carriage, peeked through the curtains, observing the city of Girivraja through the breaks in the trees. The city appeared quiet and peaceful from these hilly heights, but the envoy knew things were always deceptive when viewed from a distance. And anyway, he could see smears of black smoke still rising from a few quarters of the capital – grim reminders of the crude justice that Magadha's arsonists and lynch mobs had very recently meted out on the hapless population of Kikatas.

After his meeting with Shoorasena, Pallavan was left with no doubt that the killing of the Kikatas was taking the form of a systematic extermination, with the full backing of the palace of Magadha. What he wasn't sure about was the cause behind this sudden animosity. He knew that the Kikatas were largely peaceloving, had integrated well into Magadhan society, and were, by and large, unresponsive to the few voices of dissent raised against Magadhan rule.

So, even if the late king's bodyguard had been part of that lunatic fringe, there was no reason for Magadha to turn against all its Kikata subjects...

Pallavan was lost in his thoughts when his carriage drew to a sudden, unexpected halt. At the same instant, the envoy heard a minor commotion from somewhere up ahead. Pulling a curtain aside, he poked his head out and craned his neck to see what was happening; however, a bend in the road obstructed his view.

Sliding across the seat, the envoy pushed open the curtain on the other side and looked out. He saw five horsemen from his escort milling around a puny man, who seemed to be making an entreaty of some sort. The escorts appeared to be arguing and pushing the man away.

"What's happening?" Pallavan inquired of an escort who was standing by his carriage.

The horseman rode up to the group and exchanged a few words with one of the escorts in front. Pallavan noticed that the small man stood to one side, defenseless and miserable, his hands joined in supplication. Shortly, the horseman turned back.

"That man is obstructing our path, sir," the horseman explained. "He insists on meeting you, and he won't let us pass, even when whipped. He says his life is in danger and that you must save him."

"Who is he?"

"He says he is a traveling musician, sir."

Baffled, Pallavan looked at the man cringing by the side of the road. Then, obeying an instinct that even he couldn't fully explain, the envoy raised his voice and addressed the escorts in front.

"Let him come."

The horsemen reluctantly allowed the man to pass, and he immediately approached the carriage, cowering and trembling with fear.

"What do you want?" Pallavan asked kindly.

"You must help me, good sir. I am a musician. I heard you are from Kosala. My grandmother was from Kosala too. I have come running to you. You must help me, please."

"Okay, but what do you want from me?" the envoy urged patiently.

"My life is at risk in Magadha, sir. I want you to take me to Kosala with you." This time the man was a little more lucid.

"Are you a Kikata?"

"No sir. But I have seen something and I fear I will be

discovered..." A look of terror eclipsed the man's face as he looked around and shivered. "If they find out that I saw what really happened in the palace, they will kill me the way they killed the old king's bodyguard."

For a fraction of a second, Pallavan's face froze as he processed the implications of the man's words. Then, looking around swiftly to check if they were being observed, he swung open the carriage door.

"Get inside," he said sharply. He knew that the cavalcade had diplomatic immunity and that it wouldn't be stopped and searched without good reason.

Once the man had clambered onto the carriage, Pallavan looked up at his escorts. "We ride full speed here onwards. No slowing down till we are beyond Magadha's borders."

As the cavalcade gathered momentum, the envoy cursed and drew the flimsy curtains close together. He then looked expectantly at the man seated on the floor of the carriage.

"As long as you keep your head down, you are safe inside my carriage. Now tell me what happened in the palace... what you saw. Tell me everything."

* * *

A shaft of golden yellow sunshine burst through the gloomy, westerly sky, drenching the plain outside Ujjayini in its fleeting exuberance, as the four councilors rode past the city's eastern gate to meet the Ashvin cavalry. The Acharya's horse was marginally in front, with Kshapanaka following him, flanked by Shanku and Dhanavantri. A small posse of soldiers brought up the rear.

Behind the cavalcade, high on the ramparts, archers of the City Watch crouched behind the fortifications, carefully observing the Ashvins clustered in the distance. Down below, Avanti's infantry and cavalry stood in orderly lines behind the heavily barricaded gate.

Seeing the small group emerge from the city's shadows into the sunlight, Nasatya, who sat astride his horse, leaning an elbow on his thigh, casually flicked back a lock of hair from his handsome face and looked across at his brother with a smirk.

It looks like the human king is here to negotiate a settlement.

Dasra returned a cold smile of triumph, his eyes on the approaching entourage.

It looks more like a case of abject surrender, brother. He appears to have come to us in the company of women – perhaps he seeks to appease us with more than just the dagger.

When they were almost within hailing distance of the Ashvins, Vetala Bhatta reined in his horse briefly. Raising his hand, he signaled the escorts to hold their ground, before nudging his horse forward. Shanku, Kshapanaka and Dhanavantri followed suit.

But having taken barely a dozen paces, the raj-guru halted once again as the other three councilors drew abreast. The four councilors and the Ashvins appraised one another across the brightly lit plain, shadows stretching long on the ground as the sun made one last valiant attempt at overthrowing the day's murk. The stillness was broken only by the faint whistling of the wind, interspersed with the rasping shrieks of two mynahs foraging for food.

Seeing that the humans from Avanti were making no further effort at bridging the intervening gap, Nasatya reluctantly prodded his horse forward. Dasra fell into step beside his brother, and the twins drew closer to the councilors.

"I presume you are King Vikramaditya of Avanti," Nasatya addressed the Acharya in a haughty tone.

"I'm afraid you presume wrongly, deva," Vetala Bhatta replied with a thin smile.

Nasatya's brows furrowed in confusion, his eyes flitting between the faces of the councilors. "Then who are you?" he demanded.

"I am Vetala Bhatta, and these are Dhanavantri, Kshapanaka and Shanku," the chief advisor pointed to his companions. "We are councilors to Samrat Vikramaditya."

"And your samrat...?" Nasatya shifted his gaze first to the knot of escorts waiting behind the councilors, then toward the city gates, searching for evidence of a royal personage.

"He is not here. Our samrat has more pressing matters to attend to in his palace."

The raj-guru had the pleasure of observing the incredulity that overcame Nasatya and Dasra's expressions. The Ashvin commanders had all along been expecting Vikramaditya to come rushing to them – instead, they were being told that the human king didn't deem them worthy of his time. The Acharya knew his gamble had paid off.

For a long moment, silence reigned as Nasatya scrambled to regain his composure.

"Have you brought us Veeshada's dagger?" he demanded gruffly, desperate to wrest the initiative back.

Vetala Bhatta considered the two devas for a moment before shaking his head. "I think we had made it quite clear to Narada that we do not intend parting with the dagger," he said. "Where does the question of bringing it to you arise?"

"You refuse the Brotherhood of the Ashvins at your own peril," Dasra scowled, his eyes shifting to the thin, long spear that the Acharya carried in his right hand. He felt there was something forbidding about the two skulls that decorated the weapon. He also noticed, for the first time, the shield that Shanku bore, and the rows of throwing knives that she wore around her narrow waist.

"We request you to leave us in peace, deva," the Acharya answered in a civil tone. "But should the need arise, we are prepared to defend Avanti and the dagger to the last man."

"It looks to me as if Avanti is already down to its last few men," Nasatya chortled, casting a sidelong glance at his brother. "See who's here to defend Veeshada's dagger – not the king, who prefers to hide in his palace, but an old man, a fat man and... two *women*."

Vetala Bhatta sensed Shanku and Kshapanaka stiffening at the deva's mockery. But before either woman could respond to the barb, Dhanavantri spoke from the Acharya's right.

"Forget about our king for the moment... First test your competence against this fat man, this old man and these two women here." The physician's voice was calm and cheerful, his face alight with amusement. "But whatever you do, make sure you don't get beaten by the women. That wouldn't make a very inspiring tale for the children growing up in Devaloka."

Watching Nasatya and Dasra's faces harden as the taunt hit home, the raj-guru knew the die had been truly cast. As if to confirm this, Dasra's hand went to the hilt of the sword dangling at his waist.

"Let's settle this straightaway then," he muttered darkly.

Out of the corner of his eye, the Acharya sensed the Ashvin cavalry ranged in the distance straighten on their saddles and reach for their scabbards.

"Don't do anything foolish, deva," Vetala Bhatta raised a cautioning hand. "At the slightest sign of aggression, Avanti's archers will let fly their arrows."

The Ashvin commanders raised their eyes to the top of Ujjayini's walls to see a long row of archers standing with their bows drawn, arrows pointing downward in their direction. Nasatya smiled inwardly in mild admiration, realizing that by holding his ground and refusing to come further into the plain, the old councilor had cleverly drawn him and Dasra into the archers' range.

Gesturing toward the ramparts, the raj-guru continued, "There are more than ten thousand soldiers behind Ujjayini's walls. I believe the five hundred horsemen you have with you will find them more than a match. So, for your own good, I urge you to return to Devaloka in peace."

The sun chose that moment to slip behind the heavy clouds, and the dark pall of dusk fell over the plain. The Ashvin commanders sat on their mounts, mirthless lips sealed tight, glaring at Vetala Bhatta. Then, quite inexplicably, a cunning smile appeared on Nasatya's face, spreading slowly till it touched his eyes.

These humans know and suspect nothing, brothers...
How about giving them a surprise?

The Acharya frowned, troubled by the same sly smile now playing on Dasra's lips. But before he could give it more thought, Nasatya addressed him.

"You will not part with the dagger and we will not leave without it – I can see only one way around this problem," the deva shrugged, still smiling. Turning his horse around, he cast one final glance over his shoulder. "Councilors, prepare to defend your city from the wrath of the Brotherhood."

With that, the Ashvin commanders rode back to their ranks in a thunder of hooves.

Siege

What do you think they are doing, raj-guru?"

The question came from a senior captain of the City Watch, a short man with a neatly trimmed gray beard and a broken nose. The captain was in the company of Vetala Bhatta and Dhanavantri, who were standing on the walkway behind the battlements, looking out into the eastern plain. Light was failing rapidly over Ujjayini, and a fine powdery spray fell from above, gradually dampening their clothes and hair, adding to the discomfort.

"They don't seem to be doing anything," perplexed, Vetala Bhatta shook his head, peering at the Ashvins gathered in the plain.

Three-quarters of an hour had passed since the verbal faceoff between the councilors and the Ashvin commanders. On returning to the safety of Ujjayini's walls, the Acharya and Dhanavantri had busied themselves with overseeing the defense of the eastern gate, while Kshapanaka had ridden off to secure the southern and western gates. Shanku had been tasked with strengthening the northern gate, besides leading an evacuation of the houses that spilled beyond the periphery of Ujjayini's northern wall – a natural expansion of a populous and prosperous city that was sprouting new urban localities.

The raj-guru and Dhanavantri had debated the prospect of leading a preemptive charge against the Ashvins, but had discarded the idea on seeing the night falling quickly around them. It was better to wait for the devas behind the security of the walls than risk losing lives in the darkness of the open plain, they concluded.

Strangely enough, in all the time that Ujjayini was being fortified against attack, the Ashvins themselves had displayed little inclination or enthusiasm for battle – Nasatya's dire warning notwithstanding. The deva force had just stood around as the day drew to a close around them, and from what the Acharya could make out, it looked as if the horsemen were waiting for something.

"It doesn't seem as if they are in any hurry to mount an attack," said Dhanavantri, wiping the spray that had accumulated on his broad forehead. Turning to the raj-guru, he raised one eyebrow. "Do you think they are having second thoughts about attacking us? Maybe they've realized that they underestimated our strength…"

"No," Vetala Bhatta shook his head with certainty. "They are waiting for someone or something. That much I'm sure of."

Just then, a soldier clambered out of a narrow staircase that led up to the battlements from the streets and alleyways below. Stepping on to the walkway, the soldier approached the raj-guru and bowed. "We have the reports from the scouts, your honor," he gasped, catching his breath.

The moment he had ascertained that the Ashvin cavalry was no greater than five hundred in number, Vetala Bhatta had ordered scouts to fan out in all eight directions to search for reinforcements. He was certain that even the devas weren't foolhardy enough to come to battle in such small numbers; he sensed that the Ashvins had split into smaller groups to escape detection and surround Ujjayini from all four sides. That the horsemen in the plain hadn't launched their attack so far only strengthened his belief.

"What do the scouts report?" he inquired.

"None of the scouts has reported the presence of any suspicious horsemen or troops anywhere within ten miles of Ujjayini," the soldier said. "And there are no signs of any suspicious boats on either bank of the sacred Kshipra, your honor."

The Acharya blinked in disbelief. "That can't be. They *must* have reinforcements."

"All the reports are with the Scouts Master, your honor. All the reports are negative."

Vetala Bhatta nodded. "You may leave."

The raj-guru returned his gaze to the plain, his bushy gray eyebrows knitting together in a deep, unhappy frown.

"No reinforcements," he muttered half to himself. "But how's that possible? There are so few of them…"

Dhanavantri and the captain of the City Watch watched the Ashvins, a clump of moving shadows in the surrounding gloom. It was becoming harder and harder to pick them in the twilight.

"That means they can't be waiting for something," said the physician. "Unless it's darkness they're waiting for, so that they can slink away undetected like foxes…"

"That's it, Dhanavantri," the Acharya insisted, a slight

note of triumph in his voice. "That's *precisely* it. They are waiting for nightfall. They plan to attack under cover of darkness."

"Five hundred horsemen against a fortified city with ten thousand defenders – not much of a plan," scoffed the captain. "What tactical advantage could darkness give them?"

"I don't know," replied the raj-guru, recalling the strange smile on the Ashvin commanders' faces just before they had parted on the plain. A wave of uneasiness swept over him, and suddenly he felt a lot less sure about defending Ujjayini.

* * *

The command center at Sristhali was moderately large in size and was situated on the western flank of the border town, nudging the foothills of the Arbuda Range. A rivulet, rarely ever in spate, formed a natural boundary between the command center and the main town, renowned all over Sindhuvarta for its marble craftsmanship.

Night having descended, the marble workshops of Sristhali had fallen silent, both artisans and apprentices back in the comfort of their homes. The last of the mule trains from the abundant marble quarries to the south had also returned, and the narrow streets were quickly emptying as the townsfolk wound down for the day.

It was just as well for Sristhali's diligent citizenry that the command center was some distance from the town – else, their repose would have been unduly disturbed by the fearful roar of Amara Simha's voice splitting the tranquil night air.

"Did or didn't the message say that I wanted the prisoner fit for interrogation?"

The voice came from a large, square building in the middle of the compound, an open window affording a view of Amara Simha, who stood scowling before a shamefaced officer of the Frontier Guard. In the background, Ghatakarpara and Governor Satyaveda stood quietly, watching the officer squirm and sweat under Amara Simha's glare.

"Yes, your honor," the officer stammered. "But… the prisoner… But we thought…"

"But you thought *what*, Commander Dattaka?" Amara Simha thundered. "Why didn't your physician attend to the prisoner? Why wasn't something done to fix his broken leg, and why wasn't he administered some medication to reduce the pain?"

"He is a Huna, so we thought he didn't deserve any kindness, your honor," the officer mumbled.

"Treating his leg had nothing to do with showing kindness, you fool," the councilor smacked his forehead in frustration. "It was to keep him in a state where we could interrogate him." Throwing his hands up in the air, he began pacing the floor, but within moments he was back in front of Dattaka.

"And to top it all, you tried beating information out of him. Is it a wonder that he's fallen unconscious? What in hell's name were you thinking?"

"We had the translator, so we thought… maybe we could get something out of him before you arrived, your honor," Dattaka hung his head.

"Ah, you wanted to impress me with your efficiency when I walked in here." The councilor folded his big hands across his broad chest. "Well, you have failed miserably in impressing me, commander. First you find some silly reason for not sending the prisoner to Udaypuri…"

"We don't have a wagon for escorting an injured prison..." Dattaka began protesting weakly, but Amara Simha raised a hand to stop him.

"No, I really don't have a problem with that, so let that be. But I have ridden long and hard to come here and question the Huna. Now if something happens to him because of your stupidity and he fails to regain consciousness... you will be in big, *big* trouble."

"He'll be all right, your honor," Dattaka assured, even though his voice didn't carry much conviction. Pointing to a small elderly man who stood in the shadows, he added, "Our physician says he will."

Amara Simha turned to the man, who stepped into the circle of light. Everything about the physician's appearance pointed to a timid and careworn life, and the councilor intuitively softened his voice as he addressed the man.

"The prisoner will regain consciousness, won't he?"

"He should. I think he will," the physician replied, although Amara Simha was discouraged by the slight shrug of the thin shoulders.

"And when can we expect him to return to consciousness?"

This time, even more dishearteningly, the shrug was more pronounced. "I can't say. Maybe in a few hours, maybe tomorrow..."

"I hope he's under observation."

"Yes, yes... the guards have been given the strictest instructions, your honor." Knowing that he had done at least one thing right, Dattaka leaped at the opportunity to salvage his reputation and rise in Amara Simha's esteem.

"Keep it that way," the councilor said curtly. "And the moment he recovers consciousness, inform the kind physi-

cian and me. Understood? Now get someone to show us to
our quarters. We've had a long day and would like to eat
and retire for the night."

* * *

Night had occupied Avanti's sky for nearly an hour when
someone spotted the lights out in the plain.

Vetala Bhatta was busy issuing instructions to a group
of archers when he heard a murmur spread along the wall,
growing steadily in volume as word was passed between
the soldiers. Turning around, he stared into the plain, his
jaw dropping open in astonishment.

The darkness that had enveloped the plain just moments
ago was now punctuated by hundreds and hundreds of
pinpricks of phosphorescent light, winking eerily through
the fine drizzle like silver-green fireflies. Though it was hard
to be sure, to the Acharya's eyes the row of lights appeared
to stretch for miles in both directions, following the natural
curve of Ujjayini's walls like a flickering girdle of fire.

"What is this?" one of the archers by Vetala Bhatta's
side whispered in awe.

"Take your places and be prepared," the raj-guru barked
in response. Whirling around, he was about to retrace his
steps to the eastern gate when, almost magically, the lights
began lifting into the air, their synchronized movement
mimicking that of a fountain. A hush fell over the walkway
as Avanti's defenders followed the flight of the lights with
dazed eyes.

The lights soared, phantom-like, high over the plain...
and then, almost imperceptibly, they changed direction
and started their descent. Growing in size and sharpness
with every passing second, they came arcing down toward

Ujjayini's walls with great force, the air filling with an unmistakable rushing, whistling sound.

"Take cover," the Acharya shouted at the top of his voice, hurling himself flat against the protective masonry of the ramparts. "They are fire arrows!"

In a matter of seconds the arrows rained down on the walkway and on both sides of the wall. The arrowheads exploded on impact, sending bursts of sizzling, phosphorescent sparks in all directions, the ember-hot particles searing bare flesh and setting fire to everything combustible.

The soldiers of the City Watch scrambled for cover, but the screams and shouts echoing along the walkway suggested that quite a few of them had been hit before they could take defensive positions. From the corner of his eye, the Acharya saw one soldier, his clothes on fire, flounder along the walkway before toppling helplessly over the edge and falling to his death. Inside the wall, a couple of the arrows had ignited a house, while another had set alight a wagon loaded with weapons from the armory.

"Quick, douse that fire," somebody shouted from below, running toward the wagon. "We can't lose so many arrows and spears."

A bout of panic swept along the wall as many soldiers broke cover and ran helter-skelter. The more strong-willed among them, however, crouched behind the parapet and drew their own bows. Vetala Bhatta cast a quick glance into the plain. Seeing that all was dark, he stood up and ran along the walkway, issuing a series of commands.

"Get back to your places. Keep your heads down and your bows ready. Shoot if you see the enemy making a charge for the gates."

A semblance of order was restored as the Acharya's

commands were relayed by officers of the City Watch. Down below, soldiers bearing swords and spears rushed to the city's eastern gate.

Vetala Bhatta had almost reached the gates when he saw a fresh row of lights blink in the plain. As the Ashvins launched the second wave of flaming arrows skyward, the raj-guru shouted down to the men inside the walls.

"Take cover. More arrows are coming."

Ducking behind the parapet, the Acharya poked his head out – but instead of gazing up at the arrows, this time he focused his attention on the dark plain below. As the arrows climbed and reached the peak of their trajectory, for a fraction of a second the entire plain was bathed with their dim phosphorescence. And in that light Vetala Bhatta saw the plain teeming with an army of horsemen.

An army of *several thousand* horsemen, arrayed to the north and south of the gate.

As the blazing arrows showered down upon Ujjayini, the raj-guru huddled behind the parapet, wondering how the Ashvin cavalry had multiplied from a mere five hundred to many thousands in less than an hour.

* * *

Shanku watched the houses and hutments clustered outside Ujjayini's northern wall going up in a blaze, her eyes smarting with tears of outrage, sorrow and frustration.

The Ashvins had smartly picked the defenseless quarter as their target, and despite the abundant dampness everywhere, the fire from their arrows had spread rapidly through the dense jumble of buildings. A patch of twenty-odd houses had already succumbed to the ravenous flames, while long tongues of fire licked appreciatively at the structures that stood intact around the fringes of the conflagration. Thick, black smoke belched and billowed from the burning debris, rolling through the township's cramped bylanes like a formless, vengeful entity.

The only consolation in all this was that the fire hadn't claimed any lives so far – every single resident of the quarter had been successfully evacuated and lodged behind the safety of the city's walls. But Shanku knew that most of the householders were in serious risk of losing all their possessions and would have to rebuild their lives from scratch.

If Ujjayini was able to weather the Ashvin onslaught, she told herself.

Cursing the injustice of it all, Shanku turned her gaze to the right and peered into the overwhelming darkness that lay to the east, from where the horsemen had launched their flaming missiles. Waving off the pungent smoke eddying around her, she addressed the bulky soldier standing beside her on the watchtower that overlooked the northern gate.

"How far away are they?" she asked. "Are they within our archers' range?"

"It's hard to say in this darkness," the soldier replied with a shrug. "I need to get a better sighting before I can be sure."

At precisely that moment, as if on cue, the Ashvin cavalry shot a fresh round of arrows into the air. This attack, unlike the one that had preceded it, was aimed at Ujjayini's wall, forcing the defenders on the walkway to scurry for cover.

"I don't think they are within range of our bows and arrows," the soldier said as he and Shanku ducked behind a parapet. "We will only end up wasting arrows if we try shooting back. We must wait for them to draw closer."

Shanku nodded, but didn't reply. She waited for the

arrows to stop falling before rising and stepping off the watchtower. She climbed down the narrow metal ladder, and on reaching ground level, she walked briskly to the northern gate, where a couple of officers of the City Watch stood conferring.

"I'm going out into the plain," she announced without preamble. "I need ten of the best horse archers you can muster to ride with me."

The officers stared at Shanku, shaking their heads in incomprehension. Some of the soldiers standing nearby had overheard her and exchanged bewildered glances. Finally, one of the officers spoke.

"But your honor, the raj-guru has sent an order forbidding us from opening the gates or venturing into the plain," he said. His fellow officers nodded vigorously in mounting alarm.

"I know that. But we can't just sit back and watch those arrows reduce Ujjayini to ashes." Shanku began tightening the harness of her horse as she spoke. "We need to engage the enemy in battle and start inflicting some losses on them."

"And you intend doing that by riding out there with just ten horse archers?" The officer's voice strained with incredulity.

"Yes, I have a plan. But first get me the men I want. And ask the archers on the wall to be on full alert."

* * *

There was nothing remarkable about the two long swords that lay on the table, side by side. Their sheaths were made of some ancient animal hide, shiny brown in some places, dark and scuffed in others. The blades themselves were concealed from view, but the heavy iron hilts, though free of oxidation, were plain and lacking in adornment.

The swords simply didn't look as if they were worthy of belonging to a king.

Yet, when Vikramaditya strode into the anteroom next to his bedchamber, he made straight for the table and picked up one of the weapons. Taking a firm grip on the hilt, he drew the sword a little way out of its scabbard to inspect it. The burnished blade, gleaming dull yellow in the light of the lamps, caught the reflection of the king's eyes, seething with cold rage.

But a moment later, the metal turned deep orange in color, and then fiery red, burning with incandescence as small blue-green flames erupted and danced, ghostlike, on its surface.

You are the one I have sought for so many years, good king. You are the one destined to wield the Hellfires. Accept them, for they are rightfully yours.

Vikramaditya thrust the weapon back into its sheath, snuffing out the flames and killing the glow of the blade. The swords hadn't been used in years, yet, to his relief, they still retained their powers. Not that he had cause to doubt what the demon Laayushi had told him of the Hellfires…

Without wasting more time, the samrat buckled the swords to his belt, one on each side of his waist, harnessed in a manner that allowed for an easy cross-handed draw. Then, pulling on his metal armguards, he walked out of the room. He was halfway down one of the inner galleries when Angamitra, the young *samsaptaka* captain, accosted him. The captain was in the company of an old man with a fine white beard and gray eyes – Sadguna, the chief of the Palace Guards.

"Samrat, please don't go out there alone," the captain pleaded, falling in step a little behind the king. "I have four hundred of my men waiting to ride with you. Please take them along."

"Yes, samrat," enjoined Sadguna, who was trailing Angamitra's heels. "It isn't wise going out there alone. Let the *samsaptakas* fight by your side."

Vikramaditya shook his head firmly, without breaking his stride or glancing back at the captain and the chief of the Palace Guards.

"Samrat, please," Angamitra desperately tried reasoning. "Councilor Kalidasa would never forgive me if he learned that I allowed you to ride out alone. The men I have picked are the very best, your honor. You have my word that they will fight until their last breath..."

"I have never doubted a *samsaptaka*'s willingness and ability to fight, captain," the king cut in, slowing his pace by a fraction. "And I am certain the men you have put at my disposal will make Avanti proud. But if they accompany me right now, they will be less of a help and more of a handicap for me."

Crestfallen, Angamitra fell silent. Sensing the captain's disappointment, Vikramaditya stopped and turned to face him and Sadguna.

"There's a reason I want to ride out of Ujjayini's gates alone," the king explained, pointing in a southerly direction. "On dark nights like this, it's hard to tell the difference between friend and foe, and one could easily end up maiming one's own people in battle. When I'm out there in the darkness of the plain, I want to be sure that I have only Avanti's enemies around me. Only then will I be free to use my swords without fear, to bring pain and punishment on the Ashvins."

＊＊

The walkway along Ujjayini's western wall was slippery and uneven from years of peacetime neglect. Loose stones sloped treacherously in places, while in others, pools of green slime and moss deposits flourished. Not the safest of places in broad daylight, the walkway was a virtual deathtrap at night, yet Kshapanaka sprinted over it unmindful of the dangers, shouting out instructions and shooting volleys of arrows over the battlements as she ran.

"Keep the enemy away from the gate. Don't let them breach it."

Below her, outside the city's western gate, the steps leading up from the Kshipra were full of Ashvins trying to batter their way into Ujjayini.

The coordinated assaults in the north, east and south were spectacular in effect, but the main thrust of the Ashvin attack had occurred to the west, under cover of darkness. A large force of Ashvins had floated down the river, and as the diversionary arrows descended elsewhere over Ujjayini, they had launched a sudden onslaught on the western gate.

Thud.

Yet another wave of heavy metal shields collided against the wooden gate, sending tremors along the framework of the old wall. Kshapanaka cursed under her breath. The City Watch had been caught flatfooted, and if the Ashvins got past the gates, she knew there weren't enough swordsmen and lancers inside to withstand a rush.

"Have you sent word asking for reinforcements?" she demanded of the captain who was tasked with manning that section of the wall. "And have they started evacuating the houses?"

"Yes," the captain answered, but the vagueness of his reply did nothing to reassure Kshapanaka. However, looking over her shoulder, she was relieved to see a few soldiers herding a flock of scared citizens down the road, away from the gate.

Thud... Thud...

The echoes of the shields crashing on wood reverberated along the walkway, escalating in pitch, insistence and hostility with every subsequent attempt. Kshapanaka snapped an order at the captain.

"I'm running out of arrows – fetch me some. And get someone to supply fresh arrows to all the archers."

The captain scurried away to do as bidden. Wishing that the steps to the river were better lit, Kshapanaka fitted another arrow into her bowstring and shot at the dark shapes writhing and shifting below.

Thud...

Not for the first time, she also wondered at the sheer number of Ashvins who seemed to have appeared out of nowhere.

* * *

The moment she sighted the bronze armors of the Ashvin cavalry, reflected dully in the light of Ujjayini's burning hutments, Shanku raised her hand to signal the horse archers accompanying her. The archers dispersed, stretching themselves over the plain in a thin ragged line, yet staying close enough to be within earshot of one another. Riding softly, their bows drawn, the group approached the Ashvins from the rear, their ears trying to pick out the faintest of sounds in the dark.

When Shanku was certain that she was within range of the devas, she extracted four daggers from her belt and rose on her stirrups. Balancing herself with consummate ease, she flung the daggers at the Ashvins in rapid succession, each dagger finding its mark with deadly precision. At the sound of the daggers hitting their targets, the horse archers swiftly unleashed three volleys of arrows at the Ashvins, before scattering in the dark.

The stealth and suddenness of the attack caught the devas off guard, and for a few moments, there was an upheaval in their ranks as they tried to take stock of the situation. Using the confusion to her advantage, Shanku hurled four more knives at the surging mass of horsemen, bringing three of them down to the ground. Then, wheeling her horse around, she let out a shrill whoop and began galloping back toward the northern gate of Ujjayini.

In a matter of seconds, the Ashvin horsemen espied the fleeing figure and gave chase.

Shanku rode hard, but the closer she drew to Ujjayini, the more sharply she was defined by light of the fire, presenting a clear target to her pursuers. Fire arrows rained down around her, hissing and exploding, a couple of them missing her by a whisker as she dodged and weaved out of harm's way.

Keep coming after me, keep coming after me, she chanted in her mind as she watched the blank face of Ujjayini's northern wall loom out of the darkness.

As the devas bore down on Shanku, the city's northern gate began opening from the inside, a bestial, gluttonous mouth in the dancing firelight. Seeing Shanku head straight for the gate and realizing they were too far behind, the Ashvins began reining in their horses – when suddenly Shanku's horse seemed to flag, slowing down in speed.

Don't stop, you pigs, Shanku grimaced as she threw a desperate glance over her shoulder, trying to gauge

distances. *Come and get me. Don't give up*. She looked up
at the ramparts, wondering if the Ashvins were within range
of Avanti's archers, but seeing no movement up on the wall,
she realized they probably weren't.

Aware that she was taking a huge risk, Shanku dropped
speed even further. She just had to keep baiting the
Ashvins...

Observing Shanku slow down and droop across the neck
of her horse, the Ashvins sensed opportunity and spurred
their horses forward. If they were quick enough, they knew
they could get to the gate before their quarry slipped inside
and the defenders had a chance to seal the city shut again.

Shanku heard the growing beat of hooves behind her and
sneaked another backward glance. What she was attempting
demanded skillful timing – if she acted too soon, the devas
would lose heart and cease their pursuit; if she was too slow,
there would be no way of getting out of this alive. From
somewhere near the gate, she heard someone yell out to her;
perhaps one of the officers of the City Watch urging her to
hasten. She didn't respond, but she fervently hoped those
inside didn't shut the gate prematurely in a fit of panic.

From the corner of her eye, Shanku saw the Ashvins
approaching out of the ring of darkness. Someone again
hollered at her from the gate, but the words were muffled
by the pounding of hooves. Then, from somewhere high
above, she thought she heard the twang of a bow.

A second later, a series of twangs were transmitted along
the length of the wall, as the archers of the City Watch
finally had the Ashvins within their range.

"Close the gate, close the gate." Shanku pushed her
charge forward, screaming at the top of her voice as the
choked cries of the devas rose into the air behind her.

A flurry of the Ashvins' arrows followed Shanku, narrowly missing her as she ducked and scrambled to get behind the gates that were being drawn shut. But two of Avanti's soldiers positioned just inside weren't as fortunate, arrows nailing them to the ground and setting them on fire before the gates slammed on the cavalry from Devaloka.

Shanku leaped off her steed and darted to the watchtower. Pulling herself up the ladder, two rungs at a time, she emerged on to the platform above in a low crouch. Staying on all fours, feeling the cold roughness of the stony floor on her palms, she scuttled to the edge of the tower to peek outside – when she sensed an uncanny hush descend all around her.

Where moments ago the stomping of hooves, the frantic rush of feet and the shouting of commands had filled the air, now all that remained was silence.

Perhaps the Ashvins have beaten a retreat.

Keeping her head down, she looked up to see the burly soldier who had kept her company earlier standing behind a wall, staring down at the plain. His face was rigid in the glow of the fire, his eyes ringed with astonishment and unease.

"What's happened?" Shanku asked in an urgent whisper, her voice uncomfortably loud in the overbearing stillness.

"They have no mercy," the soldier hissed back, hardly moving a muscle, fear rattling drily in his throat. "And they… they are… *breaking and growing*."

"What?"

Raising her head cautiously, Shanku followed the soldiers' gaze, her eyes totally unprepared for the bizarre scene unfolding below.

The ground outside the north gate was littered with

devas, both dead and dying. However, a good number of the horsemen were unharmed, and with mounting horror, Shanku watched these survivors ride among their fallen mates, slaughtering those mortally wounded, one by one. A powerful thrust of the sword into the exposed neck, a well-placed arrow to the temple or between the eyes – the Ashvins killed their own swiftly, efficiently, without remorse.

Yet, what rattled Shanku even more was the sight of some of the wounded devas shoving their own swords into their mouths and down their own gullets. For a fleeting moment they reminded Shanku of the sword-swallowers from the Southern Kingdoms, whom she had seen performing at carnivals – only here, there were none of the sword-swallowers' delicate touches on display. The devas rammed the blades in with brute force, choking and gurgling as their lifeblood ebbed from them. There was something almost ritualistic about the chilling assuredness with which the injured Ashvins were inflicting death upon themselves.

Shanku felt the bile building inside her. But before she could gag on it, it froze in her throat as she witnessed something even more grotesque. Her first instinct was to put it down to her imagination, but as the fire flared with renewed vigor, lighting up the plain, she knew she wasn't simply seeing things.

As the able-bodied Ashvins went about their ghastly chore, they seemed to grow in size, their bodies swelling and distorting and stretching sideways, as if being pulled in opposite directions by enormous, invisible forces. It wasn't just the Ashvins – even their mounts increased in width, becoming boneless masses of flesh and tissue for a fraction of a second.

Then, as the deformed bodies acquired a mashed, doughlike consistency, each horseman separated into two distinct, identical, fully-formed entities.

They are breaking and growing.

Wide-eyed with shock, Shanku watched the Ashvin cavalry divide and multiply repeatedly, their numbers doubling in the blink of an eye. In no time the plain was again thronging with horsemen – but for some reason, instead of attacking the wall, they chose to retreat into the night. Soon all that remained in the plain were the corpses.

But Shanku knew the horsemen hadn't gone far. They would return shortly, in even greater numbers. She also saw that there would be no stopping this self-generating brotherhood of devas.

Her heart sank in despair for Ujjayini.

Hellfires

They grow their numbers by splitting themselves into two over and over again."

Vetala Bhatta looked over the battlements in awe. From the light of the big torches that had been lit near the gate and along the base of the wall, he could make out the vague forms of the Ashvin cavalry out in the plain. He could tell that the horsemen were gradually drawing closer to Ujjayini – perhaps an assault on the eastern gate was imminent as well. "So that's how they increased from a mere five hundred to surround us on all sides."

"And that's why they are capable of killing off their wounded without a shred of sympathy," Dhanavantri pointed out. "They don't need to nurse their injured back to health. They just replace them with new battle-worthy warriors."

"I see another reason why they kill off their wounded mates," the raj-guru said. "For effect – to demonstrate to their enemies how ruthless and fearless they can be."

An ominous silence ensued.

"If they can multiply at will at the speed Shanku and the troops at the northern gate say they saw, how are we ever going to get the better of them?" the physician pondered slowly.

Instead of answering, the Acharya swung around to one of his commanders. "Has the king been informed about this?"

"A rider is on his way to the south gate to update the samrat, your honor."

"And what's the latest from the west?"

"The Ashvins are still trying to break the gate down, but Councilor Kshapanaka and her men are holding them back. We have already dispatched some reinforcements, your honor."

The raj-guru returned his gaze eastward, wondering where they would turn to for reinforcements if the Ashvins chose to attack the other three gates simultaneously. More than ever, he wished Vararuchi, Kalidasa and Varahamihira had been in Ujjayini at that moment.

"No news from Vararuchi so far, I presume?" he asked, without any real hope.

"Nothing, your honor."

The Acharya sighed and his head sank to his chest. Seeing the old councilor's deflated countenance, Dhanavantri placed a reassuring hand on his shoulder.

"I'm sure they are all right. Vararuchi must have sent a rider with news – he's probably just not being able to approach the city because of the Ashvins."

Vetala Bhatta nodded. A pishacha army to the south. A multitude of Ashvin horsemen all around Ujjayini. Veeshada's dagger had already begun exacting a heavy toll on the kingdom of Avanti.

Suddenly, a low roar surged from the plain. Looking up, the raj-guru saw the horsemen's shadows begin moving toward the wall to the accompaniment of hoof beats and battle cries. The same instant, another barrage of flaming arrows shot into the air in a parabolic curve.

The east gate was under attack!

*   *   *

Unlike the flat, open plains lying to east and the north, the terrain to the south of Ujjayini was hilly, marked by steep ridges and rock-strewn slopes. These ridges afforded an unobstructed view of the city behind its high walls, and it was from here that the Ashvins led by Dasra had launched their brutal assault of arrows, setting Ujjayini's southern neighborhoods on fire and driving waves of terrified citizens into the streets.

And it was down one of these rocky slopes that the cavalry, with Dasra at its head, now charged, making straight for Ujjayini's south gate.

The gate was charred black and smoldering, its rough wooden face studded with the stubs of hundreds of burned arrows, sticking out like spines on a porcupine's back. The wood had burned to ash in many places, embers glowing bright orange around these spots, and gray smoke streamed steadily out of the fissures in the old beams. The gate had received such a battering from the fire arrows that it was ready to give in at the slightest pretext.

Holding his sword aloft, Dasra hurtled down the low gradient, buoyed by the breeze and the war cries of the Ashvins – and the sense of triumph swelling inside him. All his attention was on the charred, smoldering gate, a crumbling bulwark of a proud city that had been brought to its knees. Once past that gate, Dasra knew it was a matter of time before the Halahala was in their possession.

The cavalry had reached the point where the slope leveled out when, almost in millimetric movements, the gate began opening. Dasra reined in his horse, eyes narrowed, wondering what to expect from the beleaguered city.

Careful, brothers! This might be a last token of resistance, or it may be surrender...

As the gate swung wide open on its hinges, the fires raging within Ujjayini's walls came into view. And framed in that blazing rectangle of light, the Ashvins saw the silhouette of a lone horseman, tall and upright astride a large horse.

Dasra observed the figure keenly. Although it was too far to say for certain, the horseman didn't appear to be bearing weapons. The deva peered into the shadows of the gate, trying to discern the hunched shapes of soldiers waiting in ambush, or preparing to make a sudden rush. But there didn't seem to be any soldiers hiding around or inside the gate either. He looked up at the walls. He was certain there were archers above, but not one arrow had been shot from the battlements so far.

It's probably the surrender after all.

Still, Dasra retained a firm grip on his sword. Despite his non-threatening manner, there was something vaguely menacing about the shadowy horseman.

The Ashvins watched the figure move slowly forward. Riding at a steady, assured pace, the horseman emerged from the protection of the city into the plain. No one followed the rider, and everything appeared quiet about the ramparts.

Convinced that the rider was a messenger or courtier sent to plead a truce, Dasra began relaxing his guard when Ujjayini's gates began shutting behind the rider.

Dasra clenched his jaw. He had been right in his misgivings about the horseman. This was no surrender.

As if in confirmation, the rider pulled to a halt and drew two long swords out of his belt, brandishing them over his head in gleaming arcs. Dasra blinked as the last of the fire from behind the closing gates seemed to catch and burn on the tips of the swords like an illusion – and then it dawned on him that both blades were indeed alight with lambent flames. And although he knew he was imagining it, the deva felt the horseman's eyes boring into his own from across the dark plain.

Attack.

The bowmen on the flanks of the cavalry discharged a volley of arrows at the solitary figure. Humming like hornets, the pinpoints of light homed in on the horseman, sitting rocklike on his mount, arms outstretched, gripping his fire swords tight. At the last moment, when the arrows were nearly upon him, the horseman swung his swords at the converging missiles, cutting and swiping, splintering the shafts and shattering the arrowheads in a coruscating shower of sparks. When the last of the burning barbs fell to the ground, Dasra saw that the rider was unscathed. And far from being cowed by the assault, the warrior spurred his horse into a gallop, riding straight at the wall of the Ashvin cavalry.

Dasra shook his head at this insane show of defiance; it baffled and frustrated him.

Charge, brothers!

Goaded into a rage by the horseman's temerity, the devas rushed across the plain, their swords pointing straight at the charging rider. But the horseman didn't slow down. Instead, he began flourishing his swords in broad, sweeping moves, the flames on the blades tapering and growing in length and intensity with each successive movement of his arms. The flames simultaneously changed color – from yellow-orange to a bright, malignant green. In moments, the fires had assumed the form of long flaming whips, swirling drunkenly over the rider's head.

Dasra watched in fascination as the belts of fire detached themselves from the swords and sailed through the air, constantly growing in size as they snaked across the plain at the Ashvin cavalry. The whips descended with tremendous speed and accuracy, lashing into the vanguard of the devas' attack, hurling the horsemen off their mounts, cutting through their armor and scorching their flesh to the bone.

Agonized screams rent the night and the Ashvins fell back – but the horseman from Ujjayini didn't relent. He kept on riding forward, twirling his swords, sending more and more of the gleaming green whips into the air...

This time, however, instead of seeking out the Ashvins, the whips twisted and coiled like flaming helixes in the night sky. As the devas stared in amazement, the whips magically entwined to form three gargantuan, fire-breathing *churails*. Wailing and screaming, the fiery banshees lunged at the flanks of the cavalry, spewing green flames from their horrendous black mouths.

Dasra's face slackened in disbelief as the rampaging *churails* mowed through his army, setting the Ashvins on fire before they had a chance to multiply. Slowly, he turned his attention back to the rider, who was closing in on the central column of his cavalry. As yet another blazing belt spun out and slapped into the devas, Dasra was seized with panic.

The horseman is the Wielder of the Hellfires.

Dasra shivered at the realization, his sword going limp in his hand.

* * *

"Are you sure you know what you're doing?"

Dhanavantri's expression was a mixture of doubt and alarm as he peered at the raj-guru in the half-light. They were crouching inside a covered stairway to protect themselves from the Ashvins' arrows, and the physician had to shout to make himself heard over the noise of the cavalry battering against the gate underneath.

The Acharya nodded, bringing his face close to Dhanavantri's ear. "If each horseman is essentially a twin, each capable of dividing infinitely into multiple twins, it means all the Ashvins out there sprang from one original body... and one original *mind*. It's probable that the Ashvins share a common mind, which controls the whole army, deciding things like what should be done next, who should multiply how many times... If that's the case, I want to get inside that common mind."

"To see what they want? But that's obvious – they want to attack us and take the Halahala."

Vetala Bhatta shook his head. "I want to enter that mind and try and control it. I want to see if I can influence this army in some way."

"But how are you going to do that?" Dhanavantri sounded flabbergasted.

"I don't know. I won't know till I use the spell and enter the mind of one of those devas."

"I don't like this idea," the physician protested. "It's one thing trying to read someone's mind. Trying to influence it is a completely different game, Acharya. You know better than anyone else that the process can backfire miserably – *your* mind could end up being influenced by the other's into doing terrible things, unspeakable things."

"I know what I'm suggesting is fraught with risk," replied Vetala Bhatta, wincing as the gate was rammed by the Ashvins once again. Pointing downward toward the source of the din, he pressed, "But we have to take that chance before that gate is broken down; unless you have a better idea."

Dhanavantri stared glumly down at the depths of the stone stairway.

"Come then, there's no time to think," said the Acharya, rising to his feet and grabbing his spear. "Cover me while I cast my spell."

The two councilors stepped on to the walkway, Dhanavantri in the lead. The physician planted himself firmly along the battlement, gripped his quarterstaff with both hands, and cast an eye over the wall. He swore under his breath on seeing the Ashvin cavalry amassed outside the gate, intent on breaking in.

Positioning himself behind Dhanavantri's bulk, the rajguru also gazed into the plain. His eyes, however, singled out one particular deva who was sitting astride his horse, waiting patiently for his companions to breach the gate. Drawing himself to his full height, the Acharya closed his eyes and brought his right hand, clenched into a tight fist, to the center of his chest. At the same time, his lips began moving to a wordless mantra.

Moments later, the skulls dangling on Vetala Bhatta's spear, which he held in his left hand, started glowing, the red light flickering and wavering at first, then burning steadily.

In a flash, the Acharya was filled with a raging lust to destroy Ujjayini.

The Halahala will be ours before daybreak.

The Acharya sensed being at the head of a column of Ashvins who were charging at a huge gate. Arrows fell from above in murderous clusters as he threw himself against the barricade, the wood juddering and creaking against his shoulder. One more heave and the gate burst open.

The western gate has fallen. We are inside Ujjayini.

Elation washed over the Acharya like a tide, suffusing him with its warmth as he pushed the gate's wreckage aside and hacked at Avanti's soldiers...

"The gate is down, the enemy is inside," a soldier hollered. "Sound the alarm bells, sound the ala..." The words were cut off abruptly as Vetala Bhatta slashed open the soldier's throat. Then –

There... above us... on top of the wall.

Suddenly, the raj-guru saw two men staring down from the battlements. The one in front was short and obese, wielding a quarterstaff. The other was a tall, graybearded man standing motionless, holding a spear that had something red glowing near its tip. Fire arrows were being directed at the two men from below, but the fat man was using his staff to deflect the missiles, the staff little more than a twirling blur against the dark sky.

The next image to impose itself on the Acharya's mind was of a young, athletic woman running along rooftops, rapidly shooting arrows and issuing orders as she leaped between buildings. Catching sight of her face in the firelight, he felt a sharp stab of anger.

That's one of their councilors. She's already brought down many of us. Kill her.

It took heroic effort for Vetala Bhatta to wrench himself free of the enthrallment. His suspicions had been proved right – the horsemen shared a common mind that registered everything that every Ashvin saw and felt. But now that Ujjayini had been breached and its citizen's lives were in peril, he knew he had to bring all his focus to bear on projecting his own thoughts onto the collective mind of the Ashvins.

But to his horror, he found that his mind was incapable of conceiving anything other than the destruction of Ujjayini and the recovery of Veeshada's dagger.

We shall make the king of Avanti pay for his arrogance with his life.

Wading against the flow, he fought to channelize his thoughts. Yet the harder he tried, the stronger the minds of the devas emerged, swamping him with scenes of the devastation within Ujjayini as the city's defense fell apart.

Then, all of a sudden, the Acharya's vision was filled with a huge *churail* screaming through the night sky, her hair trailing green fire, her monstrous mouth vomiting flames. He also saw a rider charging down a plain, wielding long flaming whips in both hands. The sight struck cold fear in his heart.

The horseman is the Wielder of the Hellfires.

The thought sank in, settling like a heavy stone in the pit of his stomach. And fear gave way to terror.

Run.

As the rider with the fire whips drew nearer, the Acharya saw a broad ribbon of green flame, forked at the tip like a serpent's tongue, scythe toward him, torching a bunch of Ashvins in the sweep of its arc. Transfixed, he watched the belt swerve and leap at him, its blazing white heat singeing his skin, sending shards of pain radiating along his limbs...

Vetala Bhatta's eyes flew open in his ashen face. For a moment, he stood on the walkway, staring unseeingly at

Dhanavantri's broad back, which was pouring with sweat and heaving with exertion. Then, as the hail of arrows from below ceased, the raj-guru shuddered violently and collapsed on the walkway, his spear clattering loudly on the cold stones.

* * *

The Ashvins were stampeding through the streets of Ujjayini, a torrent of hooves pouring out from all directions and heading for the shattered remains of the city's western gate. Soldiers of the City Watch hurried to get out of the way of the devas, pressing themselves against the houses that lined the streets to keep from coming under the horses. The horsemen, for their part, didn't spare Avanti's soldiers a glance, even when a spear or two was hurled into their midst.

Kshapanaka crouched on a limb of a tree, watching this frenzied ride with keen, wide eyes. She couldn't understand it.

Unmindful of the resistance from within the walls, the devas had sustained their assault on the western gate all evening, in the hope of gaining an entry into the city. Their doggedness had ultimately paid off, and the cavalry had swarmed into Ujjayini, crushing the feeble defense of the City Watch. What flummoxed Kshapanaka was that hardly any time had lapsed since the gate had been beaten down – yet here the Ashvins already seemed intent on departing.

Perhaps they had got what they came for!

As the thought flashed through her mind, panic reared inside Kshapanaka, mingling with anger and helplessness. She swiftly nocked another arrow into her bow, even as she saw the futility of her action. If the devas had got the dagger, it was too late...

It is never too late to inflict damage on the enemy, she remembered the Acharya telling them as kids, waving his wooden sword at their faces. Every wound, every bruise you deliver makes them weaker.

Drawing the bowstring taut, Kshapanaka aimed at the head of one of the Ashvins charging down the street. She was about to release the arrow when she observed the horseman's expression in the light of a burning house. It wasn't one of gloating triumph, as she had expected. Instead, it was filled with manic fear.

Looking closely, she noticed that the faces of all the horsemen in the streets below were filled with mortal terror. And it occurred to her that the devas were taking flight, desperate to be rid of Ujjayini.

Vetala Bhatta's instructions notwithstanding, Kshapanaka heaved a sigh and relaxed her arms, lowering the bow. Standing up, she balanced herself on the branch to turn and stare at the western gate, which was clogged with jostling, fleeing horsemen. Shaking her head with relief and mystification at this dramatic turnaround, she watched the Brotherhood of the Ashvins discharge into the night.

Vishakha

A dull, leaden pain pounded through Ghatakarpara's head every time he turned, and the muscles immediately above his eyelids throbbed uncomfortably, forcing him to blink and stretch his eyes every now and then. He had trouble even holding his head erect, and his mouth still felt rough and dry, the aftertaste of acid reflux lingering in his throat.

The prolonged bath in icy cold water had been of no help whatsoever, he decided. Nor had the three glasses of buttermilk, downed in rapid succession, worked any wonders.

Pushing himself off the bed where he had been sitting with his head hanging between his knees, Ghatakarpara cursed Amara Simha for the lousiest hangover he'd ever suffered in five years of drinking.

It had all started innocuously enough over dinner the previous night. Commander Dattaka, in a bid to get back into the good books of Amara Simha, had produced a pitcher of firewater, freshly distilled from a neighborhood brewery.

Never one to refuse a drink, Amara Simha had gracefully accepted a flagon, filling one each for Ghatakarpara and Governor Satyaveda as well.

The brew was of excellent quality; one flagon had quickly increased to two, then three, then four, Amara Simha's humor returning with each successive flagon. Before long – and Ghatakarpara couldn't exactly recall how it had started – Amara Simha was challenging the prince to a drinking contest, and two more pitchers of firewater were called for. Flagons were emptied with much gusto, only to be promptly refilled...

Ghatakarpara's last memory of the night was of him staring up at the ceiling of the command center's dining room, watching the rafters swim and lurch in the torchlight.

There was a sharp rap on the door, but before the prince could acknowledge it, the door opened to reveal a soldier of the Frontier Guard standing on the threshold.

"Salutations to Prince Ghatakarpara."

The prince nodded, regretting the movement immediately as a fresh bout of pounding began between his ears.

"Councilor Amara Simha desires your presence at Commander Dattaka's office, your honor."

"I'll be there," Ghatakarpara answered thickly, pressing his temples between thumb and middle finger to ease the pain.

He watched the soldier bow and shut the door, wondering if he had detected the shadow of a smirk on the soldier's face. He cursed again, knowing he had made a complete fool of himself the previous night in front of the governor and Dattaka. Word had probably spread through the command center – and he feared soon half the Imperial Army would know that the prince couldn't hold his drink.

Ghatakarpara winced at the bright morning sunlight as he stepped into the open courtyard, across which lay the building that housed Dattaka's office. Having negotiated the courtyard without accident, the prince picked his way into the building and arrived at the commander's office to see Amara Simha hunched at the table, back in a foul temper. Governor Satyaveda sat in another chair, drumming his fingers on his knees, while Dattaka stood to one side, his head hanging dolefully.

Amara Simha cocked an eyebrow at the prince as he entered, then turned and glowered at Dattaka.

"Make preparations to return to Udaypuri. We shall leave immediately." Although he was staring at the commander, there was little doubt that Amara Simha had addressed the prince.

"But what about... interrogating the prisoner?" Ghatakarpara asked in confusion.

"What interrogation, what prisoner?" the burly councilor snapped. "Because of the foolishness of Commander Dattaka here, there is no prisoner left to interrogate. The Huna scout died sometime this morning without regaining consciousness."

Not knowing how to react, Ghatakarpara merely stared at the commander, who licked his lips nervously and glanced back at the prince before dropping his eyes.

"Are you aware of how much information we could have got out of that scout?" Amara Simha continued admonishing Dattaka. "We might have learned invaluable information about the Hunas' plans if your stupidity hadn't come in the way."

"True, true," tut-tutted Satyaveda solemnly. "Very silly, very stupid."

For all the regret that he was displaying, Ghatakarpara got the distinct feeling that the governor was enjoying Dattaka's humiliation very much. Or was there something else here, something that seemed to give Satyaveda immense satisfaction... Ghatakarpara put the thought away as the commander spoke.

"My deepest apologies to you, councilors. I regret what has happened, but unfortunately it cannot be undone. As chief of this command center, I take full responsibility. I shall abide by whatever punitive action is taken against me."

Taken aback by Dattaka's earnest apology and willingness to shoulder the blame, Amara Simha merely nodded.

"Have a full report on this sent to Udaypuri without delay," he said, rising from his chair. Turning to Satyaveda, he asked, "Are you returning with us as well?"

"No, your honor. As I told you, I have some work with the town panchayat here," the governor pointed in the direction of Sristhali. "I have to go through revenue receipts, meet local civic authorities for road repairs... Then I leave for Sarmista in the afternoon – there's work pending there as well."

"Yes, yes, I see," Amara Simha interrupted, looking most relieved. "You'll come from Sarmista by yourself. Carry on." With that he walked briskly out of the room, appearing none the worse for last night's excesses.

Not much later, as Ghatakarpara, Amara Simha and their escorts stood by their horses, readying for departure, they saw Commander Dattaka approach them in a hurry.

"Councilors, I have news for you," the commander's face shone with excitement. Seeing Amara Simha raise his eyebrows, he continued, "As luck would have it, it seems another Huna scout has been apprehended by soldiers of the Frontier Guard."

"Where?" Amara Simha's voice crackled with hope.

"Near the border village of Uttashi, further to the south. An hour's ride away."

"Are they sure he's a Huna scout?"

"No, your honor. The man speaks the local dialect well, but the soldiers are certain he's not from these parts. He claims to be a traveling carpenter, but he was caught snooping around the Frontier Guard post last night. Of course he insists he had only lost his way in the dark."

"Hmmm… suspicious," Amara Simha twirled his big red moustache as he processed the information. "Maybe he's lying, maybe he's not. There's only one way of knowing." Looking from the Dattaka to the prince, he added, "Let us ride to Uttashi and meet this carpenter."

"I will get my horse right away, your honor." The commander wheeled around, but he'd barely taken three steps when Amara Simha hailed him.

"Wait… Has the dead scout's body been disposed of yet?"

"No, your honor. I was about to give the orders…"

"Then I have a better idea," Amara Simha interjected. "I want you to take twenty of your best men to Uttashi and bring this man to Sristhali. We shall find out the truth about him here. But make sure there are no mistakes this time."

"Yes, your honor." Dattaka nodded, looking befuddled at the sudden change in the councilor's decision.

"But before leaving, instruct your men *not* to dispose of the dead Huna's body. This is very important. Now hurry up, commander. I'm very eager to meet this traveling carpenter."

Ghatakarpara frowned as he watched Dattaka depart. Turning to Amara Simha, he said, "I don't understand this."

"You will, my boy," Amara Simha smiled mysteriously,

throwing an arm around the prince's shoulder and shepherding him into the shade of the buildings. "Let's go inside. You have two hours to get rid of that hangover of yours."

"Why do you want to preserve the dead scout's body?" Ghatakarpara asked irritably, hating the fact that the hangover was so obvious to everyone around.

"Because I believe a dead Huna might also be able to reveal great secrets to us."

* * *

The corner bedroom was a large but frugal affair, conspicuously out of place in the ornate environs of the palace of Ujjayini. Its expansive marble floor was completely bare, as were its plain white walls, finely washed with lime. Big, airy windows lined two of these walls, and were strung with flimsy curtains that flapped gently in the morning breeze. No furniture adorned the room other than a low divan and a simple writing table pushed against one wall, and a high bed placed nearly at the room's center.

The absence of clutter in the room seemed to reflect its occupant's outlook to life – which wasn't entirely surprising, considering the man who lay on the high bed, propped up on pillows and bolsters, was Acharya Vetala Bhatta, his hollow eyes staring tiredly out of their sockets.

The bed was surrounded by the samrat and the rest of the council, with Kalidasa, Vararuchi and Varahamihira looking understandably shocked and perplexed at the unexpected turn of events in Ujjayini. They had left a city that was strong and impregnable, only to return fifteen hours later to find it savaged and reduced to cinders.

"You really shouldn't have done what you did, raj-guru," Vikramaditya chided, though his tone implied affectionate concern rather than indignation or disapproval. "It was way too dangerous."

"I warned him against it, but who's to listen," said Dhanavantri, who was administering an unction of sandalwood and herbs on the Acharya's forehead. Contrary to the implication, there was no grumpiness about the physician either. Wiping his hands clean on a towel and shrugging nonchalantly, he added, "No one bothers about what physicians have to say anyway."

"The Ashvins had to be stopped and I couldn't think of doing it any other way." Vetala Bhatta's voice was thin but coherent, the words forming with a firmness and clarity that was reassuring. He turned to Dhanavantri, a faint smile playing on his wan, pinched face. "And speaking of following your instructions, I solemnly promise to stay in bed today and not exert myself."

"See what I meant by no one listens?" Dhanavantri shook his head in exasperation. "I didn't say rest for *today*. I said you have to rest *until* you have fully regained your strength."

The councilors exchanged smiles at the lighthearted banter, relieved to see that the raj-guru was in no great distress. Vararuchi, who was standing to the left of the bed, waited for the chuckles to die down before speaking.

"Even if it was risky and unwise, we must thank you for doing what you did, Acharya," he said. "By controlling the minds of the Ashvins, you spared Ujjayini from suffering even greater calamity at their hands."

"And you prevented them from claiming the dagger," Varahamihira added quickly, as the others nodded in agreement.

"Indeed, we arc all grateful…" Vikramaditya began, but stopped upon seeing Vetala Bhatta shake his head forcefully.

"No, no... it wasn't me. I did nothing. Yes, I tried to control their collective mind, but I failed."

Taken aback, the king and the councilors stared at one another.

"You're being modest, raj-guru," the samrat said slowly.

"I am not," Vetala Bhatta's voice was adamant. "I told you I failed."

A brief silence ensued, which was broken by the king. "Then what made the Ashvins take flight so abruptly?"

"It was you, Vikrama. You and your Hellfires."

The samrat looked down at the swords that still hung at his hips. "I don't understand..."

"I felt the fear – the terror – that took hold of the Ashvins' minds when you charged at them with the Hellfires," said the Acharya, shuddering at the recollection. "I saw the *churails* turn their cavalry to ashes, I felt their horrible pain as they died burning. It was the terror of the Hellfires that made me lose my consciousness."

Observing everyone stare at him blankly before looking at one another in confusion, the raj-guru sighed.

"I was right in guessing that the Ashvin brotherhood shared a common mind – that's how they worked so efficiently despite their large numbers, spread across such a wide area. What one Ashvin saw, felt or thought, all other Ashvins saw, felt and thought. That's the real reason why wounded Ashvins either kill themselves or are killed by their mates – so that the collective mind doesn't get crippled by the pain of the wounded."

"So, you're saying that when the Ashvins at the south gate were terrorized at the sight of the samrat with the Hellfires, their fear instantly spread to the rest of the cavalry, causing all of them to flee?" asked Kshapanaka.

Vetala Bhatta nodded. "It is possible just one Ashvin was scared, but that was enough to ignite terror in their collective mind." He paused and shook his head. "Their greatest strength ultimately became their greatest weakness."

A thoughtful stillness subsided over the group, as they mulled over what the chief advisor had just revealed.

"How are things outside?" the raj-guru asked, tilting his head toward the windows. "Bad?"

Vikramaditya nodded. He had spent the entire morning riding through the city, taking stock of the situation, offering his sympathies and paying his condolences where necessary, and assuring the petrified citizenry that Ujjayini was safe once again. Large parts of the southern and northern districts had been laid to waste by the fires, and he had witnessed much mourning and desolation. He knew it would take a while for the city to get back on its feet.

And much longer for the scars to heal.

"What are the losses we've suffered?" asked Vetala Bhatta.

"The bodies are still being counted, but we estimate close to a thousand deaths," the king stared morosely out the window. "A third of them would be civilians, most claimed by the fires. We still haven't begun making an assessment of the economic losses."

"People are bound to be scared," noted Vararuchi.

"Not just the civilians, even the soldiers are in dread," Kshapanaka pointed out. "They've never experienced anything like this in all their years in uniform."

"I agree," Kalidasa finally broke his silence. "The cavalrymen who went with us to fight the pishachas are also asking questions. There's a lot of confusion and uncertainty everywhere."

"Rumors are spreading across the city that the attackers

were the Hunas who have gained magical powers," said Shanku. "Others are talking about Avanti being cursed."

"We need to put the rumors and uncertainty to rest," said Vikramaditya decisively. "The only way of doing that is by telling the subjects of Avanti the truth about who attacked us and why."

"We will tell them about the Halahala?" Vararuchi looked at his brother doubtfully.

"We have to," the samrat replied. "We owe our people an explanation for the suffering they have undergone. If we tell them the truth, they are likely to understand and respect us for honoring the promise made to the Omniscient One."

Vararuchi nodded. "I shall have the town criers sent out right away. Would you want word to be sent all over Avanti?"

"Yes, to every town and village." The king paused, deep in thought. "Also have emissaries sent to the courts of Heheya, Matsya, Vatsa, Kosala, Magadha and the Anarta Federation. Our allies deserve to know the news as well, considering Heheya has already borne some of the brunt of the pishacha attack. In fact..." the king looked straight at Kalidasa. "...I would like you to deliver the news to King Harihara personally."

"I shall leave this evening," the giant affirmed the command.

"Vikrama, you must realize that all our allies may not be appreciative of us protecting the dagger, especially if that means dealing with threats of the sort faced by Heheya," warned the Acharya.

"Then let us use the opportunity to find out who our real allies are," answered Vikramaditya stonily.

Just then, the door opened to admit a palace attendant.

He looked tired and deflated, which was probably how everyone felt in Ujjayini that morning.

"Salutations to Samrat Vikramaditya and the Council of Nine," he said. "I bring word for the samrat." Seeing the king nod, he announced, "The queen has asked for you, your honor."

"Let the queen mother know that I shall be with her shortly," said the samrat.

Instead of following the king's orders, the attendant stood hesitating at the door. As all eyes in the room turned toward him in disapproval, he cleared his throat apologetically and stammered two sentences.

"I didn't... it was not the queen mother I meant, your honor. It is Queen Vishakha who has asked for you."

Vikramaditya and his councilors gaped at the attendant, stupefied.

* * *

The Kikata village that was going up in flames was located half a mile from the base of the hillock on which General Daipayana sat atop his horse.

The general, one of the most cunning strategists and feared warriors in Magadha, watched the burning village with satisfaction, his large, fair face flushed in excitement as he observed the tribesmen running here and there in mindless terror. Magadhan soldiers had surrounded the village from three sides, cleverly leaving just one way open for the Kikatas to flee – in an easterly direction, toward the border separating Magadha from the republic of Vanga.

Twenty-four hours earlier, six columns of the Magadhan army – each three thousand strong and comprising cavalry, infantry and archer units – had marched out of Girivraja under General Daipayana's command. The army had made its way steadily across Magadha, moving in a southeasterly direction, and a lot of ground had been covered in the first eighteen hours of travel. But the pace had dropped considerably in the last six hours, once the columns had entered the southern lowlands, the traditional homeland of the Kikatas.

On reaching the lowlands, the army had broken into smaller detachments and fanned out across the region, methodically scouring the area for Kikata settlements. In those six hours, scores of Kikata villages and hamlets had been raided and burned to the ground, hundreds of tribals had been killed or taken captive, while thousands had fled eastward.

"We must push the women, the children, the infirm and the old among the Kikatas across the border into Vanga," Daipayana had explained his strategy to an appreciative audience at the Magadhan royal council. "Vanga should be flooded with Kikata refugees – so many of them that feeding and providing them shelter should become a crisis for Vanga's governing council. Vanga must have its hands full dealing with the refugees, so that when we attack, their granaries are depleted and their supply chains are stretched to breaking point. That's how I aim to weaken Vanga's defenses."

As some of Magadha's soldiers torched the rice fields around the village, others rounded up all the able-bodied men and women and herded them to two large mango trees, where officers of the Magadhan army sat in the shade. The officers would decide how to allocate the villagers for slave labor. A couple of villagers, who appeared to put up a semblance of resistance, were summarily beheaded, their deaths serving two ends – it made the other captives more pliant and inspired the rest of the village to flee.

"At this rate, we won't have to raid many more villages," the general stroked his luxuriant, curling moustache as he addressed a subaltern who was standing beside him. "Those who have escaped will spread the word, and we all know that rumor flies on a hundred wings. Soon, there will be an exodus of Kikatas into Vanga."

"Your immaculate plan couldn't fail even if the gods so willed, lord," the flunkey gushed without a hint of shame, as he dexterously applied slaked lime on a betel leaf. "Magadha's army is blessed to have your leadership."

Daipayana grinned, pleased at the flattery. His teeth were stained dark brown, the effect of a lifelong habit of chewing *tambulam*. He reached down and accepted the flunkey's preparation, tucking the squat bundle of betel leaf and nut expertly into his right cheek.

"Look what we have for you from the village, general."

Daipayana turned around to see two junior officers standing behind him. Behind the officers, three Kikata women stood trembling at the tips of six spears and swords, wielded by half-a-dozen Magadhan soldiers.

The general's grin widened as he letched at the women, his eyes feasting on their curves. One was nearing forty, well built, bordering on buxom. The second was in her late twenties, short but slender. The third was but a girl of fifteen, frail and waif-like.

"What do you think, general?" one of the officers asked with a wicked wink.

"Very good indeed," replied Daipayana, leering obscenely. "Ideal soil to sow good Magadhan seed."

"Take your pick, general," offered the other officer.

"Which ones do *you* both want?" Daipayana asked playfully.

"Not the one the general wants," one of the officers parried.

Daipayana smiled in acknowledgment of the other's cleverness. His eyes returned to the eldest of the three women. He was always partial to bigger women. Moreover, he knew this one would be experienced. Best of all, he liked the sight of fear in her eyes.

He licked his lips in anticipation, hoping the fear would last until the end. That's the way he liked it best with women.

* * *

Vikramaditya sat on the edge of the bed, holding Vishakha's small hands in his own, staring into her blank face, searching for a glimmer of awareness in those eyes that had captivated him with their charm for so many years.

"Look, I am here," he repeated for the third time, squeezing the queen's hands softly.

There was still no response from the bed.

The samrat raised his eyes and surveyed the ring of people standing around the bed, before letting go of Vishakha's hands. Heaving a sigh filled with pain and hopelessness, he looked around the chamber.

"What exactly happened? What did she say?" he asked.

One of the two maids, the cleverer and more voluble of the two, pushed her way forward.

"I was sitting by the queen, your honor," she began her explanation. "Ever since the last time she spoke, we have been sitting by her side and observing her every moment, exactly as the honorable physician told us to, your honor."

"Good, good," said Dhanavantri, encouraging the maid

to hurry up with her narrative. "So what happened when you were sitting by the queen?"

"She suddenly spoke again. It was more like she called out."

"She asked for the king by name?" Queen Upashruti looked at the maid in mild annoyance for her inability to get to the point.

"Not at first, Queen Mother," the girl replied. "Her first words sounded to me like 'Ittitai'." Judging by the maid's expression, it was obvious that the words made no sense to her.

"Ittitai?" Queen Upashruti frowned in puzzlement for a moment, then her face cleared and she looked at Kshapanaka. "Child, wasn't Itti your mother's personal maid in the palace of Nishada?"

Kshapanaka, who was standing by the foot of the bed, nodded as she struggled to contain the tides of hope and despair that were crashing against one another inside her. Keeping her eyes on Vishakha, she walked around to her sister's side, bent down, and stroked Vishakha's forehead gently.

"Mother used to call her Itti *tai* because she was almost like her elder sister. So we also ended up addressing her as Itti *tai*." Kshapanaka's voice choked as memories of happier times came flooding back. Swallowing hard, she said, "If the queen called out for Itti *tai*, it's possible that she recalled something from our childhood."

Drooping shoulders straightened and sagging spirits lifted at Kshapanaka's words. In two full years, this was the first shred of tangible evidence pointing to Vishakha's slow and painful recovery.

"What did the queen say after that?" Vikramaditya's eyes seemed to plead with the maid.

"I was surprised by the suddenness of the queen's words, your honor. I wasn't certain if I had heard correctly either, so I asked the queen to repeat her words. She looked at me for a moment, her eyes fully alert. She then asked me where you were, your honor. Her exact words were, 'Where is Prince Vikrama?' So I asked the guards to inform you."

"What happened next?"

"Nothing, your honor. She didn't speak again... and her eyes lost their sparkle."

At a complete loss, the samrat returned his gaze to Vishakha. She had asked for him, but now that he was here, she had chosen to retreat into silence, closing the door behind her. It reminded him of the times when they used to play hide-and-seek as kids and it was his turn to do the seeking. A giggle, a rustle of clothes or a patter of feet would invariably expose Vishakha's concealment, but when he rushed over to look, he rarely ever found her where he'd thought she was hiding. Vishakha had a real knack of leaving clues and disappearing.

Rising stiffly, the king walked over to a window and leaned out, watching the branches of a nearby gulmohar sway in the breeze. The sadness in his chest felt incredibly heavy, weighing him down to the very ground he stood on.

"Why did she say *Prince* Vikrama?" he asked, turning around to face the room.

"She called for Itti *tai* before that, so as Kshapanaka said, the queen has probably started remembering things from her childhood, her distant past," offered Dhanavantri. "When she was growing up you were Prince Vikrama, so it's logical."

"What can we do to help her remember faster and recover sooner?" the king asked, striding back to the middle of the room. "There *has* to be a way."

"I'm trying all I can, my king," said Dhanavantri soothingly. "She is showing signs of recovery – we can all see that. But it will take time. You must have patience."

Though his expression suggested he was far from satisfied with the physician's advice, Vikramaditya inclined his head, allowing the matter to rest for the time being.

"I think we should all leave now," said the Queen Mother. "Let's give the queen some rest." As Dhanavantri nodded in agreement, she turned to Kshapanaka. "You may stay if you wish to, child."

"Thank you, mother," said the princess, taking a seat by the bed.

The rest of the councilors began filing out, but seeing Vikramaditya stand disconsolately by Vishakha's bed, Vararuchi paused. Laying a hand on Kalidasa's shoulder, he held the giant back. The two men exchanged meaningful glances before approaching the king.

"Why don't you be with the queen for a while, brother?" Vararuchi suggested. "Maybe your being here would help."

"Yes, why don't you?" said Dhanavantri, joining the group. Placing a comforting hand on the king's arm, he added, "More than any of my medicines, it is your faith that has brought her back this far."

Vikramaditya turned and looked out the southern window. In the distance, he could see a fog of dense, gray smoke suspended over the city, hovering like an enormous predatory bird in search of a feast among the charred and gutted ruins below. He knew a similar fog hung over the northern quarter of Ujjayini as well.

"Don't worry about the city, friend," said Kalidasa, reading the king's thoughts. "Leave that to me, Vararuchi and Shanku. We will take care of everything."

The samrat assessed the three councilors before looking down at Vishakha, lying quietly in the bed, cold and indifferent to the agony she was causing. Tearing his eyes away from her, Vikramaditya shook his head.

"Right now, the city and its people need me," he said. With that, he marched out of the door.

* * *

"I admit we judged the human king poorly," muttered Shukracharya with a regretful shake of his head. "If it's any consolation, we weren't the only ones to make that mistake. The devas too greatly underestimated his ability and determination to protect the Halahala – and they probably paid a higher price for it than we did."

"That is no consolation, mahaguru," answered Hiranyaksha, fixing a baleful eye on the high priest. "We have lost a feared rakshasa in Andhaka, the pishacha force has been routed and demoralized, and the dagger is nowhere within our grasp."

The sage and the asura lord were alone in the latter's court. Hiranyaksha sat on his crystal throne nursing a goblet of *soma*, while Shukracharya paced the floor, hands clasped behind him, deep in thought.

"The Omniscient One chose wisely when he picked Vikramaditya to protect the dagger," the sage said, half to himself.

"Yet, he's only a *human being*." Hiranyaksha smacked his thigh and stood up in agitation, spilling some of the *soma*. "No human has ever dared to stand in the way of the asuras."

"This king is no ordinary human," the sage cautioned. "Don't forget he wields the Hellfires, which were forged in the eternal flames of Naraka by your very own mother."

"I wonder how the Hellfires found their way into this human's hands," Hiranyaksha frowned, descending the steps from his throne.

"They were given to him by the demon Laayushi." Seeing the asura lord's eyes narrow in surprise, Shukracharya nodded. "Yes, the same Laayushi – your half-brother Paurava's servant. I just learned about it from the bones."

"How come the bones didn't tell you all this when you consulted them the first time?" The asura's voice trembled with displeasure.

"The bones don't volunteer information, I've said this before. They only reveal answers to specific questions, that too in cryptic riddles. Knowing nothing about the Hellfires being in the king's possession, I naturally had no reason to inquire about them earlier." Shukracharya once again shook his head ruefully. "But yes, I do wish I had tried to learn more about the human king before sending Andhaka to his death."

Though he couldn't fault the high priest's logic, Hiranyaksha still looked unhappy. Then, a fresh thought occurred to him and he appraised Shukracharya again. "But Andhaka and the pishachas didn't fight Vikramaditya – you say they were confronted by three of his generals, one of them lame in one leg. How did these generals get the better of Andhaka and an army of fearsome pishachas?"

"The three generals are a part of Vikramaditya's Council of Nine – nine intrepid warriors, each the bearer of one of the Nine Sacred Pearls."

"They bear the Nine Pearls, these nine warriors?" The asura lord scrutinized Shukracharya with a mixture of wonder and unease.

"They draw their unique strengths and capabilities from

the pearls, yes..." Shukracharya paused to permit himself an ironic smile. "Yet, not one of them has any knowledge of the existence of the Nine Pearls. The nine know nothing of the remarkable powers that each of them has at their disposal. Should they ever learn how to fully harness the pearls' powers, the Council of Nine would be impossible to defeat."

"A king who wields the Hellfires – and nine councilors who aren't aware of their own strengths but still manage handing us a defeat..." A female voice rang through the empty court, clear as a bell. "Are you saying that the full might of the asura army cannot crush these humans, mahaguru?"

The sage and Hiranyaksha turned to see Holika approach them, the golden-eyed infant in her arms. A little behind her was an asura child not very much older than the infant, trotting on chubby legs. The child's skin was golden and eyes blue like Holika's, but it had a thick mop of coarse golden hair distinct from hers, which was black. Two stubby horns thrust out from under the golden growth, giving the child an impish innocence.

"Oh, I'm sure they can be crushed," Shukracharya gave a dismissive wave of his hand.

"Good," said Hiranyaksha, planting himself firmly in front of the high priest, his voice echoing in the galleries above. "Then let us storm Sindhuvarta and put an end to this bit of nonsense that has already gone too far."

"That is one option..."

Hiranyaksha stared hard at the sage. "Are there others, mahaguru?"

"Friendship," Shukracharya shrugged. "Why go to war against the humans when we can bring them to our side? The king and his council are brave warriors and can make worthy allies in our fight against the devas."

"But why would Vikramaditya accept our hand in friendship when he turned down a similar offer from the devas?" asked the Witch Queen. "Didn't he tell Narada that he wouldn't part with the Halahala in exchange for friendship?"

Seeing the sage nod, the asura lord scratched his cheek in bewilderment. "Then why would we succeed where Narada failed?"

"Narada failed because he didn't think of employing one little ploy, which I'm sure would have had the desired result," the high priest gave a sly smile.

"I fail to comprehend you, mahaguru."

"Every human being has a weakness that can be exploited, a soft spot that makes him or her utterly vulnerable," said Shukracharya, seating himself on one of the courtiers' chairs. "The bones have exposed the chink in the human king's armor."

"What is his weakness?" Hiranyaksha asked in rising excitement.

"His deep love for Vishakha, his invalid wife. The bones tell me that King Vikramaditya will go to any lengths to have her cured..." The sage stroked his beard, a scheming, faraway look in his eyes. "It's time I paid the court of Avanti a visit."

Scouts

Hundreds of brightly colored kites, wheeling and tugging and soaring in the wind, filled the dazzling blue sky above Sravasti. Down below, the kite flyers lined the northern and southern banks of the Ajiravati, which meandered through Sravasti, splitting the capital of Kosala into two almost equal halves. The kite flyers, who represented teams from the two parts of the city, wrestled with the strings, trying their best to bring down the kites flown by their rivals from across the river. Spectators on both sides cheered these efforts, and the air was distinctly festive and generous.

However, barely half a mile from the river, deep in the heart of the royal palace of Kosala, the mood was contrastingly somber. A dozen courtiers sat in silence around King Bhoomipala and Pallavan, the former pulling at his thick, graying beard as he pondered over what he had just been told.

"Could this man be lying?" the king looked up at Pallavan. "Perhaps he has some personal grudge or an agenda of his own?"

"I don't think so, your honor," the diplomat considered the question before answering. "There was genuine fear in his eyes when he threw himself before the cavalcade yesterday. Moreover, what could he possibly gain by falsely accusing Shoorasena of murdering his father? He's not even a Kikata, which rules out the motive of vengeance for the killings taking place all over Magadha." Pallavan's face wrinkled in distaste at the memory of the lynch mobs he had seen through his carriage windows. "No, your honor. I'm certain he's nothing more than a moderately talented traveling musician who entertains at palaces."

The king mulled this over. "What was he doing in the palace garden that morning?"

"He had been put up at the palace of Girivraja because King Siddhasena had, in his kindness, offered him shelter for the night after a performance. It is sheer coincidence that he chose to take a walk in the palace garden the next morning and saw what really occurred on the garden steps."

"It does make sense," Bhoomipala nodded slowly. "Shoorasena probably chose that spot to kill Siddhasena, because he knew the garden would be deserted at that time of day. What he didn't account for was the possibility of an outsider being present and accidentally witnessing his dastardly deed."

Another brief silence enveloped the room, until the king posed a question. "But why did he do it? Siddhasena was ailing and didn't have much longer to live... Was Shoorasena so desperate to become king of Magadha?"

"Shocking though it is, your honor, this has less to do with the death of King Siddhasena, and is more about the cold-blooded killing of the Kikata bodyguard that followed," said Pallavan, displaying remarkable perspicacity. "The musician speaks of how Shoorasena pinned the king's death on the bodyguard and whipped up passions against the Kikatas in no time. King Siddhasena wasn't killed because Shoorasena wanted Magadha's throne – he was killed so that Shoorasena could pursue war against the Kikatas and Vanga."

"You're right," said Bhoomipala, recalling how Shoora-sena had made his intent of waging war against the republic clear at Vikramaditya's *rajasuya yajna*. "And you say Shoorasena has refused to honor his father's promise of sending soldiers to defend Sindhuvarta against the Hunas and the Sakas?"

"In no uncertain terms, your honor."

The king sighed. "It looks like we have lost an ally with the passing of Siddhasena."

"What do you propose we do now, your honor?" asked one of the courtiers.

"For one, we will have to keep an ear close to the ground for developments in the east. I want our network of spies in Magadha strengthened immediately. And have some spies sent to Vanga as well. We will also need reports more regularly. See to that."

"What about the musician?" the courtier asked.

"For his own good, he had better give up on traveling for some time," shrugged Bhoomipala. "Keep him in Sravasti for a while, until we can think of what to do with him. But as long as he isn't in the habit of talking too much, I think he's safe."

"Shouldn't we also inform the rest of our allies about Magadha's decision not to assist in defending Sindhuvarta?" Pallavan reminded.

"Why just that...? We must inform them about what we have learned of Siddhasena's death as well." Bhoomipala's face hardened as he spoke. "The king was an old and trusted friend. Shoorasena's sins are piling up, and in my opinion, he has to pay dearly for them."

* * *

The heavy wooden door, fortified with thick iron ribs and sturdy bolts, swung open to admit Commander Dattaka.

The commander looked around the medium-sized cell with its rough stone floor and walls. Amara Simha stood leaning against one of the walls, arms crossed on his chest, while Ghatakarpara and the command center's translator sat facing each other across a crude wooden table. Seeing all three men turn to him inquiringly, Dattaka nodded silently.

Ghatakarpara immediately vacated his place at the table, and was replaced by Amara Simha. The four men once again exchanged glances before Amara Simha glared at the translator.

"I'm warning you one last time – don't test my patience. Who are you and what are you doing in Sristhali?"

"*Ma'a ugr an'hi, keberez*," the translator babbled, injecting the right amount of panic in his voice. His words roughly translated as 'I can't understand you, have mercy.'

"I know you can speak the Avanti tongue, so stop this gibberish," Amara Simha raised his voice. "You are spying for the Hunas, aren't you?"

"*Ma'a ugr an'hi...*" the translator began again, but he was cut short by Amara Simha's roar.

"Enough!" The councilor smacked a heavy fist into his left palm. The brief echo of the slap was drowned out by the translator's agonized wail.

"*Keberez, keberez...*" he whimpered, and for a split second, Amara Simha was thrown aback by the ring of authenticity in the plea. The translator was proving to be a far better actor than expected.

"Speak out, you pig! Out with the truth!"

"*Edha unnu a'gaia h'lum. Ma'a gois khaar'i waa.*" Don't beat me anymore; I'm only a petty thief on the run.

"I'll tear you to shreds, dog."

Amara Simha banged the table so hard it made both Dattaka and Ghatakarpara jump in surprise. The translator stared in shock at the deep crack that had appeared in the wood, but gathering his wits quickly, he yelped in pain.

"*Amgo pa'ith... amgo pa'ith...*" My hand, my hand.

"Speak, you Huna dog, speak..."

For a few more minutes, Amara Simha and the translator went on and on, the former smacking his fists, hammering the table and hurling abuses, the latter screaming and begging for mercy. The cell's walls were made of stone, but there was enough ventilation near the roof for sounds to escape – Amara Simha made it a point to amplify all noises – to the neighboring cell, where Dattaka's men had deposited the suspected scout from Uttashi.

Amara Simha stepped around the table and locked the translator's head in a mock death grip. "I'll have the truth or I'll have your head," he growled. "You're not the only Huna scout in the world. We will find more and get them to talk, and you will lose your life for nothing. So tell us what you know and I'll let you go."

The translator gurgled something unintelligible, the words ending in yet another choking scream.

"To hell with him," Amara Simha shouted at Dattaka. "If he won't talk, string him up in the courtyard." With that, he banged open the door of the cell and marched out.

Shortly, two soldiers carried the body of the scout who had died earlier that morning across the courtyard, in full view of the cell where the traveling carpenter from Uttashi was housed. The body was between the soldiers, carried with its arms draped across their shoulders, head slumped forward, feet dragging in the mud, one swollen leg twisted horribly.

To all appearances, the scout was alive, though severely tortured and on the brink of losing all consciousness.

The soldiers took the body to the far end of the courtyard and hoisted it up on a gibbet. Once the body was in place, Amara Simha marched up to the gibbet. He slapped the dead man's face a couple of times, demanding answers to his questions – and then he stepped back and drew a sword from his belt.

Without warning, he plunged the sword into the corpse's belly, once, twice, three times. Then grabbing the head by the hair, he severed the corpse's head off its trunk.

Barely a minute had elapsed before Dattaka opened the door to the carpenter's cell. The hostage was cowering by the window that looked out into the courtyard, his face pale, fear in his small brown eyes. His expression turned to outright terror when he observed Dattaka step back from the door to admit the burly girth of Amara Simha.

The councilor walked into the cell holding the severed head in one hand and the sword in the other. Both head and sword dripped a trail of blood – though the hostage had no way of knowing that both had merely been dipped in the blood of a freshly-slaughtered goat.

"Are you the carpenter?" Amara Simha demanded sternly. The goat's blood was splattered liberally across his torso, and a few big drops clung to his flaming beard as well.

The hostage nodded.

"Good, that means you also understand the Avanti tongue, unlike this bastard." Amara Simha lifted the head of the dead scout and plonked it on the bare wooden table, the blood smearing its surface in unruly streaks and swishes.

Again the hostage nodded, his eyes transfixed on the head.

"Are you going to talk, or would you prefer a fate similar to your friend's?"

As the hostage nodded a third time, he retched heavily. At the same time, he wet himself with fear, the stain spreading down the front of his dirty dhoti. He grabbed the edge of the table to steady himself, the urine pooling at his feet.

"I will tell you everything," he wheezed. "Everything... I promise. Just don't kill me, please."

***

Under his rich golden beard, Indra's face was a deep shade of red, his blue eyes dark and stormy. Heavy lines creased his brow, and the cords in his neck stood out stiffly as he hunched his muscular shoulders, clenching his fists into tight balls so the knuckles turned white. He took large, loping strides around the great hallway of his palace, circling a small knot of devas who stood fidgeting, their eyes following their king with apprehension.

"You have brought humiliation upon yourselves and

all of Devaloka," he spat out, flinging a furious glance in the direction of Nasatya and Dasra, who were part of the group huddled in the center of the hall. "I don't know which appalls me more – your flight from the human army or the shamelessness with which you present yourself here!"

"It was the Hellfires, mighty king," Nasatya mumbled, his head hanging in dejection. He made it a point to avoid any eye contact with Indra.

The lord of the devas spun around to face the group. "It's heartening to know that two miserable fire swords are all it takes to give the Ashvin cavalry wings," he said sarcastically. "And here I always counted the Brotherhood among the most fearless of my warriors."

"Please believe us when we say we had the city at our mercy, lord," Dasra entreated. "It was only when the Wielder…"

"No more," ordered Indra, raising one heavy hand. "Hearing about your grand failure over and over again gives me no pleasure. Take your leave. I have more pressing matters to discuss with Guru Brihaspati and Narada."

Nasatya and Dasra bowed deeply. Keeping their eyes averted, the disgraced twins vacated the hall, their footsteps receding down the corridor at the far end.

Once silence had regained the hall, a deva from the group took a step forward. He was short and plump and bowlegged, though it was hard to say if the last was by virtue of his weight or his age. He looked old, yet his skin was strangely free of wrinkles, his fair face smooth and shiny, merging seamlessly with his bald head ringed with a thin crescent of white hair.

"Pardon me for saying so, lord, but I think you were harsh on the Ashvins," he said.

In all of Devaloka, this particular deva was probably the only one capable of venturing such a statement without fear of censure. For as royal chamberlain of the devas, Guru Brihaspati was accorded immense esteem by Indra – by all accounts the rarest of rare privileges.

"Hmph!" said Indra, folding his hands across his chest in annoyance.

"Admittedly they didn't cover themselves with glory by fleeing from battle, but there's no escaping the fact that they were against the Hellfires," Brihaspati reasoned. "We're all fully aware of the capabilities of those demonic swords."

"The Hellfires," Indra repeated with the shake of his head. "I didn't even know those swords still existed somewhere the three worlds." Pausing for a fraction of a second, he demanded hotly, "How can we even be certain they were the Hellfires? Maybe they were not and the Ashvins made a mistake."

"You heard Nasatya and Dasra describing them, lord," replied Brihaspati. "The flaming whips, the malevolent *churails* … They can be nothing but Diti's thoughtless creations."

As Indra subsided into a grim silence, a lilting voice, clear as tinkling glass and fresh as the dewdrops on lotus buds, broke the silence.

"What are these Hellfires and why do they worry our lordship so much, gurudev?"

All those present turned to the far recesses of the hallway, where Urvashi graced a broad teakwood swing. The apsara was draped delectably across the swing, its gentle to-and-fro motion making the light and shadow fall alternately on her shapely form, accentuating the curve of her hips, and highlighting the softness of her waist and her generous breasts. The devas' flagging spirits lifted by just watching her, as she considered them with a provocative tilt of the head.

Seeing that she had everyone's undivided attention, Urvashi swung her long legs off the swing and stood up. Walking to the accompaniment of dainty bronze anklets, she approached the group, her deep black eyes on Brihaspati. Despite the seductive sway of her hips, her expression was one of earnest curiosity.

"The Hellfires," Brihaspati sighed, as if not knowing where to begin. "They were... they *are* a pair of magical swords that the sorceress Diti, second wife of Sage Kashyapa, fashioned for her oldest sons, the asura lords Hiranyakashipu and Hiranyaksha. Bathed by her blood and the milk of her breast, infused with the most terrible of mantras, and fanned and tempered by the fires of Naraka, the Hellfires are possessed by the spirits of fiery *churails*. He who wields the swords can unleash these *churails* of Naraka to tame the mightiest of armies."

"And the purpose of these swords was to help Hiranyakashipu and Hiranyaksha in their campaigns against us devas, I presume?" asked Urvashi.

"Indeed," said Narada, leaping into the conversation, eager to have a share of the beautiful apsara's attention. "Diti meant the Hellfires to be the most potent weapons in the asura arsenal. Her intention was to annihilate us with the swords."

Urvashi's eyes grew wide with fear, but it was mostly for effect, in keeping with the dramatic moment. Deep inside, there was rapt, childlike excitement and anticipation about the unfolding narrative.

"And Diti would have succeeded in her scheme – had it not been for that one mistake of hers," Brihaspati reclaimed the thread of the narrative. It almost appeared as if he and Narada were openly vying for the right to tell Urvashi the story. "She took the swords to her husband to have them blessed by him as well."

"Of course, Sage Kashyapa, in his infinite wisdom, instantly saw the threat that the Hellfires posed to righteousness," Narada once again elbowed his way in. "But he also knew he had to keep Diti happy. So, with great ingenuity, he blessed the swords – commanding them to obey nothing but the will of the most virtuous of warriors."

"You're saying that with his blessing, the sage rendered the Hellfires ineffective in the hands of the cruel Hiranyakashipu and Hiranyaksha?" Urvashi looked at Narada, her eyes wide with admiration. "A true masterstroke!"

"Not just Hiranyakashipu and Hiranyaksha," Narada chuckled, enjoying the attention the apsara was lavishing on him. "The swords were useless in the hands of every asura except Diti's youngest son, the noble Paurava. That, of course, was never a concern for us as Paurava led the life of a harmless ascetic, caring nothing for war and asura glory. So thanks to Sage Kashyapa's presence of mind, the power of the Hellfires had been blunted."

Urvashi considered this for a moment. "If the swords are so potent, how come we devas never tried to get our hands on them?" She studied the faces around her one by one, her own face a picture of doe-like innocence. "Wouldn't they have been priceless in our battle against the asuras?"

The assembled devas shuffled their feet and glanced at one another out of the corners of their eyes. Neither Brihaspati nor Narada, who until now had been so eager to engage the apsara in conversation, opened their mouths. Even Indra, who had been hanging back and observing the goings-on in surly silence, quickly resumed pacing the floor to avoid answering the apsara.

"It would have been supremely ironical to have used the Hellfires against the asuras, and I hear we did try, didn't we, father?"

The speaker was a young deva, fair and of medium build, who had entered the hallway unnoticed. He had a prominent, hooked nose, but his cheeks hadn't lost their adolescent softness, and his lips were pink, fleshy and feminine. His eyes, however, were peevish and challenging as they appraised the lord of the devas. This was Jayanta, first-born son of Indra of his lawfully wedded wife, Shachi.

The king cast a reproachful glance at his son, but didn't reply.

"I'm sure we tried, isn't it, gurudev?" Jayanta turned to Brihaspati with a slight smirk.

"Yes," said the chamberlain, clearing his throat reluctantly. "Unfortunately, the swords didn't... had stopped being responsive. Probably they had dulled with age and lack of use."

"Yet, after all these years, they seem to have responded admirably to the will of the human king," Jayanta remarked with a facetious grin.

Urvashi's eyes flickered over the prince's smug face before returning to the sage, who looked distinctly ill at ease with the turn the conversation had taken. "Do we know how the human king came to possess the swords, gurudev?"

"I'm afraid not," Brihaspati replied, his manner stilted. "We had lost interest in the Hellfires a long time ago, so we never kept track of them."

"Nor does it matter," snapped Indra, stopping in his stride. He hadn't liked the tone of Jayanta's needling, and he liked the hint of awe in Urvashi's voice, as she spoke of the human king, even less. "Too much is being made of these swords; too much has *always* been made of them. We must concern ourselves with retrieving Veeshada's dagger instead. That's all that matters."

"Let me lead an army to Sindhuvarta," said Jayanta promptly, a swagger in his voice. "I shall show the human king his place and return with the Halahala – and the Hellfires."

An awkward silence prevailed in the hallway in the wake of the prince's words. As the others held their breaths, Indra gave his son a withering look.

"This is no job for a callow boy," he said. Without pausing for a response, he clapped his hands loudly. Immediately, a large garuda appeared at a doorway and made its way to the center of the hall.

"Yes, mighty king?" the garuda said, bowing respectfully.

"Send word to the Maruts," ordered Indra. "Let them know that I have summoned them to the palace."

The garuda bowed and straightened. "As you wish, my king... But the Maruts are not in Devaloka at the moment. They are..."

"I don't care where they are. Find them and have them sent to me."

Before anything more could be said, the lord of the devas stalked out of the hall without ceremony. The garuda watched the retreating figure for a moment before withdrawing quietly. Narada, Brihaspati and a couple of other devas exchanged unsure glances, and slowly the group broke up, everyone finding some excuse or the other to make what under the circumstances could pass off as a graceful exit.

Eventually, only Urvashi and Jayanta were left standing in the hall.

The apsara slowly approached the young prince, who stood with drooping shoulders, a resentful expression on his face. Coming very close, she raised her hand and traced a finger down his left cheek.

"Boy," she whispered, pouting and tut-tutting coquettishly. "My lordship called you a *boy*."

Jayanta, whose lips were quivering with hurt, snapped his head back and grabbed Urvashi's wrist. "I am not a boy and I can show you that – if only you'd let me," he hissed fiercely.

The apsara struggled to free herself, but Jayanta gripped her hand tight and pulled her close. The swell of her breast pressed against his arm, the intoxicating scent of her hair filling his senses. He could feel the warm breath escaping from her luscious, half-open lips, inches away from his own.

"You know I love you, Urvashi," he said, his breath ragged. "And I know you can't resist thinking of me, even when you're in father's bed. So why do you deny the love that is rightfully ours?"

"I'm mistress to the mighty lord of the devas," Urvashi murmured. "What makes you think I would fancy you, callow boy?"

"I can see the desire in your eyes. The way you look at me... the way you are looking at me right now. You are drawn to me, you want me."

The apsara stared deep into Jayanta's eyes and the prince felt her melting in his arms. Then all of a sudden, Urvashi twisted and pulled and slipped from his grasp. As Jayanta stared at her in dismay, she shook a finger at him playfully, her agile face alight with a teasing smile.

"Don't let my lordship ever catch you like this with me," she giggled. "You know he is very jealous and possessive about me. The consequences could be severe for you."

With that she turned around and departed, leaving Jayanta with an empty, bitter ache in his chest. And an unfulfilled longing in his loins.

* * *

"Can we believe what the scout has told us?" Ghatakarpara eyed Amara Simha, who sat chewing his lower lip.

"There's no reason not to. He's scared out of his wits. Given his state, it would be hard for him to conceal anything out of fear of ending up short of a head."

"Using the dead scout was a very clever ploy to open him up, your honor," marveled Dattaka, in whose room the two councilors now sat. "We had him singing without even laying a finger on him."

"More than threats and torture, proof of death is an effective method of extracting the truth," said Amara Simha. "A ruthless killing tells your hostage that human life is entirely dispensable to you. And when done right, it also plants the idea that you may not put enough premium on the information he possesses to spare his life. I use the tactic whenever there's a dead body handy."

For a while, the three men mulled over what they had learned from their hostage.

"A force of approximately twenty thousand Hunas is stationed in the Great Desert, four days' ride from the frontier," Ghatakarpara cocked an eyebrow at his companions. "That's not very far, especially if they choose to ride hard."

"But the scout also said that they have been encamped for

over two months, and that there have been no indications of moving the troops closer to the Arbudas," Dattaka pointed out. "If they plan to attack, they'll have to establish bases a lot closer to the frontier; a four-day ride in the desert heat will leave anyone exhausted and incapable of fighting. To me, the camp the scout spoke of looks more like a node for coordinating movements and setting up supply chains."

"You're probably right," agreed Amara Simha. "Also, twenty thousand troops is too insufficient a number to stage a full-fledged invasion into enemy territory. They'll need three or four times as many if they want to come deep into Sindhuvarta and hold captured ground – which I believe is the Hunas' intent."

Dattaka gave an emphatic nod. "Moreover, if you remember, the scout let it slip that troops seem to be in short supply, as soldiers are being diverted to shore up a planned assault on the Anartas. So, while we must be on our toes, I'd rule out an immediate threat here."

A brief, contemplative silence was broken by Ghatakarpara.

"Do you do think the scout was being truthful about the Hunas' plan to attack the Anarta Federation by sea?" Seeing an indecisive furrow on Amara Simha's brow, the prince said, "They've never attempted anything like this before. The Hunas and Sakas aren't seafaring people, and they've never had a navy to speak of."

"That doesn't mean they aren't planning to do it," the big man answered. "Over the last ten years, they may have acquired the technology to build large boats and the skill to navigate them. And it's logical – an attack from the sea is the only way the Hunas can gain quick access to the fertile hinterland and rich trading centers of the five Anarta city states."

"It is also the quickest way of crippling the kingdoms of Sindhuvarta economically," added Dattaka. "The Anarta Federation has always been relatively safe from the Hunas and Sakas, giving us and our other allies significant strategic and financial depth. But if the Anarta states were to fall to the Hunas, our trade routes to the west through the ports of Dvarka and Bhrigukaksha would get blocked. Supply of essential raw materials would stop, while earnings from exports would be hit, adding to the strain on the royal exchequer."

Amara Simha stared at the commander with newfound respect. But for the stupidity that had resulted in the death of the first scout, Dattaka had displayed great efficiency, and now from his words, it seemed his analytical skills were considerable.

"Absolutely right, commander," said Amara Simha, sitting up in his chair. "I'm now beginning to see why the Hunas attacked our outpost and delivered that threat through the captain of the Guards. It's not like them to issue warnings before an attack, and that's been bothering me. It was a decoy to draw all our attention to the frontier, so they could spring a surprise naval attack on the Anarta states. By the time we redeployed, the Anartas would have been taken. Look at it – they alert us saying they are coming, but there are just twenty thousand Hunas out on the Marusthali. See, everything falls perfectly into place!"

Spurred by his thoughts, the burly councilor leaped up from his seat. "Yugandhara and the other Anarta chiefs need to be told about this threat immediately, so that they can take necessary precautions." He peered out of the window at the gathering dusk and gave a rueful snort. "The sun's already set – too late to use the *suryayantra* now. But the news must be relayed to Ujjayini as soon as the sun is up tomorrow morning, commander. Without fail. Make sure the operators send…"

Amara Simha was interrupted by a sharp rap on the door. As he turned, the door opened unbidden to reveal the command center's physician standing on the threshold. The old man was about to step in when he noticed Amara Simha regarding him with a stern gaze. In two minds, the physician held back, looking at Dattaka with indecisive eyes.

"Yes, what is it?" asked the commander, rising and going to the door. "We are a bit busy."

The physician still hesitated, casting doubtful glances in the direction of the two councilors, not excusing himself, not taking the hint, not leaving.

"What's happened, good sir?" Amara Simha raised an eyebrow, sensing that something was troubling the man.

"It's not very important, really," the physician mumbled, even as he allowed Dattaka to take him by the shoulder and draw him gently into the room. "I didn't mean to intrude, but…"

"It's fine. Tell us what the matter is."

"I…" the physician licked his lips nervously. "I suspect the scout we captured… I mean the one who died this morning… he died of poisoning."

Amara Simha, Ghatakarpara and Dattaka stared at one another, perplexed.

"How did you figure this out?"

"I was examining the dead body before it was sent for cremation when I found a suspicious wound on the scout's right foot."

"What kind of wound?"

"They were marks left by the fangs of a snake. What

made me certain was the skin around the wound – it had been discolored by the venom."

"Snakebite?" Ghatakarpara stared in surprise. "That explains how the scout ended up in the ditch where he was found by our guardsmen. It also explains the broken leg; he must have fallen badly. And his delirium…"

"There's a problem in that," the physician interposed. "I gathered traces of the venom and analyzed it. The snake that bit the scout was a king cobra, and the venom of the king cobra kills in a few hours – whereas the scout was alive here the whole of yesterday. And no one here treated him for snakebite."

Amara Simha walked over to the open window, which overlooked the rivulet and the town of Sristhali. Five mules, laden with blocks of marble, were crossing the bridge into the town.

"So, the scout was not bitten by the snake in the hills," the older councilor surmised, gazing out. He turned to Dattaka. "When was the last time anyone checked if the scout was alive?"

"The physician and I went to his cell after the two of you and Governor Satyaveda had retired for the night," the commander vouched. "It was a little after midnight. The scout was unconscious, but most definitely alive, your honor."

"Yet, early this morning he was dead." Amara Simha breathed in deeply and looked at the three men facing him. "So, he was bitten sometime between midnight and daybreak, and he died without regaining consciousness."

"Did anyone notice a king cobra anywhere this morning?" asked Ghatakarpara.

Dattaka shrugged. "Not in the scout's cell, I can say for sure."

"I wonder if a wild king cobra could slip into those cells, bite an inmate and slip out again unnoticed," said Amara Simha. "The doors are solid, there are no convenient cracks and holes in the walls, and the windows are placed very high. It somehow seems too easy."

"Another thing, your honor," the commander's face was suddenly serious. "The king cobra is a native of dense, tropical forests. These dry mountains aren't its natural habitat. In fact, I've never seen a wild king cobra in these parts – *ever*."

"So, the one that bit the scout was probably brought here and let into the cell with the intention of murder. The idea was to pass the death off as one brought about by the beating the scout had received earlier yesterday."

"But who would kill the scout in such a manner? And why?" The commander stared at Amara Simha in astonishment.

"I can tell you why – to keep him from revealing anything to us once he returned to consciousness. The 'who' would be trickier to detect and hard to prove. It would require some investigation. But I can guarantee that whoever did this is working for the Hunas. And he is among us in this command center."

In the hush that ensued, Amara Simha's words came out loud, though he had dropped his voice to an undertone. "We won't use the *suryayantra* to send word of the threat to the Anartas, commander. It's no longer safe to communicate so openly. We'll dispatch a trusted rider to Ujjayini instead. I will prepare a detailed report for the samrat, and he can then send an emissary to Chief Yugandhara's court."

Dattaka began nodding in agreement, but stopped on seeing Ghatakarpara frown.

"Wouldn't we lose precious time this way?" the prince

asked. "The rider will first travel east to Ujjayini for a day-and-a-half, maybe two. Then, the emissary will travel west to Dvarka, covering the distance in two or three days. The news won't reach Chief Yugandhara for nearly a week."

"What do you suggest?" quizzed Amara Simha.

"I can leave for Dvarka right now – or perhaps at the crack of dawn tomorrow. It won't take me more than two days to deliver the same message directly to Chief Yugandhara. I have the royal seal of Avanti, so I can represent the samrat's court, can't I?"

"That's possible," admitted Amara Simha, wondering why the bright idea hadn't occurred to him first. Perhaps it was age catching up, slowing him down. "Yes, I think that would work well. But you're not going alone."

"I won't." The prince looked excited at the prospect of finally doing something of relevance all by himself, instead of merely tagging along like a passenger. "I'll take half a dozen of Dattaka's men as escort."

"Sure," agreed the commander. "My men will be ready whenever you are."

* * *

"How is Vishakha?" the Acharya inquired. "Any further... signs of improvement?"

Vikramaditya shook his head, his face drawn and tired in the light of the two lamps in the room. "Nothing since this morning."

The Acharya was sitting up in his bed. He looked rested, and his face had recovered some of its vigor. He was holding an earthenware cup, which he periodically raised to his lips, shuddering each time the thick, bitter potion passed down his gullet.

"What does Dhanavantri say?"

"He asks for faith and patience," the samrat replied. From his tone, he appeared disenchanted.

"Then we must have faith and patience, Vikrama," said the raj-guru, assessing the king's mood. "Dhanavantri knows what he's saying – and he's doing what he can."

The king swallowed heavily and nodded.

"I could probably have tried reading her mind had I been stronger," the Acharya ventured halfheartedly, the lack of enthusiasm betraying what he really thought of the idea.

"We need you to regain your health first," the samrat answered with another shake of his head. "Right now that's more important."

"How's the city coping?" Vetala Bhatta changed the topic after a pause.

Vikramaditya looked out the open window. The action was reflexive, though. The king appeared to be absorbed in some keen inner debate, his vision unfocussed as he stared into the darkness outside. "It's limping back," he said at last. "We're doing everything we can to instill courage."

"And how's the news of our having been attacked by the devas and asuras being taken by the people?"

"It's still early to gauge and the full significance of what's happening is probably yet to filter down, but the reaction is mixed." A small smile appeared on the king's face. "In some quarters, there's genuine pride that the Omniscient One chose Avanti to protect the Halahala. And of course, there's a sense of triumph at having won both the battles. But there are others who are in absolute fear of reprisals and refuse to be assured. Kalidasa and Vararuchi tell me that many among this lot are bound to leave the city and return to the safety of their villages."

"There isn't much we can do about that," the Acharya noted. "In fact, those who choose to leave might be the smarter ones."

The bluntness of the words hung in the stillness of the room like a portentous cloud.

Vikramaditya slowly rose from his chair and reached out for the empty cup in the chief advisor's hand. Placing the cup on a small table by the bedside, he turned to the raj-guru.

"That's why you have to regain your health quickly, Acharya," he said. "I need you to help me make a journey to the Borderworld."

"The Borderworld?" Vetala Bhatta's eyebrows rose sharply over his troubled eyes.

"I foresee the devas and the asuras returning – the Omniscient One predicted as much when he gave me the dagger. The Ashvins breached the city's gates and weren't very far from where we now sit. I fear the palace is too vulnerable. The only safe place I can think of for the Halahala is the Borderworld."

The Acharya sighed deeply. "You intend leaving the dagger in the custody of the Ghoulmaster?"

Vikramaditya nodded. "It's time to redeem the pledge that the Betaal had made to me."

Oracle

The procession that wound through the ragged hills consisted of four palanquin bearers and a dozen horsemen of the Imperial Army, six each riding in front of and behind the empty palanquin. The palanquin, its domed roof painted with the sun-crest of Avanti to denote its official status, was modest. Shorn of the extravagant craftsmanship commonly associated with palace palanquins, it was built of plain wood, with plain cotton upholstery and light muslin curtains. Vikramaditya had chosen it with great care, knowing that if he were to succeed in this mission, a balance between pomp and simplicity would be of essence.

Progress was slow, the palanquin bearers impeded by the uneven terrain. As an outcome, the procession had been greatly outpaced by Vikramaditya and Shanku, who were now nearly half a mile ahead, making their way across a flat expanse of gently sloping rock. The surrounding hills were silent, the metallic echo of the horseshoes magnifying in the stillness.

Shanku reined in her horse and the king followed suit. He watched the girl raise her head and whistle, mimicking the koel's call to perfection. She then tilted her head, listening intently, and the samrat did likewise. But however hard he tried, Vikramaditya could hear nothing but the low, rhythmic '*hoi-hui… hoi-hui… hoi-hui*' chant coming from the palanquin bearers as they kept in step with the beat.

Then, from somewhere far in the distance, he thought he heard the cry of another bird, faint yet harsh. Shanku pointed to her left, indicating the way forward.

Waiting for the rest of the procession to catch up, the king glanced at Shanku, marveling at the young girl's talents. Observing her quiet countenance and her large eyes burning with quiet intensity, he could see why Kalidasa was attracted to this woman. Though opposites in build, the two shared a rocklike resolve, both had deep reservoirs of patience and commonsense, and their outlook to life was molded by an early loss of identity – and a gradual coming-to-terms with that loss.

However, seeing her sitting astride her horse that morning, Vikramaditya thought he also detected a sense of resignation in Shanku's manner.

"You don't think the Mother Oracle can be convinced," he said.

The words hadn't exactly been framed as a question, yet the girl gave it a moment's thought. "No, my king," she said. It was always 'my king' or 'your honor' with her, even when there was no one else around.

The samrat was silent for a while.

"It's not as if we want her to abandon the Wandering Tribe and come to the palace permanently," he said. "And if she wants to stay close to the tribe, we can arrange for all of them…"

"It has nothing to do with the Wandering Tribe, your honor." A rare, uncharacteristic interruption, Shanku's voice was ringed with exasperation. "It's the palace. She hates it."

Vikramaditya looked both startled and confused.

"She believes the palace was responsible for bringing disgrace to the Wandering Tribe."

"Because of your… the Warden?" the king asked cautiously.

Shanku bit her lip and nodded, before turning her face away. But she hadn't been quick enough, and the samrat saw the shame in her eyes. And he realized that deep in her heart, Shanku also probably hated the palace for reminding her of the tainted blood that coursed through her veins.

The blood of her father Brichcha, who still languished in the palace dungeons, deep in the bowels of Ujjayini.

A common soldier of Avanti during the reign of King Mahendraditya, Brichcha had risen rapidly through the ranks once the war against the Hunas and Sakas had commenced. After the death of the king, at the time of Vararuchi's regency, Brichcha was appointed Warden of the Imperial Stables, in charge of overseeing the maintenance of the Imperial Army's horses. He continued to hold the prestigious office even after Vikramaditya's succession to the throne – a privilege which, however, he systematically started abusing in exchange of money from the Hunas.

Privy to all cavalry movements within Sindhuvarta, Brichcha secretly began passing the information onto the enemy, as a result of which Avanti's army suffered quite a few severe reverses. Yet, Brichcha's deceptions would never have been discovered had greed not got the better of him. Eager to further fatten his purse, Brichcha, at the behest of the Hunas, began bribing stable masters to add opium to the horses' diet to make the beasts slow and unreliable in battle.

Then one fine day, the wheels came off his little wagon, when one of the stable masters was caught red-handed mixing opium into a feeding trough.

Brichcha was stripped of his commission and put on trial, where inevitably, he was condemned to the harshest penalty in Sindhuvarta – banishment to Dandaka, the Forest of the Exiles. But before he could be transported to Payoshni Pass, his wife, a proud daughter of the Wandering Tribe, hanged herself in shame, leaving behind their eight-year-old daughter, Shankubala.

Brichcha pleaded to Vikramaditya for pardon, and moved by the thought of the small, helpless girl on the verge of being orphaned, the king transmuted the traitorous warden's sentence to imprisonment in the dungeons for life. He also ordered for Shanku to be moved to the palace so that she could meet her father regularly. Thus, Shanku had come to live in the royal stables, where her skills at riding horses and throwing knives had caught Vetala Bhatta's eye. Slowly she was inducted into the tutelage of the raj-guru, and over time she had earned the respect of Vikramaditya, who made her a part of his council.

Yet, the irony was that except for the first few years, Shanku hardly ever went to see her father, the visits to the dark cell growing less frequent with every passing year. Vikramaditya knew that she had roundly refused to see Brichcha for nearly three years, despite repeated pleas and petitions from the prisoner.

As the palanquin and its escort rounded a hill and came

into view, the samrat guessed that even if the palace were
to grant Brichcha amnesty, Shanku would never forgive her
father.

It was almost an hour later that Vikramaditya and
Shanku were ushered into the tent of the Mother Oracle
– but not before the king had been feted with a traditional
meal baked on dung fires. The king and his councilor were
joined in the Mother Oracle's tent by four senior tribesmen,
each present on the invitation of the king.

"I was told of your coming by the wind," the old woman
was blunt, not resorting to formalities. "I hope the meal
that I asked to be prepared for you was to your liking? Or
was it too simple for your taste?"

"It was perfect, mother," replied Vikramaditya. "No
one appreciates simplicity better than one who leads a
complicated life."

"Clever, clever," the Mother Oracle cackled with laughter,
her old watery eyes full of mirth. Then, sobering down a bit,
she asked, "What does the clever king want?"

"Well, mother…" The samrat paused, before deciding to
come straight to the point. "I want you to come with me to
the palace."

The king's words were greeted with dead silence,
filled only with the labored wheezing of the eldest of the
tribesmen.

"You have done a lot to assist Avanti, mother, and I
can't thank you enough for that," Vikramaditya continued
speaking. "But I fear there will be much greater need for
your counsel in the days to come, and I cannot have your
granddaughter constantly riding out of the palace in search
of you. That would be a colossal waste of her talents –
not to mention a colossal waste of time that could put the

precious lives of my soldiers and people at risk. So please, mother..."

The Mother Oracle was quiet for a while. Then, with a shake of her head, she spoke. "I am old and have but a few years to live. I want to be with my tribe..."

"Mother, I know you dislike the palace – your granddaughter told me so," the king butted in. "Still I request you to come."

As glances were exchanged, the woman nodded. "Yes, the palace has been unkind to me. It brought *that man* into my daughter's life," she spoke as if she found the idea of mentioning Brichcha by name revolting. "It took away my daughter and brought humiliation upon the tribe for no fault of ours."

"The palace also gave the tribe justice by penalizing Brichcha," Vikramaditya reasoned.

"The penalty was for his treachery against the palace," the Mother Oracle corrected. "We know the honor of the tribe was never under consideration. We may be nomadic people, my king, but we like to hold our heads high with pride."

The gathered tribesmen rumbled in appreciation and support of the old woman's words.

"Indeed, mother," the king conceded. "But where vengeance was to be had, the palace showed mercy by sparing the traitor's life for the sake of the tribe's granddaughter."

A small murmur of approval went around the tent as the Mother Oracle brooded. The samrat sensed a slight thaw in the atmosphere and decided to press home the advantage.

"You speak of the sun of the Aditya dynasty falling under an eclipse, mother. Yet you wouldn't lift a finger to help dispel the gloom that is to come to this land? You speak of the tribe being disgraced on account of the conduct of a palace representative, yet you turn your face to the one opportunity the tribe has to return to grace by assisting the palace? You speak of holding your honor and pride dear, yet you squander the chance to earn both by helping me protect the gift of the Ancient God?"

For a long while after the king spoke, the Mother Oracle sat hunched on her straw mat, eyes closed, her body rocking gently, back and forth. The tribesmen shifted in their seats, not knowing what to make of the Mother Oracle's silence. Shanku was almost convinced that her grandmother had lulled herself to sleep when the hag opened her eyes and took a good, long look at Vikramaditya.

"You are wise with your words and your thoughts, my king," she said at last. "I shall come to the palace with you."

* * *

"From what I understand, the devas and the asuras will not stop until one or the other has claimed this dagger. Is that correct?" King Harihara looked anxious as he studied Kalidasa's face.

"Yes, your honor."

Breathing deep, the king leaned his elbow on the arm of his chair and pinched his lower lip as he considered the implications of all that the councilor had just revealed.

"You say a good part of Ujjayini has already suffered great destruction from the first attack," he said at length. "At this rate, the city will be devastated before long."

Kalidasa opened his mouth to respond, but checked himself. Arguing against Harihara was foolish denial. It was plain that if the attacks persisted, Ujjayini would be in grave danger of collapsing. Yet, an open admission would do nothing to allay the jittery king. Under the circumstances, Kalidasa said nothing.

Unfortunately, Harihara construed the silence as a sign of tacit agreement. Throwing up his hands, he asked, "How does Vikramaditya intend defending the dagger?"

"With courage and with faith." This time Kalidasa knew he had a good answer. "That's how we rid ourselves of the pishachas and the Ashvin cavalry."

The king of Heheya rose and began pacing the narrow confines of the private chamber that Kalidasa had been shown into upon his arrival at Mahishmati earlier in the morning.

"And the Hunas and the Sakas?" the king asked in agitation.

"*What* about the Hunas and the Sakas, your honor?" Kalidasa asked cautiously.

"Will Avanti now abandon its campaign against them?" Harihara clarified.

"There's no question of that happening, your honor. Avanti will fight to the very end to keep Sindhuvarta free of invaders."

"Vikramaditya will fight the Hunas, the Sakas, the devas and the asuras, all at the same time? How?" Shaking his head, the king slumped back into his seat. Then, as a new thought occurred to him, he sat up. "There will be more attacks on Heheya too, I presume?"

"From the devas and the asuras? We doubt it, your honor. Their only interest lies in the Halahala, which is in Ujjayini."

"Yet the pishacha army led by that blind rakshasa ravaged half of my kingdom," Harihara sounded petulant. "Who is to say we won't suffer more such attacks by asuras or devas bound for Ujjayini?"

"The kingdom of Avanti deeply regrets the suffering that Heheya has been subjected to, your honor," Kalidasa spoke stiffly. Though he understood Harihara's concerns, he had begun developing a sharp dislike of the king's display of pettiness. He got the distinct impression that Harihara was increasingly behaving as an ungrateful, fair-weather friend.

"Regrets are all fine, Councilor Kalidasa, but you must realize Heheya is but a small kingdom with limited resources. We don't possess the wherewithal to deal with such eventualities."

"I offer Avanti's sincere apologies and a small token of our appreciation of Heheya's friendship," Kalidasa replied, making a mental note of the way the king had addressed him as 'councilor'. The old warmth in Harihara's tone was missing. "There's a wagon waiting downstairs that has a chest of gold for your treasury, your honor. I hope it can be put to use in rebuilding the garrisons and villages that were destroyed by the pishacha army."

The king appeared mollified at the mention of the contribution from Avanti. "That will definitely be of help to us," he admitted. Pausing for a moment, he asked, "Now that Vikramaditya has decided to take on the might of the devas and the asuras, what does he want from his allies?"

Kalidasa abruptly got up from his seat opposite Harihara. Rising to his full height, he towered over the old king. "The samrat wants nothing, your honor," he said, interpreting the import of Harihara's question correctly. "I came as an escort for the cart downstairs, and to give you the news of the Halahala. My work is done. I would now like to take your leave."

Without waiting for an acknowledgment, the giant bowed and left the chamber.

* * *

The Magadhan army was amassed on a broad, open plain on the western bank of the river Asya. Across the river lay another flat, treeless plain, receding into a ridge of gently sloping hills, beyond which lay the rich iron mines of Vanga and the mining town of Dandakabhukti.

As the shadows lengthened around them, the soldiers of Magadha cast their weapons and shields aside and eased their tired limbs by stretching themselves on the river bank. Quite a few of the men were already in the knee-deep water, washing away the dust and fatigue accumulated over the course of the long march. Behind them, tents were being pitched for the night, while large copper cauldrons were already perched on big wood fires.

Despite the vastness of the army spread on the river bank, the landscape was dominated by the twelve *mahashilakantakas* that towered over the tents. Made of hard ironwood, the lumbering catapults were drawn by teams of four elephants each, and were capable of hurling massive boulders over great distances. It was a different matter that the catapults were of little practical use in this particular campaign – Vanga had no formidable forts that needed siege weapons to breach. Yet, General Daipayana had insisted on bringing them along for effect; he knew the sight of the *mahashilakantakas* was often enough to instill fear and break the back of resistance.

"We shall cross the Asya and begin our eastward march at midnight tonight," Daipayana announced, tapping his index finger on an embroidered map that lay spread out on a small table. He was inside a large pavilion, surrounded by half a dozen commanders and captains of the Magadhan army. To his left stood Kapila, who had ridden down from Girivraja to join the general in their opening assault on Vanga.

"My plan is to cover half the distance to Dandakabhukti before the hot sun is up tomorrow," Daipayana continued. "And by reaching the base of those hills under cover of darkness, I also want to surprise whatever scouts and soldiers Vanga has stationed in the hills."

"Vanga's scouts will be shocked to see the Magadhan army at their doorstep at daybreak," leered Kapila, stroking his thick moustache as he studied the map.

"Indeed, your lordship," the general agreed. Turning back to one of the captains, he began issuing orders. "Your job is to make sure there are enough fires lit along the river bank, and that there's someone here all night to tend to the fires. And of course, there'll be no dismantling of the tents. To anyone watching us, it must seem as if the army is still very much on *this* bank and has no intention of moving before dawn. Clear?"

Seeing the captain nod, Daipayana addressed two senior commanders. "You will divide the army into four groups and oversee the river crossing. Remember the bank will be lit with fires, so the crossing will have to happen further upstream and downstream, away from the firelight. Identify the crossing points beforehand – everything has to happen swiftly. I want to be in those hills at sunrise."

"How do we go about the attack if we meet resistance in the hills, general?" one commander asked.

"I'm coming to that," Daipayana replied. "Whatever happens, under no circumstances is the cavalry to engage

in any skirmishes with Vanga's soldiers. That should be left
to the infantry and archers. The cavalry's task is simple –
once it is over the hills, it has to ride hard, fast and straight
to Dandakabhukti and take control of the town's defenses.
Next, it should secure all the mines and block all exit points
toward the rest of Vanga. Nothing should be able to enter
or leave the mines and the town without our consent."

"What about the townsfolk of Dandakabhukti?"

"Who cares, as long as they obey orders and stay out of
the way. But if anyone puts up resistance, show no mercy. We
aren't here to take prisoners. We're here to take Vanga."

* * *

Because he wasn't being able to make up his mind about
anything, Amara Simha had resorted to curses and moody
contemplation as he downed goblet after goblet of firewater.

His problems had started early in the day when he
awoke with a sore throat, and since then things had gone
progressively downhill. First, he and Commander Dattaka
had made no headway in their investigation into the
Huna scout's death, despite spending the entire morning
interviewing the six guards who'd been on duty that night.
No one appeared to have seen a king cobra anywhere
near the command center, and all six guards categorically
denied the possibility of any suspicious visitor to the scout's
cell. Yet the mystery of the killer snake persisted, with no
satisfactory explanation to the reptile's entry into and exit
from the cell undetected.

Amara Simha was almost certain some of the guards
weren't being entirely honest, but frustrating as it was, he
knew he couldn't pursue the matter more forcefully without
some form of evidence at his disposal.

Then, a little after noon, his mood took a turn for the worse when news of the pishacha and Ashvin attacks came in from Ujjayini. The reports of death and devastation had rattled everyone, and all afternoon soldiers were seen huddled in conversation. While there was obvious alarm in the soldiers' faces – and concern about the fate of loved ones in the capital – Amara Simha was also heartened by the awe and pride he saw when the men discussed the samrat and the manner in which the victories had been secured.

Strangely enough, the tidings from Ujjayini had left Amara Simha feeling both glad and depressed. Although he was relieved that the attacks had been repelled, the fact that he had had no role in either battle rankled. He had left Ujjayini with the prospect of action in the frontier, but all he'd done so far was behead a corpse and bully a scout. His fellow councilors, meanwhile, had been awarded with not one, but two opportunities to test the strength of their swords. And the Hunas, for whom he had come all this way, weren't even close to the border...

"It's just so unfair," Amara Simha grumbled to himself as he emptied the goblet he was holding and looked around for the pitcher for a refill.

"Pardon me, your honor?"

The councilor turned to see Dattaka standing in the doorway. He shook his head.

"Nothing. Care to join me?" As the commander took a seat across the table, Amara Simha waved the pitcher around invitingly. "Call for an empty goblet."

Dattaka looked out the window. The sky was fading to deep purple, but there was still enough light to tell the town of Sristhali from the shadows of the surrounding hills.

"In a little while, your honor," he said, deciding it wasn't late enough to warrant a drink.

Amara Simha shrugged and splashed a generous helping into his goblet.

"Something's troubling the councilor?"

"It's this king cobra thing," answered Amara Simha unhappily. "I can't decide whether I should spend more time here investigating it, or return to Udaypuri. It's been a while since I left the garrison in charge of Commander Atulyateja, and there's a lot of work to be done along the frontier. Yet, something happened here the other night, and I think it's important to find out who was behind it."

"If it helps, I could continue investigating the matter for you," Dattaka offered. "If I uncover something, I will let you know immediately."

"Yes, perhaps you can," said Amara Simha, taking another big gulp from the goblet. But the cheer didn't return.

The two men sat quietly for a while before the commander noticed a small pile of palm leaves and a stylus lying by Amara Simha's elbow. He could see the leaves were filled with Sanskrit words, arranged in tables in descending order.

"If I may ask, what are you working on, your honor?"

For a moment the burly councilor looked nonplused. Then, as he understood Dattaka, he glanced down at the palm leaves. "I'm creating a vocabulary of Sanskrit word roots," he explained. "It's a bit of grammar and a bit of poetry. I've been at it for the last two years."

"Not many men who wear the sword can do that." The commander's voice was filled with wonder. "You must be very learned."

"This is nothing – you must see what Councilor Kalidasa

writes. But yes, I have been fortunate to learn from masters like the late Srigupta."

"You studied under Guru Srigupta of Bhojapuri?"

Amara Simha nodded, detecting a hint of excitement in Dattaka's voice. "You know of Guru Srigupta?"

"He was a distant uncle of mine... though I admit I won't be able to draw the family tree to prove it," the commander smiled. "I have met him a couple of times as a small boy, when my mother took me to his house in Bhojapuri. I don't remember him too well – he was old and had a long white beard... But he had a daughter I won't easily forget. She was one of the nicest, kindest people I have ever met. Always smiling, full of laughter and sweets for us kids."

"Yes, she was one of the nicest people I have ever met." Amara Simha repeated. His voice had acquired a melancholy that Dattaka failed to notice.

"Of course, you studied under my uncle, so you would have known her too. Do you remember her name?"

"Swaha," the councilor looked down at his goblet. "It's hard to forget the name of someone you dearly loved and got married to."

"You're married to her? Oh, that makes us relatives!" Dattaka's eyes lit up, but then he paused. "Wait... why do you say someone you dearly *loved*, your honor?"

"Swaha died two years after our marriage, during childbirth. She and the baby, both."

The commander dropped his eyes. The silence of the evening filled the room as the two men sat opposite one another, one not knowing what to say, the other left with nothing to say.

At last, Amara Simha raised the goblet to his lips and drained its contents. Rising to his feet, he began gathering the palm leaves together. "I have decided to return to Udaypuri tomorrow morning," he said. "I will be taking the Huna scout with me. When Ghatakarpara returns from Dvarka, ask him to come to Udaypuri."

"And the investigation?"

"I believe I can trust a relation by marriage to do what's needed to uncover the truth," the councilor replied with a small smile.

* * *

Nearly half the night had passed by the time Captain Angamitra and four of his *samsaptakas* reached the city of Kausambi and made their way to the palace of King Chandravardhan. Kalidasa had entrusted his deputy with the task of delivering the news of the twin attacks on Avanti to Chandravardhan, and the young captain had diligently followed orders, resting sparingly through the long journey to the court of Vatsa.

The *samsaptakas* had been stopped at the gates of Kausambi, but once they proved their bona fides – and established the urgency of their mission – they were formally escorted to the palace, large but otherwise shapeless in the dark of the night. Dismounting from his horse, Angamitra divined that they were close to the Yamuna by the splashing of water against a stone embankment.

The soldiers from Avanti were shown into a large, almost empty room and told to wait for a palace official to attend to them. For nearly ten minutes, they were left to themselves, before they heard footsteps echoing down a corridor that gave into the room. Pushing aside the rich brocade curtain that hung over the doorway to the corridor, a thin elderly man entered the room.

"Captain Angamitra?" the man inquired, searching the faces in front of him.

The captain stepped forward and the man turned in his direction. However, on account of his pronounced squint, the man's eyes appeared to settle on the *samsaptaka* standing to Angamitra's right.

"Greetings," the man said and took a step in the direction of the captain, continuing to look at the other *samsaptaka*. "I am Councilor Yashobhavi, minister to King Chandravardhan. I take it that you have a message for the king from Samrat Vikramaditya?"

"Indeed, councilor," replied Angamitra. "We apologize for turning up at the palace at such a late hour, but the message is of considerable importance. We would like to deliver the message to King Chandravardhan right away, if that is possible."

"I'm afraid that would not be possible, captain," Yashobhavi said solemnly.

"Well..." Angamitra was a little taken aback. "Maybe we can deliver it to him in the morning then?" He found the minister's squint quite disconcerting.

"Even that wouldn't be possible."

"The king isn't in the palace?"

"Oh, he is," replied Yashobhavi. "But the problem is that earlier in the day, our king suffered a severe paralytic stroke. He isn't responding well at all, and the royal physicians say his condition is very critical."

The *samsaptakas* looked at one another. They hadn't planned for such an eventuality, and it was plain they had no idea of what to do next.

"What I can do is have the attendants show you to your rooms," Yashobhavi came to their rescue. "Rest for the night, for you must be tired. Meanwhile, Prince Shashivardhan is expected to reach the palace by dawn tomorrow. Perhaps you can meet him in the morning and give him Samrat Vikramaditya's message."

Healer

Stunned disbelief had taken permanent hold of Pallavan's face as he listened to Vetala Bhatta and Vararuchi recount the chain of events that had led to the Ashvin and pishacha attacks on Avanti. The diplomat's eyes strayed regularly to the windows of the council chamber, as if seeking validation for what he was being told, but Pallavan had seen enough of the battered city in his ride to the palace to know that it was the truth.

When the Acharya concluded his narrative, Pallavan sat in silence, cracking his knuckles absentmindedly as he stared at the intricate patterns of the sun-crest embossed on the council table.

"We can show you the dagger, if you wish to see it for yourself," Vikramaditya's solemn voice dispelled the quietness.

The diplomat raised his head and considered the king. He then shook his head hurriedly. "No samrat, I have no reason to disbelieve all of you. Pardon me if I gave you that impression – I'd never doubt your word. It's just that all this is… upsetting…" Pallavan's voice trailed away as the enormity of the situation reasserted itself in his mind.

"The suddenness of it all must be a shock to you," the king nodded gently. "But we had no intention of keeping anyone in the dark about all this, believe us. Just yesterday, we dispatched an emissary to King Bhoomipala's court with the news. But you would have left Sravasti even earlier, so there is no way you would have known of any of this."

"Indeed not, your honor. No…" Pallavan shook his head in bafflement.

Yet, when he addressed Vikramaditya again, the diplomat's tone had undergone a subtle change. Filled with awe, it was now almost deeply reverential. "Samrat, you are blessed. You saw the Omniscient One, which is rare for most humans. You have been chosen to fulfill a duty by the Omniscient One, which is rarer still. I consider it an honor to have even lived in your lifetime, and it is my king's immense good fortune to have you as a trusted friend."

"I'm glad and honored that Kosala sees a friend in Avanti," the samrat inclined his head gracefully. He had known Pallavan long enough to tell that the diplomat enjoyed the complete trust of Bhoomipala, and that Pallavan would never commit to something unless he was convinced that he would have Bhoomipala's full backing.

"Do let us know if Kosala can be of any assistance to you, samrat. It would be our privilege to help you honor your promise to the Omniscient One in whatever small way possible."

"I shall not hesitate to seek Kosala's help, should the need ever arise," Vikramaditya assured the guest with a smile. "But enough of our troubles... Do tell us, what do we owe this unexpected visit of yours to?"

Pallavan blinked as he remembered the errand that had brought him to Ujjayini. "I've come here bearing disturbing news – though I admit after what I've seen and heard this morning, I doubt your capacity to be disturbed any further," he admitted.

"And this news is...?" the king prodded.

Swiftly and without digression, Pallavan gave Vikramaditya and his council an account of his visit to Girivraja, his encounter with the musician, their flight across the border of Magadha, and the musician's revelation of King Siddhasena's cold-blooded murder at the hands of Shoorasena.

"King Bhoomipala is right," Vikramaditya observed solemnly, after having heard the diplomat out. "It is plain that Shoorasena is bent on invading Vanga, but the old king must have been a deterrent. By removing him, Shoorasena has not only cleared his path of all obstacles, he has achieved his goal of mobilizing public opinion within Magadha against the republic and the Kikatas."

"My king thinks Shoorasena deserves to be punished for what he has done," said Pallavan, appraising the faces around the table closely. His tone indicated that he had decided to throw the dice on the table. "King Siddhasena was a good friend of my king, and he was also dearly liked by the samrat's late father. My king believes Siddhasena's death shouldn't go unavenged."

Vikramaditya leaned his elbows on the council table and fixed a keen gaze on the diplomat. "Would you be kind enough to tell us exactly what King Bhoomipala is proposing?"

"My king proposes initiating military action against Shoorasena and the royal council of Magadha. We must build a consensus with the kingdoms of Vatsa, Matsya, Heheya and the Anartas to bring Shoorasena to justice."

Vararuchi and Kalidasa nodded vigorously in agreement, but the samrat looked circumspect. When he spoke, he chose his words carefully. "I agree we cannot allow Shoorasena to get away with this horrific murder, more so when he uses it as a pretext to orchestrate genocide against the Kikatas and invade a harmless neighbor like Vanga. Yet, we mustn't act rashly, for the kingdom of Magadha is still an ally of ours."

"Hasn't Shoorasena virtually annulled all alliances with us by refusing to send his troops for the defense of Sindhuvarta?" Vararuchi protested.

"True. But the subjects of Magadha, who were until recently ruled by the benevolent King Siddhasena, are still our allies. We can't have the blood of Magadha's innocents on our hands. We owe that much to Siddhasena."

"From what I could tell, there are hardly any innocents left in Magadha," Pallavan observed bitterly, remembering the sights of plunder in Girivraja.

"You're right," Vikramaditya conceded. "At this moment, the misguided subjects of Magadha are probably *supportive* of Shoorasena and the royal council. This makes it even more imperative for us to avoid rushing headlong into a military confrontation. Shoorasena will cleverly manipulate his people into believing their kingdom is being threatened solely because he refused to divert Magadhan soldiers to defend Sindhuvarta. He could go even so far as to show us siding with the Kikatas and Vanga. Then, for all practical purposes, *we* would become the aggressors in the eyes of Magadha's subjects, and he the hapless victim. We must deny Shoorasena the opportunity to gain more support from his people."

The uncomfortable silence that briefly claimed the council chamber was broken by Kalidasa. "If open hostilities are not an option, we could send a handful of *samsaptakas* to Girivraja to secretly assassinate Shoorasena," he offered. "No one would be the wiser for it."

The samrat weighed the proposal carefully before shaking his head. "The situation here is quite different from the one in Heheya, when Kulabheda engineered his coup against King Harihara. Kulabheda had very little support in Heheya, whereas Shoorasena appears to have the full backing of the royal council – and his people. If Shoorasena were to be assassinated, he would easily end up becoming a martyr in the minds of Magadha's subjects. And by blaming his death on the Kikatas, the royal council can always exploit the people's hatred toward the Kikatas even more to serve whatever ends the council has in mind. That would be counterproductive. We mustn't do anything that adds to the misery of the Kikatas."

"But samrat, if we don't act against Shoorasena, we would be giving a murderer the license to do as he pleases," Pallavan argued a trifle testily. "Are we going to grant him the freedom to break the peace of Sindhuvarta?"

"No," the king's voice was emphatic, commanding. "Shoorasena has to be reined in and he *must* answer for his deeds. But the course of action we choose shouldn't add to his glory in Magadha. By killing the old king and lying about it, Shoorasena has cheated his people – his punishment should come in a manner by which his subjects are exposed to his treachery. Shoorasena's downfall must be welcomed and celebrated by his own people. That's when true justice will be delivered to King Siddhasena."

"How are we to achieve this, your honor?" Pallavan asked, this time with more respect.

"There have to be loyalists of King Siddhasena somewhere in Magadha," the samrat answered. "Even one or two men of influence who stood by the old king would suffice. Maybe in the royal council, maybe in the Magadhan army... We have to find these men quickly and let them know the truth about their king's death. With their help, we can turn public opinion against Shoorasena."

"I might know a couple of such men." The diplomat sat meditatively, but his eyes sparkled as he warmed to the idea. "I can begin by..."

Pallavan was, however, interrupted by a knock on the council chamber's door. Looking up, the men saw the door open to admit Queen Upashruti. As the men rose from their seats out of respect, the queen walked into the room, but on catching Pallavan's eye, she drew to an abrupt halt.

"Greetings from King Bhoomipala and the subjects of Kosala, queen mother," said the diplomat with a formal bow.

"My greetings to you and your king," replied the queen. "Do accept my deepest apologies for barging in like this. I had no idea you were here." Motioning with her hand to resume their seats, she added, "Please continue. I shall come back later."

But even as Queen Upashruti turned around to depart, Pallavan spoke again. "No mother, it is nothing," he protested. "I presume you are here for something that demands the samrat and the council's attention. I shall wait most willingly. Please don't leave."

The queen paused and looked at Vikramaditya, who gave a small shrug and nodded. The envoy's words had clearly ruled out any further debate over the matter.

"Thank you," she smiled at Pallavan. "This won't take long." Returning her eyes to the king, she said, "You have heard the news about the one-eyed Healer, I suppose."

Mystified, Vikramaditya stared at his mother for a couple of moments, before turning to Vetala Bhatta and Vararuchi for illumination. The two councilors, however, looked just as confused.

"You know nothing about the Healer?" The Queen Mother's tone was of surprise and exasperation in equal measure as she cast her eye around the room. Seeing the blank expressions and shakes of the head, she said, "The whole city is talking about him."

"No mother, I'm afraid the talk hasn't reached our ears," the samrat said a shade stiffly.

"Well, this man has recently come to Ujjayini – by all accounts, he is very new to these parts. It seems he has been treating our citizens for all sorts of ailments, and word is his cures are almost miraculous. They say he has even brought relief to those affected by the Ashvin attacks; apparently he has administered remedies to some of our soldiers as well."

"Who is this man?" Vikramaditya knitted his brows and glanced at Dhanavantri, but the physician returned an expression of complete bewilderment. "Where has he come from?"

"No one seems to know," said the queen. "He's a stranger to these parts... He's only being referred to as the Healer. Or the one-eyed Healer, for he is blind in one eye."

"If I may ask, why have you brought him to our notice,

queen mother?" asked the Acharya, speaking for the first time in long while.

"A son of one of my palanquin bearers overheard the Healer say something, raj-guru. The Healer claimed he might have a cure for the young lady in the palace."

Queen Upashruti paused to let the words sink in. Then, looking straight into Vikramaditya's eyes, she added, "You must invite this man to the palace. He couldn't have been referring to anyone but Vishakha."

***

For over three hours, Angamitra had been sitting in a room overlooking the Yamuna, watching the boats and barges plying on the swollen river. While the smaller boats scuttled between the two banks ferrying passengers, the big barges, laden with goods, floated sluggishly upstream and down between Matsya and the minor principalities of Surasena and Chedi to the west, and Magadha and Vanga to the east. With every passing hour the sun had climbed higher in the sky, and was now almost directly above Kausambi, but its heat was tempered by the cool river breeze. The breeze, working in combination with the boredom, had lulled the captain into a light doze, so it was with a start that he awoke on hearing a voice accompanied by a rush of footsteps.

"Please do pardon me for keeping you waiting so long, captain."

Angamitra looked over his shoulder to see a young man hurrying across the room, Councilor Yashobhavi following two steps behind. The man was in his early thirties, tall and willowy, with long brown hair that fell up to his shoulders. His thin face was adorned with a trim beard, while his large eyes had an expression of perpetual sadness about them.

The captain couldn't help observe how different Prince Shashivardhan and his father were when it came to build and physical appearance.

"Your honor, it is perfectly..." The captain began rising to his feet, but the prince waved him back into his seat.

"I know this is no way to treat a guest from Avanti – father would never approve of it," Shashivardhan dropped into a vacant chair opposite Angamitra. "But what could I do? I just got back this morning, and I've practically been with the physicians ever since."

Listening to the prince, Angamitra missed neither the slight slur in Shashivardhan's speech, nor the distinct whiff of *soma* on his breath. Realizing the prince wasn't being entirely truthful about how the morning had been spent, the captain looked up at Yashobhavi, but the councilor squinted stoically to Angamitra's right.

"I can understand, your honor," Angamitra returned his gaze to Shashivardhan. "How is King Chandravardhan now?"

"Not good, I'm afraid," the prince heaved a sigh and leaned back. "The physicians aren't happy with his progress. And there are so many things to take care of in the palace, so much that demands attention..."

Shashivardhan passed a weary hand over his forehead, his worried eyes looking out over the river. Angamitra concluded that the prince seemed overwhelmed by the responsibility of having to make official decisions in the absence of the king. Suddenly, the captain was no longer sure if he should burden the prince with the news that had brought him to Vatsa, but the matter was decided when Shashivardhan addressed him.

"Anyway, our good councilor Yashobhavi says you came

bearing an important message for father," Shashivardhan looked at Angamitra inquiringly. "The message must be important enough for you to wait for me all morning – what is it?"

Sticking to his brief – and speaking almost by rote – the captain narrated everything of importance that pertained to the dagger that was now in Vikramaditya's keeping. Both Shashivardhan and Yashobhavi listened with keen interest, their mouths dropping in amazement as Angamitra told them about the encounters with the Ashvins and the pishacha army.

When the captain fell silent, the prince and the councilor turned what they had just heard over in their heads, their expressions full of wonder. Finally, after casting a brief glance at the councilor, Shashivardhan spoke.

"What you've told us is frankly amazing. It's no surprise to me that father holds Samrat Vikramaditya in such great esteem. But…" Here the prince's voice faltered a bit. "…is there something that the samrat wants from us? I mean, are you here for…?"

Angamitra shook his head. "The samrat only wants his allies to know the truth about the dagger, and I was deputed to come here to share the news with King Chandravardhan, your honor. There's nothing more to my visit."

Shashivardhan nodded, his face and shoulders relaxing with relief. Angamitra sensed the prince was just glad that he wasn't expected to make an important decision on behalf of his father. But as the captain began mentally preparing to take his leave, Shashivardhan addressed him again.

"Nevertheless, Avanti and Vatsa have been allies for as long as I can remember. Father and King Mahendraditya were always on very good terms, and as I've already said, father has the utmost respect for the samrat. Our kingdoms have also forged ties of blood through marriage, so..."

The prince came to a fumbling halt, as if suddenly fearful of the fact that in the rush of good intentions, he was committing himself to something that would later incur King Chandravardhan's displeasure. He looked up at Yashobhavi with doubtful eyes, but seeing the councilor's imperceptible nod of encouragement, his face cleared.

"So it is Vatsa's duty to offer Avanti any assistance it needs," Shashivardhan renewed with confidence. "Let Samrat Vikramaditya know we will be happy to extend help in whatever way we can – I'm sure father would not have wished it otherwise had he been here."

"It is an honor to have trusted friends like King Chandravardhan and you, prince," replied Angamitra, rising from his seat. "Now if you will permit me, I would like to return to Ujjayini with your pledge of allegiance."

* * *

"I am known as the Healer, your honor. I hail from the misty valleys through which the mighty Lauhitya flows before it enters the kingdom of Pragjyotishpura."

The man who had spoken stood in the center of Ujjayini's cavernous Throne Room, his strong voice echoing off the high, vaulted ceiling, making the ornate crystal lamps hanging overhead quiver faintly as if in fright. He was short but broadly built, with a thick gray beard and moustache covering his fair face. He also wore a black eye-patch over his left eye.

"You don't have a name other than the Healer?" asked Vetala Bhatta shrewdly.

"Isn't a man ultimately known by his deeds, your honor?"

The awkward silence that followed was broken by Vikramaditya.

"And you say you can cure the queen of Avanti of her illness?" The king leaned forward in the royal throne, a large chunk of hewn and polished black marble, cushioned with rich velvet and satin pillows. The marble was heavily inlaid with gold and ivory, the white and yellow strands rising and intertwining to form a large sun-crest behind the king's head. Vikramaditya's eyes were keen as they appraised the stranger.

"I believe I could, your honor – though I can't say with any surety until I have had a chance to see the queen."

"Are you a physician?" The Acharya fixed a suspicious gaze on the newcomer, before glancing briefly at Dhanavantri. "If I may ask, where did you master your craft?"

"Some call me a physician, some a healer... still others a tantric. What does it matter?" the Healer shrugged and gestured in the direction of Dhanavantri. "The honorable court physician would agree that the only thing that finally counts is faith in the remedy. The people of this city have a capacity for immense faith; else, none of my cures would have worked."

"For someone of your talents, it is strange how we have never heard of you before," remarked Vetala Bhatta, continuing to scrutinize the stranger closely.

"That is beyond my control," the Healer gave a small smile of helplessness.

The raj-guru nodded. "What brings you to Ujjayini?"

"I am a traveler, your honor. Wherever I go, I try and bring succor to the ailing and the infirm. I happened to be heading west for the Anartas when I heard of the calamity that has befallen this beautiful city of yours. So, I decided to come here."

"How did you learn of the queen's ailment?" asked Queen Upashruti

"The subjects of this kingdom love their king and queen dearly, mother," the Healer replied. "Their concern for the queen easily finds words."

"I hope you realize that the queen's illness isn't minor," said Vetala Bhatta. "She has been in the care of our court physician for two years and has shown little improvement. And there's probably no better physician in Sindhuvarta than Dhanavantri."

"I can but try where others have failed."

Although the stranger spoke the words in a matter-of-fact manner, the raj-guru thought he detected a subtle attempt at putting Dhanavantri down. He also saw how the Healer had cleverly deflected every pointed question that had been posed to him. But before he could probe any further, the samrat spoke.

"I expect you would want to be rewarded if you are able to cure the queen. So what would your price be?"

"That would be premature, your honor," the Healer answered. "I am still to see the queen. And even if I do think I can be of assistance..." he paused to look fleetingly at the Acharya. "...I think *you* would like to see some evidence of progress in the queen's recovery before you decide whether it's worth having me in the palace treating her. So it would only be fair to discuss this at a later time."

Vetala Bhatta opened his mouth to lodge a protest, but he was beaten to it by the king.

"As you wish," said Vikramaditya, rising from the throne. "Now if you will allow me, let me escort you to the queen's chamber. Dhanavantri, would you care to join us please?"

"Yes, samrat."

The king and the Healer filed out of the Throne Room, closely followed by Dhanavantri. As the Queen Mother and the rest of the councilors and courtiers emptied into the hall outside, the Acharya stroked his beard thoughtfully. Though he couldn't put a finger to it, there was something smarmy about the stranger that the raj-guru found quite distasteful.

Making a mental note to keep a close watch on the visitor, the Acharya shuffled out of the Throne Room and joined the group making its way to Vishakha's bedchamber.

***

With the sweep of its glazed marble floor, its broad arched windows that let in the scented breeze blowing down from Mount Meru, and the sixteen massive columns holding up its domed ceiling, the central hall of the palace of Amaravati was by no means small. Yet, as Indra looked down from the head of the grand staircase, everything about the hall below appeared to shrink in size, dwarfed by the seven hulking rakshasas who stood at the foot of the stairway in a crude semicircle.

Tall and imposing though each one of the seven was, their size wasn't all that made them remarkable. What also caught the eye were the hard, bony exoskeletons that covered their bulky torsos, the ultramarine blue of their skins, and the four black horns that sprouted from their heads – two sweeping upward and back, two curving down toward their shoulders, pointing forward. Their handsome faces were dark and brooding, and their eyes were filled with the dull gleam of quicksilver.

Indra smiled to himself as he descended the stairs, watching the rakshasas go down on one knee and bow

their heads in obeisance. It was the first time the lord of
Devaloka had looked at ease since the Ashvins had returned
from their disastrous outing to Sindhuvarta.

"Rise, sons of Diti," commanded Indra with a wave of
his hand.

The rakshasas, however, stayed on their knees until
Indra came to a halt at the bottommost stair. They then got
to their feet and stood with bowed heads, each a good two
hands taller than their king.

"Greetings, my lord," one of the rakshasas spoke in a
low rumble. "What can we do for you?"

Instead of replying, Indra stepped onto the hall. Two of
the giants immediately made way, allowing the deva to walk
past them to one of the hall's windows. For a while, the
deva stared out the window, arms crossed behind his back,
his eyes on the cliffs protecting the palace. Then wheeling
around suddenly, he looked at the rakshasas.

"I want you to destroy the city of Ujjayini," he said, his
voice cold with anger. "Destroy the city, kill its king, and
retrieve the Halahala and the Hellfires for me."

The figures by the staircase glanced at one another.
"By the Hellfires you mean... our mother's swords?" the
rakshasa who had spoken earlier asked.

"Are there any other by that name?" Indra frowned
in irritation. With a slight shake of his head, he cleared
his mind of the distraction. "Yes, Diti's swords. And the
Halahala that is stored in Veeshada's dagger."

"Who is this king who has possession of the Halahala
and the Hellfires, my lord?"

"He is a human and his name is Vikramaditya." Retracing
his steps from the window, Indra began pacing the breadth
of the hall. Over the course of the next few minutes, he gave

the giants a sketch of the Halahala's narrative, culminating
in the devas' failures at recovering the dagger.

"By fleeing the way they did, the Ashvins made a mockery
of us devas in front of the human army," Indra concluded,
gritting his teeth. "It is now up to you Maruts to restore the
pride of Devaloka by killing the human king and bringing
me the dagger and the two swords."

"As you command, my lord," replied the leader of the
rakshasas. "We shall proceed for Ujjayini right away."

"Make sure the attack is swift and ruthless," the deva
raised a cautionary finger. "The Ashvins made the mistake
of giving Vikramaditya's army time to strengthen the city's
defenses. You will take them by surprise, when they are
least expecting it. And while you're at it, make the humans
pay for their arrogance."

Once the rakshasas had lumbered out of the hall, Indra
mounted the staircase to a balcony that overlooked the
palace courtyard, pausing just long enough to pick up a
goblet of soma along the way. Leaning against the parapet,
he prided himself on his decision to send the Maruts to
Sindhuvarta.

Conceived by Diti after severe penance and ritualistic
sacrifices, the Maruts had originally been one single demonic
entity growing in her womb. Endowed with immense
strength and great magical abilities, the demon child was
being borne by the sorceress with one purpose in mind – the
destruction of Indra and Devaloka.

Indra, however, had got wind of her scheme and engaged
a yaksha from Kubera's court to seduce Diti – in the hope
that the yaksha's mystical semen would secretly poison the
fetus. Diti expectedly fell for the virile yaksha's charms, and
while they made passionate love, the yaksha tried destroying

the demonic fetus inside her. But so great was its strength that his semen only managed sundering it into seven lesser parts – from each of which a Marut was born.

Distraught and enraged at seeing her plan of giving birth to an all-powerful rakshasa being foiled, Diti abandoned the seven babies, leaving them to their fate inside a draughty cave in the ridges of the Himalayas. It was in this cave that Indra had found the unwanted Maruts, blue and stiff from the cold, starved and barely alive. In a rare stroke of selflessness and compassion, the lord of the devas brought the babies to Devaloka, where they were nursed back to health.

As he raised the goblet to his lips and savored the *soma*, Indra smiled to himself once again. Bringing the Maruts to Devaloka had proved to be a masterstroke. Fed on a routine diet of hatred for their heartless mother, the seven rakshasa babies had grown up abhorring the asura blood that coursed through their veins. And now as powerful giants, they swore unflinching fealty to Amaravati and its ruler, leading the devas in many successful campaigns against their own brethren from Patala.

Tossing down the contents of the goblet, Indra wondered why it hadn't struck him to send the Maruts to Ujjayini the first time around. There was nothing any human army could do against the fearsome might and wizardry of Diti's seven rakshasa sons.

* * *

Ujjayini was reveling in the glow of twilight, the palace's western wall splashed vermillion, when Vishakha turned her head to look at the Healer.

At first this development went unnoticed; the Healer's eyes

were closed as he sat on the floor by the queen's bedside, deep in meditation. The only other person in the bedchamber, the elderly nurse, had her back to Vishakha as she went about setting the small table for the queen's evening meal.

The silence within the bedchamber was in stark contrast to the hivelike activity that had prevailed earlier in the afternoon, when the Healer had been ushered in to take a look at Vishakha. The palace household, buoyed by expectation, had crammed itself into the room, while the passageways had ebbed and flowed with palace attendants eager to catch a glimpse of the happenings inside.

Once the Healer had made a cursory examination, he had asked for Vishakha's face to be treated with a sandalwood and turmeric salve. Drawing a tantric *mandala* on the floor by the bed, the Healer had placed a red hibiscus in each of Vishakha's hands, before seating himself in front of the *mandala*. Then, after uttering a few invocations and propitiating the Dasa-Mahavidyas, he had slipped into a meditative trance.

With the passing of the hours, the pulsing anticipation had dissipated, and people had slowly trickled out of the bedchamber and returned to their duties, Kshapanaka being the last to leave. Had she stayed a while longer, Kshapanaka would have been the one to observe her sister staring at the Healer, but as luck would have it, it was a servant bearing Vishakha's meal who noticed the change in her queen.

Barely breathing, her round eyes on Vishakha, the servant tiptoed over to the nurse.

"The queen..." she whispered.

"What?" The nurse turned sharply, catching the urgency in the maid's tone.

She gazed at Vishakha for a moment, eyes widening with excitement. Then, unburdening the servant of the tray, she leaned close to her ear.

"Fetch the queen mother," she hissed. "Don't waste any time and don't tell anyone else about this. Now hurry."

In a matter of minutes, Queen Upashruti and Kshapanaka were standing by the foot of the bed, looking indecisively from Vishakha to the Healer. Kshapanaka took a step toward her sister, but the Queen Mother placed a restraining hand on her shoulder. Shortly, they were joined by Vikramaditya and Dhanavantri, and the four exchanged anxious glances.

"Why is she staring at the Healer?" Vikramaditya asked, drawing Dhanavantri aside.

The physician shrugged in response.

"She looks a lot more alert," murmured the king. "Should we try to get her attention?"

"No," Dhanavantri shook his head vehemently. "Let us wait and see what's happening."

Just then, the Healer opened his eyes. For a moment, he stared unseeingly in front of him, before raising his head to look at Vishakha. The queen's eyes locked with the Healer's fleetingly – and then, as if a spell had been broken, she blinked and turned to look at the other faces observing her. She displayed no signs of recognition, but the brightness in her expression and the mild curiosity in her eyes were completely new.

The royal household looked at the Healer for guidance. Seeing him incline his head, Queen Upashruti released her hold on Kshapanaka's shoulder. The princess went to her sister's side and reached out tentatively for her hand, but Vishakha pulled away, her face clouding with alarm.

The Guardians of the Halahala   325

Kshapanaka's face fell, but withdrawing her hand, she proffered a reassuring smile.

Vishakha stared back, showing no intent at reciprocation. She then cast her doubtful eyes around the room before returning to Kshapanaka.

"Water," she spoke clearly, even though her voice was that of a timid, frightened child.

As the room held its breath in anticipation, Kshapanaka leaned closer to Vishakha.

"Do you want some water?" she asked, choking with emotion.

Seeing her sister nod, tears rolled freely down Kshapanaka's cheeks. It was the first time Vishakha had responded to anything since that fateful, sunny morning.

"Water for the queen," Dhanavantri looked at the nurse, feeling the lump in his throat.

A goblet of water was handed to Vishakha. She drank deeply, studying the ring of faces around her. At last, lowering the goblet, she looked from Kshapanaka to the Healer.

"Where am I?" she asked in a trembling voice.

"Among friends," the Healer replied, placing a comforting hand on her head. "Now you must rest."

As Vishakha slumped obediently onto the pillow, the Healer turned to Vikramaditya. "Let the queen rest, your honor."

"What about her meal and her medications?" asked Dhanavantri.

"She can be given her meal. Your medications..." the Healer shrugged. "They won't harm her, I suppose. But sleep is what she needs most. Please make sure she sleeps well. I shall see her again tomorrow morning." With that, he bowed and walked out of the room.

The samrat watched the Healer depart before turning his attention to the bed, where Vishakha was still appraising everyone in confusion. When their eyes met, Vikramaditya saw a slight frown develop on Vishakha's brow. As she looked away, he wondered what was going through her mind. Turning around, he followed the Healer out of the bedchamber.

"Can you tell me what has just happened?" Vikramaditya asked as he caught up with the retreating figure of the Healer. "Is her memory... returning?"

The Healer slowed to a halt and turned to the king. "Right now, the queen doesn't even know who she is, your honor," he spoke patiently. "I've only brought her one step forward by making her conscious of her surroundings. It's going to take a while before things start coming back to her."

"But they *will* come back, won't they?" The samrat's eyes, swimming with hope and anxiety, bored into the Healer's. "She will recover fully, won't she?"

The Healer smiled inwardly as he detected the desperation in Vikramaditya's tone. He liked it. It told him that he had been right in making the journey to Avanti.

"We will know only when she recovers fully, your honor."

* * *

Shukracharya permitted himself another smile, this one more open, as he was in the privacy of the bedroom that had been furnished to him in the eastern wing of the palace.

The bedroom was large and well-ventilated, with a comfortable bed, though Shukracharya had preferred a palm leaf mat to sleep on. He now lay on this mat, hands crossed behind his head, staring up at the shadows that danced across the ceiling in the light of the low lamp. Outside, much of the palace had retired for the night, with only crickets and cicadas keeping the sentries and gatekeepers company.

She will recover fully, won't she?

Indeed she will recover, Samrat Vikramaditya, but only if you want her to badly enough. Indeed, she will recover, but only if you will give me what I have come for.

Not for a moment did Shukracharya doubt that the samrat badly wanted the queen to get well – the bones never lied, and he had seen evidence of the king's devotion in plenty all day. What he wasn't sure about was whether the king would be willing to trade the dagger for...

Shukracharya's thoughts were interrupted by a low knock on the carved wooden door of the bedroom. Raising his head, he looked at the door, unsure if he had heard correctly. Two low knocks, one following the other in quick succession, told him someone was at the door.

"Enter please," he said. Getting up from the mat, he raised the lamp's wick as the door opened to admit a wiry figure of medium build. As the light fell on the figure, Shukracharya remembered seeing the man in the Throne Room, and later in Vishakha's bedchamber.

"Yes, what can I do for you?" he asked.

"I am Vararuchi, brother of Samrat Vikramaditya," the man introduced himself as he approached Shukracharya. "I have heard of how the queen is showing signs of recovery after you examined her."

"The road is long and filled with uncertainties, but I'm happy there's been some progress," Shukracharya inclined his head. So this was Vararuchi – one of the councilors who battled and killed Andhaka. "Is there some way I can be of help to you?"

"Well..." Vararuchi hesitated. "You are... your healing powers are quite incredible, so I want... I would like you to come and visit my mother."

"Your mother... You mean the queen mother? But she seems to be in fairly good health."

A shadow flitted across Vararuchi's dark face, though Shukracharya couldn't tell for sure whether it was just the flickering light playing tricks.

"No, I meant *my* mother – the samrat and I are half-brothers. My mother isn't here in the palace."

"I see." Shukracharya processed this information, realizing it was something that could come in handy sometime. "What ails her?"

"Arthritis."

"Easily remedied," Shukracharya reassured. "How far away is your mother?"

"A two-hour ride to the west, across the holy Kshipra."

"Shall we go and see her tomorrow evening then?"

"I would be grateful if you came. Thank you." Vararuchi folded his hands, bowed and left the room.

Shukracharya returned to the mat, but instead of lying down, he drew his plain cotton traveling bag to him. Emptying the contents of the bag on the mat, he rummaged through the pile until he found the six pieces of human vertebrae he was looking for. Using a pinch of vermilion, he drew a *mandala* on the marble floor, before cupping the bones in hands and shaking them as he uttered a mantra.

Throwing the bones inside the *mandala*, he leaned forward and began studying the pattern, trying to divine something more about the man who had just paid him a visit.

There was something about the king's half-brother that tickled Shukracharya's curiosity.

Warnings

For longer than anyone in Vanga could remember, the
tradition had been for the Grand Assembly to meet once
every fortnight to debate policy matters with the utmost
dignity and decorum. But that sunny morning in Tamralipti,
both tradition and protocol had been uncharacteristically
breached. For one, the Grand Assembly had been convened
out of turn and at short notice; for another, the chiefs of the
republic's eighteen principalities were all talking at once,
shouting to make themselves heard over one another. The
cool river breeze blowing through the assembly hall failed
to dispel the apprehension and outrage hanging in the air.

"Calm down... Please calm down," an official of the
Assembly entreated. "Allow Chancellor Sudasan a chance
to speak."

"How can you ask us to calm down?" one of the chiefs
who had gathered demanded hotly. "Dandakabhukti has
been taken by the Magadhan army, and reports say nearly
fifty of our soldiers and civilians have been killed there. God

knows which one of us is next on their sights. How can we be calm when our safety is at risk?"

"Please... we are all here to discuss the matter," the official urged.

"All we're going to do is *discuss* the matter?" asked another chief. "Who wants discussions? I want to know what is the Grand Assembly going to *do* about the matter."

Before the official could reply, an elderly man who had been standing a little behind stepped forward and placed a gentle hand on the official's shoulder. The man had the bearing of a noble, his aged face lined with responsibility, yet his bright eyes were full of sagacity. With a slight incline of his head, the man indicated to the official that he was taking charge of the proceedings. As the official withdrew, the din in the hall petered down to a low murmur.

"Chiefs, you ask what the Grand Assembly is going to do about the matter," he spoke in a stentorian voice as he smoothened down his thinning hair with his palm. "But you forget that you *are* the Grand Assembly... so only *you* can answer that question."

The gathered heads shuffled their feet and exchanged sheepish glances. At last, one of the chiefs rose to his feet.

"Excuse us for the oversight, Chancellor Sudasan," he said, addressing the man who had restored order in the hall. "Please understand that we are all worried with what's happened at Dandakabhukti. Me, most of all, as Dandakabhukti comes directly under my jurisdiction."

"I share your concern, brother," replied Sudasan. "That's why this Assembly has been summoned."

"Do we know why Magadha has attacked us, Chancellor?" another of the chiefs asked. "And why Dandakabhukti has been captured?"

"We don't know, to be entirely honest. We have never meant Magadha any harm – we have never meant *anyone* any harm. Vanga has always maintained a cordial relationship with the kingdoms of Sindhuvarta."

"Could it be that Magadha grudges the fact that we have offered shelter to the Kikata refugees?" the chief who had spoken first asked. "Magadha's old king is believed to have been killed by his Kikata bodyguard."

"Why are we granting the Kikatas refuge in Vanga anyway?" demanded the chieftain under whose purview Dandakabhukti fell. Seeing heads nod in approval, he continued, "They are draining our resources and spreading disease... and because of them we have now incurred the displeasure of Magadha. We should send them back."

"Send them back where?" asked Sudasan, conscious of the support that the idea had received. "Back to Magadha to be slaughtered? The Kikatas are a peaceful tribe and our association with them goes back a long way. Now they are being driven out of their homeland and have nowhere to go. We shouldn't let worry and fear impair our judgment."

"So what do we do now? How do we find out what Magadha's motivations are?"

"We have already dispatched two senior emissaries to Dandakabhukti to meet the Magadhan army commander," the chancellor replied. "It's possible the whole thing is only a terrible misunderstanding that can be resolved by sitting across the table."

"And we haven't heard from the emissaries so far?"

"They left for Dandakabhukti only yesterday evening."

"What happens if the emissaries return with the news that Magadha intends keeping up hostilities?"

As a wave of uneasiness washed through the hall,

Sudasan took a deep breath. "In that eventuality, Vanga will have to prepare to defend itself. As a precautionary measure, we have already started strengthening our defenses around Dandakabhukti. The Assembly hereby proposes to increase troops across all the principalities that border Magadha with immediate effect. Further, the Assembly proposes that more troops be deployed to defend the towns of Chandrakanta, Medinipuri and Tamralipti."

"We approve all your proposals," the chiefs shouted almost in unison.

Sudasan nodded to one of the Assembly officials, signaling the passing of the resolution. As the official hurried out of the hall to execute the order, someone raised a question.

"Are we adequately equipped to defend the republic against an extended attack?"

The chancellor had been dreading that question. The Magadhan army was among the mightiest in Sindhuvarta, capable of posing a challenge in the best of times. Now with Dandakabhukti captured, the central armory in the town was also out of bounds, putting additional pressure on Vanga's army.

"Everything depends on the strength and intent of the Magadhan army," he replied. "But to answer your question, we will have to retake Dandakabhukti and claim the armory if we are to survive a protracted war."

Ominous looks were exchanged once again.

"Can't we seek assistance from kingdoms of Kalinga and Odra?" the chief of Dandakabhukti broke his silence. "They could help us."

"We could try asking," Sudasan said, though he didn't sound very hopeful. The problem was that Vanga had always remained neutral in conflicts, and while nonalignment was a clever little strategy that did away with the need to pick sides, it made it harder to seek committed alliances when trouble came calling at your door.

Just then, a small murmur broke out in one corner of the assembly hall. Turning around, the chancellor saw a soldier speaking to a couple of officials.

"What is the matter?" Sudasan raised his voice.

"The soldier is a rider from near Dandakabhukti, Chancellor," one of the officials replied.

"Come down here, soldier," Sudasan beckoned the soldier. "What have you got for us?"

"I bring news of the emissaries who were sent to Dandakabhukti yesterday, your honor," the soldier said. "Their horses returned from Dandakabhukti this morning."

"Their horses...? What about the two emissaries?"

"Your honor, the horses were dragging their bodies in the mud behind them." As sharp intakes of breath sounded from around the room, the soldier continued, "Both of them were headless. We identified them through their official insignia... and this."

Sudasan reached out for the scroll that the rider held in his extended hand. Even as his fingers closed over the scroll, the chancellor knew it was the official letter that the emissaries had taken with them, registering Vanga's protest at the infringement, and offering to resolve the issue through talks.

Opening the scroll, the chancellor looked at the splotches of dried blood that were splattered over the letter. At the bottom, scrawled with a quill dipped in blood, was a terse message.

Your emissaries have paid the price of trespassing through Magadhan territory. Stay clear of Dandakabhukti.

* * *

"Are you certain this Huna scout spoke of plans to attack us by sea?" Yugandhara considered Ghatakarpara with his gentle brown eyes.

"Yes, your honor," the prince looked across the table at the Anarta chieftain and nodded.

The two men were seated in a private balcony situated high on the western corner of Yugandhara's palace in Dvarka, a lavish lunch spread out on the table between them. The bustle of the busy trading port was far below them, and the only sounds to be heard were the sighing of the wind and the occasional squawk of black-headed gulls.

Yugandhara leaned back, his brows furrowing as he concentrated on the problem. "But the Hunas and Sakas have no knowledge of the sea... It doesn't make sense."

Ghatakarpara's eyes strayed out toward the blue expanse of water stretching away to the horizon, his expression reflecting the typical wonder of one who has spent his entire life in landlocked places. His mind was partly on the news of the deva and asura attacks on Avanti – of which he had learned through Yugandhara just hours earlier – so he didn't respond to the chieftain right away.

"Indeed it doesn't make sense," the prince said finally. "But Councilor Amara Simha thinks the Hunas may have spent the last few years mastering the craft."

"You don't understand," Yugandhara shook his head. "Seamanship cannot be mastered by staying on land – one has to step aboard a ship and sail in the seas. We are seafarers..." he paused to sweep his hand in the direction of the bay, where half a dozen large ships could be seen anchored. "Ships from Anarta ply these seas every day, and the sailors are familiar with every cove and inlet along the coast on both sides. None of them has ever reported seeing Huna ships anywhere in these waters. Then, where are the ships that the Huna scout spoke of moored?"

Ghatakarpara shrugged, suddenly feeling foolish having come so far bearing news that was incorrect. The holes that Yugandhara was picking in the scout's story were now glaringly obvious.

"Navigating the smallest of vessels takes practice, and from what I know, the Hunas haven't been practicing at all," the chieftain continued. "So, either the Hunas are extremely foolhardy to attempt naval warfare, or your scout was lying through his teeth. Unless... unless..."

As a new possibility suddenly crossed his mind, Yugandhara's expression changed, and he stared intently up at the balcony's domed ceiling. "...unless the Hunas have been perfecting the craft in the waters of the Dark River."

From what they had heard the nomads tell, the people of Sindhuvarta knew that the Dark River flowed right through the middle of the Great Desert – where the Hunas and Sakas first came from, and where they returned to after being driven out of Sindhuvarta.

Ghatakarpara studied the chieftain carefully. Taking a deep breath of the salty air, he asked, "Is that possible?"

"It's possible. Sailing on a river is not the same thing as sailing in the seas, but it equips you with the necessary skills. And the Dark River is rumored to be a big river with powerful currents." As the idea took root, Yugandhara's eyes grew wide with anxiety. "So yes, it's possible."

"But wouldn't your sailors have known?"

"No sailor of Anarta ventures beyond the mouth of that accursed river whose foul waters gave birth to the Great Desert."

The chieftain turned to stare at the ocean, screwing his eyes against the sun's glare reflecting off the deep water. If the Hunas did come as was being suggested, Dvarka would bear the brunt of the attack. Dvarka – the shining jewel, pride of the Anartas.

"Councilor Amara Simha has already dispatched a rider to Ujjayini, alerting the samrat to the potential threat you face," said the prince, hoping to allay some of the chieftain's unease. "I'm sure the samrat will act on it and send forth reinforcements."

Yugandhara nodded, thinking of the deva and asura attacks on Avanti. Vikramaditya was already dealing with a lot, and he wasn't sure the king would have time to spare for the Anartas' miseries. Staring gloomily at Ghatakarpara sitting across the table, Yugandhara realized he had suddenly lost his appetite for lunch.

* * *

"You sent word for me, mother?"

The Mother Oracle raised her head to see Vikramaditya standing inside the door of her room. She sat on a plain straw mat that had been laid out on the cool marble floor, a copper pestle and mortar in her hands. She nodded, and as the samrat entered the room, she returned to grinding the contents of the mortar. The king stopped in front of the old woman and waited patiently for her to speak.

"Do sit down," the Mother Oracle finally gestured to a teakwood stool nearby. With a toothless grin she added, "It's your own palace."

Vikramaditya smiled as he drew the stool forward and sat down. Yet, he made no attempt at interrupting the woman, watching her quietly as she pounded away with the pestle. After a few moments had passed, she tilted her head and assessed the king with shrewd eyes.

"I hear the queen is getting better?"

"Yes, she is showing some definite signs of recovery," Vikramaditya's eyes brightened as he spoke. "She's still hardly speaking anything, but she appears to be more aware of what is happening around her... at least sometimes." He paused as doubt crept back on him. "It's the best I've seen her in two years."

"I'm happy to hear that," the Mother Oracle nodded, peering into the mortar. Setting the pestle aside, she upturned the mortar, emptying its contents into the cup of her right hand. The king saw that she had been crushing dried betel nuts. Tossing the small pieces into her mouth, the woman considered Vikramaditya.

"I'm happy to hear the queen is better," she repeated. "But beware of the stranger in the palace, wise king."

The samrat knitted his brows. "Do you mean the Healer, mother?"

"The breeze blowing through the palace speaks of bad intentions," the Mother Oracle replied obliquely. "Be on your guard."

Vikramaditya studied the old woman's face, expecting her to add to what she had said, but she had already closed her eyes and was chewing on the betel nuts, rocking back and forth in contentment. He looked down at his clasped hands, pondering over her words.

"Will that be all, mother?" he asked finally.

Opening her eyes, the Mother Oracle said, "There's also danger lurking in the clouds. Watch out for the lightning."

The samrat inclined his head. "Thank you, mother."

Stepping out of the oracle's room, Vikramaditya traced a path to an open portico with a large sundial mounted in its center. Leaning against the railings, the king shielded his eyes and looked heavenward, turning all the way around to thoroughly survey every little portion of the firmament.

Other than the blazing directly overhead, there was nothing in the spotless blue sky.

Vikramaditya was still observing the sky when he heard approaching footsteps. Looking around, he saw a palace attendant hurrying into the portico.

"Your honor, you are wanted in the queen's chamber," the attendant informed.

"Is the queen all right?" the king spoke with concern as he strode forward.

"Yes, your honor. It seems she spoke again."

When Vikramaditya hurried into the bedchamber, he saw Kshapanaka seated on the bed next to Vishakha, while Queen Upashruti stood close beside. The Queen Mother had one hand on Kshapanaka's shoulder as she leaned over and spoke gently to Vishakha.

"This is your sister Kshapanaka, my child," the king heard his mother saying.

Vishakha looked dubiously at Kshapanaka for a while before turning back to Queen Upashruti. "No, my sister is much younger," she said with a shake of her head.

Noticing Vetala Bhatta and Dhanavantri standing to one side, the samrat went up to them. "What's happened, raj-guru?" he asked.

"It seems she suddenly asked for Kshapanaka and her mother," the Acharya replied. "She has been expressing the desire to return to Nishada."

"She wants to go back to Nishada?" Vikramaditya looked incredulous.

"Obviously some memories from her childhood have returned," Dhanavantri proffered an explanation. "Memories of her mother and Kshapanaka... In her mind, Kshapanaka is still a small child, which is why she is finding it hard to accept what the queen mother is saying."

The three men returned their gaze to the bed. Vishakha shook her head once again. "No, my parents are in the palace in Nishada," she protested, tears welling up in her eyes. "I want to see them. Please take me there."

As Queen Upashruti and Kshapanaka turned to the men in helplessness, Vikramaditya asked, "Where's the Healer?"

"We've sent for him," replied Dhanavantri a trifle stiffly. "He should be... ah, there he is."

The Healer entered the room and marched straight to Vishakha's side, without bothering to acknowledge the others in the room. "Yes child, what is the matter?" he asked, looking down kindly at the queen.

"I want to go home, but these people aren't letting me," whimpered Vishakha. "Please tell them to take me home."

"Of course they will let you go," the Healer exclaimed reassuringly. "It's just that they want you to rest a while. Once you have woken from your sleep, you can go. Is that all right?"

Vishakha sniffled and nodded.

"Good. But hold these in your hands while you sleep."

The Healer placed two red hibiscuses in Vishakha's hands. "Now sleep."

The queen willingly subsided into the bed and turned on her side. In a matter of moments, she was asleep. As the Queen Mother and Kshapanaka left the bed, Vikramaditya watched the Healer begin drawing a *mandala* on the floor. The king's eyes were cloudy.

"What's the matter, Vikrama?" the raj-guru asked once they exited the bedchamber. The king, the Acharya and the royal physician were walking down one of the passageways. "Is something troubling you?"

Beware of the stranger in the palace, wise king.

"I happened to meet the Mother Oracle a little while ago," said the samrat.

"What did she say?" the Acharya probed.

The breeze blowing through the palace speaks of bad intentions.

"She…" Vikramaditya hesitated, caught in two minds. "She warned that there is danger in the clouds and that we must be careful of the lightning."

"Clouds?" Dhanavantri peered out of one of the windows lining the passageway. "There are no clouds for miles around."

"But if the Mother Oracle says we must be careful, we have to be," Vetala Bhatta reminded. "She's rarely been proved wrong."

"True." Vikramaditya licked his lips and avoided looking at his companions. "That's why I'll need your assistance, raj-guru. I intend taking the dagger to the Borderworld tonight."

* * *

"Don't look so downcast, my friend," Varahamihira said with a shake of his head. "No matter what the Healer has achieved, there's no debate over the fact that you're the best physician in the kingdom of Avanti."

Dhanavantri inclined his head, but the sag of his mouth indicated that Varahamihira's words hadn't reassured him the least bit. The two councilors were seated in the verandah of the physician's house – Varahamihira on a large swing, nursing a cup of *soma*, Dhanavantri on a fluffy mattress, drinking a concoction of honey and lime. A strong breeze blew from the north, cooling the night air around Ujjayini.

"Look, the truth is that the Healer has worked wonders," Dhanavantri spoke at last. "And I mean not just in the palace – everyone in the city is talking about him and his cures."

"Yes... but..." Varahamihira groped for a counterargument. "But take Vishakha's example. She'd been showing signs of recovery well before the Healer's shadow fell across Ujjayini's gates."

"Very minor signs," the physician butted in to clarify.

"Okay, but signs nonetheless. It's possible she was getting better under your care and the Healer simply happened by at the right time. That is a possibility, isn't it?"

The physician conceded the point with a shrug. "But it's the speed of her recovery under the Healer that's amazing. You can't discount that."

"Well, he's been using tantric powers. That doesn't exactly count as *medicine*."

"But it counts as a *cure*," Dhanavantri said glumly, sinking lower into the mattress.

"Okay, so the Healer is... good," Varahamihira spoke after a short pause. "But why are you letting that weigh you down?"

"Because he's worried the palace will start paying greater heed to the Healer," said Madari, speaking from the doorway that led into the house. She had appeared quietly, without either of the men noticing her presence, and as she leaned against the door, her expression was one of frustration and sympathy at her husband's predicament.

Dhanavantri glanced up at his wife in annoyance, but didn't retort.

Varahamihira turned his gaze from Madari and looked at the physician inquiringly.

"Well, the samrat and the queen mother have been turning to the Healer a lot more the last two days," Dhanavantri admitted grudgingly.

"That's natural as he has played a role in Vishakha's recovery," Varahamihira's tone was matter-of-fact.

"Exactly the point I've been trying to make all this while," the physician said in exasperation. Now that the issue had been forced into the open, his tongue loosened. "The Healer has succeeded where I have failed. And his appeal is not limited to just the king and the queen mother – even Vararuchi has been taken in by his curative powers."

"In what way?"

"Vararuchi has persuaded the Healer to see his mother." Seeing Varahamihira's confusion, Dhanavantri added, "To cure *badi-maa* of her arthritis. They left by boat a little while ago. I wasn't even told about it, even though I have been tending to her ailment."

Varahamihira opened his mouth to say something, but decided against it. He could see the royal physician's concerns weren't entirely without basis.

"Well, whatever his powers might be, I doubt the Healer

has it in him to restore the leg I have lost," he said at last, trying to inject some lightheartedness into the conversation. "And you have my assurance that I shall not consult him should a need ever arise. I dislike the sight of him."

It was Dhanavantri's turn to study Varahamihira closely. "Why do you use the word dislike?"

"I don't know. There's something *fishy* about him. He's just so oversure of everything, so glib... He gives me the impression that he's too good to be true."

"Exactly what I thought of him too," the physician looked pleasantly surprised, even relieved. "I just didn't say so."

"Wise of you – it would have been put down to professional rivalry," Varahamihira nodded. Taking a final swig out of his cup, he proceeded to get off the swing. "Come, let's not allow the lovely dinner that sister has cooked to go cold. If I had to eat cold food, I needn't have accepted your invitation to dinner."

"That's why you should have got married when you had the chance to," Madari teased playfully.

"A hefty price to pay for two warm meals a day, sister," Varahamihira quipped, as he stood up with the help of his crutch. "And even if I had wanted marriage, no woman would have put up with my obsession for my little inventions."

As Madari and the older councilor went indoors, Dhanavantri rose from his mattress. The breeze had stiffened to a draughty wind that was kicking up little puffs of dust in the courtyard outside. From somewhere inside, an unlatched window banged in the wind.

The physician went inside and scouted around the house until he found the troublesome window. As he fastened it shut, he thought he heard the faraway rumble of thunder. At first, he thought nothing of it. But just as he was entering the dining room where Madari and a kitchen help were serving dinner, he stiffened as Vikramaditya's words from earlier in the day came back to him.

She warned that there is danger in the clouds and that we must be careful of the lightning.

If what he had heard was thunder, there had to be lightning out there as well.

***

Thick charcoal-red light flowed from the sockets of the skulls on Vetala Bhatta's spear, percolating through the yellow glow of the solitary lamp that occupied a far recess in Vikramaditya's bedchamber. The combined effect was a dim, ocher illumination that swirled around the Acharya as he sat at the head of the king's bed, one hand holding the spear, the other placed palm downward on the king's fevered forehead. The raj-guru had his eyes closed, and his lips moved to a barely audible mantra.

The samrat lay inert, his body rigid and shoulders squared, the tendons stiff in his neck. Even in the diffused light, the pallor on his face was evident, and his breath came in shallow, erratic spurts. The king's hands, which were by his sides, were clenched tight – and from the right fist a thin blade protruded, the metal winking wickedly in the heavy, ocher light.

For a long while, neither man moved. Then, all of a sudden, the Acharya's brow contorted and his eyes flickered open.

Beware of the stranger in the palace, wise king.

Alarm flashed across Vetala Bhatta's face, but before the

phrase could anchor itself in his mind, Vikramaditya's body convulsed violently. The raj-guru immediately screwed his eyes shut, fighting to overcome the distraction. The exertion brought beads of perspiration to the Acharya's forehead, but with his concentration returning, the tremors running through the king's body weakened and receded.

The glow from the skulls gradually increased in intensity, and the Acharya felt the king's skin go damp and clammy under his palm. A few moments later, Vikramaditya heaved a huge sigh, and his body went limp. Opening his eyes, Vetala Bhatta saw that the king was hardly breathing, and his muscles had acquired the slackness of deep slumber.

More than slumber, the slackness of death...

Yet, Vikramaditya retained a tight grip on the dagger in his hand.

Breathing in huge gulps of air, the Acharya mopped the sweat from his brow. Then, careful not to disturb the stillness of the room, he made his way to the door of the bedchamber and opened it. In the passageway outside stood Kalidasa, leaning against a pillar, his great arms folded across his broad chest.

On seeing Vetala Bhatta framing the doorway, the commander of the *samsaptakas* straightened and raised an eyebrow in inquiry.

"He has crossed over into the Borderworld," the Acharya announced softly, dabbing his face dry with a cloth.

"Is he fine?" the giant asked, craning his neck to look into the bedchamber.

The raj-guru nodded, a faraway look on his face. Was that the roll of distant thunder? He cocked an ear, but heard nothing but the strong wind rustling through the trees outside.

Glancing over his shoulder, the Acharya said, "Yes he is, but this is the most delicate and dangerous part. Nothing should upset Vikrama's death-sleep. Otherwise... he may never be able to come back."

"Do not fear, Acharya," Kalidasa replied, planting himself in the middle of the passageway, one hand resting lightly on the pommel of his scimitar. "I will be here to make sure nothing disturbs our king."

Borderworld

Vikramaditya picked his way down the weed-infested bathing *ghat* with caution, stepping over the tentacled sprawl of tree roots, and skirting the larger clumps of soggy, putrefying vegetation that carpeted the stairs. In many places, the old, cracked stone had come loose, while rubble from Ujjayini's crumbling ramparts littered the *ghat*'s steps.

Despite all his caution, the king's foot skidded every now and then to dislodge an avalanche of pebbles, which rolled down and disappeared into the fetid, gray-black waters of the Kshipra. The river barely moved, and even the ripples from the falling pebbles died prematurely on its sludgy surface.

Reaching the water's edge, the samrat peered around, looking for a means of getting across the river. Although the sun was directly overhead, the light was pale and feeble, failing to penetrate the shadows of the gnarled and withering trees lurking along the river's banks. Even the sun's heat was absent, and as he looked directly up at the anemic yellow orb in the faded white sky, the king shivered at the moldy dampness in the air.

All around him was the overpowering stench of decay and ruin.

Scouring the bank, Vikramaditya finally found what he was looking for: a small boat, almost camouflaged, imprisoned within a dense infestation of reeds and undergrowth. It was with considerable effort that the king liberated the vessel, its rotting wood crumbling under his fingers as he tugged it into the river. He surveyed the boat as it bobbed in the undulating water like a bloated carcass, his eye taking in the layer of slimy moss that masked the faint outline of the sun-crest of Avanti that had once been proudly inscribed on its hull. The boat was missing a couple of boards on one side, but seeing it still had one broken oar and was dry on the inside, the samrat decided it would serve to transport him to the opposite bank.

The row across the Kshipra was negotiated without event; however, just as he docked the boat and prepared to step ashore, a roll of thunder fell on Vikramaditya's ears. The same instant, the river underneath seemed to pitch and heave, throwing the rickety boat sideways and making the samrat lose his balance. The king made a grab at the boat's gunwales, steadying himself and the rocking boat –

– when he felt the dagger that he had stuck in his belt come loose and slip from his waist!

Looking down, Vikramaditya saw the slender blade cartwheel in little arcs of light, plunging straight toward the wedge between the boat and the river bank. Drawing his breath, the king lunged after the knife, his fingers grabbing and missing, catching and slipping...

The desperate juggle over the rancid, insidious Kshipra seemed to last forever, but with the dagger just inches from the water, the king's fingers caught its obsidian hilt and it was plucked back to safety. For a moment the samrat just stood in the swaying boat, clutching the dagger to his chest where his heart was hammering away from anxiety and exertion.

Having calmed himself, Vikramaditya stepped on to firm land and secured the dagger to his belt. He then turned to survey the bleached ruins of Ujjayini, choked by the encroaching forest of dead trees, desolate and utterly devoid of any form of life.

This was the fate that would befall his beloved city one day, the king realized sadly.

Then, looking up at the wan, dying sun, he saw that this was the fate that would one day befall everything that had ever come into being. What he was witnessing was nothing but Creation caught in the transition between life and death.

For this was the Borderworld, the eternal realm of the undead ghouls, the gloaming separating the world of the living from the world of the dead. The bridge over which everything that had been created had to pass when going from a state of existence to a state of destruction. A mirror world where things already existed in their doomed, decomposing state...

Vikramaditya turned and began ploughing through the coarse, knee-high grass that grew in profusion beyond the tree-lined bank. He realized he still had a fair distance to cover in his journey to the cremation grounds, presided over by the Ghoulmaster.

***

Shukracharya and Vararuchi rode at a steady canter through the night, the whistling of the quickening wind and the soft pounding of hooves filling the silence that stretched between them. The two had hardly exchanged a word since leaving Ushantha's house, and on the two occasions that Shukracharya had tried to make conversation, Vararuchi's replies had been offhand and indefinite.

The high priest wished he knew what was occupying the councilor's mind.

The bones had told him a lot about Vararuchi the previous night, yet there was much that the bones were incapable of revealing. So, while Shukracharya knew that the councilor had ruled the kingdom of Avanti until his half-brother was old enough to become king, he didn't know how Vararuchi felt about having to abdicate the throne to Vikramaditya. And while he had learned that Vararuchi had a wife in one of the Southern Kingdoms – from whom he had begotten a son and a daughter – the bones had said nothing about why the councilor's wife and children continued to live in the far south while he served in the court of Avanti.

For that matter, the bones had remained silent about the fact that Vararuchi kept his marriage a closely guarded secret – even from his own mother! That was something that Shukracharya had stumbled upon by sheer accident.

"It's the curse of life that we have no time for our children when they are young, and they have no time for us when we are old," Ushantha had said as the high priest had begun drawing a *mandala* on the floor of her bedroom. The woman was plainly deprived of company, and the presence of an unexpected guest had cheered her to garrulity. "To answer your question, yes, it does get lonely here at times. I do wish Vararuchi got married – at least then I'd have some grandchildren for company."

"Your son isn't married?" Shukracharya paused and looked up, his fingers hovering over the half-drawn *mandala*. Vararuchi had stepped out of the room on some errand, leaving the high priest free to probe the matter.

"No," Ushantha exclaimed. "Whenever I raise the subject, he says he's too busy at the palace, and that he won't have time for a wife and children. How silly is that! It's just an excuse, I say. You're a Healer – can't you do something about this?"

The high priest searched the woman's face for artifice, but all he found was forthrightness staring straight back at him. He shook his head and smiled.

"I'm afraid not, mother. I have cures for most ailments, but I confess there is none for chronic stubbornness."

Now as they rode back toward Ujjayini, Shukracharya peered at the back of the councilor's head with narrowed eyes. He knew the bones couldn't have been wrong – they never were.

"I take it that you are married, your honor?"

Shukracharya posed the question diplomatically, inflecting his tone with innocent curiosity, yet he was certain he saw Vararuchi flinch in his saddle.

"I'm not," the councilor mumbled tersely after a brief pause.

"For some strange reason I always thought you were," said the high priest, feigning surprise. "In fact, I could almost have been certain…"

"Wouldn't I know if I was?" Vararuchi turned to face his

companion, his voice harsh and cold. "What gave you the idea? Have you heard anything being mentioned...?"

This time, the high priest thought he detected a hint of anxiety in the councilor's voice.

"No, your honor."

"Well, even if you did, it couldn't have been anything but a silly rumor," Vararuchi snapped. "Everyone knows I'm not married." With that, he simply turned away and continued riding.

Shukracharya smiled in the dark – a dark, secret smile. The half-brother of the samrat intrigued him more and more.

They had been riding through a densely forested gorge with steep ridges on both sides, but moments later, they emerged into flat, open countryside. Immediately, the two riders were drawn to the northern sky, where flashes of lightning lit up a low bank of clouds.

"We must move fast," said Vararuchi in a tense and edgy voice as soon as he had caught sight of the lightning. Without waiting for a response from Shukracharya, the councilor spurred his mount into a gallop.

Digging his heels into his horse's belly, the high priest gave chase, wondering why Vararuchi was in a tearing hurry to get back to Ujjayini all of a sudden. As far as he could tell, it wasn't the prospect of getting caught in a storm that was bothering the councilor.

It had to be something else...

* * *

The three drunkards were the last to vacate the tavern, having been coaxed and cajoled into leaving on the innkeeper's promise of a free pitcher of firewater to last them their way home. The three men now swayed down one of the narrow roads in Ujjayini's eastern quarter, clutching one another for support and passing the innkeeper's inducement from hand to hand, quickly depleting the last of the day's quota of grog. All around them the bracing wind blew, tearing at the treetops, moaning down alleyways and blowing detritus across the streets.

"Aaah…" sighed one of them, licking a final drop off the rim of the upturned pitcher. Shaking the empty pitcher to ensure that it had no more firewater to yield, he flung it to one side, the earthenware hitting a low wall and breaking with a loud clatter.

"That was good," he beamed, smacking his lips in satisfaction and wiping his mouth with the back of his hand.

"Wish we had another pitcher," slurred one of his mates, casting a forlorn look at the smashed pitcher lying by the roadside. With a burst of petulance, he added, "We should have asked the innkeeper to give us *two* of those."

"Shhh…" said the third, placing a finger on his lips. Casting a bleary eye into the darkness around, he continued, "Shhh… no noise. If any soldiers of the City Watch hear us, we'll be in trouble for disrupting the peace."

As luck would have it, no member of the City Watch appeared to be in the vicinity, and the men weaved and stumbled unhindered, alternating between silence and boisterousness. Passing an overgrown garden, one of them pulled himself free of the grasp of the other two. Using mime to indicate that he wanted to answer nature's call, he made for the shrubbery separating the garden from the road. Too impatient to wait, his partners simply continued teetering forward.

Ever since they had left the tavern, dull flashes of lightning and a near-constant roll of thunder had filled the heavens overhead. Now, as the drunk stood relieving himself, a sudden blinding flash of lightning hit the ground not far to his right. Reeling under the impact of rushing air, his skin tingling with heat, the explosive crack of thunder flooding his ears, the man turned and stared numbly into the darkness.

As his eyes – which had miraculously escaped injury – adjusted to the feeble light, he thought he saw a hulking shape rise from the spot where the lightning had struck. Blinking rapidly, the drunk watched as the shape gained height and form and assumed humanoid proportions. Then, as another flash of lightning backlit the sky, he noticed the four large horns protruding from the figure's head.

Rooted to the spot, his face contorting in terror, the drunk watched as the four-horned figure turned its head slowly and surveyed him with cold eyes that shone like dull, metallic moonlight. Almost the same instant, the beast bared its teeth in a noiseless snarl and lunged at the drunkard.

The drunkard let out a scream – but his own voice was lost in the flat hollow silence that now filled his ears.

His friends, who had come to a halt a little way down the road, heard the scream though. It was a high-pitched shriek of horror that tore through the rasping growl coming from the beast's mouth. The shriek leaped skyward and pierced the canopy of trees overhead, sending a flock of roosting birds into frenzied flight.

As his two friends stood arm in arm, watching in shocked silence, the beast swatted the drunkard with its large hand. The blow lifted the drunkard off the ground and sent him tumbling and rolling into the middle of the road. He immediately tried to scramble back to his feet, but the beast took two loping strides and kicked him brutally so that he once again fell on his face. He lay sprawled in the dirt for a moment, whimpering and mewling for help.

Then, clawing at the mud for support, he began to raise himself again... But before he could push himself off the ground, the beast raised its large foot and brought it down heavily on his back. The weight of the foot broke the drunkard's spine, and his torso imploded to the sound of cracking bones.

The two friends down the road trembled in unison and looked at one another. When they returned their gaze to the spot where their partner now lay dead, their eyes grew even wider in alarm.

The giant, four-horned beast had turned its cold, quicksilver eyes upon them!

Panic gripped the men's hearts as the beast began striding down the road toward them, shoulders hunched, arms swinging purposefully, hands clenched in fists. Paying heed to the frantic signals being transmitted by their brains, they turned and lurched away, screaming and moaning in abject terror. But the beast continued its steady charge, rapidly gaining ground on the two fleeing figures.

The beast was almost upon the babbling drunks when it unexpectedly broke its stride and drew to a stop, displaying a sudden change of intent. One of the drunkards threw a petrified glance over his shoulder to see the beast suddenly leap sideways and clamber onto the large trees lining the park. Then, as the two cowering men watched in wonder, the creature moved among the treetops with remarkable agility, pushing deeper and deeper into the park to the accompaniment of angry grunts and the snapping and cracking of branches.

The next instant, six more bolts of lightning descended on Ujjayini, each following the other in quick succession, each landing in a different part of the city. Almost immediately, the sky opened up in a sudden, heavy shower.

Their bodies quaking with fright, their breath catching raggedly at their throats, the two surviving drunks stumbled into a clumsy embrace. Clutching each other, drawing and imparting hope and support at the same time, not believing their good fortune, they shivered and watched the rain puddle around the broken body of their friend lying in the middle of the road.

* * *

A trail of dripping water followed Dhanavantri as he stepped out of the rain and entered the palace. Mopping the rainwater off his head, face and arms, wringing out his clothes to allow free movement, the physician brushed past the guards milling around the doorway, toward a hall filled with the bobbing shadows of Avanti's courtiers.

"We have to first ascertain what exactly is happening," Dhanavantri heard the echo of Varahamihira's voice rise above the jittery hum. "We can't act until we have more details, so please stay calm. Councilor Kshapanaka and Councilor Dhanavantri have gone to investigate matters. We should hear from them soon… ah, there is the royal physician!"

Dhanavantri ploughed through the assembly instead of waiting for the courtiers to make way. The gathering fell back, allowing the physician access to Varahamihira, who stood in the middle of the hall in the company of Shanku, Queen Upashruti, the chief of the Palace Guards and a couple of senior courtiers. Looking at the circle of inquiring eyes, the physician spoke bluntly.

"We are under attack," he announced.

"Again?"

The question exploded softly from somewhere to Dhanavantri's right, muffled by gasps and hisses of dismay. An incredulous silence followed, filled with the patter of rain and the plaintive pealing of the alarm bells in the distance. The shock of the Ashvin attack was still fresh in memory, Dhanavantri reflected, so in spite of the warning of the brass bells, the courtiers had probably been hoping to hear that nothing was the matter after all.

"Who is attacking us?" asked Varahamihira, leaning on his crutch as if the weight of the news was an additional burden on his shoulders.

"We don't know," Dhanavantri shook his head. "But it seems some... *things*... are attacking the city randomly. Big and large and very violent things."

A collective sigh of despair fluttered through the hall before settling on slumped shoulders.

"Where have the attacks occurred?" pressed Varahamihira.

"Everywhere. In every quarter of the city. Houses, shops, City Watch pickets... anything and everything is being attacked. They are just maiming, killing and destroying. Soldiers of the City Watch are trying to engage them in combat, but these things are simply too powerful."

"How many of them are there?"

"No one knows," Dhanavantri shrugged unhappily. "But given the scale of the attack, too many."

"What *are* these things?" This was one of the senior courtiers, his voice strained. "Surely someone must have seen them, respected Councilor."

"It's dark and raining heavily," the physician replied.

"And these things apparently move very fast. No one's caught a clear sight of them – no one who's alive, at least."

"Someone who's still alive has." Kshapanaka's voice came from far back near the door. "These things are asuras, in all probability."

Heads swiveled and the courtiers quietly parted way for the councilor. Kshapanaka walked into the hall, bow in one hand, sword dangling at her hip. Like Dhanavantri, she was wet with rainwater, her clothes clinging to her sensuous form.

"A soldier of the City Watch reports that two drunkards in the eastern quarter saw one of these things appear," she explained. "According to the drunks, the thing materialized in a bolt of lightning." Seeing Dhanavantri cock an eyebrow, she inclined her head. "The thing apparently crushed one of their friends to death under its foot."

"Can drunkards be believed?" one skeptic courtier protested. "They may well have imagined the whole thing."

"The soldier of the City Watch confirms that a horribly mangled body has been found on a road by a park in the eastern quarter, where the drunks claim their friend was killed," Kshapanaka spoke evenly. "The man was crushed by something impossibly heavy – like a huge boulder or a tree trunk or a heavy foot. And no boulders or tree trunks were found near the body."

She paused to let this sink in. "The drunks say the beast had a human body, but was much larger and heavier, with eyes that shine like moonlight. It also had four horns on its head."

"Yes, rakshasas from Patala," Varahamihira exchanged glances with the physician. Raising his voice so he could be heard clearly, he added. "They're here for the dagger, courtiers."

More anxious looks passed around the room. Sadguna, the elderly chief of the Palace Guards, cleared his throat. "We must raise the samrat," he appealed to Varahamihira.

"We can't," the councilor answered sharply. Reining his voice in and dropping it to a conspiratorial whisper, he took in the ring of distressed faces. "The samrat mustn't be disturbed in his journey to the Borderworld. It's too dangerous – you all know that. The Acharya can bring the samrat back only when he is ready to return."

"Can't Councilor Kalidasa do something?" Sadguna pressed. The swell of approval in the hall made it obvious that the courtiers were pinning a lot of hope on the commander of the *samsaptakas*.

"He has instructions to prevent anyone... or any*thing* from disturbing the samrat and the Acharya."

"Why did Vararuchi pick such a time to visit his mother?" Queen Upashruti's lips were thin lines of disapproval; she made it a point not to mention Ushantha by name. "He should be in the palace during times of crisis. Surely he was aware of the Mother Oracle's warning."

"He must have had some important reason to visit *badi-maa*." Varahamihira stole a glance at Dhanavantri, who averted his gaze. "He also probably didn't expect an attack so soon. To be honest, even I didn't."

The Queen Mother didn't reply, but the petulance with which she crossed her hands and looked away told Varahamihira that she didn't appreciate his opinion on the subject.

"It doesn't matter who *isn't* here," Kshapanaka's voice

rose by a few octaves, the ring of authority masking a slight exasperation. "*We* are here. If the asuras want the dagger, they are bound to come to the palace. We have to protect the palace with everything we've got. Let us prepare for that."

Almost as if they had found sustenance in her words, the courtiers nodded in agreement. Relieved though he was, Varahamihira raised a cautionary hand.

"Yes, but we have to try and stop those rakshasas from wreaking havoc in the city as well."

"How can we do both?" asked one courtier. "We can defend either the city or the palace."

"We have to defend both," Varahamihira was adamant. "If it's our job to protect the dagger, it's also our job to protect the citizens of Avanti. There's no question of choosing one over the other."

"I agree, honorable courtiers," said Shanku, speaking for the first time. She turned to Varahamihira. "Let me ride into the city, your honor."

"I shall come with you," Dhanavantri stepped forward. "I will help you marshal the City Watch." Looking from Kshapanaka to Varahamihira, he added, "The raj-guru and Kalidasa can't leave the samrat's side, so it's up to the two of you and the palace guards to defend the palace. But I shall dispatch some *samsaptaka* units to assist you."

"We will do our best," assured Varahamihira. "Fight well, my friends."

As Shanku and the physician left the hall, Varahamihira addressed a courtier. "Have word of the asura attack sent to Kalidasa and the Acharya. They should know of the nature of the threat we're facing."

Turning to Sadguna, the councilor continued reeling off

instructions. "Please escort the queen mother and all the other members of the royal household to the safety of the Labyrinth. Have your men make sure that the palace is emptied, the Labyrinth is sealed and booby-trapped, and no one is at risk."

The chief turned to Queen Upashruti, and the two made their way to the staircase leading to the chambers above accompanied by a posse of palace guards. They were halfway up the stairs when Varahamihira called after Sadguna.

"I shall be in the council chamber with Councilor Kshapanaka. Meet me there once the palace has been secured."

Palace guards jumped to obey instructions and junior courtiers huddled around in hurried discussion as Kshapanaka, Varahamihira and three senior courtiers adjourned to the council chamber. Outside the palace, the rain kept pelting down, and the pealing of the brass bells increased in number and intensity all across Ujjayini.

* * *

"Has the dagger been handed over to the Ghoulmaster yet, raj-guru?"

Vetala Bhatta started on hearing the low voice. He had been staring uneasily at the closed window, consumed by the sound of the alarm bells outside, wondering what impending danger they portended. But what also worried him was their growing clamor – if it permeated and disrupted his king's death-sleep, the samrat might never be able to find his way out of the Borderworld.

There was one more thing that troubled the Acharya. A phrase he had picked up just as the king had crossed over, a half-remembered warning that nibbled at the fringes of his mind...

Beware of... Beware of the...

Turning to his left, he saw Kalidasa's form towering down from the middle of the bedchamber. The giant wielded his scimitar in one hand, while the other held a broad shield made of bronze. The sight of the weapons disconcerted the Acharya.

Glancing down at the inert form of Vikramaditya, the raj-guru motioned with his hands, instructing Kalidasa to leave the room. Getting up softly, he followed the giant out of the bedchamber. It wasn't until they were in the passageway outside that Vetala Bhatta spoke.

"No, the dagger is still with the king. Perhaps he hasn't met the Betaal so far. Perhaps the Betaal hasn't taken possession of the dagger yet."

"Would he refuse to accept the dagger?" asked Kalidasa. "Could he?"

"He could." The Acharya shrugged. "He is not bound to accept it. But Vikrama appeared certain that the Betaal would honor the pledge. That's why he has braved this journey into the Borderworld."

Kalidasa nodded and cast his eyes around the corners of the passageway.

The raj-guru looked at the scimitar. "What's outside?" he gestured with his head.

"Rakshasas," the giant replied. "They have stormed the city and are causing mayhem. I was told we've already lost many lives, both soldier and civilian." His grip tightened on his sword, jaw hardening in anger and impatience. "Dhanavantri and Shanku have ridden into the city.

Kshapanaka and Varahamihira are below, fortifying the palace against attack."

"And Vararuchi?"

"It seems he has gone to visit *badi-maa*." Kalidasa's broad chest rose and fell as he heaved a big sigh. His eyes looked disturbed. "I don't know if he will make it back in time."

"I know you want to be out there with the others, fighting off the attack and saving lives," said Vetala Bhatta, his tone kind but firm. "But we can't, you and I. We are needed here."

Seeing Kalidasa nod, the raj-guru turned back to the bedchamber, closing the door behind him. He knew what he'd said had been unnecessary – no matter what happened, Kalidasa could be trusted to stand outside that door and fight for his king until his last breath.

Vetala Bhatta remembered the day he had first set eyes on the little orphan, a scrawny boy of around eight, but tall for his age. Vikramaditya had brought the boy to the royal library where the children of the royal household were tutored, and had introduced him as Kalidasa. The young Vikrama had explained that he had found the boy hiding in a temple near Lava, and that the boy had no recollection of his past. So he had brought him to Ujjayini, and he wondered if the Acharya would accept Kalidasa as one of his wards as well.

The raj-guru had his reservations – fairly deep ones at that. Kalidasa hardly spoke, and his social skills were awkward at best. But the Acharya had persevered, partly out of respect for the young Vikrama's faith and affection for the boy. Not that Kalidasa ever showed signs of reciprocation; the boy was almost obstinately uncommunicative and withdrawn. Things came to such a pass that the Acharya was close to

telling the prince that he couldn't tutor Kalidasa any longer
when, one evening, Amara Simha paid him an unexpected
visit. The councilor handed Vetala Bhatta a palm leaf scroll,
on which was penned a short, but incredibly touching poem
on gratitude and friendship.

Seeing the caliber of the work, Vetala Bhatta had
begun heaping praise on Amara Simha for his writing
when the grammarian had restrained him – revealing that
the poem had actually been authored by Kalidasa for
Vikramaditya!

That evening, a little over a year after he had been
brought to Ujjayini, something had shifted inside Kalidasa.

Outside the palace, the rain increased in intensity,
muting the sound of the alarm bells a little. The raj-guru
smiled to himself and shook his head. That evening,
something had shifted inside Kalidasa *permanently*. The
young boy had found a key to unlock the kinship he felt for
Vikramaditya.

That evening, Kalidasa had been reborn as the Kalidasa
they had come to love, admire and respect – the Kalidasa
who now stood outside the door of the bedchamber, willing
to fight until his last breath for his king.

For his oldest friend.

* * *

The ringing of the bells had reached Vararuchi and
Shukracharya's ears long before Ujjayini had come into
their sights. The councilor had charged through the dark
and the rain, driving his mount harder and harder as they
neared the city, and Shukracharya had struggled to keep
pace. The high priest had hollered to Vararuchi a couple
of times, demanding to know what was happening, but the

king's half-brother had merely beckoned with his hand, urging greater speed.

Now as they reined in their horses to a thundering halt on the west bank of the Kshipra, Vararuchi leaped off his mount and strode to the river's edge, where in the light of a covered lamp a boat could be seen riding the water. A couple of soldiers of the City Watch stood by the boat, waiting. Across the Kshipra, the lights of Ujjayini reflected and diffused through the rain, spilling softly over the city's ramparts like a river of ocher mist breaking its banks.

The bells continued their incessant clanging.

Getting off his horse, Shukracharya scuttled down the embankment to where Vararuchi was now in earnest conversation with the soldiers of the City Watch.

"Would you tell me what's happening?" the high priest asked as he neared the group.

"Our city is under attack," Vararuchi explained brusquely.

"Who?" Shukracharya shook his head to clear the confusion. "I mean, by whom?"

"You might not want to come with us," replied the councilor, evading the question. "I'm told it's pretty bad inside. It's best you stay here. Safer."

"But your honor, why are you being attacked?" Shukracharya persisted. "And how is it possible? Everything was peaceful a few hours ago when we left."

"We are being attacked by asuras." Seeing the head priest's eye fly open in surprise, Vararuchi nodded grimly. "See what I meant? It's safer to stay here than come inside."

The councilor and the soldiers began stepping into the boat when Shukracharya took a few steps forward. "But... I would like to come too."

"Why?" Vararuchi snapped irritably. Waving his arm in the direction of Ujjayini, he asked, "Do you want to die? It's nasty in there... many lives have already been lost, it seems. Stay here. You can come in if the city is still standing tomorrow."

"I can help."

"What help?" One leg already in the boat, the councilor turned to look at Shukracharya in vexation. "Don't tell me you will help in the fighting."

"You forget I am a healer, your honor." The head priest paused as the small group turned their eyes on him. "I can help with the wounded. Especially the soldiers."

The boat pushed away from its moorings and nosed into the black water, the boatmen paddling furiously toward the darkened bathing *ghats*. Shukracharya sat in the center, flanked by Vararuchi and one of the soldiers of the City Watch.

"How do you know it's an asura attack?" the head priest ventured.

"The attackers are giant rakshasas with four horns on their heads," the soldier beside him answered.

"Is that all?"

"Well, they have hard, shell-like bodies that spears and arrows can't seem to penetrate. Swords just shatter against them. And they have eyes that glow like white moonlight."

Shukracharya could feel his heartbeat quicken. "Are they... dark blue in color? Their skin?"

The soldier shook his head. "No idea. It's too dark to tell, and anyway their bodies are mostly covered by that shell-like armor."

"Why do you ask?" Vararuchi turned and looked at the high priest with keen interest.

"No particular reason. I just... In my travels I've heard people speak of asuras having moonlight eyes and blue skin." Shukracharya fumbled and recovered. "So I was curious."

The councilor dismissed the healer with a shake of his head. "We must have some idea of the approximate numbers dead," he looked at the soldiers hopefully.

"There are all kinds of numbers being bandied around, your honor," the soldier seated near the prow of the boat replied. "Some put the toll at fifty, some say it's closer to seventy-five. According to one report, thirty people have died in the eastern quarter alone. All we know for certain is that the numbers are mounting."

Looking up at the city, Vararuchi let out an effusive oath.

"It's the invisible fire that is causing the most damage," said the other soldier in a voice that trembled slightly with awe and fear. "Because it can't be seen..."

"*Invisible* fire?" the councilor interjected.

"The asuras throw something that is invisible to the eye, but which scorches the skin on contact," the soldier by the prow confirmed. "I chanced upon three bodies in an alley that were charred beyond recognition. Soldiers of the Watch – I could tell by their swords."

"Invisible fire," Vararuchi muttered in disbelief.

"They're also armed with swords, your honor. Giant, jagged swords, sharp as steel. But they look as if they've been fashioned out of bones."

Shukracharya held his breath, not heeding another word being spoken by the men. Asuras with four horns on their heads, shell-like bodies that were impenetrable, eyes that glowed like white moonlight... and jagged swords shaped out of bone.

Diti's seven demonic sons. The dreaded Maruts. Asura by birth, deva by allegiance.

The irony of it brought a small sneer to Shukracharya's lips. After all, he was a deva by birth, but asura by allegiance. Loyalty was everything and nothing.

The humor passed quickly, and cold, numbing anxiety took its place. He had been banking on the fact that the human king could fend off the attack with the Hellfires. But now that he knew the identity of the attackers, Shukracharya saw the Hellfires would be useless in this battle – for Diti had cleverly infused the two swords with mantras to keep the *churails* from causing harm to those born out of her womb.

Shukracharya marveled at Indra's tactic of sending the Maruts to Ujjayini. There was nothing the humans could do to protect the dagger.

It was now entirely up to him to get to Ujjayini and prevent the seven rakshasas from claiming the Halahala for their master.

Maruts

The sun had faded and lost form long before the fog had crept in around Vikramaditya. Now all that existed was a dull, white, disembodied half-light that shifted around the king, watching him like a wary sentinel as he walked through the flat, wet marshland. The air was thick with damp, and a fine drizzle fell from the whiteness above, settling on the samrat like a clammy shroud.

The earth beneath Vikramaditya's feet was soft and alkaline, pockmarked with cesspools that held small quantities of dark green water in their shallow basins. Other than the moss, lichen and clumps of dwarf-reed that clung to the edges of the pools, the ground was devoid of vegetation, with no tree or shrub to break the sweeping, weeping monotony of the soggy marsh.

Strangely enough, even though he had no way of finding his bearings in this featureless desolation, the king's feet instinctively knew where to lead him.

Vikramaditya had lost track of how long he had been

walking when somewhere ahead and a little to his left, he fancied he saw a nebulous orange glow punctuate the curtain of fog. The glow flickered and died as the fog thickened, and the samrat shrugged it off as a trick of his mind. But a little further on, another glow appeared up to his right. Then yet another, straight ahead. Unlike the first glow, these two persisted in his vision.

The king realized he had finally arrived at the cremation grounds.

Almost at once, as if obeying some silent command, the fog receded like an ebbing tide, and the cremation ground revealed itself to Vikramaditya. Hundreds of smokeless funeral pyres stretched away in all four directions, dwindling into the marshland haze. Many of the pyres were burning low, but many others were in full flame. Around these, the king could see small groups of ghouls hovering, wraithlike, tending to the fires and making certain the passing over of the dead was complete and without incident. The monastic ghouls paid the samrat no attention – their work was with the dead who arrived on pyres, not the living who walked on their feet.

Vikramaditya didn't concern himself with the ghoul attendants either. His focus was on a solitary banyan tree of impossible proportions that sprouted in the middle of the burning pyres. The tree was of majestic height, its upper reaches lost in the fog overhead. But its lower branches were visible, spreading like a mammoth umbrella over the cremation ground. From these, colossal aerial roots plunged to the ground, forming a protective ring of pillars – ring after ring, radiating outward in concentric circles. These ash-gray roots were so densely stacked that the tree's trunk was fully hidden from view.

Patting the dagger in his belt, Vikramaditya made for the tree, wondering how he was to find his way in.

But as he approached the outermost ring of the jumbled aerial roots, the roots directly in front of him parted miraculously, creating a narrow cavelike mouth to allow passage. It was pitch black inside the opening, but Vikramaditya stepped in with bowed head and began walking. Behind him, the roots fell quietly back in place like curtains drawing shut, but ahead more roots made way, so that the king progressed through a gloomy tunnel that opened and closed in his immediate vicinity.

The walk seemed to last forever, so when the tunnel abruptly opened into bright orange light, Vikramaditya was both blinded and surprised. He blinked for a moment, shielding his eyes as they adjusted to the surroundings. Then, slowly lowering his hands, he walked toward the light.

And its source.

The king was in a bare, open space of indeterminate size, the mud underneath disappearing into shadow on all sides. And in the middle of this open space hovered a large ghoul, the top of its head alight with fire in place of hair. Thick locks of flame collapsed in abundance over its shoulders and back, casting a cheery glow around the chamber.

The ghoul's body was silvery and vaporous, with no distinguishable anatomy other than two long ghostly hands that ended in curiously curved, razor-sharp claws. Its features were more clearly defined though – a thin, skeletal face set to a permanent grin that revealed sharp teeth and fangs. Tiny pinpoints of red light burned in the black hollows of its eyes, which were trained on the samrat.

"My greetings to the Wielder of the Hellfires," the ghoul

spoke in an old, bony voice. "Now that you are here, I remembered that you would come."

"My greetings to you, Ghoulmaster," Vikramaditya smiled. "So if you remembered I would come, you would also know what brings me here?"

"I don't, wise king." The samrat detected dry humor in the Betaal's tone. "But when you tell me, I will remember."

* * *

A clatter of hooves on stone chased Shanku as she rode at the head of a posse of twenty horsemen of the City Watch. Now that the city had been adequately warned of the dangers it faced, the alarm bells had started dying down. The rain had also let up a bit, improving visibility, and to Shanku's relief, the streets of Ujjayini were mostly clear of its citizens, who were hiding deep in the bowels of their houses. Open streets meant unimpeded progress for units of the City Watch, the *samsaptakas* and the soldiers of the Imperial Army, who had also been pressed into service.

That was the good news. The bad news, unfortunately, continued to outweigh the good.

The attacks were spread across the city, and no one still had the faintest clue of how many asuras the city was up against. It didn't help that these rakshasas moved at incredible speeds, making the job of tracking them virtually impossible. Fresh reports of indiscriminate attacks in some new corner of Ujjayini kept streaming in, and from what had been gathered so far, nearly sixty lives had been lost.

Judging by the nature of the multiple attacks, Shanku suspected that the asuras' objective was to draw the defenders away from the palace and spread them thin over a large area. Once this had been achieved, the weakened palace would be open to attack – and it would be nigh impossible for the defenders to rally and return to the palace in time. The strategy, as she saw it, was working brilliantly.

From somewhere to the left, not far from the city's southern wall, voices could be heard shouting. Something crashed heavily, followed by more screams and shouting. Up ahead, where the street she was riding in emptied into another street, Shanku saw a group of people running. Men, women, a few children. Citizens running scared.

Cursing under her breath, Shanku dug her heels into her horse's flanks.

Emerging onto the main street, she turned in the direction of the shouts. The horsemen followed in her wake, up the winding street, but their progress was slowed by another rush of panic-stricken citizens coming from the opposite direction. The sight of reinforcements arriving didn't seem to reassure those in flight, and that bothered Shanku.

But when she turned the corner and set eyes on the scene in front of her, she understood the fear she had seen on the people's faces.

The street was strewn with debris – rubble and masonry, an overturned horse cart with a dead horse still hitched to the shafts, a smashed potter's wheel, a pair of upturned wheelbarrows... and half a dozen human bodies. Shanku could tell that two of the bodies belonged to children not yet into their teens.

And rising above this carnage was one of the wrathful beasts!

She had heard the attackers being described as giants, but the rakshasa standing in the middle of the street – hulking over a doorway that barely reached up to its chest – was far bigger than anything she had pictured in her mind's eye. With bulk to match and the huge horns framing its face, the demon was downright diabolical in appearance; watching it batter the door and the surrounding wall with its huge fist, a tremor ran through Shanku. Even from this distance, she could hear the muffled wails of terror issuing from behind the door.

"We must distract that creature," Shanku threw a frantic glance over her shoulder. "I want two of you to go around and approach from the other side. While we draw the thing this way, you must free those trapped inside that house. Go!"

Two horsemen detached themselves and rode away. Shanku stared at the asura for a moment before turning her horse to face the remaining riders. "We have to lure that thing into a trap. Do we know where the closest City Watch picket is?"

"There's one a few streets down that way," one of the soldiers replied doubtfully. "But I'm not sure if it's still standing... and if it is, whether it's still manned."

"We'll have to take our chances," said Shanku. "Let's try to attack the beast and draw it toward the picket. You –" she picked out one soldier at random. "Inform the picket to be prepared."

The soldier departed, his relief in plain sight. Shanku appraised the rest of the horsemen, their doleful expressions and the hesitant glances they exchanged barely concealing their reservations. Shanku realized her idea bordered on the suicidal, but then something had to be done to stop these asuras...

"Come on," she said turning her horse around. And her eyes widened in dismay.

The rakshasa had stopped pounding the door and was

loping away, shaking its horned head in sullen rage. That it had lost interest in the house and its inmates was good, of course. But now it was moving in the direction from where the two horsemen she had dispatched would appear. And they would blunder straight into the beast's path – toward certain death.

Shanku spurred her horse into a gallop and charged down the street, yelling at the top of her voice to attract the demon's attention. Behind her, the horsemen followed with more circumspection.

As she rode, Shanku's hand closed around one of the thick, circular blades that occupied a wide-mouthed pouch in her saddle. Fashioned out of iron, its outer edge wickedly sharp, the *chakram* was an ancient range weapon of the Wandering Tribe, very deadly, but incredibly hard to wield. Hefting the *chakram* out of the saddle, balancing herself carefully, Shanku went after the murderous beast.

* * *

Vararuchi clutched the short *katari* in his right hand and surveyed the rooftops of the buildings that bordered the open market square.

The lethal *urumi* was his most favored weapon for combat, but for all its virtues, Vararuchi knew no *urumi* could cut through the thick, bony armor of the rakshasa that stood glowering amid the ruins of Ujjayini's biggest marketplace. His best bet was the *katari* – as long as he was able to move in really close and get his aim right.

With this beast though, even that posed a serious challenge.

Vararuchi had seen the demon in action, laying the market to waste. Soldiers of the Watch and a dozen *samsaptakas* had tried to collar the beast, but the ferocity of its counter-attack had been stupefying. The rakshasa had swatted the soldiers aside, cleaving the head of a *samsaptaka* into two and frying four soldiers to death with invisible energy bolts.

It wasn't just the city's defenders who suffered the rakshasa's onslaught. Three innocent laborers sheltering in a shop had tried to make their escape at an inopportune moment; catching sight of the fleeing trio, the beast had pursued and slaughtered them ruthlessly, displaying a vindictiveness that had left Vararuchi aghast. The councilor could see at least fifteen soldiers lying in the market square, and something told him those brave men of Avanti would never rise again. Anger surged through his veins at that thought, and he set his jaw in determination.

He would bring this asura down if it was the last thing he did.

His eyes alighted on a building that stood a little to the left of the beast. Its rooftop was of the right height, and it was located close enough for him to try and have a go at the demon. Without wasting another moment, Vararuchi slipped through the shadows, circling the square, making for the building...

***

Varahamihira's eyes were wide with amazement and horror as he watched the battle raging on the palace causeway.

The rakshasa was already halfway across the bridge, hacking and slicing with its massive serrated sword, and the speed with which the palace guards were being forced back was alarming. Archers from the palace roofs and windows had tried to slow the demon's progress, but now, even they had ceased attacking for fear of wounding Avanti's own.

Maimed and mutilated soldiers lay on the causeway and floated in the lake's dark waters.

"Fall back, fall back…" the chief of the Palace Guards could be heard instructing his men. "Fall back… we're closing the palace gates."

Directly below Varahamihira were the heavy palace gates, and the councilor could see anxious soldiers and palace attendants bracing themselves against it, eager to shut it before the beast could get any closer. It was only the thought of leaving those outside at the rakshasa's mercy that prevented them from prematurely shutting the gates.

"The gates must be closed quickly," Kshapanaka's strained voice sounded in Varahamihira's ear as she leaned out of the window next to him. "We can't let that demon get inside."

Their superior's commands were finally heard over the din of battle, and the soldiers on the causeway began withdrawing to the safety of the palace. However, with resistance melting, the rakshasa gained ground even faster, quickly reducing the distance to the gates.

"Hurry, hurry," Sadguna exhorted. "Quick, get behind the gates."

As soldiers started tumbling back into the palace, Kshapanaka left the window and ran the length of the gallery that overlooked the gates. "Start closing the gates… fast," she shouted at the men manning the heavy doors. "Don't allow that thing to enter the palace."

A desperate scramble ensued on the causeway, with soldiers abandoning fight and running for protection before the gates closed them out. Behind them the demon stormed, swiping at their unprotected backs, cutting them to pieces. Varahamihira lost count of the number who fell to that terrible, jagged sword.

"Jump into the lake," yelled Sadguna. The gates were closing rapidly, and it was plain that the last of the guards would never make it to safety in time. "Jump, jump..." The chief's voice rang with fatherly concern for his men.

Soldiers leaped into the water with loud splashes, and the causeway emptied. Inside the palace, more shoulders were thrown against the gates to get it to shut faster. Looking down from the gallery, Varahamihira observed the rakshasa slow down, as if assessing the next plan of action. Then, lowering its head, it charged down the causeway.

"Hurry up, hurry up... Shut the gates, *now*!" Varahamihira shouted his lungs out. "The asura is coming."

He held his breath, watching the doors draw inexorably together...until, with a final heave, they shut to an echoing clang. In no time, the guards slid the heavy bolts into place.

Outside on the causeway, still some distance from the closed gate, the rakshasa drew to a halt.

Varahamihira exhaled deeply, as Kshapanaka's voice rang through the palace. "Archers, you have a clear target. Shoot your arrows."

Missiles screamed down onto the causeway, but for all their fury they did a miserable job, barely leaving any scratches on the asura's bone armor. The beast, for its part, just stood its ground, glaring at the gate in oafish stubbornness.

Continuing to ignore the fusillade, the rakshasa raised one hand high above its head, as if holding aloft a large rock. Then, with a sudden downward jerk of the arm, it hurled whatever it was holding – something that was invisible to the eye – at the palace. All Varahamihira could make out was the slight warping and tunneling of the air, marking the passage of the speeding projectile...

The next instant, something bearing tremendous weight and force slammed into the gate with a resounding bang!

Varahamihira saw the gate rattle and sway, its metal surface bulging grotesquely under the impact. The guards and palace attendants who had been standing nearby staggered back and fell, as if knocked over by a horde of stampeding bulls.

A horrified hush overcame the gallery and the atrium below. Before anyone could recover their senses, the gate was buffeted by a second blow. This time the gate shuddered on its hinges, the bolts straining at their hoops and snapping loose. A bloodcurdling bellow rose from the causeway as the gates parted, the crack widening slowly to reveal the rakshasa standing on the threshold, sword in hand...

Pushing aside the broken gate, the beast crossed into the palace.

* * *

At the other extremity of the palace, hidden from all eyes, the horned head of a Marut silently broke the surface of the dark lake close to the palace walls.

Instead of moving immediately, the Marut drifted in the water for a while, surveying the edifice above, watching for movement in the windows and terraces, waiting to hear a shout which would suggest that it had been sighted. The sounds of the battle on the causeway were clearly audible to the rakshasa, while from across the lake, the prolonged roar of one of its brothers shook the night air.

Having established that the coast was clear, the Marut hauled itself out of the water and began scaling the palace wall. It pulled further and further up with surprising agility and surefootedness, using the narrowest of protrusions and toeholds for support. Finally, with the help of the thick vines that grew in profusion along that wall, the rakshasa hoisted itself onto an open, unguarded terrace.

Checking to see that it hadn't been detected, the Marut padded soundlessly toward a doorway that led into the palace, its right hand reaching to the back of its neck as it walked. The rakshasa's nails ripped into the dark blue skin of its nape, fingers digging deep into the flesh until the hand locked around something long and hard buried underneath. With a smooth, effortless tug, the Marut yanked the thing free of the surrounding flesh.

The light from a cluster of lamps mounted on a wall fell on the rakshasa as it crossed the terrace and entered the doorway. The light illuminated the object that the Marut had extracted from its back – a big, jagged, sharp sword. A sword built out of the Marut's own backbone!

Swinging the bone-sword in small arcs, the rakshasa walked down a passageway, picking up the vibes emanating from the Hellfires. Ever since they had descended upon Ujjayini, the Maruts had sensed the swords' vibes – they were, after all, the creation of their accursed mother Diti, washed by her blood and her breast milk. Now, with every step forward, the Marut detected the Hellfires' vibes grow stronger, pulsing in the ether around him.

The swords were very close. Which meant the human king would also be nearby.

The Marut turned a corner and took two steps before coming to a halt. The Hellfires were behind one of the two doors down the passageway – but there was someone guarding the passageway. A large, strongly built human with a dark face, his hair swept back into a high ponytail. He carried a heavy scimitar in one hand and a big bronze shield in the other.

Their eyes locked.

The rakshasa watched as the human threw his chest out and drew himself to his full height, shield held ready to block an attack, scimitar rock-steady and poised to strike. The human's bearing held the promise of a good fight, which gladdened the rakshasa. Nothing nourished the bone-swords like the blood of brave warriors...

With mounting anticipation, the Marut gripped the bone-sword in both hands and took a step toward the human. The man responded by taking two forward.

Drawing close, they slowly began circling one another.

* * *

Once the boat had been docked and they had entered Ujjayini, it had been easy enough for Shukracharya to give Vararuchi and the soldiers of the City Watch the slip. Stopping the carnage being uppermost in Vararuchi's mind, the councilor had quickly rallied his men and ridden off, hardly sparing a second glance at the head priest.

Shukracharya now squatted on his haunches in a deserted back alley in the western quarter of the city, his back hunched as he wrestled with ideas to counter the Maruts – while testing the strength of a nifty new plan that had begun formulating in his head. Before him, drawn on the mud of a shop's darkened courtyard, was a *mandala* more complex than any he had had occasion to draw in Avanti.

He had weighed his options, and it was evident that whatever he did, the outcome wouldn't be favorable to the humans. With their superlative strength and magical powers, victory for the Maruts was inevitable. He could, of course, try and change the course of the battle by intervening directly, but he wasn't certain even that would succeed. Moreover, that meant drawing attention to himself, exposing his true identity to the human king and alerting the devas to his presence in Avanti. The head priest wasn't sure if he wanted to take that risk. Not when he wasn't assured of getting the dagger in return.

Yet, he knew that unless he acted quickly, Diti's sons would prevail and the Halahala might be lost forever.

A sudden change in the direction of the wind bore the tumult of battle to Shukracharya's ears with renewed vigor, nudging him into a decision. There was only one route left open. He had to help the humans tackle the Maruts. Not so they could defeat them – that would have been fanciful thinking. But helping them to the extent of prolonging the battle long enough for him to take advantage of the prevailing chaos, slip into the palace... and seek Veeshada's dagger out for himself.

Pinning his hopes on this slender prospect, Shukracharya lowered himself to the ground, crossed his legs and closed his eyes. He would start by making the humans more resistant to the attack, more hardy, more resilient. He would help them regain lost strength and nerve, so they could fight and frustrate Diti's sons longer. His hands hovering over the *mandala*, the head priest began invoking the Dasa-Mahavidyas.

He then began casting the Regeneration Spell over the human population of Ujjayini.

Ghoulmaster

Indeed, I remember everything you have just told me about the dagger and why you have brought it to me."

The Betaal stood in front of Vikramaditya, its flaming head throwing flickering shadows around the bare chamber. It had listened to the king's narrative in silence, without interruption, and although its skeletal face was inscrutable, Vikramaditya detected a trace of melancholy – even resignation – in the Ghoulmaster's voice.

"Will you accept my request to keep the dagger in your protection?"

For a long while, the Betaal remained silent. When it finally spoke, its tone was kind, reassuring and full of gratitude.

"I also remember a promise that I had made a long time ago, wise king," it said. "A promise to be of assistance to you should the need ever arise. Now that you have come to me with so much hope, how could I let you return disappointed? I owe my existence to you, Samrat Vikramaditya. I shall gladly take charge of safekeeping the Halahala."

The king smiled as he felt a burden lift from his shoulders. Reaching into his belt, he withdrew the dagger and extended it toward the Ghoulmaster. As the dagger changed hands, the samrat thought he saw the iridescence in its hilt wink at him wickedly.

"I shall not remind you to be careful with it. You already know about the promise I have made to the Omniscient One. I trust you to help me honor my word."

"I am as ancient as the Ancient Gods," the Betaal replied, cradling the dagger in its hands. "If one of them has entrusted you with this, it would be an honor to be of service to you."

"But do remember that I didn't bring the dagger to the Borderworld to transfer its responsibility to you," Vikramaditya reminded. "The responsibility of the Halahala will continue to be mine and mine alone. The devas and asuras believe the dagger is with me, and I will never give them a reason to assume otherwise. You have my word that those who covet the Halahala will never disturb the peace of the Borderworld for that dagger."

"I have never doubted your word or your fairness, wise king," the Ghoulmaster replied. "Now go in peace."

The samrat bowed his head in appreciation and turned to depart. The Betaal followed him. But just as they neared the edge of the chamber where the curtain of roots came into view, the king paused and considered the Ghoulmaster.

"You knew about my coming, you knew about the dagger and of my request. Did you also know that you would accept the Halahala?"

"I did, when I remembered that I had already agreed to keep it for you."

"You know everything that has already happened. Don't you know how all this ends?"

The Betaal lingered thoughtfully for a moment before shaking its head. "I see what you mean," it said. "Everything in Borderworld has already occurred – it is, in a way, the future of all the other three worlds. But no, unfortunately I remember things only as they happen – the way you humans sometimes remember having seen or experienced a situation before, even though what you've remembered has just occurred in front of your eyes. You know what I speak of... like a fragment of a forgotten dream unfolding and coming to life?"

Vikramaditya nodded in understanding.

"For me, every moment is like that," said the Ghoulmaster. "Everything I see and hear and say and do, I have seen happen before. It's like living the same reality over and over again. It can be very disconcerting at times. Farewell, wise king."

The samrat nodded again and stepped forward as the roots parted way again.

* * *

Shanku couldn't tell if it was the pounding of her horse's hooves or her yelling that took effect, but the beast she was pursuing finally stopped and turned. It was the moment she was waiting for.

Bracing herself, she flung the *chakram* into the air. The ring arced far to the demon's left, whispering softly, nothing in its trajectory indicating it would venture anywhere near the rakshasa... But at the last moment, the *chakram* changed direction, dipping and scything viciously toward the beast's head. Yet, when the ring was just a few feet from its target, the rakshasa ducked, and the ring sailed harmlessly away into the night.

Shanku cursed. The *chakram* was one of the most deceptive of weapons, almost impossible to read. However, this asura had evaded it with utmost casualness. Plucking another *chakram* out, Shanku hurled it at the beast. But her frustration impaired her judgment and the ring went straight at the demon's chest, hitting and bouncing off the thick exoskeleton.

The councilor was reaching for a third ring when the rakshasa broke in to a hurtling run – and came straight at her.

Shanku had been warned that these beasts were fast, but again there was a gap between what she had mentally prepared for and the reality of what she saw.

The demon leaped and bounded down the street, narrowing the distance at an incredible pace. Shanku could feel the ground shake every time the beast's foot landed on the earth, looming closer and closer, its quicksilver eyes holding her own. She heard the horsemen behind her shouting and urging, but she was utterly mesmerized by the sight of the demon bearing down on her.

"Run, councilor... Please run!"

The voice of one of the soldiers finally invaded Shanku's mind, snapping her back to her senses. She wheeled her horse around frantically and urged it into a gallop. Before her, the horsemen of the City Watch were already scattering, tearing down the street in search of exits that would deliver them from the menace. From behind, she heard the stomping of the rakshasa's feet and the guttural growl emanating from its throat.

Then something heavy – it felt like a broad beam to Shanku, or perhaps a large sack loaded with stones – slammed into her mount.

Neighing in agony, the horse reeled and buckled under her, its hind legs swept from underneath by whatever had struck it. The acrid smell of burning hair and flesh rose to Shanku's nostrils as she toppled backwards and fell off the saddle. Her horse, hind legs and rump scorched to the bone, keeled over to one side, never to rise.

Shanku hit the wet ground flat on her back. For a moment she lay in a daze. Then, as her eyes swam into focus, she saw the demon's face upside-down, bending over her, its eyes burning silver-white, lips pulled back in a vicious snarl of rage.

Gnashing its teeth, the asura raised its right foot high over Shanku's head and brought it down on her with unbridled violence.

* * *

A crushing wave of dismay washed over Vararuchi as he crouched on the rooftop. He had sprinted around the market square as fast as he could, climbing up to the rooftop without pausing to catch his breath, yet looking down into the square, he could see the rakshasa moving further and further away from him. The few remaining soldiers and *samsaptakas* had withdrawn to a safe distance and appeared in no mood to engage the beast. It was clear that the asura had lost interest in the market and was preparing to spread its havoc in some other part of the city.

I can't let that thing get away!

Vararuchi made a quick assessment of the distance between the rooftop and the beast. It was a yawning gulf, too wide for him to bridge in one leap. And with every passing moment, the gap was widening. It wasn't humanly possible...

I can't let that thing get away!

Gripping the *katari* tightly in his hand, Vararuchi stood up. Taking five steps back to get some momentum, he ran to the edge of the roof and flung himself toward the rakshasa.

Below him, the market which lay in shambles passed by in a rush of air. He observed a couple of soldiers of the City Watch look up at him, their mouths falling open in amazement. He saw the demon's broad back – and he saw the demon swivel its horned head around as if sensing danger. And then he began his descent.

For all his determination, Vararuchi had expected to fall well short of the rakshasa and hit the ground in a jarring, bone-crushing fall. But as he drew closer and closer to the giant, he realized that he had somehow made a perfect leap.

He would land on the asura's back, as planned.

The impact of their bodies made a heavy, cracking sound that slapped against the walls of the buildings lining the square. Vararuchi felt pain shoot through his limbs as his body came into contact with the demon's shell-like armor. Ignoring the pain, he locked his left arm around the beast's neck and hung onto its back. With all his might, he choked the rakshasa with his forearm, pushing its head upward and back. Then, quick as lightning, he raised the *katari* and plunged it into the right side of the beast's exposed neck, pushing and skewering deeper until the short blade was buried up to the hilt.

The rakshasa let out an agonized roar and spun its body around. The sudden move loosened Vararuchi's grip, and he slipped to the ground, yanking the *katari* free as he went down. The councilor fell between the powerful legs of the asura, but he instantly twisted and scrambled out of harm's way. Wheeling around, he prepared to face the wrath of the beast.

But the asura just stood in the middle of the square clutching the right side of its neck, its fingers pressed into the deep, ragged gash left by the *katari*. Vararuchi could see a thick, silvery liquid gush and spurt from between its fingers, the liquid the same color as the beast's eyes.

The soldiers in the square stared wide-eyed as the demon swayed uncertainly for a few moments. It then turned its head to look at Vararuchi with eyes that were losing their luster and growing dark and smoky. The councilor was preparing to make an evasive move when a bolt of lightning streaked down from the heavens and hit the rakshasa.

The men in the square flinched, half expecting to be annihilated by the blinding bolt. But as the crack of thunder exploded around them and rolled over the city, they saw that they were mistaken. Miraculously enough, none of them had come to any harm.

They also realized they were alone. There was no sign of the four-horned asura that had terrorized the square.

* * *

At the palace gates, there was complete pandemonium.

The asura waded into the defenders, slashing left and right, dismembering guards who were now fleeing in panic. Archers rained arrows down from the galleries above, but the beast kept advancing, the arrows snapping like twigs on its bone armor. The rakshasa loosened two bolts of energy into the galleries to good effect – the sight of a dozen of their mates shrivel and burn took the resistance out of the archers, and the arrows dried up. In a matter of moments, the demon had crossed the atrium of the palace and was making its way toward a stairway leading to the floors and galleries above.

Sensing a rout and desperate to rally the defense, the chief of the Palace Guards sprang at the beast, trying to block its path.

"Surround the thing, men," he shouted, slashing at the asura. "The fight isn't over yet. We can still get it…"

One foot on the lowermost stair, the rakshasa spun around to face the challenge from Sadguna. Four guards responded to their commander's call – but all four were slow in reacting. With an effortless swipe of its sword, the demon first disarmed the old warrior. Then, as the chief stood petrified and weaponless, the cruel beast struck again, decapitating him.

Shock and outrage boiled over Kshapanaka at the sight of the old, faithful soldier's head rolling across the atrium, a wheezing scream escaping those lifeless lips. Nocking another arrow into her bow, she ran through one of the galleries, her mind clamoring for revenge. But beneath the anger and the lust to settle scores, a sane part of her mind reminded her of the more pressing task: stopping the beast from coming upstairs.

Rounding the head of the stairway, Kshapanaka saw the asura come tearing up the steps, its eyes on her, its bloodied sword waving drunkenly in the air. The councilor wondered if she should swap her bow with her sword – she had already emptied many quivers on the beast to no avail. On the other hand a sword would… She promptly abandoned the idea. Her short sword would be no match for the demon's giant one, she realized.

She also thought she heard a voice instructing her to use an arrow.

Drawing the bowstring back, Kshapanaka let the arrow fly at the rakshasa's head. The shot had been aimed straight between the eyes, but the beast had been expecting it. Raising its left arm, it blocked and deflected the arrow's flight. The arrow just grazed the exoskeleton.

Kshapanaka felt the anxiety and fear well up inside her. At any moment now, the beast would be upon her. There was no time to nock a fresh arrow into her bow. There was no place to run. This was the end.

But to her surprise, the rakshasa had come to an abrupt halt on the stairway. She was within striking distance of the demon's fiendish sword, but instead of attacking her, the asura was staring down at its left forearm in what looked like puzzlement.

Following the asura's gaze, Kshapanaka saw that the exoskeleton that covered the beast's forearm had started discoloring at the point where her arrow had struck. The white, bony shell was turning brown, and had begun flaking and crumbling. A filigree of widening cracks branched out from the spot, spreading rapidly across the rest of the asura's armor, and the discoloration chased the cracks, turning the entire exoskeleton brown and brittle.

Without wasting a moment, Kshapanaka slipped another arrow into place and shot it at the rakshasa. This one hit the beast in the middle of its chest, and the molding, decaying armor splintered. The same instant, the beast dropped its sword, which fell on the marble stairs with a rattle and broke into pieces. As more arrows thudded into the asura, piercing its weakened armor, it turned and dashed down the stairs, across the bloodied atrium and out of the shattered palace gates.

Wary, disbelieving eyes followed the asura's progress

onto the palace causeway. The demon was halfway across the bridge when it was struck by a bolt of lightning. The next instant, the causeway was empty, except for the bodies of Avanti's fallen sprawled across it.

***

Outside the king's bedchamber, Kalidasa was locked in a fierce struggle with the Marut from the lake.

The councilor had been the first to attack, moving in suddenly with the intention of surprising his opponent. The Marut, however, had been sharp, and Kalidasa had lost his scimitar to a well-placed blow from the Marut's sword. Seeing its foe unarmed, the rakshasa had launched a savage assault, but far from being overwhelmed, the councilor had successfully parried the withering blows with his shield, until the bone-sword had shattered on its dented face. Casting the broken sword aside, the Marut had made a rush at Kalidasa, and the two now grappled barehanded.

The Marut tried to subdue Kalidasa with a series of head butts, but the councilor avoided the lethal horns, using his big arms to restrict the rakshasa's movements. However, the Marut had the advantage of bulk and height, and using its long arms, it delivered a series of crippling blows to Kalidasa's midriff and ribs. The blows knocked the councilor's breath out and sent jabs of pain along his body, causing him to double over. Seizing the opportunity, the Marut trapped Kalidasa from behind in a vicelike grip. The councilor fought to free himself from the rakshasa's grasp, but the more he struggled, the tighter those powerful arms went around him, squeezing, crushing, choking, sapping the life force out of him...

Drawing from the last reserves of strength, Kalidasa

wrenched off the hands that were clasped around his chest and throat. Breaking free of the death grip, he twisted around and curled his right hand into a tight fist, which he slammed into the Marut's plated stomach. An agonizing current shot up the councilor's arm as the flesh over his knuckles split open, but he had the satisfaction of seeing the rakshasa's armor crack under the impact of his blow. He immediately drove his left fist into the same spot. More stinging pain, but Kalidasa's hand went in deeper this time, the chitinous shell caving in and breaking.

The Marut staggered back in surprise, but instead of giving it time to recover, Kalidasa rammed his shoulder into the rakshasa, driving it backwards. The Marut tried to break the charge by smashing its fists into Kalidasa's back, but the councilor pushed with every ounce of strength, exerting pressure, his hands locked around the demon's torso for leverage. Gaining momentum, the two hurtled down to the end of the passageway and out onto an open terrace. Still Kalidasa pushed on, relentless in his intent, driving the Marut in front of him until they came to the stone parapet bordering the terrace.

The two combatants broke through the parapet, sending a shower of masonry into the water below. For a moment they teetered on the edge of the terrace – and then with final heave from Kalidasa, they tumbled into the lake in a colossal splash.

On hitting the cold water, Kalidasa's grip on the Marut weakened and the rakshasa broke loose, kicking itself free. As the councilor went underwater, he looked up, searching for the Marut. Seeing the attacker pulling away, Kalidasa propelled himself upward to give chase when the water's surface lit up with a flash from above. The same instant, a jolt of numbing pain surged through the councilor's body and he felt the water boil around him.

Thrusting the pain and heat out of his mind, Kalidasa broke the surface of the water. Taking in huge gulps of air, he scanned the sizzling lake for the Marut. But the beast was nowhere in sight.

***

Shaking her head in bewilderment, Shanku stared at her surroundings.

She was standing in a narrow alley lined with small houses that crowded into one another. The houses all appeared deserted, and from what she could tell in the darkness, many of them were in a state of ruin, some listing dangerously, others nothing but broken skeletons jutting into the night. There was a smell of old, burned wood in the air, and as she walked down the alley, she thought she could taste ash on her lips.

It wasn't until she exited the winding alley and came into a plain that Shanku realized where she was. To her right, she saw the jumble of houses extend to a huge wall, with a big gate built into it. A row of watchtowers poked out from behind the wall like cautious heads.

Shanku understood she was looking at the northern gate of Ujjayini, where she had made a stand against the Brotherhood of the Ashvins not many nights ago. And the huts that surrounded her were the charred remains of the same Ashvin attack.

She shook her head once again in confusion.

Moments earlier, she had been in the southern quarter of the city, lying in a wet, rain-soaked street, staring up at the face of one of the attacking asuras. She had watched in horror as the beast had raised its large foot to trample her to death. She had seen the foot descend, blotting out the sky above... The next moment, she had found herself alone in the charred and deserted alley, way outside Ujjayini's northern wall, with no sign of the beast or the soldiers of the City Watch.

Shanku wondered if she was dreaming. Perhaps she was dead, crushed under the rakshasa's foot, and this was her soul, rid of her body, roaming her beloved Avanti in freedom?

But if she was nothing but soul, why did her head hurt at the spot where it had hit the cobbled street when she had fallen off her horse? Lifting her hand, she gingerly touched the tender spot and flinched. When she brought her hand down, she could feel the sticky wetness of blood on her fingers. She was bleeding and she could feel pain. She wasn't dead, that much was certain.

Just then, a bolt of lightning came down upon Ujjayini. Even as its crash shook the ground, Shanku saw a second and a third bolt hit the city – then a fourth, in quick succession. In all, she counted seven.

She remembered that the asuras had appeared in Ujjayini in bolts of lightning. Could this mean more were coming? She broke into a run, heading for the north gate, still wondering if it was all a dream that she would wake up from.

* * *

Vetala Bhatta's hand quivered on the king's forehead and his lips moved in frantic incantations. The light from the sockets of the skulls waxed and waned, sometimes glowing bright red, at other times dwindling almost all the way to black.

The dagger had disappeared from Vikramaditya's hand around the time a violent struggle had commenced in the passageway outside, and the raj-guru had tried his utmost to shut out the noise so that he could concentrate his energies on leading the samrat back. He had almost succeeded when the lightning had commenced once again, two bolts hitting very close to the palace. The Acharya did not know what to make of them, but it was becoming harder for him to focus on the king's revival from death-sleep.

Vikramaditya was barely breathing, his body slumped on the bed, face deathly pale.

The Acharya kept his eyes closed and stayed with the task until he felt a cold sweat break on the king's brow. Opening his eyes, the raj-guru saw the bedchamber flood with an intense red glow and his spirits soared. But the next instant the light dimmed, and then died out completely. The samrat convulsed and went rigid, then fell back on the bed.

Licking his parched lips, his face white with anxiety, Vetala Bhatta closed his eyes and went back to reciting the mantras.

"How long was I in the Borderworld, raj-guru?"

Relief flooded Vetala Bhatta's heart. For a moment he sat still, eyes shut, calming his strained nerves. At last he looked at the king, who had propped himself up on an elbow and was studying the chief councilor with tired eyes.

"You're back, Vikrama!"

"Yes, but how long was I in the Borderworld?" the samrat asked again.

"Too long, I'm afraid. Ujjayini has come under attack while you were away."

"Who's attacked us?"

The king's expression brimmed with anxiety and he made an attempt to rise, but his tortured body would have none of it. As his head flopped down on the pillow in fatigue, the Acharya reached out a steadying hand.

"No Vikrama, you mustn't," his tone was gentle but firm. "You've just recovered from death-sleep..."

"But who's attacked us, Acharya?" Vikramaditya insisted with growing agitation.

Before the Acharya could answer, the door to the bedchamber swung open. The raj-guru turned, his spear raised in defense, to see Kshapanaka in the doorway, arrow nocked and pointed into the room. Behind her were a handful of palace guards.

"Oh, the samrat is back." Lowering the bow in relief, she entered the room. "We came to see if everything was all right here." Looking from the Acharya to the samrat, she asked, "Is the dagger safe?"

Vetala Bhatta nodded. "What's happening outside? Where's Kalidasa?"

"He isn't here," Kshapanaka glanced in the direction of the passageway, as if half-expecting Kalidasa to appear and contradict her. "But it looks like we've beaten the asuras back once again, raj-guru."

"They've left?" the Acharya's shoulders relaxed. "All of them?"

"The rakshasa that attacked the palace gates certainly has – in a flash of lightning. There was more than one bolt over Ujjayini, and Varahamihira thinks they've all gone back the way they came."

Rage

Dandakabhukti was an ugly, unpleasant town, a shabby clutter of buildings, hovels and shanties that staggered down from the hills amid the slag heaps and foundries, and spilled like effluvium onto the plains below. Long before the first iron mine, the place had been a peaceful, nondescript village, but now there was evidence of nothing but economic greed raking the earth that had yielded life-sustaining crops and fruit trees. It was clear that the inhabitants of this town were more interested in what was below the ground than above it.

Dandakabhukti was a blight upon the landscape, yet Shoorasena looked at it with great joy and pride as he sat in the shade of a verandah of the central armory. Even under Vanga rule, the armory had been the administrative epicenter of Dandakabhukti – it now served as the makeshift headquarters of the Magadhan campaign into the republic.

"Have there been many casualties?" Shoorasena asked, tearing his appreciative gaze away from the town to glance at Kapila and General Daipayana, who were keeping him company. The glare from the hot morning sun made him blink and squint a little.

"We lost four men when they…" Kapila began, but he was cut short by an impatient wave of his brother's hand.

"I'm not talking about *our* losses. Did a lot of the locals die?" The Magadhan prince looked briefly toward the south, where carrion crows could still be seen in the air, searching for scraps among the bones of those recently dead. "Especially workers?"

"We killed all the soldiers and official representatives of Vanga," replied Daipayana. "That's always recommended, to enforce *compliance* among the populace. But no, I don't think more than half-a-dozen workers were killed. Those who died were rebellious and had to be made examples of."

"For compliance," Shoorasena nodded. "But make sure we don't make examples of too many of them. We need labor to continue working the mines and the foundries. And I hope the mine engineers are still around. They're needed for another two days, at least, until our own replacements come from Girivraja."

"I understand, my lord," said the general.

For a while, the three aristocrats sat in silence, sipping cool, fermented coconut water from large goblets. At last Kapila spoke.

"This messenger of Vikramaditya who came to the palace with news about the deva and the asura attacks on Avanti… was he seeking Magadha's assistance in some way?"

"That's what I expected, given Vikramaditya's obsession to defend Sindhuvarta from the Hunas and Sakas," replied Shoorasena. "But the messenger just said that Vikramaditya wanted Avanti's allied kingdoms to know about the attacks and the reasons behind them. There were no requests made for soldiers... or anything."

"Could it be true, this story about the Omniscient One giving Vikramaditya the Halahala?" Kapila seemed both skeptical and awed at the same time. "Why would an Ancient God trust a human?"

Shoorasena shrugged. "I have ordered scouts to verify the facts, but I see no reason why Vikramaditya would lie – his righteousness would never permit him to do that," he snorted. A sly smile spread slowly across his face. "In fact, I hope everything we've been told is true."

Kapila and Daipayana looked at Shoorasena in anticipation.

"One thing has always worried me in this campaign against Vanga," said Shoorasena, rising from his seat.

Kapila and the general's eyes followed him as he leaned against a railing and squinted into the sunlight at the row of *mahashilakantakas* ranged along the town's northern limits. "That fool Sudasan could end up appealing to Vikramaditya for help, offering who knows what concessions in lieu of Avanti's support. And if Avanti steps in, we can expect the puppets across Sindhuvarta to throw their weight behind Vanga."

Shoorasena turned to face the other two men. "But if Vikramaditya does indeed have the Omniscient One's dagger and the devas and asuras want it, he will have a lot more to worry about than Chancellor Sudasan's plight in faraway Vanga. Between the Halahala and the threat from the Hunas and the Sakas, I expect we would be free to pursue Magadha's expansion unhindered. Vanga first, Kalinga and Odra after that. Then perhaps Pragjyotishpura..."

"In that case, shall we begin preparations to take Tamralipti, my lord?" Daipayana asked, rubbing his hands in eagerness.

"We should, general. Without delay."

* * *

"Is this the final tally?"

Vikramaditya glanced up from the palm leaves that lay scattered before him on the council table. He surveyed the faces around him with tired, sleepless eyes, his own countenance drawn and sallow from the previous night's exertions. The palm leaves were scrawled with figures and annotations, with numbers marked against the names of various precincts and localities of Ujjayini.

Vararuchi nodded. "I think that's all – unless more bodies are found in some new location."

"Let's not forget that the lake is still being trawled," said the Acharya. "More bodies might be fished out."

The samrat sighed and returned his gaze to the leaves. "Nearly three hundred and forty dead across the city, more than a hundred of them at the palace gates alone." He shook his head. "So far, we've lost a thousand and three hundred lives in the three attacks on Avanti."

A gloomy silence enveloped the council chamber. Outside, a pale forenoon sun shone through the vestiges of the previous day's rainclouds, though even these were scattering quickly on account of a balmy breeze blowing from the east. The morning had been spent attending to a terrified populace and taking stock of the night's damage, and the councilors had just returned to the palace to give their king a report.

"People are in a state of shock," said Kshapanaka. "There's nothing but fear out there."

"Those who have somewhere else to go have started leaving the city," Varahamihira added. "One helper in my workshop has left a message saying he's going away and doesn't intend coming back to Ujjayini."

Vikramaditya bit his lip and looked down at his clasped hands, saying nothing. Yet, his eyes spoke eloquently of the torture he was undergoing on hearing the plight of his people.

"It could have been much worse, had we not managed driving them away," the physician remarked, in a bid to get everyone to see the brighter side of things.

"That's true," the king's face glowed with pride and gratitude. "You fought like lions for your city."

"I still can't believe I made that leap," Vararuchi rubbed the stubble on his chin in wonder. "Nothing I have trained in could have equipped me to do what I did."

"If what the soldiers are saying is true, you leaped halfway across that market square to bring down that asura," said Dhanavantri.

"That would be an exaggeration, I suppose," shrugged Vararuchi. "But not by much."

"I'm also very intrigued at what happened to the asura who broke down the palace gates," said Vetala Bhatta. "You say its armor disintegrated all of a sudden?"

"Yes Acharya," Varahamihira spoke emphatically. "Right before our eyes, for no conceivable reason. We tried everything to stop the beast, but nothing had worked. Then Kshapanaka shoots one arrow and its armor just falls apart."

"Was there anything unique about that arrow?" Vikramaditya looked at Kshapanaka.

"Nothing at all. It was part of a set made in the royal guild, just like everyone else's. In fact, the arrows I used

before that one belonged to the same set. But yes..."
Kshapanaka paused. "The arrow that I used *after* the first
one also seemed to affect the rakshasa's armor. The armor
simply shattered."

"Fascinating," the raj-guru observed.

"If that is fascinating, what do you make of what
happened to Shanku?" the samrat pointed out, looking at
the girl sitting quietly with a bandage around her head.

"Indeed," exclaimed Varahamihira, turning to Shanku
in bafflement. "How *did* you end up outside the northern
gate?"

"I don't know, your honor," Shanku shook her head,
wincing a little. "I recall nothing."

"The soldiers who were with her say they saw her
disappear moments before the demon's foot could crush
her," Kalidasa shook his head in incomprehension. More
than wonder, Vikramaditya sensed relief in Kalidasa's voice.

"You didn't do too badly yourself, my friend," said the
king. "These asuras were plainly strong brutes, but you
broke one's armor with your bare hands and wrestled it
into the lake."

"There's nothing to be amazed in that," Dhanavantri
gave a lighthearted chuckle. "That was just Kalidasa being
himself. One shouldn't be surprised when he and Amara
Simha do these things."

"Any news from him?" the king inquired. Seeing the
others shake their heads, he frowned. "It's been a while,
hasn't it? It's unlike Amara Simha not to send regular
updates in times like this."

"Maybe there's nothing to update us about," said the
physician, a glint of amusement in his eyes. "Funny how
Amara Simha went to the frontier with battle in mind; since

the day he left, we've had our hands full of battle, while he's probably swatting flies in the garrison of Udaypuri."

The mood lifted at the thought of their fellow councilor's predicament, but the significance of what the Acharya said next ushered the solemnity back.

"I think it might be a good idea to call Amara Simha back. He will be of better use here – at least until we hear some concrete news of Huna and Saka movements from the frontier."

Vikramaditya gazed down at his knuckles in silence.

"You know they will return, my king. That's why you thought it best to journey into the Borderworld last night. That's why you've brought the Mother Oracle to the palace." The Acharya paused as something stirred in his memory – *a warning!* – but in a flash it was gone. "Ujjayini needs as many men as possible to defend it, and Amara Simha is as good as twenty of the best."

The samrat nodded. "You're right, raj-guru. I was only wondering if it was a good idea leaving Ghatakarpara unsupervised. He is still young…"

"At his age, you were fighting the Hunas and the Sakas," Vetala Bhatta reminded. "And he's not alone. He is in the company of Atulyateja, and from everything Amara Simha tells us, Atulyateja is a capable commander. I think we should trust Ghatakarpara a lot more."

"We will do as you suggest," the king inclined his head and turned to Vararuchi. "Please send news to Udaypuri summoning Amara Simha back."

With Vararuchi's departure, the assembly began breaking up. As the councilors rose to their feet, Varahamihira addressed at the king. "In all this confusion I forgot to ask you about Vishakha. My apologies… How is she?"

"She is well, though there's been no further improvement in her since yesterday," replied Vikramaditya. "I fear the evacuation to the Labyrinth might have affected her. Which reminds me – I haven't seen the Healer since last evening..." Worry creased his brow as he looked at the councilors. "I hope he's still in the palace and is safe. Send word for him."

Varahamihira stole a sidelong glance at Dhanavantri. The physician had lost his cheer, and as he followed the others out of the chamber, he cut a sorry, forlorn figure. Varahamihira wished he hadn't brought up the matter of Vishakha's condition.

As he hobbled out on his crutch, Varahamihira cursed the Healer under his breath.

* * *

The jacaranda tree was located at the northeastern end of the promenade surrounding the lake. Set apart from the palace thoroughfares and hidden by an overgrowth of ornamental bamboo, it afforded Shukracharya solitude and concealment – both of which he had sought all morning. He had a lot weighing on his mind and didn't want to be disturbed.

Seated under the jacaranda, the head priest wondered at the manner in which the Maruts had abandoned their quest for the Halahala. They had departed so suddenly and unexpectedly – barely minutes after he had cast the Regeneration Spell over Ujjayini – that he had briefly worried they had got what they had come for.

Their defeat pleased Shukracharya no end, of course, even though it had put an abrupt stop to his own plan of stealing the dagger. But he really didn't mind that; he had the more elaborate scheme involving Vishakha to fall back upon. What he enjoyed was the slap the humans had dealt Indra's bloated ego.

Still, the capitulation by Diti's sons was incomprehensible, more so when all his calculations had ruled out a human victory. Moreover, the head priest had learned that Vikramaditya himself had not been involved in any of the battles – *where had the king been during the attacks?* – which meant that it was his councilors who had repulsed the formidable attack.

And there were the rumors that he had caught flying around. The king's half-brother had leaped an impossible leap to attack one of the Maruts... The giant had fought and thrown another Marut into the palace lake... The young girl had vanished from under the feet of a third... Shukracharya intuitively understood that his spell had played a part in the rout. He just didn't know how the pieces fitted together.

The other thing that was bothering him was how he would go about convincing the king and his council that the asuras had had no hand in the nocturnal attack. For things to go according to plan, it was imperative that the humans viewed the asuras favorably; but now, thanks to the Maruts, the asuras had ended up being projected in an unflattering light.

Yet, he couldn't just walk up to the council and tell them the Maruts had come to Ujjayini on Indra's bidding...

The head priest rose from the wrought-iron bench to return to the palace. He needed answers. He needed to consult the bones over everything that had transpired last night.

* * *

From where he stood, high on a turret at the pinnacle of his palace, Indra could take in the sweep of Amaravati, twinkling like a sequined bedspread in the light of the westerly sun. But the deva was in no mood for beauty, his brooding gaze fixed at a point high above the city, his mind full of dark thoughts and horrible deeds.

He had been that way ever since Narada had barged in upon him, as he watched Urvashi and two other apsaras disrobe one another, their exquisite and promising foreplay interrupted and spoiled by the news of the debacle in Avanti. Hearing Narada recount the fate that the Maruts had suffered, the lord of Devaloka had dismissed the nubile apsaras and broken a dozen swords in rage and frustration – before withdrawing into seclusion to plot his next move.

Vikramaditya. The Wielder of the Hellfires.

How he hated the sound of the human king's name. The king who had shamed him twice already. The king who had stubbornly denied the Brotherhood of the Ashvins and the Maruts their victories... who wouldn't yield him the dagger...

Such stubbornness had to be punished. With death.

Drawing a deep breath, Indra made up his mind. He would make the trip to Alaka to meet Kubera, lord of the magical yakshas. The idea wasn't in the least bit palatable, but he would swallow his pride and pay the loathsome and pompous yaksha king a visit.

Kubera's assistance would be crucial for the vengeance Indra had in mind for Vikramaditya.

End of Book 1

Glossary of Indian Terms
(In alphabetical order)

alankara	embellishment techniques in the context of Indian classical music
apsara	beautiful, supernatural female beings in Hinduism
ashwagandha	a herb used in Ayurvedic medicine
badi-maa	elder mother; a form of address
ber	jujube; Indian plum
bhoota	ghost
chakram	a throwing weapon, circular in shape
chaturanga	ancient Indian strategy game; ancestor of chess
chhoti-maa	younger mother; a form of address
damaru	a small two-headed drum, symbolic of Lord Shiva
danava	mythical race in Hinduism
Dasa-Mahavidyas	wisdom goddesses; the ten aspects of the Divine Mother Kali
garuda	large mythical humanoid bird in Hinduism

ghat	steps leading down to a body of water like a holy river
guggul	a herb used in Ayurvedic medicine
gurudev	master or teacher; also a form of address
jamun	black plum; Java plum
katari	a fist dagger
Mahadeva	great God; another name for Lord Shiva
mahaguru	grandmaster or teacher; also a form of address
mahashilakantaka	a trebuchet or catapult
mandala	a spiritual and ritual symbol in Hinduism representing the universe
pishachas	mythical flesh eating demon in Hinduism
raga	melodic mode used in Indian classical music
rajasuya yajna	ritual sacrifice performed by ancient Indian kings before being anointed emperor
raj-guru	royal tutor; also a form of address
rakshasa	mythical humanoid being in Hinduism
rudra veena	a large plucked string instrument
rudraksh	prayer bead
sambrani	a balsamic resin used as incense
samrat	emperor or overlord
samsaptaka	a tribe of mythical warriors
soma	Vedic ritual drink
suryayantra	sun-device; heliotrope
tambulam	paan; a betel leaf and areca nut preparation
tilaka	mark worn on the forehead in Hinduism
urumi	a longsword with a flexible whip-like blade
yogi	ascetic

VIKRAMADITYA VEERGATHA
BOOK 2

THE

CONSPIRACY
AT
MERU

VICTORY IS TEMPORARY
THE BATTLE IS ETERNAL

Vikramaditya and his Council of Nine have fought valiantly to repel the rampaging hordes from Devaloka and Patala – but Avanti has been brought to its knees. Ujjayini lies battered; its citizens are scared, and morale is badly shaken. Meanwhile, the barbaric Hunas and Sakas are gathering on the horizon, and cracks are emerging between the allied kingdoms of Sindhuvarta...

The only silver lining is that the deadly Halahala is safe. *For now.*

Bent on vengeance, Indra is already scheming to destroy Vikramaditya, while Shukracharya has a plan that can spell the doom for the Guardians of the Halahala. How long can the human army hold out against the ferocity and cunning of the devas and asuras? And will Vikramaditya's love for his queen come in the way of his promise to Shiva?

JAICO PUBLISHING HOUSE
Elevate Your Life. Transform Your World.

ESTABLISHED IN 1946, Jaico Publishing House is home to world-transforming authors such as Sri Sri Paramahansa Yogananda, Osho, The Dalai Lama, Sri Sri Ravi Shankar, Sadhguru, Robin Sharma, Deepak Chopra, Jack Canfield, Eknath Easwaran, Devdutt Pattanaik, Khushwant Singh, John Maxwell, Brian Tracy and Stephen Hawking.

Our late founder Mr. Jaman Shah first established Jaico as a book distribution company. Sensing that independence was around the corner, he aptly named his company Jaico ('Jai' means victory in Hindi). In order to service the significant demand for affordable books in a developing nation, Mr. Shah initiated Jaico's own publications. Jaico was India's first publisher of paperback books in the English language.

While self-help, religion and philosophy, mind/body/spirit, and business titles form the cornerstone of our non-fiction list, we publish an exciting range of travel, current affairs, biography, and popular science books as well. Our renewed focus on popular fiction is evident in our new titles by a host of fresh young talent from India and abroad. Jaico's recently established Translations Division translates selected English content into nine regional languages.

Jaico's Higher Education Division (HED) is recognized for its student-friendly textbooks in Business Management and Engineering which are in use countrywide.

In addition to being a publisher and distributor of its own titles, Jaico is a major national distributor of books of leading international and Indian publishers. With its headquarters in Mumbai, Jaico has branches and sales offices in Ahmedabad, Bangalore, Bhopal, Bhubaneswar, Chennai, Delhi, Hyderabad, Kolkata and Lucknow.

SINCE 1946